A QUEEN'S COMMAND

BOOK II OF LEGEND OF TAL

J.D.L. ROSELL

.

Copyright © 2020 by J.D.L. Rosell

All rights reserved.

Illustration © 2020 by René Aigner
Book design by J.D.L. Rosell
Map by Kaitlyn Clark

ISBN 978-1-952868-05-4 (hardback)
ISBN 978-1-952868-04-7 (paperback)
ISBN 978-1-952868-03-0 (ebook)

Published by JDL Rosell
jdlrosell.com

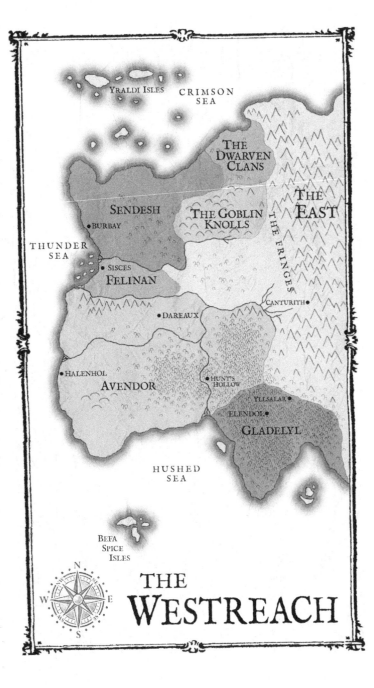

YRALDI ISLES

CRIMSON
SEA

THE
DWARVEN
CLANS

THE
EAST

SENDESH

THE GOBLIN
KNOLLS

•BURBAY

THUNDER
SEA

THE FRINGES

•SISCES

FELINAN

CANTURITH •

•DAREAUX

•HALENHOL

AVENDOR

HUNT'S
HOLLOW

YLLSALAR •

ELENDOL•

GLADELYL

HUSHED
SEA

BEFA
SPICE
ISLES

N
NW   NE
W   E
SW   SE
S

THE
WESTREACH

PROLOGUE
THE SECRETS IN THE LIES

I TREAD ON TREACHERY'S HEELS.

Tal Harrenfel, hero of fraud and deception, has reemerged in spectacular fashion. Not long ago, he appeared at the Coral Castle and made as much noise as he could, drinking wine until he could not stand and making a fool of himself by "practicing" swordplay in moonlit courtyards.

Now, two short months after his arrival, he makes off with the King's own minstrels on an unexplained trip to the elven queendom of Gladelyl.

And I travel with them.

To my immense honor, King Aldric himself requested that I join the retinue as his eyes and ears. "Watch, note, and write back to me," he said, "and your abbot and gods will be well-pleased."

I did not question him, nor would I, even if I had not taken my vows. I do as my King orders, for Silence, Solemnity, and Serenity speak through him.

But even if I did not go by my King's bidding, I confess, I would be curious to see Tal Harrenfel in Gladelyl. His history with the Eldritch Bloodline is speckled and strange. Harrenfel's sword is said to be a gift from Queen Geminia for killing the demon Heyl when he first arrived in Elendol. Devil Killer, he's hailed — and Falcon Sunstring

1

would have us believe he killed the hellish fiend by himself, and with a single blow no less:

> The demon saw him, riding at the fore
> A human on a mare amid the elves' white stags
> And Heyl laughed — 'Look!' he mocked. 'Here comes
>   my Killer!'
> And so he permitted Tal to enter his bastion of flames
>
> But Tal did not slow, but brandished his blade high
> Summoning the magic in his blood, he struck at the
>   fiend
> And, in a single blow, cleaved the horned head from his
>   shoulders
> The burning crown fell, and the fires of Elendol died to
>   ashes
>
> All stared in silence until one among them called forth
>   —
> 'Devil Killer! Devil Killer! There, the Slayer of Heyl!'
> Tal Harrenfel has saved all of Elendol!
>
> All around him, the elves took up the call
> And ushered Tal forth to the Elf Queen for his rightful
>   windfall...

Though I've confirmed Tal's presence in Elendol during the invasion, I've read no evidence that he struck the final blow, nor even dared to face Yuldor's creature. And, from all I've seen, the man has not shown himself to be the bravest of men.

Though the slaying of Heyl is the most remarkable of the stories, there are other whispers about Harrenfel in Gladelyl. Of a secret affair with one high among the Houses — an elven princess, if you will. And of the Silver Vines, the agents of the Cult of Yuldor in Elendol, Harrenfel was said to have pulled them out by the roots two decades before.

But now, traveling to Gladelyl itself, I will uncover this corner of the truth — of who Tal Harrenfel is, and what secrets he's buried beneath his legend's lies.

- Brother Causticus of the Order of Ataraxis

A DREAM OF VINES AND FLAMES

FAR AWAY IN AN AUTUMNAL WILDERNESS, SURROUNDED BY OLD friends and new enemies, a man twitched in uncomfortable slumber.

Rising in a dream, he entered a room and stood before a silver chair and the man sitting within it. The man was no king or prince, yet the dreamer knew it was a throne in which he sat. Vines twisted through the silver spindles and around the arms, choking out the light glimmering from the metal. To either side, tapestries hung tattered from the walls, the tales they told of an ancient people lost. Smoke hung like fog in the surrounding air.

Silently, the man on the throne gestured him forward, and the dreamer went, kneeling and bowing his head. His senses strained to detect the slightest movement. His hand itched to seize the sword at his side.

"You disappoint me. I expected more of you, Skaldurak."

The dreamer did not look up, did not rise, did not speak. He listened. He plotted. He waited.

The man's robes rustled as he rose and stood over him. *"By confounding my comrade, you raised my expectations. Yet here I come, entering your own mind, only to find no resistance."*

He had no response. The dreamer's senses strained toward the man, waiting to catch his every word, fearful of missing a single one.

"How did you overcome him, I wonder? I shall not be able to ask him for many years now, thanks to your efforts. But there are other ways of discovering."

The man stepped closer.

Now! the dreamer urged himself. *Rise!* His hand fell to his sword's hilt, and he loosened the blade in its scabbard. But he did not draw it, and he did not rise.

The man's voice was a harsh whisper above him, like a snake's skin rubbing against bark. *"I shall flay your mind of its secrets,* Skaldurak. *I underestimated you once before. But never again."*

His hand touched him.

Flames lanced through the dreamer's body, burning lines where his veins should have been. He tried to rise, tried to draw his sword, but his blood boiled, his skin beginning to split—

Tal twisted free of his bedroll and sat up, panting.

The sweat that beaded his skin grew cold as the night's air touched it. Shivering, he huddled back down into the thick, woolen covers and stared out over the darkness of the camp. One small campfire burned, a shadow huddled before it, revealing the poor chap who had drawn the short stick for the midnight watch.

A dream. Or a memory. Had it happened like that? He rubbed at his eyes, wishing the thought would leave him, but it needled him like a pebble in a boot. He'd been there, knelt in that room before that man. But those words, *that* word. *Skaldurak.* Even now as he formed it in his mind, it twisted like a viper threatening to bite.

Stone in the Wheel.

And that man — he knew him, too. *But he's gone from that place; I drove him out. Unless...*

Tal drew out his right hand, and despite the cold, held it bared to the night. Even in the darkness, the milky-white crystal band on his middle finger glowed gently.

Shaking his head, he hid it below the covers again, muttering, "What has the World become?"

He stared across the silhouettes of the wagons, gathered in a circle for protection of the caravan. Littered among them huddled other folks who, like him, slept outside on the ground, their wagons too full of articles to fit themselves inside. None who could avoid it enjoyed the chill, autumn air on their skin.

My friends. Despite his clouded mind, he smiled into the darkness. It had been a long time since he'd traveled with the Dancing Feathers, a long time since he'd been surrounded by friendly faces.

Or mostly friendly.

He didn't know where the monk Causticus slept, but his gaze wandered over to where Garin lay. Before Hunt's Hollow, the youth and Wren had often curled up together at night. But much had changed since they'd left their hometown behind. Now, the youth slept alone, and spent much of the days on his own, staring sightlessly ahead of them.

Listening to the voice in his head? Tal wondered. *Or plotting his revenge?* Garin had never struck him as the vengeful kind.

Much had changed, indeed.

Tal closed his eyes against the old memories, but still they came, reminding him of the betrayal that had come between them.

Flashes of light in the dark tavern. *Velori* dancing and cutting. The black spray of blood.

His oldest friend dying on the ale-stained boards.

I killed him. He didn't know if it had been his sword or one of Jin's soldiers who had struck the killing blow in the sorcerous darkness. But it didn't matter. That truth couldn't erase the stain upon him.

His hands trembled, and he clenched them, the bones clicking. He had no time for weakness, no time to show the countless flaws running through his foundations. He had to remain Tal Harrenfel, legendary soldier and sorcerer. Or pretend to be.

Red Reaver. Magebutcher. The Man of a Thousand Names.

"No more," he growled to himself. Each name was only a facet, a single side of him. Somehow, some way, he had to put the fragmented pieces together.

But if five years of a quiet life hadn't healed him, he doubted anything could.

———

He dreamed of fire and wind.

Garin floated above a burning forest, held aloft on invisible wings. The bones of a town lay below him, blackened and smoking.

A shadow swept over the land.

"Come."

Even in his dreams, he knew the Nightvoice, the Singer, though its sound had shifted. When it had first broken into his thoughts, it had been thin, little more than a whisper. Now, it held the rumble of thunder and stone, deep and sonorous, filling his mind with a single word.

"Come, little Listener. Come and see what we have become. Come and fulfill our final purpose."

He nearly fractured under the Singer's words, his tenuous consciousness threatening to fall as rain to the burning woods below.

"Come and see all we will make of you. Come and witness the power of our Song."

Only then did he notice a figure among the inferno, their arms raised, slowly spinning in a clearing. The flames did not touch them, and where the tongues of fire neared their hands, they flared up all the greater. By a stray thought, Garin found himself floating down toward the shadow, and the dancing orange light fell upon the face.

Garin's own face grinned up at him, eyes wide with a wild ecstasy.

"Come."

"NO!"

Garin jerked upright, fighting the constraints on him, only to realize it was his bedroll, tangled around his flailing limbs. He paused, panting for breath. No burning forest. No manic mirror-image of himself spinning among it.

All of it, a dream.

A shadowed form shifted a few feet away. "What is it now?" Wren groaned. "Another dream?"

He settled back down. His heart still pounded, but he was too embarrassed to move. Only then did he realize he'd shouted aloud. "Yes. Sorry."

"Try to have quieter dreams," she advised snidely. "Of sheep and pastures and all that pastoral bilge."

She turned her back on him.

He barely registered her grumpy comments. His mind was full of the burning forest in his dream and himself at its center.

I caused it, he realized. *In the dream, I am the one who starts the fire.*

The Singer only spoke to him in dreams now. While awake, he could almost forget a devil inhabited him at all. He could almost forget why they traveled to Elendol.

But the truth always found him in his sleep.

Garin turned toward Wren and stared at her outline. The dreams made them sleep apart now. He'd woken her one too many times with an errant flailing limb or a shout. A distance was growing between them, and though the cause of it remained unspoken, he had a feeling they both knew what it was.

I'll get rid of this demon, he promised her. *And then, nothing will stand in the way.*

He willed his oath toward her, urging her to hear it, until his eyes drifted slowly, inevitably closed.

———

Tal rose from his bedroll, eyes gummy and head aching with the lack of restful sleep. Yet, no matter the troubles that the night brought, a smile always found his lips.

It was another day on the road.

They'd been traveling the High Road for a month since leaving Hunt's Hollow. It had been a varied three weeks, full of long days of riding and walking, longer evenings of music, revelry, and dancing, and unending nights of chilled sleeplessness. In southeastern Avendor, autumn was giving way to winter, and the cold had swept in the first of the frosts and snowfalls. Leaves, newly fallen from trees, crunched under feet, hooves, and wagon wheels as they inched along the packed dirt road, always moving east.

Toward Gladelyl, and all the elven queendom would bring.

The going was leisurely, if not outright lethargic. Not only were they burdened by the numerous implements of the trouper's trade, but the members of the Dancing Feathers rebelled against anything resembling haste. They took frequent breaks throughout the day, and they rose late. Though Tal had gently urged Falcon to end the evening activities earlier, it had little noticeable effect on their habits. Eventually, Tal had resigned himself to the pace.

You brought this on yourself, asking Falcon along, he'd thought to himself more than once, always with an indulgent grin.

Slowly, the troupers drew him back into the lifestyle he'd once occupied many years before. On more than one occasion, he'd obliged to sing by the fireside with the actors, and though his scratchy, unused voice appalled him, it drew enough applause and laughter from the others to placate his smarting pride. He took part in their mock fights, giving pointers on how to make them more realistic, while they gave him dubious advice on how to make it more dramatic.

Mikael endeavored to teach him the ways of goblin humor. Ox showed him the ropes of the backstage overseer. Despite his supplications, Yelda refused to teach him how to act the leading lady. And Falcon reacquainted him with the finer points of poetry, high and low, in Reachtongue and Gladelyshi alike. Some of it was old knowledge learned again, and some of it new, for the Dancing Feathers had not been idle in perfecting their art in the intervening years since he'd ridden with them. Tal delighted in all he still had to learn, and even when he floundered, he rose from it with a grin and renewed resolve to try again.

Not since his time in Hunt's Hollow had his life allowed him to fail without consequences.

But as his days lightened with levity, his nights grew ever more burdened. Then, his guilt seeped back in and infected his dreams. How Garin avoided him, spending time among the troupe only where Tal was not, and how much longer their estrangement might continue. How he'd done next to nothing with all of his hard-won knowledge and experience.

And, most of all, what Aelyn had bound him to when they arrived in Elendol.

The morning after his dream, Tal accepted a breakfast of porridge from Hilly, an actress with a talent for the harp and juggling knives, and wove his way through the camp until he found the mage. The elf often made his camp at the periphery of the others, and with no wagon to duck into, he shaped his own shelter from dead wood and sorcery.

By the time he found him, Aelyn was already sitting on top of his wooden shelter, his porridge half-eaten, his expression of distinct dissatisfaction growing sourer when he looked up to see who had arrived.

"So you decided you've frivoled away your time long enough, pretending to be princes and poets, have you?" the mage observed with a smirk.

Tal grinned as he sat next to him. "I doubt I'll ever have enough of acting the prince. It fits me just as the curmudgeon fits you."

Aelyn snorted. Lifting a spoonful of porridge, he dripped it back into his bowl. "Peer to the Realm, Emissary to the Queen, and a Master of the Onyx Tower," he griped, "and I am forced to eat *this*."

"I don't remember you complaining about our fare on the way from Hunt's Hollow."

"Then, we made speed, not dragged on each interminable day to its breaking point."

Tal clapped Aelyn on the shoulder. "Patience, my traitorous friend. We'll arrive at your beloved Queen's capital soon enough."

"Traitor, am I?" He irritably shrugged off his hand. "Because I chained a stray dog to his hunt?"

Tal felt the smile leave his eyes, even as it remained perched on his lips. "I don't know what you chained me to, Aelyn. But I'm very interested to find out."

The mage's gaze lingered on his, then he looked off into the snow-dusted woods, his spoon stirring in his bowl. "I am no traitor, Harrenfel. Not even to you. Before long, you'll understand that."

Tal ate and let the silence speak for him.

The day passed much as the others had. Tal rode his horse, whom he'd named Loyal in a fit of self-pity, for the morning saunter, then used his own legs during the afternoon to let his mount rest. Long before dusk, they stopped again and set to the long task of setting up camp. Hilly, in her informal capacity as the troupe's chef, cooked their dinner of stew, filled with onions, potatoes, and salted mutton, and Tal gave her the sincerest false gratitude he could manage before sitting down to the dissatisfactory meal.

After an evening passed exchanging ribald jokes with Mikael and Falcon, Tal found his bedroll as the light faded completely to a moonless dusk. As with every night, an anxious vigilance rose in him as soon as everyone else became still. He didn't know if it was the dreams that caused his insomnia or some long-latent awareness of danger lurking ever near. It didn't matter that Ox sat at the watch. He was a good man and responsible in his duty, but at his core, he was still a trouper.

He hadn't seen or shed the blood that Tal had.

Long into the night, he breathed in deeply to calm himself. The air was crisp with a cold that stung his nose, but underneath it, the scents of the night came to him. Hoping it might lull him to sleep, he made a game of identifying them.

The stink of his long-used bedroll.

The smoke of the sputtering watch fire.

The animal smell of the horses and mules.

A hint of sulfur.

Tal stiffened. A prickling of heat had started in his veins, familiar in its portent. *Sorcery.* He knew its stench, knew its touch upon his blood. And unless Aelyn were up to something this late at night, it could mean nothing well.

He extracted himself from his blankets and rose. Already clothed to keep out the cold, he drew on his boots, belted on *Velori*, threw on his heavy cloak, and seized his bow and quiver. Most likely, they'd be useless in the darkness, but as his old commander had often told him, *We're all morons for being out here, but we'll be dead morons if we don't come prepared.*

As ready as he'd ever be, Tal crept out into the night.

———

"Awaken."

Garin sat up, coughing, his heart racing. The flames of his dreams left white afterimages against the darkness pressing against his eyes. His throat felt raw, like he'd been breathing in smoke. A clashing din filled his ears. Screams, the harsh ring of metal, manic laughter — the Nightsong was unrelenting.

Another dream, he despaired. But just as he lay back down, he saw something that made him stiffen in terror.

A shadow stalked through the camp.

For a moment, he could do nothing but watch while his mind flitted through the possibilities. *It's just a trouper looking to relieve their bladder,* he thought. *Or to pay someone a late-night visit.* Such liaisons weren't unheard of among the Feathers, free-spirited as they were. More than once on their trip to the elven queendom, Garin had woken to sounds that made him feel both uncomfortable and shamefully intrigued.

But this shadow didn't move like someone innocent. They moved furtively, like a cat through a cellar scrounging for scraps of food. They moved as if they wished to remain hidden.

As soon as they'd passed out of sight, Garin rose, his hand clasping his belt knife. He shivered as the late autumn night rushed over his exposed skin, and he quickly drew on his boots and cloak before he followed.

He caught sight of the shadow as soon as he peered around the wagon that sheltered Wren and him from the wind. They had paused at the outside edge of a wagon and seemed to look into the woods.

Perhaps giving a signal to others?

Garin knew he was probably overreacting. In the months of travel, those on watch had never glimpsed anything more suspicious than a squirrel. But as his eyes adjusted to the fire-limned darkness, he made out the unmistakable shape of a longbow in the shadow's hand, and the glint of a notched arrow.

Before he could decide what to do, the sneak moved away

from the wagon and toward the woods, silent and half-bent. They disappeared among the trees.

Tal. He suddenly knew it was his old mentor who had been warily watching the shadows. But what had he seen that alarmed him? What did he now mean to do?

Shivering, Garin stared out after him and waited.

Tal ghosted around the closest wagon. Without the light of the moons, he could see little, and he lacked the ingredients for a spell to improve his vision. So he contented himself with listening.

A snow-hushed forest surrounded them. The birds, squirrels, and deer had already departed before the coming winter months. An almost deafening silence filled the air, broken only by snores or the faint singing of Ox as he sat the watch.

Then a branch snapped from deep within the dark woods.

Tal withdrew behind the wagon and notched an arrow. Despite the cold of the night, a faint warmth coursed through his blood, unwelcome in what it signaled. He crept forward again, stepping carefully to avoid crunching any fallen leaves or twigs, but his footfalls remained loud in his ears, even above the blood hammering in his temples. He strained his senses forward, breathing in deeply, eyes wide, ears perked—

Crunching footsteps sounded ahead.

Tal crept closer, positioning his approach so that the small fire from the caravan didn't reveal him. He heard the footsteps constantly now, many pairs of them. *Five? Ten?* As he continued forward, their muttered speech became audible, though it was in a language he'd rarely heard.

Darktongue.

His blood burned in his veins now as he stared at the blackness where he knew they must be, steadily approaching the caravan of the Dancing Feathers. His mind spun. What were

Easterners doing here within Gladelyl's borders — their western borders, no less? The road was supposed to be safe from Halenhol until Elendol, or so King Aldric and Queen Geminia claimed.

But, like so many promises from kings and queens, Tal was finding they were less than certain.

PERILS OF THE HIGH ROAD

T<small>AL CLENCHED HIS JAW AS HE CONSIDERED THEIR PREDICAMENT.</small>

How many can I kill?

The troupers were no fighters. The only weapons they possessed had blunted edges, suitable for the stage rather than combat. And what training they had was for showmanship, not killing. Among them, only Aelyn, Wren, and Garin would put up a stout resistance.

It had been a blessedly long time since he'd killed those of the Bloodlines. But now, he had to remember when his blade had been regularly red with their blood. He had to become that man again, to save all those he'd brought into this danger.

Tal smiled into the darkness and felt again upon his lips the wild, mad grin of the Red Reaver.

He remembered climbing hand over hand onto the ships. Dodging, slicing, chopping limbs. The frantic caper of death, always balancing on its edge, and the barest slip could have sent him falling. But he'd always kept the advantage with a weapon none of his opponents possessed.

Moving the bow and arrow to one hand, he reached forward, and his hand met the cold, dried bark of a tree. Running up it until he reached the branches, he concentrated on them and imagined them burning, orange flames rippling along their silhouetted form.

"*Kald*," he whispered, then threw himself away.

Almost as soon as the flames had risen from the branches, he heard the snap of a crossbow, then the hiss of the bolt falling into the woods. As he stumbled to his feet and moved deeper into the forest, he glanced back at the tree to see fire quickly engulfing it. By the flickering light, he could see many silhouettes rushing away from it, down toward the caravan.

"Not yet, you bastards," he muttered.

Tal ran, finding another tree and setting it ablaze, then several strides further he ignited another. With each burning tree, his adversaries were revealed, their silhouettes more apparent to the caravan below. Not only would it warn them of the danger, but they'd be able to more clearly see their enemies.

But with each tree, he also became more visible.

More bolts whistled toward him from the darkness, but the flickering shadows must have confused their vision, for all of them missed. *For now.* Breath hissing through his teeth, Tal ran further into the murk, trying to get around where he'd last seen his quarry. He heard them distinctly now, shouts breaking out among their ranks. They were angry and scared — no soldier enjoyed facing a sorcerer, and there was no doubt what Tal was now.

Positioning himself to silhouette them against the fires, he tried counting the assailants. *A dozen at least — probably more.* He didn't doubt they were hardened soldiers, well beyond the experience and capabilities of Wren and Garin.

Wren and Garin. Falcon and Aelyn. He alone stood between them and the Easterners. He couldn't fail them.

Behind the partial cover of a trunk, Tal lifted his bow and drew back the string in one smooth motion. The wood tensed under his hand, and his body quivered for a moment with the strain of holding it. As he sighted a silhouette, the point of his arrow slowly dropped to the appropriate angle, close to parallel to the ground in the windless forest.

He let loose.

The arrow whistled out of sight, and a moment later, a screech of agony came from one of the Easterners. Tal pivoted back behind the trunk as he notched another arrow, then drew back as he turned around the other side. A bolt nearly found him, whistling a hand's length away from his face. He didn't flinch back, but sighted another target, aimed, and fired. A second scream joined the first.

They were coming for him now, dark shapes racing in front of the flames toward him. Tal dropped his bow and drew *Velori*, keeping the sword's glowing runes hidden beneath his cloak.

The enemies were closing in on his tree. One slipped and nearly fell flat on the icy ground while the other two continued. In the darkness and snow, there was no room for fancy footwork and fine swordplay. Only timing, luck, and savagery remained.

The first two came into view around the trunk, and Tal bared his blade and swung with all his strength.

The blue runes along *Velori's* steel went dark, and the shadowed Easterner howled as the blade cut clean through. Seeing him fall, Tal spun away to hack at the second silhouette.

The World reeled.

Pain burst through his jaw from an unseen fist, and his vision, already limited to begin with, specked with black dots. But he saw enough to duck the wild swing that whisked overhead. Tal jabbed forward into the black form before him and was rewarded by a sickening squelch and a man's whimper. Tal pulled *Velori* free and, stepping away, looked around for the last assailant.

The axe swung so close he heard it whistle by his ear as he jerked out of the way. Tal grinned with fear as he staggered, his balance lost on the frozen ground, then again found his footing. The Easterner readied another swing even as their own footing shifted beneath them. Tal waited for the inevitable blow.

The axe was little more than a glint in the darkness, fire catching on the blade. Luck as much as a keen eye guided Tal as he pivoted, caught his footing again, and retaliated. The assailant, whether from the icy snow or inexperience, had continued forward within reach, and he slid onto Tal's jabbing blade. By the firelight, Tal saw *Velori* projecting from his throat before he yanked the blade loose.

Seeing no others advancing, Tal retreated behind the nearest tree and breathed hard as a smile found his swollen lips. He wiped a trail of blood from his chin. The fighting continued a moment longer as the invaders fought among themselves, not realizing who their assailant was. A second after, a harsh command called out, and the melee ceased. A torch lit among the Easterners, then two, and Tal took the full measure of the company.

Two dozen. Even with five men down, they still outnumbered the troupers. And all of them knew how to wield a weapon.

Instead of chasing after him, the enemy company raced toward the caravan. Cursing under his breath, Tal slipped and slid through the forest in pursuit.

As soon as the first fire ignited among the trees, Garin raced back to his bedroll.

"Wren!"

Her eyes flew open. Before he could say another word, she'd thrown off her blankets and was standing, sheathed rapier in hand. Her hair was a mess and her eyes still swollen from sleep, but she already looked readier than he as she studied the camp and surrounding forest.

"We're under attack?" she asked, bending to pull on her boots.

"I think so." He quickly explained the little that he knew.

She nodded, taking it matter-of-factly. When she'd secured her boots, she motioned to his bedroll. "Shouldn't you be armed, then?"

Cursing himself for a fool, Garin scrambled to grab his sword and shield, forgotten in his shock. As he hefted the shield, the muscles in his left arm felt tight with the scar he'd earned at the Ruins of Erlodan. He shivered at the memory of that day, and at the prospect that similar horrors awaited them.

Even as he stood, Wren dashed away, and he had to sprint to keep her in sight.

Wren turned a corner, and Garin followed, only to skid to a halt. A broad figure, silhouetted by the fires from the forest, charged toward them. He looked as if he wore a horned helmet, and steel glinted above his head.

Garin's brief training came to the rescue. As the assailant struck, Garin raised his shield while his sword dove toward the attacker's knees. "High-Low" it was called by Master Krador, the Master-at-Arms of the Coral Castle, who had drilled them endlessly over it in the castle's courtyard.

But their training had been against youths, and this attacker possessed far more than a boy's strength. Garin's shoulder exploded with the impact of the blow, and bright spots appeared in his eyes. Yet he managed to cut into his opponent's leg, and his blade jarred against bone. His assailant roared as he collapsed, a sound almost inhuman, then cut off abruptly as Wren leaped forward and stabbed her rapier through his neck.

Rolling his smarting shoulder, Garin stared down at the man they'd killed — if he could be called a man. His body had the shape of a human, but instead of wearing a helmet, he found the horns were part of its head. He closely resembled a bull, down to an iron ring through its nose.

"What is it?" His voice shook as the realization of what they'd just survived sunk in.

"Minotaur." Wren spat on the corpse and looked around. "Damned Easterners. Come on — we have to find Falcon and the others."

Though a large part of him wanted to flee the other way, he followed Wren around the caravan toward the sounds of fighting. Coming around the edge of a wagon, he gained a view of the middle campfire and stared, trying to make sense of what he saw.

Tal stood with his back to the fire, his runic sword raised before him, while four shadows flanked him. The attackers' faces were strange and horrific in the flickering light, their features coming in flashes — the slitted, yellow eyes of a serpent; the horned countenance of another bull-man; the glowing eyes of a devil set in a face lost in darkness; and the white, shimmering tattoos inked over human features.

"We have to help!" Wren hissed.

For a moment, Garin debated if he should. What did he owe Tal Harrenfel? But then his gaze fell on someone he hadn't seen at first glance, who cowered next to the wagon behind Tal. Falcon Sunstring.

He'd already made his choice.

"We need to get behind them," he told Wren, pulling her back around the wagons.

"But they're closing in!"

"They'll hold out for a second. Trust me."

To his surprise, she relented, and they set into a stealthy run.

"I don't like the look of this," Falcon said at his back, a whine sneaking into his voice.

"You think I do?"

Tal gritted his teeth against the pains announcing themselves along his body and eyed the Easterners penning them in. A Nightelf, a medusal, a minotaur, and a human, they were the last of their attackers. Those whom Tal hadn't hunted down had fallen prey to Aelyn's sorcery, for the Nightelves in the enemy company posed no match for the mage's prodigious skill. But Aelyn was busy protecting the rest of the troupers — there'd be no help forthcoming from him.

"I only have one hand, you know," Falcon called to their assailants. "You wouldn't kill a man with one hand, would you?"

The minotaur snorted, its dark eyes unreadable in the scant firelight. The medusal's tongue flitted out to lick one yellow eye, the slitted pupils dilated. The serpentine Easterner and the Nightelf were nocturnal and could see Tal and Falcon much better than they could see them. He had to take them out before the Easterner human and the bull-man.

If they'd only give him the opportunity.

For the moment, they all waited, sizing each other up, edging around so they surrounded Tal and Falcon. Tal's breath hissed in his throat. His eyes were dry from the flames' heat and the smoke and staring unblinking into the darkness. Yet he couldn't allow himself a moment's respite.

Then he saw it — little more than a hand flexing — and his four enemies charged.

Blood burning through his veins, Tal thundered, "*Mord!*" and dove to one side.

Inky blackness, impenetrable even for Nightborn eyes, fell over the camp. Though the campfire still cast off light, it was muted, barely reaching beyond the burning wood. Tal, blind as the rest of them, tried to recall the layout of the camp as he stumbled around obstacles. His assailants did the same —with much less success, from their hissed Darktongue curses.

A foreign word sounded from the darkness, then a ball of werelight appeared, revealing the Nightelf's hunting pink eyes.

Tal ghosted out his line of vision, but heard other prey closer at hand, the heavy breathing of a minotaur mere feet to his right.

"*Fuln!*"

In the blinding flash of light that followed, Tal lunged at the silhouetted enemy and felt *Velori* shudder with impact as the blade ground against bones. In his sparking vision, Tal saw the counter-swing and tried to dodge, but still felt the strange, familiar splitting of flesh over his left shoulder. Gasping at the fire spreading down his arm, Tal fought the fog in his mind as he jerked his sword free and, with a parting slash, extinguished his light to retreat into the darkness.

But the Nightelf, still wreathed in phantom light, was closing in. Likely, the other two Easterners neared as well. Tal tried to quiet his breathing, but the pain from his shoulder undermined his efforts. He could only hope the pain-filled grunts of the injured minotaur nearby masked any sound he made.

As a trembling shout came from further away, the Nightelf turned, its attention drawn. Tal almost cursed aloud. *Falcon, you thrice-damned fool,* he thought, then lunged.

Velori's point sought the artery in his enemy's leg as he gashed it open. Crying in pain, the Nightelf tried to spin around and slash at him with his sword, but his leg collapsed beneath him, pitching him to the ground.

Tal was already withdrawing. At the edge of the Nightelf's werelight, he saw the last two of his enemies stalking forward. The black, slitted pupils of the medusal were wide in its yellow eyes, staring at exactly where Tal moved.

"Yuldor's prick," he muttered, then lifted the darkness.

In a moment, he took in the surrounding scene. The minotaur, a dozen paces to his right, clutched his side in one massive hand and leaned against a wagon. The Nightelf, both hands to his thigh, crawled away more sluggishly with each moment. The last two Easterners, the medusal and Imperial woman, stalked toward him, the medusal carrying a single, curved scimitar, while the human bore both spear and shield.

Behind them, Garin and Wren crept forward, blades bared.

His heart leaped into his throat. The two youths might have faced undead soldiers without fear, but these were no mindless draugars — they were trained killers, some of the best the East had to offer, if his suspicions were correct. Should Wren and Garin attempt to fight them, they'd be killed.

"*Kald!*" Tal shouted, and flames licked up *Velori* as he charged.

Neither the medusal nor human flinched before his sudden assault, but instead fanned out to either side. Cutting his dash short, Tal lunged at the medusal, hoping to strike and retreat before his companion could get within range. But the medusal slipped his sword around to turn Tal's aside, disregarding the flames running down the steel and forcing him to retreat.

Sidestepping, Tal spun away from the woman warrior's lunging spear and felt his legs nearly give way. In addition to his shoulder, a dozen wounds bled across his body. Exhaustion dragged at his limbs. He had to end this, and quickly.

Sensing weakness, the Easterners attacked, the human leading with her spear and the medusal following. Tal extinguished *Velori's* flames as he turned the spear aside and backed away, then brought his blade around for the medusal's assault. Their blades met, and the medusal drove against him until their crossguards met, then punched a scaled fist into his side.

He bore no open injury there. But deep in his flesh, an old wound remained, a scar that had never fully healed.

As the medusal's fist found it, he crumpled.

Next that he knew, he was down on his knees. His vision blurred. All the strength went out of his limbs. A last thought flickered through his mind.

Once more, Tal Harrenfel had failed to live up to his legend.

———

Garin and Wren charged toward where Tal knelt before his two assailants.

As Wren lunged at the spearwoman, Garin darted toward the lizard-man, the colorful mane of feathers running down its back making it stand out even in the scant light. Before he could reach it, the Easterner batted aside Tal's half-hearted retaliation and kicked him in the chest with a wickedly clawed foot, hitting him in the side again and leaving bloody marks in its wake. *The side with his old wound*, Garin remembered, and understood now what had felled his old mentor.

As the lizard-man drew back its sword for a strike, Garin raised his shield and threw all of his weight into it. As the blow connected, they were both sent staggering, his tortured shoulder screaming once more. Ignoring it, he used "Fort-Strike-Fort," another of Krador's techniques, his sword darting around his shield to stab at the warrior. It had looked like an easy strike, but somehow, Garin's sword skittered down the Easterner's scales. He barely raised his shield to accept the return blow, stumbling under the force of it.

He backed away, the lizard-man darting in strikes that he barely blocked. His breath came quicker, his reactions slower. Fear weighed down his limbs as much as exhaustion.

Let me assist! the Singer suddenly roared through his mind, his voice a blistering gale. *Cede me control!*

"*No!*" Garin cried his defiance with both his mind and mouth.

The tip of the curved sword darted over the top of his shield before he pushed it back. But the sudden movement threw him off balance, and as he stepped backward, his heel caught on something solid. Garin went sprawling, his shield and sword thrown wide as he tried to stop his fall.

The lizard-man stood over him. Its sword fell toward him.

Without thinking, Garin threw up his shield to block while his sword darted around. The lizard-man's yellow eyes widened, and a surprised hiss escaped its lips. The Easterner stumbled backward, Garin's sword sliding from its gut.

Movement flashed in the corner of his eye, then Wren was there, cutting the legs out from under the Easterner. The lizard-man's tail lashed the air as it fell, screaming its pain, and Wren darted back, her rapier held up warily before her as she watched it die.

Garin rose to his knees and stared at the dying creature. The stench of blood and piss and smoke were thick in his nostrils.

He looked away, and his gaze fell on Tal.

The man was still curled around his wound. His eyelids flickered, but his former mentor seemed unconscious. His sword lay by him, the runes glowing a faint cerulean amid a lattice of blood.

Kill him. Kill him, as he killed your father.

He didn't know if the voice was his or the devil's. He didn't much care. They had the right of it, didn't they? He could pay Tal back the debt he owed him and be done with it.

All he needed to do was let his blade fall.

From a distance, he heard Wren speaking, but he ignored her. This was his decision. Only he could make it.

He took a step toward him, his sword rising.

A flicker of motion caught his attention, and Garin raised his gaze to the burning trees ringed around them — and like a hammer-blow, the dream came back to him.

The burning forest. His double, spinning amid it, glorifying in it, his face contorted with wild pleasure. The power promised to him.

Garin lowered his sword and turned away as Wren seized his arm.

"Garin!" The urgency in her voice made him meet her eyes, and the fear in them brought him fully back to himself. "Are you hurt?"

He heard the unspoken question in her words: *Did the devil take you again?*

"I'm still me." His words came out harsh, his throat tortured from the smoke and fighting, and he pulled roughly away.

Wren didn't follow as he shuffled through the ashes of their camp.

ASHES OF THE PAST

PHANTOMS MOVED AROUND HIM, SPEAKING SOFTLY AS IF FROM far away. Tal tried to focus on them, to reach out and touch them, but his fingers found nothing. They were just out of grasp, if they were there at all.

"Ashelia?" he whispered.

The blurred face above him resolved, and he recoiled. Its skin was hard and edged in rough layers like the bark of a gnarled oak. Its eyes were laced with green veins as if vines grew through them. As the maggot lips smiled, the teeth were black and barbed like the stingers of bees.

"Wake up, Tal, you cursed fool," a familiar voice came from the oaken face.

Tal blinked, and the horrific face resolved into Aelyn's scowling countenance. The mage's head was bare, his pointed ears on display through his black, braided hair, and his bronze eyes narrowed as he stared down at him.

"What happened to you?" Aelyn demanded. "I purged the common corruptions, but you remain delirious."

Tal closed his eyes as the World slowly continued to spin around him.

"It's not a new poison, but an old one," he muttered. Each

word came out garbled, his tongue and mouth defying his will to form them. His skin felt both feverish and chilled, and his body ached to the bones with the fire burning inside him.

"My side," he tried to clarify as he squinted up at the mage, willing him to understand.

"The wound you took from the Thorn?" Aelyn's mouth twisted as he matter-of-factly lifted Tal's shirt away, cutting where it stuck to bloody wounds, then bent forward to examine it. "Hm. It's open again, though only slightly. You'll need the runes repaired."

He worked his tongue over his chapped lips. "Only one person should repair those."

"Yes. The one who first wrote them." The elf's smirk widened. "It seems you cannot stay away from my House-sister after all."

Tal groaned, and only in part from the pain wracking his body.

He slowly took in their surroundings. They were in one of the covered wagons. Bags of foodstuff — including onions, from the stench — lay underneath him as a makeshift bed. Aelyn, tall as he was, had to remain stooped to continue his healing. The flap was closed, but he could see a faint brightening against the canvas that was more golden than a fire's glow. Day was breaking.

The night's activities reasserted themselves. He found Aelyn's gaze. "They're all dead?"

The mage nodded. "Or fled. Unless more hung back, only two at most escaped. You performed well, Magebutcher. And you know I don't hand out compliments."

At another time, Tal would have lorded the moment of civility over him. But fear and pain weighed down his levity.

"Our people?"

Aelyn's smile fled. "There were some... casualties."

His chest clenched too tightly to breathe. "Who?"

The elf looked aside. "We fared well, all things considered.

Falcon is alive, as are Wren and Garin. But we did lose one: Mikael, the goblin, stabbed an Easterner from the shadows and paid for it. Some others took minor injuries, while the Befal human, the one they call Ox, took many wounds protecting the others. But he'll survive."

Tal stared at the canvas above him, not bothering to wipe his eyes. Mikael, the laughing jester... *No more pranks for him,* he thought bitterly. *You made sure of that.*

He'd had his fair share of deaths settled upon his shoulders. But he'd thought those days were past. Yet here it was, the blame clear and unavoidable before him. He'd asked Falcon to bring the troupe with them to Elendol as a cover for their true purposes. He'd brought them into this peril.

He'd killed Mikael as surely as if he'd driven a dagger through his heart.

Tal sat up again, fighting through a sudden wave of pain and nauseating heat. A trickle of wetness down his side made his torn shirt stick again to his skin.

Aelyn watched him with a twisted smile. "Where do you think you're going?"

"To protect the caravan," Tal wheezed as he put one leaden foot under him, then the other, and levered himself up. "There might be others out there."

"If there are, I doubt they'll attack again. Prime Helnor is at least capable of handling a perimeter defense."

Tal had to steady himself against the wagon's wall and nearly fell over as his hand sunk into the canvas. "Helnor?" he managed. "He's here?"

"He arrived an hour ago, just after we'd put out the fires. Too late to be of use, I might note."

Tal ignored him and kept his gaze on his feet as he navigated the haphazard floor. Finally, he reached the wagon's flap and nearly fell out as he pulled it back. The camp swarmed with people, the figures swimming before his unsteady vision. He could see well enough to notice most of them were strangers and clad in a way he hadn't seen in many years.

He knew them to be Warders, the guardians of Gladelyl's borders. Equipped both to ride for days at a time upon stors, their stag-like mounts, to fight any enemies they encountered, their protection consisted mostly of brown leather and amber-hued, petrified bark. The bark, made light by enchantment and cleverly arrayed like scales, came from their massive trees, the elder mangroves called "kintrees" that formed the bones of their cities and towns. It could as easily stop an arrow as a blade. Each had a sword belted at their side, light, single-edged sabers similar to those borne by Avendor's cavalry. Some Warders still wore their helmets, most made of leather and bark, each of them unique to the individual. The rigidity of uniform that plagued the armies of the human realms of Avendor and Sendesh didn't hold sway among the Gladelysh protectors, perhaps because their service could last for a century.

"Tal Harrenfel, you damned hero — come here and sit before you fall over!"

Tal turned to see a familiar Warder approaching him. Prime Helnor wore a broad grin as he approached, though in the reserved fashion of the elves, he made no move to touch him. The growing dawn's light caught in his loose, long curls, turning the blonde hair golden and brightening the tattoos inked across his face to the yellow-green of newborn leaves. Though his face was ordinarily smooth but for his white-lined scars, his brow creased as he looked Tal up and down.

"Mother's name, Tal, but what happened to you?"

He had only enough energy to shrug. "You've seen the camp."

"And could scarcely believe my eyes. Do you know how many of the *kolfash* bodies we found? Eighteen. Eighteen, Tal!" Helnor laughed, and his eyes, silver dancing through amber irises, were bright as he stared at Tal. "I would have been hard-pressed to accomplish the same myself!"

Tal winced, and not only at the praise. "I'd prefer you didn't use that word around me, Helnor. You know who my friends are."

The laughter died in the Prime's eyes. "*Kolfash?* Yes, I suppose I know. And for you, I'll keep the Mother's own patience. Besides, your half-kin friend isn't the worst to walk the streets of Elendol these days."

"I'll hear more of that later. But as good as it is to see you, old friend, I have a charge to look after. I assume you'll escort us?"

"*Kolesa* would never forgive me if I didn't, would she?"

Tal gave a wan smile, trying to hide the nervous thrill his allusion sent through him, then he made to move past Helnor. But no sooner had he placed his foot than all the strength went out of his leg.

He didn't quite reach the ground, for steady arms caught him.

"Never did know your limits," Helnor chastised.

The Prime Warder lifted him up, the tall man making easy of the task, and Tal groaned a protest. But even his dignity seemed too much effort to maintain.

"Tal!"

Though drowsiness was quickly overtaking him, he let his head fall to the side and tried focusing his vision. Wren and Falcon stood next to him, eyes spinning with concern.

The minstrel placed his one hand across Tal's forehead and shook his head. "Hell's fires, my friend, but you're a damned fool. Why didn't you stay put? Too good for a bed of onions?"

"I still have standards," Tal wheezed.

"Standards get you killed," Wren observed sagely with a raised eyebrow. But she briefly pressed his hand before stepping back.

Tal moved his eyes sluggishly around. "Garin?"

33

Wren and Falcon exchanged a glance.

"He's busy helping pack up camp," the lass said.

Tal had to give it to her — he couldn't hear the lie in her voice. He closed his eyes. "As long as he's safe," he murmured, "I haven't entirely failed him."

Then he remembered who he hadn't saved. "I heard about Mikael. I'm sorry, both of you. I couldn't protect him."

He felt his hand squeezed tightly. "Stubborn old fool," Falcon said, his voice choked. "We all knew the risks."

And what's life without the spark of risk? As his own saying came back to him, and a mocking smile curled his lips just before oblivion swallowed him once more.

Garin watched as his one-time mentor went slack in the arms of the warrior elf. His feet longed to move, his hands twitched for something to do, but he kept himself hidden behind the wagon. Tal hadn't seen him, and he had no intention of letting him.

I just don't want him to die by someone else's hand, he told himself.

The silence seemed to mock him.

Turning away, he began ambling around the camp. Ashes sifted beneath his boots, rising in small squalls to further stain his pants. Even in the dawning light, the surrounding trees looked like deathly specters, black, jagged shapes charred from the night's fires. Some of the encompassing forest had caught, but the magic of the elven scouts — Warders, he'd heard them called — had extinguished them before they'd spread much beyond their camp.

Garin looked up to find someone watching him, and he abruptly turned away. Brother Causticus' gaze was never comfortable, but it was all the less so with the black thoughts on his mind. The monk's eyes followed him until he turned out of sight behind a wagon.

Even as he breathed a sigh of relief, his thoughts turned down other dark paths. The Singer had tried to lure him again and gain control. He wondered how long it would be before he gave in. Was defeat inevitable?

He knew little of the devil, and less of the Nightsong. How were they connected? Did the devil "sing" the Song? Or was it the other way around, that the Nightsong caused the Singer to exist?

More than ever, he longed for answers. But he who might know more was the one person he couldn't speak to.

"Young *lenual*. Are you well?"

Garin startled and turned toward the lilting voice. A female Warder leaned against a wagon, her light gray eyes swirling with the gray of thunderclouds as she studied him. As with most of the elven warriors, she was taller than him, yet slender despite the toned muscles evident beneath her armor. An emerald tattoo, as intricate as the lace on the noblewomen's dresses in the Coral Castle, spiraled across the earthy brown skin of her face, forming patterns Garin could almost recognize. Her tightly curled, brown-blonde hair was bound in thick braids.

The Warder smiled, and Garin felt his tongue tie itself into further knots. She was enchanting in a way he'd only glimpsed in Wren before. A few of the women in Halenhol had been beautiful, but buttresses of paints and powders had supported their delicate elegance. This warrior elf's features were far from soft, yet she possessed about her a wild allure he couldn't explain, like the thrill of standing on a bridge over a surging river.

The elf finally broke the silence. "I've startled you — my apologies. I only wished to see if you were well."

Too late, Garin tried to dredge up his manners. "I'm sorry. I didn't mean to…"

She waved a hand. "No need for that. It was a shocking night for you."

Her words were lightly accented, pleasantly curling familiar words in his ears.

"Yes," he mumbled.

"You are Garin, are you not?"

His ears burned. "How did you know?"

She smiled again. "We had word of your coming. And there are few *lenual* youths among your party."

"*Lenual?*"

"'Human' in Gladelyshi. The first of many words you'll learn in my tongue, if you stay in Elendol long."

He hoped she didn't know why he'd come. If they'd been warned to expect him, it couldn't just be for the "dancing lessons" that King Aldric had been told he came for. But under her stormy gaze, he smiled all the same.

"Garin?"

He spun and saw Wren coming around the other end of the wagon. Something behind her eyes eased as she walked toward him, at least until she saw the elvish warrior.

"Hello," she said warily, stopping at a distance.

The Warder only smiled. "Don't worry, little half-kin. I don't share the outrage of my peers. I serve as a Warder, don't I?"

Garin knew he should keep out of whatever hovered between Wren and the elf, but he couldn't help himself. "What do you mean?"

The woman's eyes came back to him. "Elves are even more rigid in their beliefs than humans. While women often keep to certain roles, and they may be frowned upon when deviating from those, there have been exceptions in your history. The Warrior Queen Jalenna, for one, and the Witch of Jalduaen, who purified the Scourge from the Nortveld Barrows. But among our people, each is held to their caste — male and female, Highkin and Low."

"And *kolfash*," Wren observed coolly.

The Warder regarded Wren, her expression unchanging. "And half-kin, too."

As much to break their gaze as out of curiosity, Garin asked, "Do women not become warriors in Gladelyl?"

"Until recently, they were not even allowed to hold a sword, nor any blade larger than a table knife," the elf replied. "No woman has been a blacksmith, warrior, or even a tanner in the length of our history."

Garin frowned. "But a queen rules you. If women wanted to do those things, wouldn't she change the rules?"

The Warder shook her head. "Even a queen's command is limited by the ignorance of men. And not men only — many women, too, wish for things to remain as they are. In Gladelysh society, change comes slowly. Perhaps they feel threatened by the possibility of all they could have become, but now believe they cannot."

"You carry a sword," Wren observed snidely.

"Yes." The Warder's hand fell to her hilt, not threateningly, but almost as a caress. "Some time ago, long by *lenual* reckoning, I convinced a man to teach me the blade, even though it was forbidden. Ever since, I've observed the best dancers among us and practiced what I've seen. A poor education, but it was the best I could manage. Yet it was enough that when the Peers' House came to Queen Geminia with their demands to open the borders to the Empire, she countered with her own requirements: that the castes, too, be opened, and the limitations of gender with them. In one fell swoop, Elendol as we've known it changed. Time will tell if it was for the better.

"But change didn't come quite so easily. When the Peers demanded that Her Eminence show them a woman who could wield a sword, Queen Geminia, in her prescience, called me forward. I was given a blade and put before the finest of our dancers, Ulen Yulnaed — Windlofted, in the Reachtongue."

"And you bested him." Wren gave the Warder a droll smile.

The elf didn't return it. "I did not. Ulen was gentle and did me no permanent harm, but his House is among the Eastern Sympathists, and he didn't spare me any humiliation. But when I could no longer hold a sword, the Queen held up her hand and pointed to me, and said, 'She is a healer. She is a mother. She is a woman. Yet see her fire, her spirit, burning as bright as any male's. Had she been trained all her life as Ulen Windlofted has, I do not know that even he could have bested her.'

"I thought they'd laugh and jeer. I lay bruised and beaten before the Queen's court, so ashamed of my poor performance I could not lift my eyes. But at that moment, no one spoke against Her Eminence's words. And so she decreed that any woman who wished to learn to dance, or forge a blade, or skin a hunt's prey, could do so." The Warder's chin lifted, and the dark gray in her eyes swirled as if daring them to challenge her.

Garin wouldn't have dreamed of it, even if he'd had the words. And a glance at Wren showed a new emotion shining in her eyes.

"Warder Venaliel!"

The Warder pivoted, suddenly stiff at the sharp command. "Prime."

The Warder in charge of the others, Prime Helnor, stepped into view. Though a smile had often been on his lips as he'd taken over command of the caravan, his bright eyes were hard as they fell on the elvish woman. Garin's gut tightened. He longed to rush to her defense, even as he knew how little good that would do.

"If you insist on acting the Warder," the Prime said, "then you must at least *pretend* to play your part."

The Warder's eyes swirled. "I was looking after the youth, Helnor. Or were we not told to ensure Garin's safety?"

"Delaying the caravan's departure does nothing to help that. And you'll use my title when we're on patrol, *Kolesa*, or this will be your last."

"I will, Prime Venaliel. So long as you treat me as you do the others."

Helnor looked as if he would say more, but he instead clamped his mouth shut. As Garin looked between them, a realization slowly dawned on him. Their features, their tattoos, and most of all, their shared name revealed who they were to each other.

"You're related, aren't you?" he said, only thinking better of it after the words left his mouth.

Both elves turned to face him, and it was all Garin could do not to wince.

"Unfortunately," the Prime responded. His gaze snapped back to the woman. "If you can leave off your act for a moment, you might apply your Mother-given talents somewhere they're needed. He's suffering, *Kolesa*. And if he knew you were here and didn't come—"

"I told you, I can do nothing for that wound that our *belosi* could not. Once we reach civilization, I will treat him."

Helnor held her gaze for a long moment, but when she didn't move, he exhaled sharply, turned, and strode away. The female Warder looked after him for a long moment before the rigidity left her. Her eyes fell to her boots.

Garin glanced at Wren. Her eyes were wide and her mouth slightly parted. Before he could whisper a question, though, the Warder spoke.

"Helnor may be stubborn, but he's the Prime. You should both find a wagon to ride in — the Easterners released most of your horses during the attack, so there won't be any to ride."

With that, the Warder turned and followed after Prime Helnor.

His mind turned with all he'd discovered. "Do you know what just happened?" he asked Wren.

She looked at him like he was dim. "They're related, Garin, like you said. Even more, they're siblings — *kolesa* means 'sister.'"

"I'd figured out that much. But—"

"You still don't know who she is, do you? Venaliel, her House-name, means 'Starkissed' — does that ring a bell?"

A memory, a faint melody, came slowly back to him. In a lilting, half-singing voice, he murmured, "*He came to her in the night, the moon lighting his way.*"

Wren took up the verse, gold spinning in her eyes. "*Though love to them was forbidden by day.*"

"*With leaves as their blankets, and boughs as their shields.*"

"*Each took to the other, and gave all the World would not yield.*"

"*And when only the stars remained awake.*"

"*He whispered her name with a thirst he could not slake.*"

"'*Ashelia Starkissed,*'" Garin murmured, "*her very name, his wedding bell.*"

"*But in the end, love would be denied both her and Tal Harrenfel.*"

Though anger stirred in him at Tal's name, Garin focused on their discovery. "Ashelia. She's his long-lost lover of legend. But was it true?"

"Father always said it was." Wren shrugged. "But we both know you can't believe much of his stories. We'll think on it later. You heard Prime Helnor — it's time to leave. Mikael wouldn't want us to linger."

The goblin's death coming to the fore of his mind again, Garin's shoulders sagged. He nodded and followed Wren back among the caravan.

A HEALER'S TOUCH

SHE SLID FROM HIS SWORD AND CRUMPLED TO THE FLOOR.
Bloodied blade falling to his side, Tal watched as the red, killing mist rose from her body. For a moment, the fog formed into a mockery of her figure as it had been in life, and seemed to meet his gaze, accusation clear in its murky eyes.

Then it turned and descended on their enemies.

One by one, the unholy revenant dove into the Easterners, streaming in through their mouths, their noses, their eyes. As it entered, their expressions froze in sudden horror. When it eased back out, each man fell, never to rise again.

Only when the mist had murdered all the others in the chamber did it rise in a crimson cloud before Tal again. Still he stood motionless, not moving to protect himself.

From the bloodshade issued forth a voice, aged and nearly unfamiliar with the time that had passed since he'd heard it. Even so, he recognized it as Keeper's.

"*Damned fool. I died so you could possess my sister's knowledge. And what have you done with it? What have you done with your Blood?*"

Tal fell to his knees, his head bowing. He did not speak.

"*You are the Heart's Blood,*" Keeper continued, merciless. "*But you are not worthy of it coursing through your veins.*"

"I know."

As she gave him one last accusing look, the dream dissolved, and his eyelids fluttered open.

Even the dim light through the canvas of the wagon pressed painfully on his eyes. Groaning, Tal closed them again and shifted, trying to find a spot where the shuddering wagon beneath him didn't jolt his wounds so painfully. He didn't succeed.

A dream — it was only a dream. Yet just as with his dream the night of the attack, it had felt so vivid and real, all of his senses awakened to the scene. He'd smelled the smoke of the fires from the traps triggered in the tower below, felt the sweat beading down his unwashed skin. The metallic tang of blood sat on his tongue.

A bitter smile touched Tal's lips. "I'm mad," he murmured. "Even more than I was before."

Though he recognized the dream as taking place in the Blue Moon Obelisk, a place he'd long ago visited, it had been a parody of the true events. The bloodshade of Keeper, the Nightelf who had maintained the derelict tower, had never spoken. Tal hadn't just stood still as the shade slaughtered the Easterners, but had fought for his life. Yet it hadn't stopped his latent guilt from sending him a poignant message.

All I've learned, all I've striven for — and what has it gained?

He shifted uncomfortably on his bed of onions as he stewed. He'd hidden away in Hunt's Hollow, assuring himself it was to translate the tome Keeper had entrusted to him, *A Fable of Song and Blood*. But when he'd finished, he'd stayed, spinning its words repeatedly in his head. *Founts of Blood, Founts of Song* — what did it mean? Was any of it real, or the delusions of a Nightelf as devil-touched as himself?

Yet if Tal's experiences hadn't proven the truth of Hellexa

Yoreseer's *Fable*, Garin's tribulations had. And, for the youth's sake, he could no longer delay acting.

Delay doing what?

No answer came, and inevitably, he drifted off again. In and out he came from a dreamless slumber, and the light through the wagon's canvas faded. He only jolted fully awake as the wagon rumbled to a halt.

The flap opened, and Tal squinted through the painful light to see Wren peering in.

"He's still alive," she called back.

"Thanks for the wager of confidence," Tal muttered as she climbed into the wagon and began shifting him around.

"With you reeking of onion, you've got enough to thank me for already."

As Tal grimaced, a Warder he didn't recognize peered in. "The Prime told me to carry him," the elf said shortly.

Wren barely glanced back at him as she gestured to Tal, then moved out of the way. Another Warder joined the first, and between the two of them, they scooped him up in their arms and began moving him out, jostling him and sending fiery, mind-numbing stabs of pain cascading from his side throughout his body.

Tal realized he'd fallen unconscious when he woke again, swaying back and forth, cloth stretching beneath him. Feeling with his clumsy hands around him, he guessed he was on a makeshift pallet. He opened his eyes and saw the forest canopy disappearing before the high boughs of an impossibly large tree. *A kintree,* he recognized, and despite his pain and weakness, a smile curled his lips.

The kintrees, rising hundreds of feet high and as thick around as a wealthy merchant's manor, formed the homes of the Gladelysh nobility, the Highkin. Unless Tal had been unconscious much longer than he knew, this kintree was the provincial estate of a Highkin House. But though he wracked his faint memories of the Gladelysh noble families, he couldn't remember to whom it might belong.

Four Warders carried him into the shivering shade, all the way to the grand trunk. Then the litter took on an angle as they ascended a long, curving flight of stairs around the kintree. Tal tensed at each jostling step of his escort, but he couldn't keep the pain from steadily rising and claiming him again.

When he next woke, it was to a blessedly soft surface and suffocating blankets. Groaning, he pushed the quilts off half of his body, then lay panting and reveling in the cool air against his feverish skin. Someone had removed his clothes, and except for the blankets, he was exposed. The curtains had been drawn, but a faint glow escaped through them, golden with the last light of day, or perhaps the next morning. Tal's stomach rumbled, reminding him how long it had been since he'd eaten.

He heard the bare squeak of a door's hinge, and he stiffened, listening. His eyes wandered next to him, searching for a knife, or *Velori,* or anything he might use as a weapon. It didn't matter that he was among friends. He was vulnerable. It would be far too simple to rid the World of Tal Harrenfel.

A figure with a small, yellow orb of werelight in hand came into view, and Tal half-lidded his eyes and lay prone as he watched them approach the bed. In their other hand hung a heavy bag.

The figure came closer, and Tal knew once again he dreamed. He opened his eyes wide, yet she didn't disappear.

"Ashelia?" he whispered.

Her eyes, like a storm-riven sea, stared down into his. "Tal."

They held each other's gaze for a moment. Then she turned away and set the satchel on a small table behind her and began ruffling through it.

Tal stared at her back, at the braids of hair that tumbled down like vines on a tree. Silhouetted, he could only tell that she wore a set of tunic and trousers and not the dresses he'd grown accustomed to seeing her in. It didn't matter. The sight of her set his heart galloping and his mind soaring far beyond the reach of words.

Ashelia rustled through the bag for several minutes, then turned back. In one hand, she held a small pouch, its ties loose, while the other clutched a short blade. Tucked under an arm was a wooden dowel.

For a moment, Tal grappled with the realization of her intentions. "Don't you have anything to say first?" he finally managed.

"Put this between your teeth," Ashelia responded, setting the pouch down on his bed and handing him the dowel. "You'll need your tongue if we're to speak later."

His mouth worked for a moment. His voice came out in a choked whisper. "You're repairing the runes, aren't you?"

"Yes. But I must purge the wound again first."

There was nothing more to say. He accepted the dowel and put it securely between his teeth, his breath rasping around it.

"*Kald,*" he heard her say, and the hearth across the room erupted into flames. Then she stooped over him and sprinkled a white powder over his side.

Her other arm descended, then she paused. "It will only hurt a moment," she murmured.

The knife entered the wound, and lightning surged through his veins.

You're a coward, Garin told himself once more as he paced back and forth. *Only a coward would still be here.*

Long after Tal's screams had stopped, Garin lingered outside his door. He'd said he stayed for Wren, who leaned against the wall next to him, running a coin over her knuckles again and again with a jester's dexterity. Falcon waited next to his daughter, unconsciously touching the stump of his missing hand, then quickly pulling it away.

Garin said he stayed for Wren. But though he told the lie to others, he couldn't deceive himself.

An hour had passed, and night was swiftly approaching. Garin paused to stare out from their high view. Another time, he would have marveled over the sights he'd seen since crossing the border into Gladelyl's woods. The trees grew taller and thicker than any he'd seen, and the East Marsh of Avendor held its share of giants. But none came close to the size of the kintree that housed them. Its furthest boughs stretched half a mile away, keeping them in permanent shade. They'd ascended the winding staircase higher than any tower of the Coral Castle, and his stomach turned every time he looked at the distant ground below.

But he couldn't deny that it was spectacular to behold. The woods smelled rich and earthy, full of life in a way even the wild East Marsh couldn't match. The trees were in the peak of their autumnal colors, and a tapestry of fiery orange, golden yellow, and apple red spread as far as the eye could reach, swaying and rustling in the constant wind.

He turned away and began pacing again. The platform didn't creak underfoot as he expected. Like the room Tal occupied, it seemed more grown from the tree than carved or formed of planks. The stairs, too, were like smoothed nubs that had emerged from the trees. According to Falcon, they were shaped by the mages of the Emerald Tower, one of Elendol's Chromatic Towers, where elves learned to harness their inherent sorcery.

He'd heard tales of the tree-city of the elves all his life. To be standing now on one of the kintrees themselves would have once filled him with profound wonder and awe. But that had been before the devil had clawed its way into his mind. And before Tal's confession.

The door behind them opened, and Ashelia stepped out

from the rounded opening. Garin had turned toward her with as much rapt attention as Wren and Falcon, but he quickly smoothed his expression.

Ashelia wasn't looking at him, but at Falcon. From what Garin knew, they'd had little interaction before that day, only once during the Court Bard's brief visit to Elendol some months before. But each knew what the other meant to Tal.

Garin scowled and turned his gaze over the railing, staring at the shifting sea of fall leaves below.

"He survived," Ashelia announced. "He should recover swiftly now."

From the corner of his eye, Garin saw Wren step up next to her father and clasp his hand. Falcon raised his right arm toward Ashelia before jerking it back, once again forgetting that no hand lay at its end. Still, the minstrel recovered his composure and, with a series of flourishes with his other hand, bowed as deeply as he had to King Aldric.

"Thank you, m'lady. I expected nothing less of the prodigious healing hands of my friend's legendary lover, but all the same, I admit I'm relieved."

Ashelia's skin darkened even as her eyes narrowed, and the silvery gray in them whirled. "'The legendary lover' — I have you to thank for that title."

"Perhaps I had a hand in it once." He held up his handless arm with a weak smile. "But those days are past me. May we enter to see him?"

Ashelia's eyes flickered to his stump, perhaps only now realizing the bard had only one hand. Garin's lips twisted, wondering what she'd think of that story.

"Yes," she said. "But only briefly. And do not wake him."

Falcon and Wren moved past her to enter, but Garin remained where he was. Part of him longed to go in and see Tal breathing for himself. The greater part of him wished to flee down the kintree and never look back.

Ashelia neared him. "Will you go to him?"

He opened his mouth to speak, but the words caught in his throat.

She waited a moment before speaking again. "I don't know what happened between you two. But from all I've heard, Tal had taken you under his wing. Is that right?"

"It was. Now..." Garin shrugged, unable to put words to all he felt.

Ashelia stepped up to the railing next to him, staring over the colorful canopy. "You wouldn't be here if you didn't care for him, and him for you. He almost died keeping you and your friends alive. The least thanks you can give him is to see him now. He need never know."

He knew that Falcon would tell Tal if he asked. But all the same, he nodded.

Coward, he accused himself as he entered the door behind Ashelia.

The room was dark, the great window on its far side covered with heavy curtains. A fire burned in the hearth, illuminating the room in a faint yellow glow. On the opposite side, a four-poster bed lay with a figure prone in it, partially obscured by Falcon and Wren standing over him. From the corner of his eye, he saw bloodied bandages gathered on a small table in the corner.

A lump in his throat, Garin approached, peering between the minstrel and his daughter to glimpse Tal's face. His brow creased slightly amid the shallow wrinkles of age and the scars of old battles. His chest rose with steady breathing under the blankets. His hands rested above the covers, bared of his gloves for the first time in weeks.

And glimmering on one finger was a Binding Ring.

His heart hammering, Garin turned to find Ashelia behind him. They stared silently at each other for a long moment. He wondered if she knew what that crystal band meant. Falcon and Wren might not — there'd been little reason to mention it

48

back in Halenhol, and even less since they'd freed Falcon from his long entombment.

"I've seen enough," he whispered, and headed for the door.

He breathed in the fresh air outside, a fine change from the warm, stuffy air within the chamber. One question plagued him, spinning around and around in his head.

Who bound him?

It wasn't long before the other three joined him outside. He longed to ask Wren about it, but knowing he should question her alone first, he reluctantly let the thought go.

"Now that he's stable, I need to greet our benefactors," Ashelia said. "The Lathnieli are not known for excusing lapses in courtesy."

Falcon glanced down at himself. "Perhaps I should get changed into something more suitable?"

The Warder visibly winced. "I'm sorry, Falcon Sunstring. But you and your daughter won't be able to join us."

"Why not?" The thin tendrils of gold in Wren's green eyes suddenly spun. "Because we're *kolfash?*"

To her credit, Ashelia met Wren's glare. "Except for being Sympathists, the Lathnieli are traditional in most ways. Which means they hold to the exiling of all those of partial elven blood. Out of respect for my House, they've given you hospitality, but they will not admit you within their presence."

"How kind of them," Wren sneered.

"Wren," Falcon said warningly, then nodded his head to the Warder. "We understand, Ashelia Starkissed. You have my word that we won't cause any trouble."

She nodded, her expression still uncertain, as she looked to Garin. "You, however, ought to come with me."

"Me?" He glanced at Wren and, at her continued glare, stiffened his jaw. "Why should I go when they're not allowed?"

Ashelia gave him a crooked smile. "Your loyalty is admirable. But again, it is our customs that reign supreme here. Prominent guests must come before their hosts and thank them. And despite our best efforts, you, Garin Dunford, are already well-known here."

His stomach tightened like a stone sat on it. "Why? I'm just part of the Dancing Feathers."

But she shook her head. "All the Highkin know better. Every family has contacts within the Coral Castle, and Tal made little secret of you being his protege there. Though your true purpose in being here remains secret, that you are close to Aristhol is common knowledge, and enough reason to be of interest."

"Aristhol?"

Ashelia cocked her head to one side. "It translates to 'Thorn Puller' in Reachtongue, though that doesn't quite capture the meaning. It has a much grander feel in Gladelyshi."

He felt the ropes tightening around him. "Fine," he relented wearily.

"Good. Now, come along — they'll already be sitting down to dine, and it's better to be timely than well-dressed." Beckoning him over, she glanced at Falcon and Wren. "I'll make sure they send food to your rooms."

"Don't worry over us, m'lady," Falcon said with another bow, while Wren glared coldly back.

Ashelia only turned away. "This way, Garin."

They walked down the endless stairs, descending until they were level with the forest surrounding the peripheries of the kintree's furthest branches. A silence had fallen between them, but to Garin's surprise, it was not altogether uncomfortable.

Halfway down the tree, Ashelia spoke. "I know I should ask you of your ailment. I am to be your healer, you know."

The pit in his stomach that had been growing with anticipation of the dinner suddenly became heavier. Yet he also found himself relieved. "If it has to be anyone, I'm glad it's you," he replied, surprised that he meant it.

"As am I. But I won't ask questions about that now." Her

eyes briefly alighted on him, then darted away. "I just have one I hope you'll answer."

Despite her statement, she didn't speak again for a long stretch. Garin wondered if he should ask, even as part of him dreaded to know.

"When you traveled together," she finally said, "before whatever schism came between you. Did he…?"

She trailed off, seeming to struggle to find the words. Garin avoided her gaze, his face flushing. He'd never thought to see this confident woman reduced to stammering and didn't much enjoy witnessing it.

At length, Ashelia sighed. "Never mind. I shouldn't involve you."

Not wanting to leave her disappointed, Garin tried to think of a response that wouldn't further embarrass them both. He couldn't deny that tendrils of anger seeded through his chest that Tal had put him in this position at all. But Ashelia had been nothing but kind to him. Whatever his issues with his former mentor, he wouldn't do anything to harm her.

"He never spoke of you." As Ashelia's eyes grew hard at his words, he continued quickly, "But that he didn't speak of you said enough."

She didn't answer, but stared ahead. Yet Garin saw the corner of her mouth crimping in a smile.

They continued the descent in silence once more. It wasn't long after that she stopped their walk with a gesture.

"The banquet hall is just below — see how the trunk bulges outward and the platform extends? A hundred could be seated within. But don't worry — this is no feast night, but only a small gathering of our party and whatever few guests Houselord Lathniel is already hosting."

Garin nodded, wondering if it wasn't too late to plead ill. But that was the boy's way out, and he knew he had a lot to prove if he was to continue to call himself a man.

The banquet hall opened up before them as the stairs curved

around to its landing. He'd seen it on the way up, but distracted by following Tal's entourage, he'd barely given it more than a glance. Now, he craned his neck back to take in the grand chamber. An entire wall was open to the outside so they could see all the way to the windows in the back. The windows extended nearly from the floor to the domed ceiling. Even as he wondered how it could be comfortable with the late autumn winds blowing in, they stepped under the overhanging roof. A chill rushed over him like a door opening in the dead of winter, followed by an enveloping warmth and deadening of the wind. Trying not to shudder at the clamminess that clung to his skin, he found Ashelia smiling at him, a hint of amusement swirling in her stormy eyes.

"Magic?" he queried softly, and she nodded.

Tables lined either side of the grand, carpeted walk that they trod on. The carpet was formed of no fabric Garin had ever witnessed, but felt soft beneath his feet. It was dyed the same colors as the fall-painted forest that the hall overlooked and swirled in figures and shapes that were exaggerated and foreign in their features, with eyes unnaturally angled and noses fit for giants. The surrounding walls were decorated with tapestries and paintings boasting a variety of styles and mediums, one even appearing to be little more than a slab of bark. All matched the hues of the season.

Even more enthralling were the lights that hovered all around him, suspended in midair. Werelights, he recognized them, though they were unlike any he'd seen before. Each hovered over what appeared to be lamps hanging from the ceiling, as if the lamps had conjured the lights themselves. These lights, too, shone in the spectrum of fall colors, wreathing the hall in a gentle, warm glow that shifted as they moved through it. A harp's resonating music added to the ethereal aspect. It was enough for Garin to entertain the fantasy that he walked the Quiet Havens before his time.

As they approached the far end of the room, Garin shifted

his focus to the figures seated at the table upon the dais. Houselord Jondual Lathniel looked over at them as they neared. His hair was black and cascaded in oily curls down his back, and as with all the elves he'd seen, his chin was smooth and free of facial hair, revealing severely thin, pale lips. He was as tall as Helnor, who sat by his side, though willowy in the billowing red robes around him.

Prime Helnor sat on his left. Though he'd discarded his armor, the Warder's oft-jovial expression had been replaced by flinty eyes Garin had previously seen as he interacted with his sister, as if he were preparing himself for battle.

To Helnor's left sat Aelyn, scowling even more than usual as he watched their approach. From the little Garin had gathered, Aelyn and his "House-brother" did not get along well at the best of times. He doubted the present situation would improve their friendship.

Further to the left sat a young woman who looked slightly older than Garin and a boy, both elves by their pointed ears and lively eyes. They waited demurely with their hands in their laps, though the boy fidgeted and watched them with open interest.

To their host's right, two seats remained open — their seats, he suspected, with an uncomfortable squirm. Sure enough, as they neared the dais, an elf, shorter than the others he'd seen and dressed in a plain brown dress, bowed with her hands working in strange swirling motions, then murmured for them to follow her.

"Peer Ashelia Venaliel," their host said, his voice deeper and richer than Garin would have expected. "You grace House Lathniel with your presence."

"You do me honor, Lord Jondual. Forgive our state of undress — our journey has not allowed for the finer requirements of society."

Lord Jondual waved a hand, the gesture slow and measured

instead of casual. "It matters not. Society seems to be doing away with much these days."

A shadow crossed Ashelia's face, but her expression smoothed as servants seated her and Garin. He sat with the movement of the chair being pushed in and hoped it hadn't looked as awkward as it felt.

"And welcome to your companion. Garin Dunford of Avendor, I believe?"

Garin looked up to find their host's eyes on him. His gray eyes were laced with a light lavender that swirled slowly as he beheld him.

He tried to speak and found his throat had closed. Clearing it as softly as he could, he answered in a half-strangled voice, "Yes, that's right. A pleasure to meet you, Lord Lathniel."

The elf lord's lips curled, but the smile didn't touch his eyes. "The pleasure is all mine, I'm sure."

Wondering if he'd misspoken, Garin let his gaze fall to the empty plate before him. The sooner they ate, the sooner this uncomfortable affair would be over. Or so he hoped.

But more dismay met him as he studied the implements surrounding the plate. Two knives lay at the top, but where forks and spoons should have been there were only two pairs of what appeared to be shapely sticks. He desperately hoped they weren't supposed to be their utensils.

Jondual Graybark introduced everyone at the table, the young woman apparently being his daughter and the boy his "House-son," which Garin understood to mean that this was the son of another House whom the Lathnieli were looking after.

With the introductions made, only the music from the harpist filled the great hall. Then Lord Jondual turned and gave a sharp nod, and the entire staff of servants seemed to blossom from nowhere, all bearing brimming ewers of colorful liquids and full platters of food Garin could scarcely describe. Fragrant spices filled his nose, some burning with their intensity, others soothing and sweet, all strange to perceive. He watched wordlessly as one elven servant poured a dark orange liquid into his glass.

Ashelia leaned slightly toward him. "*Bakala* — pumpkin wine. It's a traditional fall drink."

At her prompting, Garin took a sip and tried to hide his wince. The wine was thick and musty, and the strength of the alcohol made his eyes water.

Before he'd recovered, the food was being served. One by one, servants approached and silently proffered their dish, and at Ashelia's prompting, Garin accepted a little of each. When his plate was overflowing with food, most of it unidentifiable and pungent, he pretended to be politely waiting for the others to be served as he eyed his dining companions.

The elven boy didn't hesitate, but immediately picked up two of the sticks in one hand and began manipulating them in a way that seemed an impossible feat of dexterity. Trying to imitate the boy's crimping position with his own hand, Garin attempted to coax a piece of what he thought was chicken between the sticks. The sauce-covered meat defied his best efforts. He thought he saw Ashelia look askance at him and was whole-heartedly glad that Wren wasn't there to witness it.

"I must admit," Lord Jondual broke the silence of their party, "I was surprised when a Prime Warder begged hospitality of me."

Helnor didn't bother hiding his frown. "As I informed you before, Lord Jondual, it's on account of an attacked caravan. One was killed and more injured, and we had need of a place to heal them."

The elf lord's gaze slid over to Ashelia. "Then it is fortunate that you have a renowned healer masquerading as a Warder in your party."

Ashelia didn't appear to feel what Garin understood to be a slight. "Yet another reason women should be more commonly accepted as Warders, don't you think, Lord Jondual?" she said evenly.

Their host's expression tightened as he took a delicate bite from his meal.

Garin finally secured the piece of meat and levered it toward his lips. As he chewed, a sudden, searing pain shot through his mouth. It was all he could do not to spit it back out as he fumbled for his glass and drained it. But no matter how much pumpkin wine he drank, his mouth grew no cooler.

Now he was certain a smile tweaked at the corner of Ashelia's mouth.

"I heard," Lord Jondual began again, "that one of your patients was a human of very particular renown. One whom you've known in the past in a rather... intimate way."

Ashelia's smile disappeared. Through his watering eyes, Garin saw her exchange a glance with Helnor and Aelyn before finally meeting Lord Jondual's eyes.

"Most already knew Tal Harrenfel was returning to Elendol," she said coolly. "Your prescience is not as great as you believe."

The elf lord gave her a wintry smile. "If that were the extent of it, perhaps."

"But if I were you, Lord Jondual, I'd extend your scrying in a different direction. It isn't who's come to your House that should concern you, but who attacked them along the road."

"Imperials, I heard."

"Yes. No doubt the same Easterners your bond allowed in through the Sun Gate, now attacking travelers on the High Road."

"Ashelia," Helnor said warningly.

Lord Jondual waved his free hand slightly. "We have no proof they did not sneak down from Avendor. Besides, Her Eminence has not suffered Venators to enter within Gladelysh borders, and from your brother's fearsome reports, these Imperials, armed and battle-trained, could be nothing else."

Venators — Garin had heard the term used by the Warders on their way to House Lathniel. He knew the famed Easterner headhunters by their Reach-name, Ravagers. As a child, his mother had told him stories of the Ravagers, how they snatched naughty children from their beds. But even after he outgrew such tales, the soldiers who fought along the Fringes told truer stories of their deadliness.

And now he'd seen it for himself.

"They were Venators," Aelyn spoke up. "Undoubtedly."

"Ah, yes, Emissary Aelyn. I forget that you fought them. And yet your party suffered such losses. Perhaps your training at the Onyx Tower has grown faint in your mind."

Aelyn's scowl deepened, but before he could speak, Helnor broke in. "Aelyn is still a Peer of the Realm, lest you've forgotten, Lord Jondual. You shall address him as such."

The elf lord's smile disappeared. "Of course. A Peer keeps her or his title, even if they are long absent from the court and their House consists of one member."

To Garin's surprise, Aelyn suddenly stood, his features even paler than before. "And who," he nearly shouted, "is responsible for that, I wonder?"

Lord Jondual didn't rise to meet the challenge, but only held Aelyn's gaze. Garin's heart thumped in his chest, and not only from the spice still burning his mouth.

"Justice, I believe, was served for that terrible crime against your family, Peer Aelyn. Was not the man who committed it caught and executed? It certainly doesn't call for shouting in my hall."

His words did little, for Aelyn remained as taut as a drawn bow. Before he could speak again, though, Helnor rose and put a hand on his adopted brother's shoulder. "Calm now," he said in a soft rumble.

The mage angrily shrugged off his hand and strode away, and everyone at the table remained silent as Aelyn walked down the carpet toward the entrance. At the great opening, he paused and flicked a hand up. All the werelights turned an ominous violet.

Frowning, Lord Jondual muttered something as he waved his own hand over the feast hall, and the lights resumed their previous colors. But Aelyn had already gone.

Helnor still stood, and at a look from Ashelia, Garin stood as well.

"I'm afraid we are quite tired from our journey," Ashelia said coolly. "You'll excuse us if we take the rest of our dinner in our rooms, I'm sure."

Lord Jondual remained seated, as did his daughter and House-son. The Lathniel daughter glared openly at all of them, while the house-son watched the proceedings with wide eyes.

"Of course," their host said at length.

As Garin followed the Warders out from the feast hall, he'd never been so happy to leave dinner with an empty belly.

PASSAGE I

IN MY SPECULATIONS, I HAVE MADE SEVERAL ASSUMPTIONS REGARDING the thing I call the Heart. But its true nature continues to elude me.

Like most of my colleagues and fellow adherents to the Path, I have made the pilgrimage to look upon the Paradise that our Lord will bring to the World when his empire stretches from the far shores of the medusals to the ends of the Westreach. The jungle there brims with plenty — water spilling in clear falls from mossy cliffs; trees and vines growing in every crack in the stone; and no winter, no matter how cold or snow-laden, can lay claim to the peak of Ikvaldar.

But Yuldor's Paradise also disguises what lays under the shaded boughs, and the Sentinel allows none past her archway. No one has laid eyes upon our god, much less the Heart that fuels his creations, in half a millennium.

Moth-bitten scrolls dating back to that time tell of the Heart being a stone that is not a stone, black in hue, with red veins running through it. Perhaps this is where the name "Heart" comes from, for unless these ancient authors were taking liberties with description, the veins pulsed with their own light, making it seem as if blood ran through the stone. The rock was not smooth, but carved so that beasts with the wings of birds and the aspects of reptiles seemed to snarl at onlookers, as if they'd been petrified while trying to escape.

If these unnamed writers are to be believed, I still hold my doubts. But if the Heart is a stone that is not a stone, what is it truly? From the little I know, I can only guess — so if I must inscribe more speculation into this fable, I will.

I believe the Heart is magic given form, its essence made material. Sorcery incarnate.

- A Fable of Song and Blood, *by Hellexa Yoreseer of the Blue Moon Obelisk, translated by Tal Harrenfel*

CHANGING SEASONS

WHEN THE MORNING LIGHT PRIED HIS CRUSTED EYELIDS OPEN, and his gaze settled on the person sitting in the chair next to his bed, Tal knew he must still be dreaming.

In his dreams, he'd held Ashelia's hand as they raced through a forest glade and leaped into a grotto's deep pool. One moment they'd been clothed; the next, the trappings of society were sinking into the depths of the pool. He'd floated next to her, only their hands touching, their gazes holding each other's, hair flat against their heads. And she'd looked just as he remembered.

Awake, he hadn't hoped to see her so close, nor meet her eyes. She was over their long-ago affair, that much she'd made clear. Yet there she sat next to his bed, her posture bowed, her eyes slitted.

As she noticed his eyes opening, Ashelia's fluttered open, and she groaned and stretched.

"Morning." His voice rasped, and his smile pulled at his skin like it was parchment.

She raised an eyebrow. "Thirsty?"

At his nod, Ashelia rose stiffly and brought him a silver

ewer with a copper cup. Pouring it, she offered it at arm's length.

He took it and gulped it down. How many days he'd lain prone, he didn't know, but it was long enough that he felt as if every droplet of moisture had been wrung from his body. When he finished his first glass, Ashelia refilled his cup.

"Try to drink it slower," she said, a slight reprimand in her voice. "You don't want to spit it back up."

Trying to take her advice, Tal accepted the copper vessel and cradled it in his hands. He couldn't help but keep his eyes unwaveringly on her, as if by looking away, she might disappear.

"You stayed."

She looked away. "I'm your healer. I had to make sure you remained stable."

"Not every healer remains by their patients all night."

For a long moment, she was silent. "You must be starving," she said finally. "I'll fetch you food."

At the suggestion, his empty stomach announced itself. But despite its pleading, he said, "Wait."

She paused at the foot of the bed, her back to him. He sat up slightly, wincing with expected pain. But though he felt weak, the fire in his side was gone. Pulling down the covers, he examined the wound and found it neatly sealed. The skin would never merge, but with fresh runes surrounding it in shimmering blue ink, the gap held together.

Tal looked up to find Ashelia watching him.

"You mended it perfectly," he murmured. "Thank you."

"Not perfectly."

"But with a wound that will never heal, you did as well as any could."

He covered himself again. It wasn't out of modesty, for he felt no shame that she had tended to him like a helpless babe. Even as long apart as they'd been, they'd been through enough to have long overcome embarrassment. But he wondered if, with him recovered, the sight of him unclothed would make her uncomfortable.

She seemed about to leave again, and he grasped for any topic to keep her there a moment longer.

"How did you treat it?"

Ashelia raised an eyebrow, but obliged him with an answer. "Aelyn purified it for common corruptions, but I had to delve deeper and remove the magical impurities."

"Chaos?"

She nodded. "Something remains lodged within the wound, Tal. I didn't notice it before when I first mended it — sorcery fails before it, and my fingers never found it. Now, it's too late to remove, for it's lodged itself in your flesh.

"But it was this remnant of the Thorn's curse that caused you to collapse. A few tendrils of chaos had spread throughout your body. It's possible that with the sorcery that runs through your veins, you might have fought it off. But that curse, whatever it is, kept feeding the corruption."

"Then you saved my life."

She sighed. "It was only necessary because I didn't complete the mending last time. But I'm a healer, Tal. If you think you owe me anything, you don't."

Tal regarded her silently for a few moments. "And to seal it, you used the same binding runes as before?"

"Similar, but modified." A ghost of a smile lifted her lips. "I haven't been idle in the decades since I last painted those, and the enchantment had eroded. Now, you will find the wound won't open even with a direct hit to it. I'd wager a blade would have difficulty prying it open."

"Let's not find out, shall we?"

Almost, the silence that fell between them was comfortable. Tal closed his eyes, savoring the moment, knowing how fleeting it would be.

When he opened them, it was gone. Ashelia's face had

smoothed, her smile lost. Her eyes held his a moment longer, a storm swirling inside them.

"I saw what's on your finger, Tal," she said quietly.

His hand self-consciously reached for it. Already exposed, he traced a finger over the smooth crystal band of the Binding Ring. He felt strangely guilty that she'd seen it.

"Who bound you?"

"Someone with whom you're intimate." His mouth twisted in a bitter smile. "Your House-brother yoked me to the service of a certain queen."

"Queen Geminia? Why would she command that?"

He shrugged. "Your guess is as good as mine."

But he saw from the wariness in her eyes it wasn't a sufficient answer, even if it was the only one he had.

"I'll fetch your food now," she said, then abruptly exited.

Tal watched the door even after it closed, willing it to open again. But once more, Mother World ignored his wishes.

Rising from his bed, he moved about the room hunched over. Hunger and pain made him feel as if he'd aged decades. He reached the set of tunic and trousers, cut in the elven styles, and pull them on, albeit by collapsing again on the bed.

No sooner had he dressed than he heard a knock at the door. Without waiting for a response, it opened, and he expected it to be a servant. Instead, Wren, Falcon, and Aelyn came in. Wren balanced a wooden platter heaped full of hot, fragrant food that nearly had Tal bolting across the chamber. The elven spices permeated the room, and he found he'd missed the spicy-sweet delicacies of Gladelyl.

"Good morning!" Tal greeted them as heartily as he could as he sat upright on the bed. "I see you bring a fitting reward for my valiant efforts!"

Aelyn's lips curled. Falcon grinned. Wren only raised an eyebrow.

"Just let me set this down," she griped as she made for the

bed and settled it on the sheets, then shook out her arms. "I don't know how servants do it!"

"By not spending their days idling with their lover," Falcon observed, and Tal grinned as Wren colored and glared at her father.

A moment later, his smile faded. Garin wasn't among his visitors.

"As much as I enjoy watching your buffoonery," Aelyn said, words dripping with irony, "I came to say as soon as you're well, we'll leave. Ashelia has healed the other injured troupers, and our party waits on you to depart."

Falcon leaned close and said in a stage whisper, "He's only eager because he and our lord host had a falling out."

Tal raised an eyebrow, the only response available to him, for his mouth was already full of the spicy fare.

Aelyn glared at the bard. "How would you know? You weren't there."

Falcon tapped the side of his nose. "I have my ways, my irritable friend."

"The boy told you."

Falcon rolled his eyes. "Of course he did. You think he'd keep something like that secret?"

Tal choked down his mouthful, determined to hear as little of Garin as he could, and asked, "What was it over?"

"You don't know?" Wren looked skeptical.

He shook his head as he took another bite, keeping his suspicions to himself.

"It was nothing," Aelyn snapped. "Only travel weariness. And now, if you'll excuse me, I'm eager to return to the road." The mage strode for the door and roughly closed it after him.

Tal swallowed. "He's as cheerful as ever."

"As cheerful as a spring blizzard." Falcon sat at the foot of the bed and snatched a roll from the platter, taking a bite as he stared at Tal.

Tal raised an eyebrow back. "What?"

"Is the fire alive?"

Wren rolled her eyes and backed toward the door. "I don't think I want to be here for this conversation."

Falcon waved his bun at his daughter, and the youth disappeared through the door.

All amusement had drained from Tal, and the pleasant heat of the spice in his mouth had dulled. "I think I'd best lay those hopes to rest."

Falcon frowned as he chewed. "Surely you don't mean that."

"The Extinguished who stole your face told me she has a son."

"You mentioned that. And from what I remember, that much is true. But what of it? You know elven customs as well as I do. Peers of the Realm may take lovers if they so wish, and so long as they take their herbs and don't conceive by them, no harm is done. It's how you held your liaison before."

"Things have changed since then."

"What — you've grown old?"

A snarling beast reared in his chest, and it took all of Tal's effort to hold its chain tightly in check.

"No. That I never came back, and she moved on."

Falcon's expression softened. "Have you told her why you didn't return?"

Tal turned his head aside. Despite eating half the platter already, his gut still felt empty, and now his appetite had abated.

His friend reached over and gripped Tal's hand. "I can speak to her if you'd like. I saw you during those intervening years. I know why you didn't return, and eloquence has never been something I lacked for."

Tal squeezed Falcon's hand back, then pulled away. "I appreciate the offer, but no. If anyone is to tell her, it will be me."

"If?"

He sighed. "Permitted or no, Yinin never liked us together when they were promised to each other. Now, they're bonded and have a son. Even if she wished to pick up where we left off, it would be far more threatening to their House. I'd only cause trouble for everyone."

"Then I'm to understand you rarely cause trouble wherever you go?"

Tal couldn't help a small smile. "I try not to, for those I care about."

Falcon rose from the bed and shook his head. "You're a fool, Tal Harrenfel. A damned fool."

"I've never claimed to be wise."

Garin had never thought he'd be so happy to be traveling.

Not long after Tal had risen from his fever and wounds, the wagons were loaded and the caravan prepared, and the Dancing Feathers and their escort of Warders set back on the road. Garin rode among them, taking turns with Wren driving a wagon — Mikael's wagon, all of them knew, but no one mentioned it.

Elendol was only a few days further. Now that they were within the elven queendom, the roads had vastly improved, paved with white stones that shimmered where a ray of light broke through the thick canopy above. Despite their friend's death weighing on their spirits, the fear of another attack was on all of their minds, and their pace quickened from the months before.

Garin avoided driving near Tal, and Wren never strayed near as well. With each other for company, they talked of small things, of all that they'd heard of Gladelyl and the ever-changing sights that surrounded them.

Neither of them spoke of what awaited Garin in the elven city. And with his devil silent, he could almost forget their true purpose.

One topic they returned to again and again was the Binding

Ring on Tal's finger. After Garin had explained the significance and she'd chastised him for not telling her of the man's trick on Aelyn, they tried working out who might be behind it.

"My wager's on the mage," Wren declared. "He doesn't enjoy being made a fool. I'll bet he took the first opportunity he could to pay Tal back in full."

Garin shrugged. "Could be. The original oath ended when we reached Hunt's Hollow — at least, it should have, from what I recall. But we've all worn gloves against the cold since then. It might have happened sometime along the road, or perhaps while he lay sick in bed."

"And who would have done it then?"

Little as he wanted to consider it, he knew he had to. "Ashelia attended him."

"And why would she bind him?"

"How should I know? But they were lovers once — don't strange things happen between people who are intimate?"

He stopped then, realizing how his words might apply to them. An uncomfortable silence fell, interrupted by the creaking of the wagon, the clomping of the horses, and the chatter of the caravan.

Wren spoke first. "Anyway, it could have been any of the Lathniel staff. If Tal still had the ring on him, all they'd have to do is go through his belongings and bind him while he slept."

"And the Lathnieli *are* Sympathists."

They'd learned a little of Elendol politics since joining with the Warders. The city seemed to have split into two factions: the Sympathists, who favored the opening of the elven nation to the Eastern peoples; and the Royalists, who supported the Queen in opposing it. The finer reasons why either position held weight had eluded them, but he'd gathered that Ashelia and Helnor were Royalists, while their recent hosts held the opposition stance.

Wren nodded. "They'd assume Tal would take Ashelia's side and try to secure him against them."

"Maybe. Unless it was Aelyn or Ashelia."

"We could just ask Tal, you know. He might tell us."

Garin tightened his jaw and looked away. To his relief, Wren let the subject drop.

Later that day, Ashelia surprised them with a visit. She weaved her mount skillfully through the caravan to ride up alongside their wagon, the stor she rode eyeing them as it trotted along. It was nearly as bulky as a horse, but with long, graceful legs, and upon its head grew an impressive set of antlers. All the Warders rode them instead of horses, and Garin wondered if there were any horses or mules in Gladelyl.

They exchanged pleasantries, though with their slight suspicion of her, Garin found his wariness made him stiff and formal. But, as she'd done before, Ashelia dispelled his guarded attitude with a coaxing question.

"What have you heard of our Queen?"

Garin exchanged a glance with Wren. "Not much," he admitted. "Only that she's ancient, like…"

He hesitated, about to say "like most elves," but he suddenly wondered if that might give offense.

Ashelia seemed to guess his thoughts. "Age isn't shameful among elves as it sometimes is among humans — on the contrary, it's welcome. After long, well-lived lives, our elders are revered for all they've done for our people, and they're provided for in their every need. But while Queen Geminia is aged even by our standards, she remains in the prime of her life. You might think her younger than me when you see her."

"Than you?" Wren looked incredulous. "But you don't look over thirty."

She smiled. "I'm far older than thirty, Wren. Elves age much slower than humans. You've seen this in Aelyn, no doubt."

Curiosity itched at Garin. "How old is he?"

"You don't know? Well, let's say that when Tal was born, Aelyn had already spent a decade studying at the Onyx Tower."

"A decade?" He did some quick figures. "That must make him at least sixty years old."

"Older. An elf isn't inducted into one of the Chromatic Towers before they've lived twenty-one springs."

Wren's brow furrowed as she studied Ashelia. "How old is the Queen, then?"

The Warder turned her stormy eyes back on her. "When the Eternal Animus between the East and the Westreach last erupted into war, Queen Geminia had just ascended to the throne."

"The War to the Sea?" Wren gave Garin an incredulous look.

"What's that?" He felt stupid for not knowing what they referred to, but he cared more to understand than hide his ignorance. "How long ago was the War to the Sea?"

Wren seemed too amazed even to tease him. "The War to the Sea is when the Empire of the Rising Sun burned their way across Gladelyl and Avendor to Halenhol itself. But that was two centuries ago."

Ashelia nodded. "It was thanks to the Gem of Elendol that they didn't penetrate Halenhol's walls. After she drove back the invaders from our home, Queen Geminia left only a paltry force behind and rode forth with all the might of Gladelyl to come to Avendor's aid. Only by her sorcery and soldiers was your kingdom saved."

Garin strained to understand the length of such a life. "How long do elves live, then?"

"Three hundred years, sometimes four if the Eldritch runs strong within them."

He stared at Ashelia, wondering at all she'd experienced, all she would see, even after he and Wren were dead. Then he wondered how long Wren might live, being part-elf herself.

If any of us survive Yuldor and his Chosen.

He pushed down the chilling thought and asked, "Is there no king in Gladelyl?"

"Garin!" Wren looked at him, aghast.

He turned to her, surprised. "What did I say?"

But Ashelia only smiled. "Do not fear, little sister. Our ways are different. No, Garin, there is no king in Gladelyl. Even if the Queen's bond were still alive, he would be the Prince Consort. Women have always ruled the queendom, and so long as there is a monarchy, they always will."

Garin thought a moment over that before deciding not to risk further censure. "Her bond... is that like a husband?"

"Exactly so."

"What happened to him?" Wren asked softly, the earlier flush fading from her cheeks.

Ashelia wore a grim look. "Twenty years ago, the Cult of Yuldor had wormed their roots deep into Elendol. Calling themselves the Silver Vines, they coaxed and coerced Gladelysh at every echelon of society to bend to their will, gathering more power to themselves with each day. The Queen did her best to combat it using her network of agents, the Ilthasi, against the cultists. But Yuldor's promises are insidious, and the corruption continued to spread. Until finally, it reached even the royal kintree."

The Warder's eyes fell to her stor's antlers, which bobbed with each step, and spoke softly. "Prince Nevendal was killed by the fire devil Heyl, who was summoned by the Thorn."

"The Thorn?" Wren's eyes were wide, and Garin detected more avidity than fear in their golden swirl. "One of the Extinguished?"

Ashelia nodded.

"And that was the same Heyl that Tal slew, wasn't it?" Garin asked.

She sighed. "You might now understand why our Queen felt so grateful as to bestow one of our treasured artifacts upon him."

A flicker of pride ran through him — but a moment later, he felt revolted. *Pride for the man who killed your father?* a part of him taunted.

He drew in a ragged breath and tried to push it from his mind.

"I need to check our perimeter." With a last nod toward them, Ashelia turned her mount and threaded her way through the caravan once more.

"Are you alright?" Wren placed a hand on his arm.

He gave her a weak smile. "Fine."

As the wagon rolled on, though, he couldn't help but turn the question over and over in his head.

Is Tal a devil? Or a devil killer?

He was getting an uncomfortable suspicion that he just might be both.

In the days following his illness, Tal felt as if he'd risen a new man.

The woods of Gladelyl had always held a mysterious beauty for him. But now, as he rode upon a wagon through them, he beheld them in outright awe. He admired the fall colors that were all around. Red, orange, and gold proliferated on the trees' branches, winter's first breath not yet having swept them away. A freshly fallen carpet was forming on the white cobblestones of the High Road, crunching pleasantly underfoot. When he breathed in, the fresh forest scents filled his lungs.

Autumn, however, would soon lose its grip. Surrounding Elendol, the forest never slept, and winter could lay no claim. Long ago, the First Queen of Gladelyl had united the Chromatic Towers into casting an enchantment around the Sanguine City, suspending it in eternal spring. Rains came often, but snow was rare, and the trees and foliage remained green all year long.

As much pleasure as he took in their surroundings, however, his range of companionship was less gratifying. As before, Garin rode wherever Tal was not, and hadn't even met his eye since his recovery. Ashelia was just as often absent, only checking in briefly each night to ensure his wound remained sealed. Though he usually tried to coax her into staying a little longer, she kept their encounters brief and focused on his health, and rarely strayed from that topic. Wren only flitted by his company occasionally, for she was more often with Garin, and made it clear without words she didn't wish a conflict between them.

That left only Falcon and Aelyn sitting on the wagon with him. Ordinarily, Tal might have made the most of it and banded together with the bard to wage an interminable campaign against the irritable elf. But even if his own good humor wasn't flagging, Falcon had grown uncharacteristically morose.

Tal didn't have to wonder why. Not only had they buried one of his friends, but he was still coming to terms with the loss of his hand — and with it, the loss of his music. And there was also how he'd soon be treated in Elendol as one of the *kolfash*, or "half-kin," forbidden entry from the lofty lives and homes of the Highkin and forced instead to dwell in the marshy under-city of the Lowkin. It was hardly the standard of living that the Court Bard of Avendor deserved, especially when he'd so recently been interned in a tomb for months on end.

To make matters worse, Aelyn had grown beyond intolerable. Though he mostly holed himself up in the back of the wagon, werelight illuminating one of his books, when he did emerge, he snapped at them like a poorly tamed hound.

Elendol, it seemed, was ill-looked forward to.

But Tal took what pleasures he could find. The air was cool and moist, but comfortable. Every breeze seemed to set the leaves aflame. The trees grew ever taller and grander, and vines and moss proliferated on the ancient trunks. Forest creatures, both large and small, skirted around their company. Gladelysh monkeys swung through the trees overhead, and the boldest of them snuck into their camp at night to steal small morsels left unguarded. He glimpsed a wild stor, the same caribou-like creature the Warders used as mounts instead of horses. The buck observed their passage as if wondering what its kin was doing by allowing the two-legged creatures astride their backs.

When they stopped for camp each night, Tal sought Helnor, and the Prime Warder seemed happy to receive him. Uncorking a flask of *bakala*, they passed back and forth the potent pumpkin wine and reminisced over the past like old men.

"Do you remember that time I caught you climbing our kintree?" Helnor grinned as he handed Tal the flask and leaned back against a log around their campfire. "You'd descended damn near fifty feet just to avoid being seen on the stairs!"

As he took a drink, Tal's eyes slid over to the glow where he knew Ashelia sat with the other Warders.

"How could I forget?" he said as he lowered the flask. "I was a young fool then."

"A young fool in love." The Prime Warder's smile slipped away. "I'll admit, I didn't expect you to return to us. Perhaps two decades ago, when your infatuation was still fresh. But now?"

Tal forced a smile and drank again. Helnor didn't ask why Tal had stayed away. Even as he'd always considered Tal and Ashelia's liaison a frivolous affair, he'd known what it had meant to them.

Perhaps he doesn't want to resurrect ghosts, Tal thought, *in case they come to haunt him.*

Helnor would never suffer his House to fall into shame if he could help it. Ashelia joining the Warders had gone far enough, but that it had the blessing of the Queen made it just tolerable. If she were to abandon her bond and son, however, he could only imagine the lengths the Prime Warder would go to secure his family's honor. Even friendship would not deter him.

As if she would abandon them now, he thought with a bitter twist of his lips. *What a man I've become to wish for it.*

Even so, during his visits, part of him hoped Ashelia would come around. His hope was in vain. The brother and sister seemed to have suffered a schism of late, and he quickly divined its source. When he'd first heard Ashelia had joined the Warders not as a healer, but as one of the warrior-scouts themselves, he'd been surprised and a little disconcerted. Only then did he realize he'd hoped to return and have her and Elendol exactly as he'd left it.

But the next moment, he had to grin. It was just like her to shatter the expectations others would bind her with. And hadn't he helped to set her on this path long ago when he first taught her the blade against her culture's prohibitions?

After he and the Prime called it a night, he would lie in his bedroll, sleep evading him, his thumb turning the Binding Ring on his finger round and round. He thought through all that Gladelyl's Queen might intend by binding him to her will. His conclusions weren't comforting.

The gates have opened to the East. Ravagers prey within her borders. And that dream...

Through a fog, he remembered the forest-corrupted face leaning over him, vine-riddled eyes boring into his. A face familiar and feared. A face he'd hoped never to see again.

His blood cold from the lack of sorcery around him, Tal shivered into his bedroll. That night, Yuldor's reach seemed long, indeed.

On the fourth day, the forest abruptly changed. Where fall had claimed it, now spring seized back hold. Green, in every shade and hue, abounded from the forest floor to the high boughs hundreds of feet above. The moss was a newborn yellow-green; the ferns were emerald as they blanketed the ground; the trees' leaves, gigantic oaks and maples, were dark and robust. Flowers sparkled like stars throughout the forest.

Near the edge of a river, Tal spotted a mangrove and

scooted off the wagon mid-trot, shouting that he'd be back. Running like a boy through the thick foliage, reveling in how quickly his body had recovered from its illness, he came before the wild-rooted tree and grinned. Long, white blooms filled its branches, and a divine perfume, reminiscent of honey and lemon, filled the air. *White mangrove blooms*, he thought, and though he knew it was foolish, he picked off a small bunch and hurried back to the caravan.

As he sprung back onto the cart, Falcon smiled knowingly at him, though the smile scarcely touched his eyes. "Dare I ask whom those are for?"

"All of us already know," Aelyn snapped from within the wagon. "And, as usual, he shows himself to be a fool."

Tal kept the smile lodged firmly on his lips as he breathed in the wonderful honey-scent of the flowers.

"Perhaps they're for me," he said casually.

"They do smell how I imagine Heaven's Knolls might." Falcon leaned closer and closed his eyes as he breathed in. "Ah. Too bad I will never reach that blessed place."

Tal put an arm around his friend. "Then, my sinful companion, you and I will shelter together wherever the gods see fit to place us."

He kept the blooms hidden in his pocket after that, telling himself he waited for the right moment. But even when he glimpsed Ashelia riding at the front of the caravan, he didn't move from his wagon.

In time, he thought wistfully. *In time.*

Then the wide Briar Bridge came into view, and he couldn't help but wonder if his time was running out.

The bridge seemed formed of old stone, but upon closer inspection, it showed itself to be a veneer. For beneath the pavers, it was not a stone structure that held them in place, but a network of thick and interwoven roots. During his previous visit, he'd learned that this bridge hadn't been formed by sorcery, but through scaffolding and a patience spanning decades. Some enterprising elven ancestors had coaxed two trees on the opposite shores to extend their roots across the chasm of the Sanguine River. Slowly, their roots had melded, and the two trees had become one, their bond so strong that even wagons could cross it without peril.

If only there were some way to mend every schism, Tal thought wistfully.

Glancing behind him, he saw Garin's face draw tight as the youth contemplated the bridge. But when he saw Tal looking, a scowl replaced the fear. Tal glanced away again. Rifts between him and the people he cared about most gaped all around him.

As they rattled over the Briar Bridge, river rapids roared beneath them. Thick roots grew overhead as well as under, blocking the forest and light from view, and their journey darkened. Tal couldn't help a grim smile, both anticipation and dread tingling inside him.

Then the wagon was across the bridge, and the Sanguine City, with all of its shadowed beauty and half-veiled promises, opened up before them.

THE GEM OF ELENDOL

GARIN FELT LIKE A BOY AGAIN AS HE STARED AT THE SIGHTS emerging before them.

Elendol was a city like he'd never imagined it could be. Even having witnessed the immensity of one kintree, he wasn't prepared for the sight of dozens more dominating their view. These kintrees were even larger than the Lathniel country estate, the smallest of their mangrove-like roots as thick around as any house back in Hunt's Hollow. Around each of the trunks spiraled stairs and wooden terraces a hundred times over, with openings in the trunks showing where rooms, no doubt as grand or grander than House Lathniel had boasted, were tucked away. Werelights shimmered through the air in blues and whites and yellows like a swarm of fireflies. Monkeys chattered down at them from the branches.

He breathed in, and it smelled nothing like his first whiff of Halenhol. Whereas the human city had stank of too many people packed together, Elendol was thick with the earthy scents of the forest, and strongest of all was the aroma that came after a freshly fallen rain. The air felt different, too, the moisture so thick it settled like a cool blanket over him. The sun was still high in the sky, but he could barely see it through the kintrees' giant leaves, much less feel its heat.

Despite his reason for being there, and despite the horrors they'd faced on the way, Garin found a smile spreading across his face. This was what he'd left Hunt's Hollow to see — the conviction ran down to his bones. He turned to Wren, and found her eyes as wide as he knew his must be, and his grin spread wider still.

Gladelysh guards, clad in dyed bark armor similar to the Warders', but far more ornate, saluted in the elven fashion as Prime Helnor passed them by, their heads inclined and their hands moving in slow circles toward him. They remained at attention for the rest of the caravan as the Dancing Feathers and their escort continued forward along a neatly paved road. Though perfectly maintained, at its edges the forest grew thick with vines and ferns, as if it mounted a continual assault against the white stones.

As they continued around the bend of a hill, other parts of the tree-city were revealed. A few buildings of wood and stone, similar to structures he'd seen in Halenhol, had been erected next to the road. As the road split, half of it descended toward the river and forest floor below, where more buildings lay scattered among the roots of the kintrees. Some even seemed to have made their walls and ceilings from the great roots. Signs written in what Garin assumed was Gladelyshi spoke of what these buildings were, and many of them had a glowing symbol beneath that further clued him in. A set of crates signaling a warehouse appeared first, proving Tal's adage, told to him upon entering Halenhol, correct once more: *In a city, lad, it's always about commerce.*

His gut tightened at the memory, and a little of his wonder slipped away.

As if the thought had summoned him, Garin saw Tal approach their wagon on foot. He gave Wren a look, as she was driving the wagon, but she ignored him and pulled it to a halt.

"Welcome to Elendol," Tal said with a half-hearted grin, one arm spread wide. "What do you think?"

His one-time mentor tried to meet his eye, but Garin looked away.

"It's not what I expected," Wren offered.

"It does defy the imagination." Tal's tone remained light, though from the corner of his eye, Garin saw his gaze lingered on him.

"Until we have further directions," Tal continued, "the Dancing Feathers will wait down here in Low Elendol — or the Mire, as the locals call it. Garin, you'll come with me, Aelyn, Helnor, and Ashelia to pay our respects to Queen Geminia in High Elendol at her residence, House Elendola."

He turned and pointed toward the centermost tree, which, though misty with the distance of a mile or more, appeared the largest among them.

Garin finally met his gaze. "And why are Falcon and Wren not coming with?"

Tal's eye twitched at the corner, but his smile didn't ease. "You know why, Garin. They're 'half-kin' to the elves. It would be a grave insult for them to appear before any of the nobility, much less the Queen herself."

He felt his chest growing hot. "If Wren can't come, I won't."

His words had the effect he'd hoped for, and Tal's smile dissipated. But he spoke gently as he began, "Garin…"

"Don't be an oaf." Wren gave him a small shove.

Surprised, he met her green-gold eyes. "They're barring you for something you have no control over. You can't help being part elf. Besides, what does it matter? It doesn't make you less than any of them!"

Despite her own anger, Wren grinned and took his hand roughly in hers. "I know that, and I know you know that. But for now, we have to play by their rules. You need healing, and this is the only place you can get it. So go bow and scrape before the Queen — I'll be fine here."

His stubborn words melted before her reason. "Fine. I'll return as soon as I can."

Wren rolled her eyes. "I'll be pining away after you, never fear."

Tal smiled until Garin turned and gave him a flat look, at which point his former mentor seemed to be casually observing their surroundings. Jumping off the wagon, Garin silently followed him as they walked back toward the front of the caravan.

Ashelia, Helnor, and Aelyn waited for them, with Aelyn standing a few feet apart. Ashelia spoke with her adopted brother, her brow creased, but their conversation ceased as Tal and Garin neared.

He halted, and Garin kept a few steps to the side. As usual, Tal wore a cocky smile. Once, Garin had admired it as a hero's self-assurance and wished he could wear a smirk half so well. Now, he knew it for what it was: the mask that hid his countless lies and betrayals.

"Are we ready?" Tal said with evident cheerfulness. "We wouldn't want to keep your Queen waiting longer than we must — even if you stink of the road, Aelyn."

The mage raised an eyebrow, a slight flush climbing his throat. "You can hardly talk with mud stains splattered up your trousers. But enough — you've already kept her this long. We shall not delay any longer."

"What, can a man be in control of his illness now? Surely you don't expect that even of me."

Only Helnor smiled, if slightly. Tal's grin slackened at the temperature of his audience, but he only made a sweeping gesture toward the closest staircase that led up to the tree platforms. "Please, Emissary Aelyn, be diplomatic and show us the way."

Garin took up the rear of their entourage, except for the two other Warders who followed them. He wondered uneasily if the escort was necessary. Though Gladelyl was as close to the

81

East as any nation in the Westreach, he'd always heard their borders were well-defended.

But considering the Easterners who had attacked them along the King's High Road, Garin wondered if that was just another groundless rumor.

After they'd reached the first platform, Aelyn, who had taken the lead, directed them toward one of the bridges leading away from it. Though the rest of his companions seemed at ease crossing, Garin hesitated before taking the first step. Unlike their entrance into Elendol, this bridge was made of planks and rope, and it swayed and danced with each of his companions' steps.

To his irritation, Tal noticed Garin hadn't followed and turned to call back, "It's not so bad, lad. Every thread and plank is checked weekly. It would take terrible luck to die on a Gladelysh bridge."

Scowling, Garin didn't answer, but set foot on the first plank. Once he was sure it wouldn't give, he staggered forward another step, trying not to look like he was clutching the hand ropes as tightly as he was. His eyes watched where he stepped, but it meant he saw the long drop below them, a hundred feet at least. His stomach turned and roiled along with the bridge.

When he finally made it across, he leaned over and breathed for a moment.

"Never mind," Tal said above him. "Gets most folks the first time."

Standing, Garin ignored him and walked past, only realizing a moment later that would mean Tal would get a prime opportunity to view his next awkward crossing. Gritting his teeth, but knowing there was nothing for it, he followed the elves around the platform and onto the second bridge.

Gradually, as they crossed bridge after bucking bridge, he grew used to their erratic rhythm. Caught in timing his steps to reduce the jarring in his legs, he nearly ran into Aelyn when he reached the far end, who had turned back to glare at him.

"Try not to act as much a fool as your mentor," the mage grated. "Our appearance is bad enough. You must compose yourself before Her Eminence."

Once, that fiery stare would have reduced Garin to quaking. But he'd seen enough of Aelyn to return the stare without fear. "He's not my mentor, and I'm not a fool."

The mage seemed a little taken aback, while Helnor turned and grinned at his adopted brother.

"Ah!" the Prime Warder said. "You've discovered our foundling lacks teeth, haven't you, Garin?"

"Don't call me that," Aelyn snapped back, then turned and gestured sharply. "Enough of this. The Queen waits."

As Aelyn walked around the royal kintree, Garin gained an appreciation for just how large it was. Where the Lathnieli's was wide enough for a grand room, any floor of House Elendola could fit an entire suite. The tree might have comfortably housed the entire population of Hunt's Hollow. *Not that anyone back home would be mad enough to come here*, he thought with a small smile.

They reached a set of rounded doors, not nearly as grand as those leading to King Aldric's throne room, but more lively with scenes of elves painted in bright colors across them. Garin wanted to guess what stories they told, but the guards at the doors, more ornately armored than those at the city's entrance, turned their hands in the same sign of respect as the city guards had used, then pulled open the doors to a dazzling light.

Garin blinked rapidly as he followed the elves inside. The Queen's throne room was as bright as a blue-sky day, and after the relative gloom of the rest of the city, it dazed him for a moment. The light projected from what looked like windows, but Garin knew they must be rune-inscribed sheets of glass, or some other variety of magic. The radiant beams shone down on the carpet they walked over, mossy-green and made of the same strange wool as had carpeted the Lathniel dining hall. Tapestries hung from the walls, with unfamiliar stories woven in a complicated swirl of scenes that resembled the shape of a tree. Their road-weary appearance — and stench — contrasted poorly with their lovely surroundings, and Garin wished they'd taken the time for a bath.

But as soon as his gaze settled on the silver-latticed throne before him and the woman seated on it, all other thoughts fled him.

Her eyes caught him first. Queen Geminia Elendola the Third had lavender eyes as warm as newly bloomed flowers. Opalescent clouds wound through them, as lively and brilliant as pearls. Her skin was as dark as shadowed moss in winter, and her hair spiraled up in a twisting tower like a vine-laden tree the color of burnished gold. Her dress was simple yet full of silver folds that shimmered with the slightest movement. An elegant crown perched on her brow, made of a white metal that shone like the stars. The throne behind her provided a frame, extending upward in glimmering arcs around her, the silver branches of a tree reaching skyward.

For many moments, Garin walked mindlessly, entranced by the Elf Queen. But as their party came closer, he blinked at a sudden realization. Despite her many shining qualities, Queen Geminia was not a beautiful woman. Had he seen her in a peasant's plain dress with her hair undone, he might have thought her a homely housewife. The two images, the shimmering monarch and the mundane imagining, clashed in his mind, and he struggled to reconcile them.

Then the Queen's gaze, moving from one member of their party to another, settled on him, and a slight smile curved her lips. Hastily, Garin tried wiping his mind clean. Almost, it seemed she could see what he imagined, and it amused her. Even as he thought himself silly, another part of him wondered what powers a queen of the Eldritch Bloodline might possess.

When they stood a mere dozen feet before the Queen, the three elves in front of Garin halted, then performed the same series of respectful gestures as the guards outside, only now accompanied by a deep bow at the waist. If he attempted such a gesture, he'd only make a fool of himself. Unwittingly, he met Tal's gaze, who only wore his arrogant smile with a raised eyebrow and didn't bother to bow.

I won't be as rude as him. Garin bowed as he had before King Aldric and hoped it would suffice.

"Rise, please." Queen Geminia's voice didn't tinkle like temple bells, as he thought it might, but it was gentle and pleasing all the same.

As Aelyn, Ashelia, and Helnor complied, the Queen looked at those gathered around her, whom Garin had scarcely noticed before. "Dear ministers, I must ask you to leave us now."

It sounded like a request, but the surrounding elves, each decorated in their own distinct and strange way, gave their respects and filed out. *Even a queen's requests are commands,* Garin thought.

Only one lingered, a man with sallow skin and limp, shoulder-length black hair. One of his eyelids twitched as he smiled and walked up to Ashelia to take her hands. "Ashelia, Core of my Heart, how happy I am to see you returned to me. I heard there was trouble on the road."

"Later, Yinin." Garin could only partially see Ashelia's face, but her expression seemed cold and unyielding, not at all what he'd expect her to show toward someone calling her the "Core of his Heart." *Her husband,* he guessed, though he recalled that elves used the term "bond" instead.

He glanced at Tal, and found his former mentor's smile stiff, his eyes unblinking as he watched the pair.

At length, Minister Yinin dropped his wife's hands, made a respectful gesture toward the Queen, then started to leave again. But as he passed Tal, he paused mid-step, his dark eyes widening.

"Ah," was all the minister could say.

Tal's lips curled in a mocking smile. "Hello, Yinin."

Yinin glanced at his bond, but Ashelia didn't acknowledge him. His eyes flickered back to Tal. "I didn't know you had arrived."

"Did you expect trumpets and parades? Alas, I'm disappointed, too."

The minister's mouth twitched. Garin wouldn't have blamed the elf if he'd taken a swing at Tal. Instead, he only said, "I suppose I will soon see you again."

Tal's smile hadn't slipped. "It seems so."

Yinin's gaze lingered on Tal for a moment longer, then he gestured respectfully again to the Queen before striding from the room. Garin couldn't help glancing after him to see Ashelia's bond cast one last look back at her. Ashelia once more ignored it.

Looking back toward the throne, Garin briefly met Tal's gaze, but looked away as the man gave him a brief shrug.

The Queen's pleasant expression remained, and she seemed as still and patient as if she were formed of ice. Once the doors had closed behind Yinin, she made a slight gesture, and the elves stepped closer, Garin and Tal following.

"I am gladdened to see you all well. Particularly you, Aelyn Belnuure. You have suffered much since you left my side, and all on my part."

Had they not been before a queen, Garin might have smirked at the glow of satisfaction radiating from the mage as he bowed again. "You are kind in your recognition, Your Eminence. But any pain I endured was worth it in service to you."

Helnor snorted, and everyone looked at him. Aelyn gave him an outraged glare. The Prime Warder only shrugged.

"Some things never change, little lost foundling," he said. "You'll always scrape and bow before your betters."

As Aelyn flushed, the Queen's eyes creased slightly. "Please, Prime Helnor. Control yourself."

A gentle rebuke, but Helnor stiffened under it. Garin grew more mystified by the Queen with her every word.

The Gladelysh monarch looked now to Tal. "Aristhol, you are welcome to my realm after your many years away. You should not have been so long absent."

Tal didn't react to her small emotions as the others had, but remained coolly aloof. "My apologies, Your Eminence. I have been otherwise occupied, or you can trust I would have wished once more to gaze upon the Gem of Elendol."

Despite Tal's tone, she smiled. "And *Velori* has served you well in keeping to our common goals?"

"So long as they remain goals we share in common."

The Queen was silent for a long moment. When she next spoke, it seemed to respond to something that Tal had left unsaid.

"What is past must be forgiven, for we cannot change it, but only grow from it. You have learned from your mistakes, Tal Harrenfel. If you remember those lessons, you will find your redemption."

All pretense had disappeared from Tal's face, leaving only a hunger that surprised Garin. He looked away, nameless feelings twisting in his gut.

"Thank you, Your Eminence," Tal said after another long silence. "But you know why I cannot trust your words."

Aelyn looked affronted. Garin wondered what had passed between the Queen and Tal, and Helnor seemed to wonder the same. Ashelia, however, seemed wary and watchful, as if danger stalked them even now.

If his words confused Queen Geminia, she didn't show it. "Our war calls for compromises and assurances, as you well know. I apologize, Aristhol, but I cannot take back what has been done."

Aelyn looked outraged at the apology, and from Ashelia and Helnor's expressions, such an event was rare. Even Tal seemed moved by the words.

"I suppose you can't," he said at length. "Tell me, Queen Geminia. To what end have you made this compromise?"

The Elf Queen didn't answer him, but turned her gaze upon Garin. "You are Garin Dunford," she said in a tone that didn't make it a question.

"Yes, uh, Your Eminence." Garin colored as he stumbled over his words.

Queen Geminia gave him a slight smile, and his chest filled with butterflies. Whether it was sorcery or some other strange magnetism, he was beginning to understand the Queen's influence over his companions.

"You may speak plainly to me, Garin. I am a queen, but behind the title, I am the same as you. You have suffered an affliction."

Her invitation for informality only made him feel more awkward. "Uh, yes, I suppose so."

The Queen's eyebrows lifted slightly. "Then we will do our best to heal you. Ashelia, whom you have already met, is one of our most talented healers. She will assist the masters of the Sapphire Tower in purifying you of whatever demons plague your body and mind."

Ashelia gestured in the elven manner of respect. "It would be an honor, Your Eminence."

"To maintain pretenses, we will also train you in our ways, both in culture and in dancing. You know what dancing is to us, Garin?"

"Swordplay." He found himself both excited and apprehensive at the thought. While he'd survived this long on his meager training, he'd never felt he'd been a talented swordsman.

Queen Geminia nodded. "Yes, among other things. A philosophy. A discipline. A crucible. You will learn from the best of our dancers, Ulen Yulnaed."

At the name, Garin glanced at Ashelia, remembering how she'd spoken of her humiliation at this Ulen's hands. The

Warder's face had turned stony. Tal caught their glance and frowned, and Garin looked quickly away.

"Thank you, Your Eminence." He paused, wondering if he'd been too formal again, but the Queen only smiled.

"It is my pleasure, Garin Dunford. I know you will grow well here. Now, I'm afraid I must ask you to wait without. I will not be long with your companions."

At his dismissal, Garin tried not to feel like a child banished from an adult conversation. In vain, he hoped someone would speak for him to stay, as Tal had before King Aldric. But the rest remained silent, and he could do nothing but bow, mutter his thanks, and depart.

As he walked back down the mossy carpet, Garin suspected they'd come to Elendol for more than just his healing.

———

Tal watched his one-time apprentice depart the throne room before he turned back to the Elf Queen.

Geminia's eyes were on him, the opal cloud swirling slowly, entrancing as a snake's stare. *No — mesmerizing, like the will-o'-the-wisps that lure men to their deaths in the swamps.*

He respected her, even trusted her to an extent. Queen Geminia had been the first to honor him, granting him the boon of *Velori* after Heyl's defeat, and then entrusting to him, an outsider, a task she'd given to no other.

But with the Binding Ring warm beneath his glove, he couldn't help but feel like a fly slowly sinking into sap.

Helnor looked uneasy as he glanced between him and the Queen. Ashelia gazed only at Geminia, her expression hard. Aelyn smirked knowingly.

"What would you have me do, Your Eminence?" Tal finally said.

She stared a moment longer before answering. "I will speak plainly, Aristhol, for time grows short, even here in the

Sanguine City. You will have noticed Elendol has suffered many changes since you last visited. Gladelyl has transformed more in the past year than in the century before. Under pressure from the Peers — or most of them," she amended with a slight smile at Ashelia, who nodded gravely, "I opened the Sun Gate and admitted the first immigrants from the Eastern Empire in the history of our realm. Now, foreigners live among us, bringing their cultures with them into Low Elendol and stirring unrest."

"Some philosophers say the differences between us breed opportunity and innovation," Tal offered. "And, as one of your renowned playwrights once said, 'The finest feast is full of variety.'"

Queen Geminia smiled. "Neither sages nor poets have ruled Gladelyl. I am neither intolerant nor biased, Tal Harrenfel, only practical. And this inflow of strangers with their strange customs has turned Low Elendol into a city as poor as any human one."

"Ah, to pity the Gladelysh — finally suffering as the rest of the World does."

The expressions of his elven companions grew hard — except for Ashelia, who, to his surprise, regarded him thoughtfully. A warmth spread through his chest, and his smile planted itself more firmly on his lips.

"Pity is not what I hope from you, Aristhol," the Queen replied. "For I fear the Ingress of Elendol has brought more than immigrants."

She paused, her eyes flitting around the room. For the first time, Tal saw a glimpse beyond her calm mask.

"The Silver Vines have returned," she pronounced softly. "The Cult of Yuldor has its roots in Elendol and its people once more."

Though it hadn't bothered him since Ashelia's mending four days before, the wound in Tal's side twinged at her words. Her pronouncement wasn't surprising, yet he found a chill prickling inside him. *No enemy of mine ever seems to die,* he thought bitterly.

"And the Thorn is leading them, I suppose."

The Queen of Gladelyl was well over two centuries old, despite her skin being smooth but for a few faint lines. But in that moment, all of her years showed through.

"Yes," she replied softly. "The Nameless who once plagued us has returned."

Tal shared his wince with the others in the room.

"Your Eminence," Helnor protested, but Ashelia quieted him with a gesture. In a rare moment, she looked fully at Tal. It was only that glance that gave him the courage to continue.

"Why summon me?" Tal asked. "I'm not what I used to be, and I've never been what others have claimed."

"I know you for who you are, Tal Harrenfel, whatever name and guise you've worn. I know you are only a man. But you have a piece in this. I have seen its touch over and over again across the tapestry of the World."

Tal didn't bother hiding his amusement. Before she'd ascended to the throne, the Queen had trained in the Diamond Tower, the elven school of divination, and was considered still to be one of the foremost among them. *But even if the future can be foretold,* he thought, *there's little any of us can do to change it. Even a queen.*

Only the whispers of a burned book kept him from dismissing her words entirely.

"He tried to turn me once," Tal said aloud. "But I've slain his fellow Extinguished since then. The Thorn won't make the same mistake."

"Nevertheless, you are valuable to him. He will come for you, no matter the cost. And by this, we will ensnare him."

"So I'm to be bait."

"You are to be my hunter," Queen Geminia corrected. But her eyes told another tale.

A bitter laugh escaped him. "I don't suppose I can refuse. Tell me at least you'll inform me of all you know."

"I will not leave you in the dark." The Queen pressed her lips together. "I am not King Aldric, Tal. The Named knows he cannot sway me. Between us, it will always be a war, not a game. You will have every weapon you need when I send you out to do battle, and the might of Gladelyl behind you."

Her words rang with truth. Even with the task looming over him, Tal felt his chest loosen, if slightly.

"If I'm to do battle with another Extinguished and their cult, then I'll begin with a feast and a bath, if you please."

Aelyn gave a huff of outrage, Helnor openly grinned, and Ashelia sighed with what Tal hoped was fondness. Queen Geminia smiled. "That can be arranged. And when you burn out the Silver Vines once more, you will be more richly rewarded than with a sword."

His heart rattled against his ribs. She knew what he most desired; Geminia had always had a disconcerting way of seeing to the heart of each person before her. But even if such a thing were within her power, he knew he could only accept it if willingly offered by someone else.

Tal kept his gaze carefully on the Queen as he bowed in the elven manner, his every movement respectful. Yet in his correctness, he knew she would read his true feelings.

"As my Queen commands." Without waiting for a dismissal, he rose, turned, and strode away from the Elf Queen on her throne, her enchanting eyes boring into his back.

THE LINES THAT DIVIDE

GARIN STEPPED OUT OF HIS ROOM AND, LEANING AGAINST THE railing, stared blearily over Elendol's morning gloom.

The first night spent in the tree-city had passed uneventfully, if disorienting in its oddness. After Helnor and Ashelia had invited the whole company of the Dancing Feathers to their kintree within the city, they'd feasted on more spicy elven fare — though, to Garin's relief, plainer food was provided as well. He couldn't get out of using *galli* though, which he'd learned translated to "food sticks," though he used them passably after Falcon gave mocking instruction to his troupe. Garin had hoped to watch Wren struggle, but her clever hands quickly contorted themselves to lever the sticks back and forth like a beetle's pincers.

He'd struggled through the meal as he caught up Wren on everything he'd learned inside the Queen's throne room, including how he'd been excluded for a good deal of the conversation. They speculated on what task the monarch had set before the others.

"If it even is a task," Wren pointed out around a bite of sauce-covered meat. She'd quickly formed a nasty habit of pointing with her *galli*, causing flecks of sauce to splatter across the table.

Choosing to ignore it, he asked, "What else could it be?"

"Perhaps Geminia wants to use Tal's fame just like Aldric did."

Garin winced at the lack of titles, but ignored that as well. "Or maybe it was about me."

"Could be. You *are* the reason we're here."

Garin glanced nervously at the other troupers surrounding them, though they were carousing and caught up in their own conversations.

"Keep it down, would you?" he muttered. "I don't want that spreading around."

"They think it's for both of us, wool-brain. For us youth to be trained. Not… you know."

They ate in uncomfortable silence for several moments. During their trek to Elendol, he'd been glad they'd barely spoken of the Singer. What was there to say? For the moment, he was stuck with it. That she remained with him despite it meant more than he could say.

But he couldn't know his future with Wren until he'd dealt with the devil, so he shoved thoughts of it aside for the rest of the night. Wren didn't suggest his coming to her room, but bade him a good night and descended by werelight to her own chamber.

It hadn't taken him long to miss her.

His mood matched his somber surroundings. As the sun couldn't penetrate the canopy, dawn was a muted suggestion through the leaves. Werelights, green and yellow and blue, hung over Elendol and cast the buildings, bridges, and platforms in a gossamer glow. Birds sang into the relative darkness, dozens of calls he'd never heard, and creatures scurried across the branches, chattering in unfamiliar voices.

He'd never felt more alone.

But you're never alone, he thought bitterly. *Not with a devil inside you.*

Knowing he'd find no comfort there, he ascended from his room to the dining hall. To his surprise, cheery lights already illuminated the grand chamber, and as he mounted the last stair, he looked over it with grudging admiration. The Venaliel hall was similar to the Lathnieli's provincial estate, with a whole wall exposed to the elements. But instead of the bright, gaudy colors, it had been decorated with subtle opulence. A shimmering chandelier hung overhead, glowing in patterns of ever-changing hues. Tapestries that spoke of a long history hung from the walls, and the werelight lanterns set the hall awash in golden light.

Only a few folks were awake, but a feast was already starting to form, with more brought out by the servants every moment. Not wanting to be around people, but wanting less to be alone, Garin forced himself to approach.

Wren flashed him a smile before continuing her chatter with Ashelia, who stood next to the buffet with her. Despite their initial friction, they'd seemed to have found a mutual respect.

Helnor sat next to Falcon and, to Garin's dismay, Tal. He could only hope his former mentor wouldn't try to talk to him. At the moment, he wasn't sure he could keep a civil tongue.

But as he mounded his plate with food, Wren appeared by his side to steal him away to table in the hall's far corner.

"How did you sleep?" she asked cheerily. "These elves know how to stuff a bed! What's in them, do you suppose?"

Garin grunted and shoveled food into his mouth. From the corner of his vision, he saw Wren narrow her eyes.

"Someone's in a high mood this morning," she noted acidly, her temper turning like a wind vane to match his. "Fine. Maybe I won't tell you my news."

"News?" he choked out before swallowing. When he could

speak again, he continued, "How could you have news? We only just rose."

"Some of us have been up longer." She smiled, a knife's promise in it. "After all, some of us didn't have a big day before the Elf Queen."

"It's not my fault they didn't allow you in."

"I don't care about—" Wren cut off short and blew out in exasperation. "Never mind. Listen to us — we're squabbling like two old hens. I was just trying to make conversation."

"Until you weren't," Garin muttered.

"What's wrong with you?"

Oh, nothing, he wanted to say. *Only that a curse spreads through me.* Though part of him wondered if he was overreacting, the greater part knew it to be true. The night before, he'd had a dream that he'd been back at the attack on the caravan. Only this time, he hadn't chosen to walk away from Tal.

"So you're just going to ignore me," Wren noted, the gold in her eyes swirling.

With a force of effort, Garin exhaled his frustration. "I'm sorry. It's not you. It's just... everything."

Wren sipped from her cup, steam billowing around her face before she set it back down. "It's alright," she said in a tone that said it wasn't.

Not wanting to fight anymore, he tried smoothing things over. "Why don't you tell me your news?"

But just as her expression shifted, Garin noticed Ashelia approaching their table.

"Garin," she said, her rich alto voice lively as if she'd been awake for hours. "Would you mind taking a walk with me?"

He glanced down at his half-eaten plate, then up at Wren. Her face had once again closed off, but she gave a slight nod.

"Sure." He stood and followed Ashelia as she led him from the dining hall.

Tal watched Ashelia and Garin walk out of sight of the dining hall and repressed a sigh.

It didn't escape Falcon's notice. "I'd reassure you with a clap on the shoulder," he said lightly, "but, you know…"

He held up his handless arm with a weak smile.

Helnor looked up from his food, his bright eyes swirling. "It takes a strong man to make light of a heavy wound." He gave Falcon a wide grin. "I think I'll like you, half-kin minstrel."

Tal raised an eyebrow. "Do you have to call him that?"

The Prime Warder shrugged and took another bite of his sauteed green onions. "Must I? No — just as I don't have to call you *lenual*. But it doesn't change what he is."

"You say that like it's a bad thing." Falcon, surprisingly deft at using *galli* with his left hand, took another swift bite of his sweet bun.

"Among my people, it is. And unlike most of the Peers these days, I uphold our traditions. But that doesn't mean I'm cruel. I let you sleep in my home, did I not?"

"Strictly speaking, Ashelia permitted us," Tal pointed out.

Helnor grinned. "She's the Peer, but I'm her elder brother! Nothing is done without my permission."

Falcon and Tal shared a look, and Helnor laughed. All of them knew the reality of the situation.

Tal's gaze wandered over to Wren. After Garin's departure with Ashelia, several of the other troupers had risen and joined her, but she still looked far from merry.

Meals have a way of baring the lines between us, he thought. Aelyn, though invited to stay at the Venaliel kintree, had declined and slept at his own ancestral home in the city. Yinin had returned to House Venaliel, but Tal hadn't glimpsed him. Helnor had informed them that his House-brother and his nephew would dine separately in their rooms.

Already, I'm driving a wedge between Ashelia and her bond, he thought, and felt a glimmer of shame at his lack of disappointment.

"I could speak to the boy."

Tal looked back at Falcon. "What could you say?"

The minstrel shrugged. "Something he'll listen to, at least. Perhaps I can convince him to hear you out."

"So I could say what, exactly?"

"The truth?" Falcon winced as he suggested it.

Tal shook his head. "The truth only heals when it's not poison."

Despite his words, he knew it was the only option. He couldn't let the youth remain aloof forever; there were things he had to know that only Tal could teach him. Things he didn't yet fully know himself, but that Garin might help him understand.

"For Ashelia, however, I don't think talking will ease anything," Helnor noted. "Best to let that whimsy die, my friend."

Tal winced. "Thank you both for your aid. But am I not supposed to be as eloquent as a statesman? I can find my own way."

Falcon and Helnor shared a look. Tal grinned. *Nothing brings men together like shared derision.*

He rose. "Much as I hate to leave this levity, I'd like a private moment with you, Falcon."

Helnor stood as well. "I should leave, too. My men will need rousing after their night's carousing, and we must be off before the sun shines through. Just try not to burn down my home while I'm gone."

Despite his jesting manner, the Prime gestured toward them respectfully, then took his leave, striding with a soldier's air from the dining hall.

With a forlorn look, Falcon eyed the remnants of his food and stood. "This had better be important."

"Would I pull you away from a feast for anything less?"

They passed the Dancing Feathers and grinned and waved as the troupers put up a call, both cheering and jeering at them.

Then Tal led the minstrel toward the balcony overlooking the city. As they leaned on the railing, made of wood as alive as the tree towering above them, he breathed in the air. Even in the city's heart, it was fragrant with the smells of the forest in spring, not only the earthiness and petrichor but also the faint hints of nearby blooms.

"She's a beautiful city," Falcon noted. "Song-worthy, one might even say."

"You've already written many regarding her."

"Regarding you, more like. But I believe Elendol deserves her own ballads, don't you think?"

Tal inclined his head, his eyes tracing the silver-froth river below, and began without preamble.

"While you were entombed, and the Extinguished still wore your face, he said you had come here seeking an old legend. Is that true?"

Falcon's expression had drawn, but he nodded. They'd spoken some of what he'd missed in his absence, but had avoided the topic as often as they could. "Yes. The legend of the Worldheart."

"And you learned what you knew from an elder here in Elendol?"

"Indeed. He's an old root of a man, if I'm honest, but a fine storyteller at that."

"Could you take me to him?"

Falcon's brow crinkled as he studied him. "Perhaps. Do you think there's something to the legend?"

"Maybe. I..."

He hesitated. Not that he didn't trust Falcon; his experience with the Extinguished hadn't changed that. But what he believed to be true felt ridiculous as soon as he tried to put it into words. Instead, he let his lips curl into a crooked smile. "I'll tell you if you take me to this elder."

Falcon grinned back, eyes swirling. "So that's how we're playing it! But I don't mind a bit of mystery, as you well know."

"Whose kin is he?"

"How should I know? He didn't live with anyone else that I remember."

"What, he has an entire kintree to himself?"

Falcon looked surprised. "He isn't Highkin, Tal! How would I have been able to speak with him? He's down in the Mire."

Tal found his gaze slipping to the under-city far below them. He wasn't prone to unwarranted bias, but found himself skeptical. "Lowkin might know as much as High," he conceded finally. "Especially at three centuries of life and counting. You remember the way?"

The Court Bard shook his head. "In parts. My memory frays like cobwebs ever since... you know. But I'm sure we can stumble our way there."

Gripping his friend's shoulder, Tal smiled. "Then equip yourself, my friend. I hear the Mire is not the pleasant swamp it once was."

Falcon grinned in return. "But who would ever harm a bard?"

Garin followed silently after Ashelia as she led them around platforms and over bridges, traveling further from her House with every step. They passed other early risers, some of whom respectfully greeted her and eyed him with curiosity. Garin avoided their gazes and tried to guess where they headed. Ashelia had wanted to speak, but why they needed to walk this far away to do so, he hadn't the faintest idea.

After a time, a sound built up under the quiet forest noises, a crashing din unlike anything Garin had heard before. Ahead, a platform extended out from a kintree with seemingly no purpose or destination, and as they approached, the noise grew into a roar. Garin reached the railing and stared before him, astonished. A cascade of water, hundreds of feet tall, crashed down a cliff to the river below. Even at the distance, a cold, wet wind blew from it over Garin's skin.

"Ildinfor, the source of the Sanguine River." Ashelia had to speak loudly to make herself heard over the waterfall. "This early in the morning, it's as good a place as any for a private conversation."

Garin was so busy admiring the waterfall he didn't notice her muttering and moving her hands until she turned behind them and repeated the gesture. As she turned back, Garin felt the shiver of something settle over him that had nothing to do with the waterfall's wind.

"I've cast wards of silence," she said. "No one will overhear us now."

He swallowed and met her eyes. "Overhear what?"

For a long moment, Ashelia only stared at him, the gray in her eyes rushing furiously around her pupils.

"Garin," she said carefully. "I need you to tell me about your devil."

DEMONS

G<small>ARIN</small> <small>STARED</small> <small>AT</small> A<small>SHELIA</small>, <small>THE</small> <small>CRASH</small> <small>OF</small> <small>THE</small> <small>WATERFALL</small> filling his head.

He'd suspected she knew of the Singer. After all, the Queen had said she'd assist in his cleansing, and it stood to reason she knew what it entailed. But to hear her ask about it so directly… Fear twined with some other, nameless emotion in his gut, and he had a strange feeling not all the apprehension he felt was his own.

"What do you want to know?" An uncomfortable smile forced itself on him.

Ashelia didn't return it. "All that you can tell. Anything that might assist in the cleansing."

Garin ran a hand through his hair, which had long since become shaggy from the road. He thought back to when it had begun and all that had happened since, and to Tal's warning never to tell anyone else that he was Night-touched.

Since when am I listening to Tal?

Besides, Garin trusted Ashelia. She'd shown him nothing but kindness from the moment they'd met, and she was to be his healer. No one could be trusted with the truth more.

So he began to tell her, and once he began, he couldn't make himself stop. All the fears of losing his mind, of becoming a monster; all the guilt for attacking Kaleras and trying to hurt his friends in the ruins — it spilled forth like milk from an overturned bucket. And as he confessed and laid bare what he was, his chest loosened, and a warm pressure built up behind his eyes.

"And I spoke those strange words, and the big bandit… burst." Garin wiped at his eyes and stared into the waterfall.

Ashelia didn't speak. The whole time he'd babbled, she'd only interrupted to ask clarifying questions. Now he waited nervously. *She'll condemn you,* part of him thought. *No one could accept all of what you are. Not even Wren.*

"And nothing has happened since?" she asked finally.

Garin started to shake his head, then hesitated. *It was a momentary thought,* he told himself, *a slight inclination. And even if you wanted to kill Tal, isn't it no more than he deserves?*

"That's it."

Ashelia nodded, eyes never leaving him. "You're a brave man, Garin, to bear such a heavy burden."

His knees went weak with relief.

"Brave?" He wanted to laugh at her words. He wanted to believe them even more.

"Brave. Few could hold out against the Night's influence for so long. Though the role of this Singer in Yuldor's plans appears…" She turned her frown toward the waterfall. "…complicated."

Garin hesitated, not wanting to speak his next words, but knowing he must. "Tal seems to know something of them, the Singers. He recovered a Darktongue book that spoke of them."

Ashelia glanced back toward him. "Did he?"

"We never spoke much of it. First, we had to rescue Falcon, then we all wanted to forget about the whole thing." Garin shrugged. "Then we stopped speaking."

"Why?"

He went stone-still. When he breathed in, the moment of

shock fell away, an echo of what he'd felt when he first realized what Tal had done, and the debt he must repay.

But this was something private. Something only he and Tal could settle.

"Garin," she said gently, "I don't know what lies between you. But as a healer, I know this: ignoring wounds only causes them to fester. To heal, they must be allowed to breathe. Speak with him. Whether or not it mends things, you must talk of what happened."

He looked away, not wanting to shame himself. A lump had lodged in his throat. "How?"

"That's the simplest part. Just begin."

"No." Swallowing back down all he felt, he faced her. "I mean, how can you say that, when you yourself can barely look him in the eye?"

She flinched, her gaze darting away. "It's different for us, Garin."

"I don't think it is. I think you're scared. Just like I am."

His resolve and anger petering away, he turned and watched the water surge over the hidden crest of the cliff to fall in white tendrils and mist to the river below.

"I must speak with my cohort and prepare for your cleansing," Ashelia said at length. "But come evening, I'll summon you. In the meantime, you'll have your first lesson with your dancing master. Not only must we maintain your cover for being here, but perhaps you'll find it takes your mind off things."

Garin nodded. He was as glad to let the conversation pass as she seemed to be. "Thank you, Ashelia," he said, remembering his manners.

The elf smiled over at him, the warmth not quite touching her eyes. "You can give no better thanks than to recover quickly and fully."

He nodded, then followed as she led him back to her family's kintree.

Tal stepped from the lift and surveyed his surroundings, a smile perched on his lips.

Low Elendol had changed from the last time he'd seen her, but it was still named the Mire for good reason. The stink of the swampy ground permeated the air despite the best efforts of the shops, whose windows boasted of incense or bouquets of fresh flowers. And like any bog, it had its fair share of mosquitoes and midges. Other critters like snakes and monkeys plagued its inhabitants from the overhanging roots.

The main path through the city had been built of stones, but time and negligence had shifted the pavers, making the road as rough as a river rapids. An incessant din already rose around them despite the early hour, Lowkin elves scrambling to make the best of the little that life had granted them.

His eyes quickly picked out the Easterner immigrants among them. In every way, they stuck out like brambles in a flower garden, all different shapes and sizes, and some almost grotesque in form. Ever since his first encounters with those from the Empire of the Rising Sun, Tal had made a study of their various Bloodlines, and so he recognized most of those he saw.

Minotaurs, some as tall as the Gladelysh, with the heads and horns of bulls and powerful, stout bodies.

Nightelves, who differed from their Gladelysh kin by an aubergine cast to their skin and sinisterly colored eyes. Though they shared in common pointed ears and spinning irises, they were often shorter and had a tendency of slinking about the city, whereas even the Lowkin walked with their backs straight and their chins held high.

Then there were the medusals, who resembled large, upright lizards in both looks and the way they moved. Their yellow eyes and slitted pupils peered out from shadowy alleys, their ruff of colored feathers eerily resembling that of the deadly quetzal.

Easterner humans, too, were represented, their skin a shade of ecru either too light or dark to be of the Westreach, and the shapes of their eyes and facial features unfamiliar.

Even with so many varieties, there were still others that Tal hadn't seen before. Some of them were short creatures, barely four feet tall, with wide noses and wrinkled skin, many of whom seemed to possess the foulest tempers of all. And slightly taller were willowy beings that seemed even more suited to the forest than the Gladelysh elves. Their hair took on a variety of looks, with some resembling vines, others moss, and still others sporting a tuft of golden grain. Their skin, in contrast, looked as rough and textured as bark.

The discordant tapestry dazzled Tal, and his grin grew wider. Some would have balked at the chaotic sight; Aelyn, he knew, would have been horrified, and Helnor had shown all signs of sharing those feelings. But something in him reveled in the infinite variety before him.

The World is far larger than the Westreach, he marveled.

Falcon didn't seem to share his enthusiasm. The bard's eyes were wide as he looked around, and his remaining hand felt over the place where his other should have been.

"Will we be safe, do you think?" he muttered.

Tal clapped a hand on his shoulder. "Don't tell me you harbor biases against Easterners."

Falcon raised an eyebrow. "Didn't you earlier equate the Ingress with allowing Ravagers within Gladelyl's borders?"

"And so I maintain. But what's done is done, my friend. And it'd be preposterous to believe every Easterner is an agent of the Empire. Look! Do you think she's a spy?"

He pointed at a little Nightelf girl who tugged at a Gladelysh woman's hand, her eyes wide and pleading. The Gladelysh pulled her hand away quickly, looking around to see if anyone had seen. But just as she glanced away, the girl thrust her hands forward, snipped the purse at the woman's hip, and darted into the crowd, heedless of the woman screaming after her.

"Not a spy," Falcon said drily. "But not exactly a moral lass."

Tal shrugged. "Morals are gray in the underbellies of cities. Is it worse that the Lowkin woman is deprived of her hard-earned coin, or the Easterner girl goes yet another day hungry? But we could spend all day down here opining, my friend. Where should we begin our search for your elder?"

"I'll tell you if I can ever think through this fog." Falcon shook his head morosely, and Tal gave him a sympathetic squeeze of the shoulder. The bard's tattered memories were perhaps an even sorer loss than his hand, for his mind was his greatest instrument.

Yet before long, the Court Bard seemed to recover something of himself, and he led them forward into the throng. Tal's purse had never been heavy, but with the thief-girl still in mind, he kept one hand to the purse tucked inside his trousers and the other to a knife's hilt. The Mire's streets had never been wide, but now they felt as packed in as Tal's chickens had been in their coop. Easterners and Gladelysh bumped shoulders against them, and the only thing they shared in common were the scowls they aimed at everyone else. Tension was thicker in the air than the marsh's humidity, and at every moment, Tal expected a fight to break out.

Unlike High Elendol, which was immaculately clean, muck of every kind typified the Mire. Moss layered the roofs; mud had splashed a foot high up the sides of every building. Only the kintrees rising all around them and the werelights hovering above their heads kept Tal's spirits from sinking into the morass with everything else.

It helped that not all shops had resigned themselves to the swamp. Many of the signs still displayed glowing glyphs, their meanings imprinting themselves briefly on his mind with their charms. Bright colors painted the fronts of some homesteads nestled among the kintree roots. Such spots were valued properties, Tal knew, and the paint was yet another sign that these stores were a cut above the rest.

But Low Elendol's clean shops were far outnumbered by its rundown ones. Stalls dominated the streets, some without even cloth to keep off the perpetual dampness from their goods. Foods were on display, some from the surrounding forest like mushrooms and edible roots, others grains and vegetables imported from the plains to the east. Suspicion was their greeting far more often than a smile.

With all these peoples and their clashing customs packed together, Tal wasn't surprised to witness several altercations. As they turned a corner, they saw a minotaur turn its head and snag a nearby pavilion, sending its proprietor into a screaming rage. He tensed, expecting a fight, but was surprised as the minotaur only untangled its horn, bowed its big head, and walked away, the elf still yelling at its back.

But not all instances ended so bloodlessly. In one alley they passed, two Nightelf youths brawled with an Easterner human and one of the tree-like beings, and the Easterner elves seemed to suffer the worst of the exchange. Falcon's hand tightened on Tal's arm, but Tal only pulled him on.

"Shouldn't you stop them?" Falcon whispered, the gold in his eyes swirling anxiously.

Tal shook his head. "When you don't know friend from foe, the best you can do is to not intervene. I know this must be difficult for you, Falcon — no bard has a hard heart. But you must try not to feel everything around you."

"I could as soon as stop the rain as cease feeling," the minstrel muttered, and he seemed to shrink further in on himself.

Knowing he couldn't let Falcon withdraw, Tal prompted him, "Does anything look familiar? We've been wandering for almost two hours now."

Stirring, Falcon looked up and around them. As he

muttered to himself, Tal glanced back the way they'd come. He'd kept a careful watch, but so far, he hadn't glimpsed the same face twice. Now, though, a figure darted within a moss-covered alley just as his eyes crossed over them.

Tal frowned, staring at the place where the person had disappeared. But, as his old commander had often said, *Only stab at shadows when enemies are in them.* He wouldn't go after the figure on a hunch. Yet as he turned his gaze away, he kept a watch on the spot from the corner of his eye.

"There!" Falcon declared, and Tal looked around to see him pointing down the street. "I remember now! The elder was in the Derelict Quarter, and his house built from one of the old ruins."

Tal clapped him on the shoulder. "Good man! I knew it'd come back to you."

As Falcon led them forward again, Tal risked one last glance back and glimpsed the figure once more. Before they could flee, Tal turned his gaze back forward, a crooked smile on his lips. He suspected he knew what game was at play here.

They continued through the underbelly of Elendol, and the abodes and crowds thinned. The forest encroached on the roadway, ferns growing between the streets' pavers. The stones were loose, marking how long it had been since the road saw any repairs, while the houses became made of stone rather than wood.

"The remnants of the first settlers of Elendol," Tal murmured.

Falcon glanced at him. "You know the tales of the Origins?"

"Only a little." He gestured at one of the decrepit buildings. "That they built with stone rather than wood. That they were not elves, nor humans, nor any of the Bloodlines, but our ancestors from before the Severing."

Falcon drifted close enough to brush his fingers along the mossy, cracked stone. "Thousands of years, they've stood here," he murmured. "How many stories have played out between these walls?"

"Few these days from the look of it. Besides, I'm only interested in one tale at the moment."

They headed deeper into the quarter, and Tal feigned a stretch to glance behind him. A silhouette walked just at the edge of his sight. Tal turned back, his hand tracing his sword's grip.

Falcon abruptly stopped, staring up at one of the decrepit stone buildings. "This is it," he murmured.

Tal studied the elder's home. The stone that made up the bottom half of the house resembled a broken eggshell. A curved shape like that could only have been formed by magic, perhaps the Origins' precursor to the wood-shaping sorcery the Gladelysh now used. The rest of the house rose from the eggshell in a more typical style for the Mire, timbers making up the walls and interwoven fern fronds serving as the thatching. It looked kept up, but the door hung slightly ajar.

A tremor of heat wove through him, and Tal loosened *Velori* in its scabbard as he glanced back the way they'd come. The shadow was out of sight.

"Careful," Tal murmured. "Something has happened here. And we've been followed. No, don't look! Our only hope is to maintain the element of surprise."

Falcon stared at him, his eyes wide and his face twitching. But he followed as Tal stepped forward to the door to the hut and slowly eased it open. He drew his blade as he entered. The hinges creaked, and the room slowly came into light, though darkness still pooled around the edges.

"*Fuln.*"

A bright werelight materialized from his upturned hand to hover in the middle of the room. Behind him, Falcon gasped, then gagged. Tal stepped further in, *Velori* held at the ready, as he took in the macabre scene.

At first, he thought it darkly colored moss that covered the walls, the floor, and the table. But the body, slumped in a chair opposite to the door, and the horrid stink put that hopeful wish to rest.

"They butchered him," Falcon whispered, then abruptly retched in a corner.

"Stay with me," Tal instructed, "and shut the door behind you."

He stepped carefully around the table, eyes darting everywhere. He didn't see any glyphs carved into the surfaces, but not every trap could be easily seen. Yet as he stepped toward the body, nothing happened.

He peered closer. Underneath the savage slashes that mutilated the man, Tal could tell it had been an old, male elf who had died. *Likely Falcon's elder,* he thought glumly. The wounds looked like they were inflicted by an axe. Around his neck were more peculiar injuries, a series of punctures that made it seem as if a barbed chain had been wound around his neck and squeezed until it pierced the skin.

With any luck, he thought, *he was already dead.*

The door creaked, and Tal whirled, the tip of his blade pointed at the face of the figure who stepped in.

The elf, aged enough for lines to show faintly on his skin, didn't appear startled, nor did he have any weapons drawn. His skin was the color of chestnuts, and his hair stood in a startling contrast of silver, a long tail braided down his back. His eyes were dark down to the cloudy tendrils that swirled through them, like smoke against a night sky. His clothes were common, but Tal saw many places that could pocket away convenient and dangerous items.

Tal gave him his wolf's smile.

"You finally caught up," he said, not moving the tip of his blade from the stranger's face. "Who are you?"

"You must be subtler when you track a tail," the old elf said, his voice cracking like a whip. He didn't look at the blade, but kept Tal's gaze. "Any who meant you ill would have known you sensed their approach."

"And you don't mean us harm?"

The aged man glanced at Falcon, who had retreated to a corner, his belt knife held before him. "A good thing that I don't," he said drily.

"How about you start with your name?"

"Condur."

"And your kin name?"

Condur shook his head sharply. "That won't be necessary."

The aged elf moved a hand to his sleeve, and Tal edged *Velori* closer, the tip hovering inches from Condur's face. "No hidden knives. Or you might find my blade through your eye."

The elf only gave him a disdainful look as he pulled up his sleeve. Tal glanced at the faint tattoo inked into his skin from the corner of his eye, fearing some kind of sigil of influence. Instead, he saw the pearlescent outline of a familiar insignia: a kintree, its branches rising into towers, its many roots curved into a circle with a single, intricate rune in the middle.

Tal sighed and lowered his blade. "Why didn't you say so from the beginning?"

Falcon, unable to see the tattoo from his angle, glanced at each of them as Condur covered his arm again. "We trust him?" he asked in confusion.

"Yes. He's Ilthasi — a Queen's man, one of her spies and agents. He wears her brand."

Falcon's brow furrowed. "Couldn't it be forged?"

"Only a fool would attempt it." Condur's eyes wandered around the hut, and Tal knew a man such as he was noting every detail.

"And why's that?" the bard persisted.

"It uses a similar magic as a Binding Ring," Tal said. "Only, with the Queen's rune, it's a binding specific to the Monarch of Gladelyl. Any who try to forge it, even should they succeed, would find themselves in too immense of suffering to be of any use."

"And if it wasn't perfectly replicated, we would know." Condur stepped around the table to study the slaughtered old elf, only his narrowed nostrils showing any sign of discomfort.

"And how would *we* know it's not a fake?" Falcon ventured, sounding as if he almost didn't want to know the answer.

Condur glanced up at Tal. "Your mistake," he reprimanded him, then bared his sleeve again and pressed three fingers to the rune in the middle.

A whisper sounded in his mind. "He is true," Queen Geminia's voice spoke, her tone mildly amused.

Then, as quickly as it had come, her presence faded away.

Falcon looked shaken, clearly having heard the Queen, but seemed unconvinced. "Could be an illusion," he pointed out.

Condur glanced at Tal. "Your companion has a suspicious mind."

Tal shrugged. "An Extinguished impersonated him. He has good reason to be."

"You would do well to learn from him. A trusting man is soon a dead one in the Mire." Condur peered closer at the punctures on the man's neck, a faint frown curving his lips.

"Thorns?" Tal suggested quietly.

The Queen's agent nodded. "A message."

Tal didn't have to ask from whom. His blood, which had cooled, suddenly flared anew.

"The Silver Vines?" Falcon said aloud what they'd all been thinking. "How could they have known?"

"The Thorn knows more than you could imagine. Best to assume he knows all that you do."

Condur swept his gaze around the room once more, then strode to the door, opened it, and covertly glanced outside. As he leaned back in and nodded, Tal sheathed his sword, Falcon slowly following suit with his knife.

"We will tail you whenever you are down in the Mire,"

Condur said. "But do not assume we can always protect you. You must remain vigilant, for the Silver Vines have infected every part of the city."

"High Elendol as well?"

The Queen's man hesitated, then nodded.

Tal felt a chill prickle up his spine. He'd suspected as much with the Ingress and other strange happenings in Elendol. But it made him no more comfortable to hear it.

Perhaps not even the Ilthasi are immune to the Thorn's corruption.

"Then vigilant we'll remain." Tal didn't show his continued wariness as he glanced at the mutilated elder. "What about him?"

"I'll see to him."

"And if he has any books or letters, will you let us know?"

Condur glanced around again. "I do not think he will. But if he does, then yes."

Tal cast one last lingering glance at the corpse, guilt stirring in his gut. *Poor bastard,* he thought. *Yet another man dead in my wake.*

"I'm sure we'll meet again, Condur," Tal said aloud as he led Falcon outside.

"No need. Confer instead with my associate in High Elendol, Prendyn. He'll tell you all you need to know."

Tal nodded, then turned, aware of the Queen's agent watching from within the hut as they walked away.

LIKE WATER

"Here," Ashelia said as she stopped Garin at the edge of the platform. "The Dancing Plaza."

Garin eyed it with dismay. Located between several of the kintrees, there wasn't a more visible place in High Elendol. *So everyone can witness my prowess,* he thought glumly.

Ashelia seemed to sense his thoughts. "Don't worry what others might say. No matter your performance, they'll think no worse of you than they already do."

"That's reassuring."

She smiled. "You're *lenual* — human. Male elves dance from the time they can walk. And they expect as little of females and half-kin, you know."

"I doubt I can meet even small expectations."

Ashelia raised an eyebrow. "When others are lined up to cut you down, don't do their job for them. Your first lesson for the day."

Garin gave her a guilty smile. "You're right. I'll try not to embarrass you more than I have to. And… thank you."

"No need. Do you remember the way back to my home?"

"Probably."

"If you get lost, you need only ask for directions. They'll

mock you, but no Highkin desires a human to be wandering High Elendol. You'll find it. This evening, after Wren's lesson, I'll fetch you for your cleansing."

Ashelia had turned away before her words settled in. "Wait! What do you mean, Wren's lesson?"

She turned back, a slight crease to her brow. "I thought she told you. She was quite excited to learn how to dance with me."

Her news. He felt a guilty sinking in his gut. "She tried," he admitted. "But I did a poor job listening."

Ashelia gave him a sympathetic smile. "You'll do better next time. Put it from your mind for now. You must have your full attention on the lesson before you."

He drew in a deep breath and let it out slowly. Though it did little to calm his nerves, with her steady gaze on him, there was nothing for it but to turn and walk across the last bridge onto the Dancing Plaza.

The platform was large and shaped in a hexagon, with scaffolding providing seating on all six sides, and bridges leading away at each corner. The thick canopy of the kintrees obscured most of the sunlight, as in most of Elendol, but for a patch of light at the center. Near this burst of light, an elf stood perfectly still, watching Garin approach.

He grew yet more unnerved as he realized that in the far seats, other elves sat in attendance. From their billowing, colorful robes — and from their presence in High Elendol at all — he assumed they must be Highkin, the elven nobility. But why any of them would want to watch him flail with a sword was beyond him. *Falcon should make a good trade here,* he thought. *These elves clearly need a fresh source of entertainment.*

Entering the center of the platform, he noticed a circle painted over the wood, the depiction of a kintree with its tangled roots and tall branches contained within it. Stepping along the roots, Garin hesitantly approached the lone elf standing in the middle.

For a moment, he stood before him in silence, wondering if

he should wait for his new tutor to speak first. The elf's gaze didn't shift from him, though they didn't quite meet his eyes, but stared just past him. When he didn't speak for several long moments, Garin swallowed and ventured, "Hello. Are you Master Ulen Windlofted?"

The elf cocked his head to the side. His curly, dark brown hair was unlike any others he'd seen, cropped short on the sides and long enough on top that it flopped over with his head's movement. His eyes were brown and laced with a piercing sky-blue.

"Easily startled," the elf said. "Like a rabbit."

Garin smiled tentatively, wondering if it was a joke. "I've been told that before."

"Lacks deference. Ill-disciplined. Hasty."

His smile was starting to slip. Though another question danced on his tongue, Garin clamped his mouth shut. He was starting to wonder if this really was Ulen Windlofted. The man wore robes, for one; not quite as billowing as the Highkin around the edges, but enough that it would seem to encumber his movement. There was a sword belted at his side, but wearing one seemed to be the fashion among elven nobility. And his peculiar manner was so different from Master Krador's authoritativeness back in the Coral Castle.

The elf's expression didn't shift as he stared several moments longer. Then, for no reason Garin could tell, he turned and strode away, only to stop after a dozen paces to turn and face him again.

Then he charged.

Garin backed away, heart hammering. Should he defend himself? He had no weapon, but he could take a swing if need be. Not knowing who his opponent was, or who he might offend, he decided dodging would be the best route.

Dodge quickly, or don't dodge at all, Tal had said during their combat lessons on the way to Halenhol, and Garin tried to comply. But as he twisted at the last moment out of the way, he felt the elf snag his arm and, with a mighty wrench, send Garin spinning to the ground.

Grunting at the impact, Garin rolled away and raised his head only to throw himself back, for the elf had followed up his throw with a kick. He only just raised his arm in time to take the blow, but the force of it sent pain striking up through his shoulder, still sore from their ambush on the road, and he couldn't repress a yelp.

He scrambled backward and onto his feet. He tried to catch his breath as he eyed the elf warily.

"What was that for?" he demanded.

The man's brow creased slightly. "Unfamiliar with water," he murmured.

"What are you saying? Who are you? Are you Master Ulen or not?"

"Speak when spoken to." Though the elf's words seemed a response, his eyes were no longer on Garin, but wandering the treetops above them. "I am Master Ulen Yulnaed. I will be your dancing master. From my evaluation, you know little. We will begin with water."

Garin stared at him, unsure what to do. How could this strange man be the most renowned dancer in Elendol?

"Water?" he ventured.

His new master made a jerky motion, and Garin flinched and stepped back, thinking it another attack. Then he saw a pair of servants coming toward them, something large and wooden and mounted on wheels rolling between them. *A tub*, he realized. *Full of water. Is he going to drown me now?*

When the servants had rolled the tub next to them, Ulen made another jerky motion. "In."

Garin glanced at the tub, then back at the dancing master. "What do you mean?"

"A master should not be questioned." Ulen's rebuke was dispassionate, as if he'd spoken it a thousand times before. "Enter the water."

118

Not knowing what other options he had, Garin balanced on one leg and awkwardly tugged at one of his boots.

Ulen stopped him with a gesture. "No. In."

Baffled, Garin lowered his foot and tentatively approached the tub. He snuck a glance at each of the servants, trying to detect if this was some kind of elven joke, but their expressions were as blank as the dancer's. The Highkin seated upon the scaffolding were too far away to be of any help either, though their quiet conversations and ever-watching eyes made him yet more uneasy.

Garin lifted and put one foot then the other inside the tub, wincing as water flooded over the tops of his boots and drenched his stockings.

The Dancing Master motioned, and a sinking feeling in his stomach told him what he meant. Lowering himself, he repressed a gasp as the cold water soaked through his clothes and prickled his skin into gooseflesh.

Ulen leaned over him. "Ease back. Relax your body. Feel as water feels."

Trying to hide his grimace, Garin put his head back until his hair floated free and only his face peeked above. He knew how to swim, as there were several lakes around Hunt's Hollow where he and the other boys had liked to go during the hot summers. But he hadn't spent so much time in water that he found relaxing easy.

Especially with a score of strange elves watching him.

He heard Ulen say something, but with his ears covered, he couldn't hear. "What?" he asked as he half-rose from the water.

"You are not relaxed. Your muscles are tense. Is water tense?" With a firm hand to Garin's shoulder, the Dancing Master eased him back down until water again covered his ears.

Taking a deep breath, or as deep as he could with the pressure of water and wet clothes on his belly, Garin exhaled and tried to let his muscles relax. He kept his heels against the bottom of the tub to anchor him up, though; fully relaxing would only let him drown. But all other tension he tried to breathe out from his body, his eyes watching the dappled light on the high above canopy.

A hand came from nowhere and pushed his head down.

Midway through a breath, Garin sucked in water as his head dunked under. Gagging, he kicked furiously and grappled with the edge of the tub, then wrenched himself free of the water's surface. Coughs wracked his chest as he spat water over the side of the tub.

When he'd recovered, he looked up and saw Master Ulen standing just out of range of his splashing, watching him expressionlessly. Rage, fueled by fear and helplessness, suddenly lanced through him.

"Why did you do that?" he demanded, then coughed again.

"Water is not tense, but water is not unmoving. Water will react to the slightest touch with a ripple, to a blow with equal force. You were not water. You were human."

I am human! Garin wanted to shout, but he still had enough restraint to choke the words back. "So I'm supposed to be relaxed, but also wary?" he ventured.

"Water is ready to react. Water is not wood." Ulen gestured to the tub, and Garin knew that was all the answer he would get.

Anger still simmered through him, but Garin set his teeth and did as instructed. *Get through this lesson, and you'll never have to do another one,* he bargained with himself as he eased his head back underwater, leaving only his face exposed. *Just this one lesson.*

He relaxed his muscles as best he could, but with the expectation of a hand coming to press down on his head, he found it even more difficult than before.

Ulen approached and stood over him, and he grew yet more tense, waiting for the strike he knew must come. But as the

Dancing Master moved, and Garin jerked to intercept the blow, he found Ulen had aimed for his stomach instead.

Sitting up with a pained wheeze, Garin stared resentfully at the Dancing Master, who had leaped nimbly back to stare past him again.

"Was I not water, Master?" he guessed, unable to keep the sarcasm from his voice.

"You were not water."

Again, the Dancing Master gestured, and again, Garin settled back. He didn't bother trying to relax, but watched for where the elf would strike next.

You misunderstand his game, Listener.

Garin jerked at the Singer's unexpected interruption. Not wanting to speak aloud, he tried thinking back his answer. *He's trying to humiliate me.*

No. The Eldritch is trying to draw you out of your skull. He is trying to have you live and move in the moment as water does, not try to plot your actions ahead, as you always attempt. Only if you are fully present can you hope to intercept him.

Then how do I do that?

Stop. Be. Watch, hear, smell, taste, feel. Inhabit your senses. Move as they instruct.

Garin hesitated. Devils only made deals that benefitted them; all the old tales spoke of it. But he couldn't tell how the Singer might profit here. And what other options did he really have?

His foot slapped down under Ulen's blow.

Garin didn't bother rising. *You're still in your head,* he admonished himself. *You have to at least try.*

Exhaling, he let out all the worry, the embarrassment, the anger at his predicament, and sought what his body felt. The sensations rolled in, slowly at first, then faster as his senses asserted themselves.

Golden light against his eyes. The cold water stiffening his body. The faint murmur of the lapping waves. The lift of his suspended body.

A shift in the shadows to the left—

Garin moved, arms rising to catch the blow to his chest, but his hands slipped around the Dancing Master's palm, and it slammed into his chest. Air expelled from his lungs, and he rose, gasping for air. But to his surprise, his anger had fled.

When he looked up, Ulen stared at his shoulder. Still, when the Dancer nodded, Garin couldn't help a smile.

"Water is not surprised," Ulen said. "But water only reacts. To dance, you must not only be water, but fire, always moving before another can reach you."

With an impatient gesture, his tutor bade him to rise, and Garin sloshed water out of the tub as he stood on wobbly legs. A glow of triumph warmed his chilled chest, even as he coughed up the remnants of water in his lungs.

But what triumph could it be when the Singer had helped him attain it?

———

Tal took a breath before the entrance, then entered with a crooked smile plain for all to see.

The chamber the Queen had provided in the lower reaches of House Elendola wasn't spacious, but neither was it too cramped for four to meet. A table occupied the middle of the room, at which an extravagantly decorated woman sat with her posture upright and a vapid smile perched on her lips. Standing by the table was an unfamiliar man, who also smiled as Tal entered, and Aelyn, who decidedly did not. Prendyn the Ilthasi captain, he guessed the unknown man to be, leaving the noblewoman as Balindi Aldinare, Peer of House Aldinare and an infamous gossip.

As Tal respectfully greeted the strangers, he studied them. Aelyn was no beauty, but he appeared a well-groomed stallion compared to Prendyn's mulish features. The Ilthasi captain was one of the few ugly elves Tal had seen in Elendol, his face too long in some places and too squashed in others, and neither side could agree with the other. His red-brown hair was a pleasing hue, but it hung limply like moss down to his shoulders and was bald at the pate. But the genial smile that the man wore went a long way to transforming his looks.

Balindi, on the other hand, took great care with her appearance. She made every use of the paints and powders elves were renowned for producing, with a deep, luminous purple painted over her eyes and a sparkling powder dusted over her face. Her chestnut hair was tightly curled in an ornate arrangement atop her head. But while vanity was no rarity among Highkin women, it was her plump figure that set her apart from most of her coevals, a desirable trait in a society of lean women.

Though their appearances said little for them, Tal knew better than to underestimate their value. These two were to be his tutors in the tangle of Elendol's politics, the web which he must navigate for him to satisfy Queen Geminia's command.

"Aristhol," Prendyn greeted him with unexpected warmth and respect. "You may not remember me from your last visit to Elendol, but I recall you. Caused quite a stir among our slow-changing people! First fighting Heyl, then hunting down the Thorn."

Tal's smile twisted. "I wasn't thorough enough in my hunt, apparently."

His eyes flickered to the noblewoman, wondering why a gossip like Balindi would be entrusted with state secrets. Only at Aelyn's word before the meeting had he known to speak freely before her, though he still questioned the guidance.

"You must not blame yourself! Even if you are a hero, you are only one man." Balindi was the very picture of flattery, yet Tal thought he detected a strain of irony in her words.

"But not a man alone. And how could I fail with you on my side?"

Balindi giggled. Out of her sightline, Aelyn's scowl deepened.

"We don't have much time," the mage said, his impatience barely restrained. "Let's turn to business. Much has changed since I left for Halenhol. The Ingress of Elendol has proceeded quickly."

"Yes, yes." A crease appeared in Prendyn's forehead. "There are far more immigrants than we'd expected, and far too many to track. Ilthasi resources are stretched thin."

"How long have you known that the Thorn returned?" Tal asked. "Only since the Ingress a year ago?"

Prendyn nodded. "But it's possible he was here before then."

"He must have been," Aelyn interjected. "His influence has extended quickly. And without it, these Sympathists could not have reversed a policy that has remained in place for hundreds of years — for good reason."

"Oh, yes," Balindi said with a solemn shake of her head. "It is tragic how my fellow Peers have been so easily bought."

Tal settled into his chair. "Then you know they were bribed?"

"Absolutely! With as much certainty as one can know anything in the world of politics." She gave another smile, appearing more insipid than he now suspected her to be.

"Evidence," Aelyn groused. "We need evidence, Peer Balindi, and names."

She turned her smile on the irritable mage. "Their names are easy enough to supply — all you must do is look to the Sympathists and those who voted with them. But foremost among them are the Lathnieli."

Aelyn's eyes seemed to burn as they swirled. "I suspected as much."

Tal hid his wince. Little could make him sympathize with the mage. But what the Lathnieli had done to Aelyn was one of the few things that could.

"Peer Maone Lathniel resides here in the city, while her

bond often stays at their provincial estate," Prendyn said. "We have kept watch over her comings and goings, but they've led nowhere. If she has contact with the Thorn and the Silver Vines, it is beyond our detection."

Tal stared at the grain of the wood on the table, tracing one gloved thumb over it. "It would be difficult to hide an operation within one of the kintrees. Unless everyone in their staffs are in on the plot, strangers would be easily recognized, and rumors would proliferate like mayflies in summer."

Balindi smiled, as if in recognition of her role in that.

"Thus," he concluded, "they are likely somewhere in the Mire."

"Our thoughts precisely," Prendyn affirmed.

"A mage could track them down, if they'd seen one of their agents before."

Or the Thorn, he thought, but he kept that to himself.

The Ilthasi captain gave him a pained smile. "They could. But therein lies the problem: None alive has seen one they know to belong to the Cult."

Tal felt Aelyn's eyes burning on him and pretended not to notice. He knew all too well what the mage's gaze meant.

"Then I suppose we must discover them by other means," he said lightly.

"Would you like to hear my proposal?" Balindi piped up.

The other two elves exchanged a look, but Tal gave her a grave nod, glad for the diversion. "Of course."

She leaned forward, eyes bright, the silver tendrils in them spinning. "The Queen should hold a ball!"

Aelyn scoffed aloud, but tried disguising it as a cough. Prendyn wore a strained smile.

Tal didn't bother hiding his confusion. "What would a ball do for us?"

"Nothing makes poison and knives materialize like a ball! Think of it: the Queen, the Peers, the Chromatic Masters, every Highkin of import — all gathered in one place! It would guarantee plotting and rumormongering. And, if we learn nothing from hearsay, it might at least present an opportunity for those nasty cultists to ambush those few of us still loyal to Her Eminence."

Prendyn's skin glistened with sweat. "That would be a difficult situation in which to provide protection."

"I am sure you are up to the task." Balindi's smile was cloyingly sweet.

Tal thought it over for several long moments. "It's a good idea, if only as a cloak to disguise a dagger. Peer Aldinare, might we trouble you to request it of the Queen, and organize it should she accede?"

Balindi's smile was radiant. "Nothing would delight me more!"

"I'm sure," Aelyn muttered.

While the noblewoman turned her smile on him, Tal nodded to the Ilthasi captain. "Meanwhile, I intend to explore Low Elendol for leads. My friend Falcon, Court Bard to King Aldric, has already agreed to lend any assistance he can. If I ask him and his troupers to take up residence in the taverns in the Mire, will you be able to protect them?"

Prendyn wiped a hand across his forehead. "We will do our best, but I cannot guarantee their safety."

Tal grimaced. He'd expected as much, but it made the request of his old friend harder still. Just their brief trip down there had taken its toll. How could he survive several days, perhaps weeks, among that chaos? And then there was the rest of the Dancing Feathers to consider. They were a courtly troupe, used to playing for a genteel audience, and more than a few of them wouldn't take well to serving a lower-class clientele.

But with the Binding Ring on his finger, and the lessons of a burned book on his mind, he didn't know what other options he had.

"It'll have to do," he relented. "And you, Aelyn. What's your part in this?"

Balindi seemed slightly scandalized that Tal neglected all the mage's titles, but Aelyn only returned a small smile. "Someone must watch the watcher, Tal Harrenfel. And who better than the one most trusted by Her Eminence?"

Tal gave him a broad smile back, resentment stirring through him. "Who, indeed?"

THE SAPPHIRE TOWER

His clothes were still damp and his skin chafed by the time Garin finally found his way back to his room at the Venaliel kintree.

He changed to a dry pair of clothes, then lay on his bed for a blessedly long time, allowing his tortured muscles and blistered feet to rest. He thought over the dancing lesson, Master Ulen's strange behavior, and the Singer's aid in the endeavor.

This last thought occupied him most of all. Before, the Singer had only become present when Garin's life was in danger, or when the Extinguished had commanded it — at least, before it had turned on the fell warlock. But this time had been different.

Or maybe it wasn't, he thought, watching tiny green werelights dance across the ceiling of his room. *Maybe he thought I was drowning and believed my life in danger.*

During several moments of the lesson, it had certainly seemed perilous. Master Ulen had a detached air about him, and when he spoke, it never seemed directly to Garin. When he'd dunked Garin in the tub, he hadn't been sure the Dancing Master cared much whether or not he drowned.

Yet he had to admit, Ulen's methods had worked. After only

one lesson, he had a greater awareness of his body than after dozens of lessons with Master Krador back in the Coral Castle. Swordplay, he was beginning to see, went beyond just fighting.

But as he rose and sought sustenance, his thoughts turned toward the evening, and all his weary satisfaction faded. Tonight, Ashelia and her fellow sorcerers would try to purge him of the Singer. He wondered what they'd do to him. He'd heard Tal's screams when Ashelia had healed him of his wound. He could only imagine how much more painful it would be to pry a devil from his mind.

The food he ate might have been sawdust for all he tasted it.

Wren found him in the dining hall, and they chatted for some time as they ate and drank. Garin gulped down more glasses of watered *bakala* than he knew was wise, but his nerves kept him grasping for the glass. None of it escaped Wren, but she didn't mention it. Instead, she spoke of her own morning and afternoon spent playing warlocks' cards with her fellow troupers, their rooms up for wager. With a smug smile, she announced that she'd swept more hands than not, and Ox and Melina, a human girl around Wren's age, were sleeping at her good mercy. At his prompting, she confessed her dancing lessons with Ashelia, and that the first of them had gone well. While she had been taught the "elemental forms," as he had, her instruction hadn't included nearly drowning.

Nevertheless, between her good cheer and the wine, Garin was beginning to relax.

But all calmness fled when Ashelia entered the dining hall, dressed as he'd never seen her before. Gone were the tunic and trousers, replaced by deep blue robes lined with silver and gold and a necklace set with a glittering sapphire as large as Garin's thumb. A silver circlet bound back her hair, and her expression was so solemn that when her stormy eyes fell on him, fear shivered through him.

Behind her walked Aelyn. He'd also dressed in robes, though of plainer appearance, and his spinning eyes looked eager as they settled on Garin. His stomach gave a small lurch. Whatever made the mage excited couldn't bode well for Garin.

Wren frowned at her as they approached, but Ashelia spared her only a brief nod before turning to Garin. "We're ready to begin when you are."

Garin nodded, then glanced at Aelyn. "What are you doing here?"

The mage raised an eyebrow. "I am one of the Chromatic Masters. I need not explain myself to you."

"Aelyn," Ashelia said in a warning tone.

Garin was surprised when her House-brother only shrugged in response and looked aside. *Almost as if he has a capacity for shame.*

Ashelia looked back to Garin. "He's attending in an advisory role. As he witnessed the initial incident in the Ruins of Erlodan and your behavior since, Aelyn might provide additional insights that could aid in your cleansing."

Garin nodded, then cast Wren one last look. He hoped that he looked braver than he felt as he rose on unsteady legs and followed them.

His head was woozy from the wine, and the planks of the bridges seemed to leap underfoot more than normal. Ashelia and Aelyn spoke quietly among themselves as they led him across the bridges and platforms. Instead of moving toward the edge of the kintrees where the waterfall had been, or to the center where the Dancing Plaza hung suspended, they now traveled around the middle. Garin lifted his gaze when he could, trying to spot their destination.

As they moved out from behind one massive trunk, he saw it. It looked like a pillar of stone, jutting up from the ground half as high as a kintree, though nearly as wide and jagged at the top like the pinnacle had been chopped off. Yet it was unlike any stone he'd seen. Glimmers of glowing blue light laced through it, and the stone's surface was rough and textured in a way that reminded him more of a tree's bark than any rock he'd known.

Glancing back, Ashelia noticed his curious stare. "Petrified wood," she explained. "Each of the Chromatic Towers is formed of a dead kintree, preserved by magic and the kintree's own resources. Every time a kintree dies, a new Tower is founded. Or so it is said. None have died in many generations, perhaps a thousand years, and I don't know what school of sorcery they might establish if one did."

"And the blue light?"

A faint smile curved her lips as she glanced back. "That's for the magician's vanity. Never underestimate it."

They both looked at Aelyn, whose lips curled.

"*Ostentatious* vanity," the mage said stiffly, "is not one of my failings, as you both well know."

Ashelia laughed and placed a hand on his arm. "A lack of good humor might be, however."

To Garin's wonder, not only did Aelyn not cringe from her touch, but he gave her a grudging smile in response. *Maybe he does love one person in the World,* he marveled.

Now that conversation had begun, Garin found himself full of questions. "So you're part of the Sapphire Tower still? I thought, since you became a Warder, you might..."

"Be excluded?" Ashelia finished for him. "No — once an elf earns a position, it's rare for them to abdicate it." Noticing his confusion, she continued, "We view such things differently than *lenuali*. With our long lives, we don't feel the need to bind ourselves to one calling for all of our days. Thus, I am a healer of the Sapphire Tower, but also a Peer of the Realm, a mother, and now a Warder. And Aelyn remains a master of the Onyx Tower and a Peer of the Realm as well as our emissary to Avendor."

"What is it like to live so long?" The question was out of his mouth before he could wonder if it was rude.

Aelyn gave him a condescending smile. "It means that the short lives of humans become ever more meaningless to us."

"No," Ashelia contradicted him softly. "All lives are respected among elves. In fact, our long lives can sometimes be... taxing."

Her House-brother glanced over at her curiously. Garin noticed a small furrow crinkled her brow as she continued.

"There are moments when it's glorious to think of all I might accomplish in my lifetime. Other times, it's tedious, each day like the one before it. But given the choice between something and nothing, it's the rare person who gives up the choice entirely."

Garin tried to picture it, living so long as to run out of things he wanted to do. His own life stretched long before him; only fifteen, he had many times his present years still ahead of him. *If I survive this healing,* he thought, and his mood took a steep dive.

"We'll give you back your choice," Ashelia said, as if responding to his thoughts, then gestured before them.

They'd reached the platform that encircled the Sapphire Tower. A door, made of the same petrified wood as the rest of the tower and just large enough to admit one at a time, nearly faded into the side of it. No windows opened along its walls, and Garin felt a clammy fear at being contained within. He was a lad of the open meadows of Hunt's Hollow. The forest canopy far overhead had already made him feel cramped; this pillar seemed like a prison.

"Come," Ashelia murmured, then gestured him ahead.

The door had no handle that Garin could see, but Ashelia reached into her robe and produced a small token that she pressed to it. The door swung open with a slight groan, like a tree leaning under a heavy gust, and a yellow glow of light emitted from within. Garin blinked in the sudden brightness, but at Ashelia's urging, he stepped inside first.

For a moment, he stared around in amazement. The inside

of the tower was nothing like it appeared from without. Where its exterior was mysterious and daunting, inside it was as bright as a sunny day, and various plant forms occupied every available space. Red, green, and gold leaves were all on display, as were blooms of more hues than Garin had thought possible. Vines crawled up the tall walls, across the domed ceiling, and around the bannister leading up the stairs that encircled the wall on the far side.

When he tore his gaze away, he saw Ashelia wore a smile and Aelyn a smirk.

"Not what you expected, is it?" Ashelia asked softly.

He mutely shook his head.

"Healers have divined what helps most in our art over millennia. And though we Gladelysh are people of the forest, all beings crave sunlight. The plants serve the purposes of our medicinals as well as promote a sense of vitality."

Aelyn snorted. "So you healers claim."

"And so we have shown," she responded with a raised eyebrow.

"I feel better already," Garin said truthfully, then added, "Perhaps I won't need the purging."

A weak joke deserved a weak smile, and Ashelia gave it just that. Aelyn merely scowled.

"The ritual will take place above," the healer said. "Follow me."

She led him and Aelyn up the stairs, which seemed formed of the petrified tree itself. Yellow werelights landed on his skin as they ascended, and Garin caught one, reminded of catching fireflies during summers as a boy. He closed his hand as if he might keep hold of it, but when he opened it again, the light had disappeared.

They ascended one floor, then another, and yet another. Though not all overflowed with plants like the welcoming chamber, they all boasted flowers and vines amid the desks, bookshelves, tables, and chairs. No one else seemed to occupy the Tower — but Garin realized a moment later they must all be waiting above. His stomach turned again.

Finally, they topped the last of the stairs and entered the ritual room. Four other blue-robed elves stood with cowls pulled over their heads, though their faces remained visible. Several of them smiled reassuringly at Garin, and he tried to return them.

The ceiling here was taller, though stairs told of rooms still further above. Trees grew around the edges of the chamber. Interspersed between them were five fireplaces, each lit and roaring, filling the room with a stuffy heat and adding a sinister orange glow to the cheery yellow werelights. A carved circle occupied the center of the room, with arcs ribbing the floor all the way to its center — like the rings of a tree stump, Garin recognized. Around the edges of the circle were five pedestals that looked formed of petrified wood and were rooted in place by a strange red vine. Atop each pedestal was an open book, and a smaller pedestal beside held a mortar bowl full of petals, powders, and capped vials of liquid.

Ashelia introduced each of the Sapphire sorcerers, but Garin couldn't fix their names in his mind. His gaze kept roaming the room as if searching for an escape. He wondered if he'd return here in his nightmares. He wondered if he'd leave the tower at all. Already, he felt as if the Singer was clawing at his insides, determined to keep its hold on him, or tear him apart if it couldn't manage that.

Ashelia smiled at him, but her stormy eyes whirled, betraying her own unease. "Garin, if you could move to the center of the circle and sit, however is most comfortable for you."

Silently, he obeyed, sitting cross-legged and staring into one of the hearths. The flames seemed to beckon him. He wondered if he'd be better off throwing himself into them now. Sweat trickled down his forehead and into his eyes, and he wiped impatiently at it, wishing they'd get this over with.

The magicians moved into position behind their pedestals and talked among themselves. Aelyn shifted back into one corner of the room. Garin dropped his gaze to the floor. Between the raised circles, countless runes had been etched into the wood, faintly glimmering with a light that was the pale blue of a robin's egg. He put a finger over one of them, tracing it. An echo of a word, almost recognizable, sounded in his mind. He traced another, and another, running his hand over them, and almost it seemed like a faint song hummed in his ears.

Like the Nightsong. He jerked his hand away as if burned.

The healers, preoccupied with their preparations, had mashed up the petals with pestles and poured the vials of liquid into their bowls. Garin felt Ashelia's eyes on him but ignored her gaze, staring again into the flames. No safety lay there, either. He found his fingers tracing the scar on his left arm and thinking of the battle around the Ruins of Erlodan. *Cheery thoughts,* he mocked himself. But somehow, the memories reassured him as they didn't in his nightmares. He'd fought the Extinguished and his monsters and survived.

He could survive this.

The mages settled their bowls back onto the side pedestals, then kept one hand over them while the other stretched back toward the hearths behind them. Garin watched as, under Ashelia's hand, the air distorted like it might under intense heat. He jerked as the glyphs beneath him glowed, brighter and brighter, until they became uncomfortable to look at.

Then, in tandem, the mages began to chant. Each word was spoken precisely, slowly, moving at a stately march, with a gap of silence in between as the echoes from the previous word faded. He knew it was the Worldtongue by the way it twisted in his mind, teasing him with its meaning, then dying away before the next word came.

But though the sounds quieted, their effects did not. One by one, the words of power were tossed like stones into a pond, their ripples colliding and multiplying one another. The energy of the spell built on Garin's skin, uncomfortable and dangerous. He didn't dare move.

One word, two words, three. Tal had once told him three words poorly cast were enough to kill a sorcerer. He wondered if the danger was magnified when five mages directed their words at the same person. He looked at Aelyn and found the mage staring back at him, his eyes whirling as if alive with flames. For once, he showed no condescension, but gave him a nod that was almost reassuring.

Garin could barely notice it. His senses felt overwhelmed, his skin on fire. His eyes swelled in their sockets like they might burst out.

As the mages spoke the fourth word, an unwitting scream erupted from Garin's throat. He tried to rise, but something froze his limbs. It only made him furious, and he roared wordlessly at the mages. Part of him recoiled at what he did, but he couldn't help it. He was no more in control now than a rider atop a spooked horse. His muscles strained against his invisible bonds, and he squeezed his eyes shut against the suddenly too-bright room.

He felt the Singer rise within him, and a rumble resounded throughout the room.

He is mine! The Singer's challenge boomed in his skull, but it seemed as if he spoke to the Sapphire mages. *You cannot take him from me!*

Prying his eyelids open, Garin squinted at Ashelia. Her face was drenched in sweat, and her posture slackened, as if her legs might give way. Yet her eyes swirled with determination, and she chanted the fifth word with her peers.

The Singer seized his limbs and, with a surge of fury and force, broke his invisible bonds.

As he came to his feet, his eyes wide open, the sorcerers stared back at him, fear shining in their eyes. Aelyn's arms had risen, and his lips were moving, though he couldn't hear his words. Garin took a step forward, moving from the center of the ring, but none of the Sapphire mages hesitated in speaking the sixth word, though a howl filled the room and stole the sound of it away from Garin's ears.

He found himself suddenly thrust down onto his knees, a great weight bearing down. The Singer roared again, pain twined with ire, but seeming no weaker.

I have claimed him! the Singer thundered. *And all shall know my mark!*

Garin suddenly felt thrust outside of himself. From above, he saw the circle, the five sorcerers surrounding him, his body between them, kneeling. As he watched, his body rose again, his shoulders bowed and his knees trembling, the weight of the World seeming to press down on him. Even separate, he felt something building inside him, burning to get out.

As he came fully upright, it burst free. Like great wings unfurled from his chest and buffeted the mages with mighty flaps, everyone in the room was thrown back against the walls.

Abruptly, Garin was yanked back into his body, He swayed as the Singer's control receded. But it didn't disappear.

You are mine, Jenduit. *I have marked you and made you my own, and you shall hear my mortal name. Singer I am to you no more; know me now as Ilvuan.*

Garin could make no response, but the Singer seemed to need none. He felt it retreat further still so that it almost dissipated. But at the edge of his consciousness, its presence was a faint prickle, like the tips of claws pressing lightly on his skin.

He sucked in a breath, and suddenly he was in command of himself again.

The room had filled with smoke, and he leaned over, coughing. When he could breathe again, he looked up with watering eyes. The healers of the Sapphire Tower were groaning as they rose. One held their arm, wincing with pain, and a silver-haired elf clutched his head, a hint of blood trickling down his face. But that all five were alive was more than he'd dared hope for.

Aelyn was cursing loudly. "Damned boy," he directed at Garin as he staggered back to his feet, his scowl deepening as he touched gingerly at the back of his head.

The rest of the room had not fared so well. The trees' leaves were brown and shriveled, and the vines all dead. The fires had sputtered to coals, billowing smoke into the room. And as his gaze fell to his feet, the glyphs in the floor no longer glowed, and through them ran deep furrows, like the scratches from a terrible beast.

"Garin?"

He turned at Ashelia's voice and roused himself. "I'm here."

"Did it… did we succeed?"

He hesitated. The Singer's presence lingered still. He feared it always would now.

"Yes." He forced a smile. "The devil's gone."

The surrounding healers looked at each other with evident relief. Ashelia matched his smile with one of her own. Only Aelyn still scowled, his eyes turning with suspicion.

A thin tendril of amusement that wasn't his own coiled inside Garin's mind.

A TROUPERS' WAR

FALCON HESITATED AT THE DOORWAY AND TURNED TO TAL. "ARE you certain about this?"

They stood outside the room where the Dancing Feathers had gathered for their daily practice of music, elocution, and other amusing or artistic pursuits. Tal listened to the sounds of revelry echoing out onto the platform as he formed his response.

He'd always tried to be honest with Falcon. No matter how they'd aggrandized his legend, their friendship had never been a lie. But listening to the sounds of the troupers and seeing his friend's resigned expression, he knew the truth would only hurt him.

And if Falcon knew the extent of the danger, he might not agree to his request.

Tal smiled and gripped his friend's shoulder. "Of course! Never more. You saw Condur's capability already — the Ilthasi have more than enough resources to protect all of you."

The bard studied him, eyes squinting, as the gold spun anxiously in his irises. He'd always known Tal too well to be fully duped. But through everything that had happened to them, the trust remained. As Tal had known it would.

"Very well. Silence, Solemnity, and Serenity, I hope you're right."

Turning, Falcon led them into the room, where the company greeted them with a general cheer. Pushing down his guilt, Tal grinned and gripped the hands of several who rose from their tables. As usual, the Dancing Feathers immediately made him feel as if he were among not only friends, but family.

Amid the friendly company, however, he felt a hostile gaze. Scanning the room, he found the Mute's hard eyes glaring at him from one corner. He'd successfully put off Brother Causticus from delving into his legend thus far, mostly thanks to Falcon's efforts to distract him and the troupers' help in the endeavor. But he always seemed to remain near at hand. Brother Nat, the younger monk who attended him, gave Tal a nervous smile.

Tal turned away at the hail of another friend. *He won't be the first enemy I've turned my back on, and hardly the most dangerous one*, he thought wryly.

After they'd settled back to their drinks and games, Falcon said in a carrying voice, "Troupers! Our friend here has a task for us. A duty that, no matter how many we've shirked before, we cannot now put aside."

The theatrics immediately caught their attention, and several furrowed their brows, wondering what task might warrant such a speech. Others smiled, sensing a forthcoming jest.

"It will not be easy," Falcon continued, beginning to pace before them. "It will not be safe. But it is a task only we can do — that we *must* do."

"Quit pulling our pricks, Sunstring!" Bendor called, to a mixture of laughter and groans. The small man grinned and continued, "What do you have in mind, Falcon One-Hand?"

The Court Bard wore a patient smile until they'd quieted again, then waited several moments longer, drawing out the suspense until it was taut. Then he raised his arms and declared, "We are to be spies!"

Silence reigned as the troupers exchanged looks. For a moment, no one spoke.

Then Yelda stood on top of a bench, augmenting her diminutive dwarven height, and declared, "A leading lady is never a spy!"

"Is that so?" Falcon countered. "And what about in *Nights in a Vineyard?* Was Jezzala not a spy for the Sendeshi Protector? Or *The Sorcerer's Wife?* Even *Kingmakers and Queenslayers* has a lady spy, which I hear you all just performed!"

Yelda sat again, her pout continuing, but she remained silent for the moment.

"I say spies," Falcon continued, "but, in truth, we will continue to act as the minstrels we are. Our task is to go down to the Mire, ingratiate ourselves with the local taverns, and listen for all the rumors among the rabble, particularly regarding the Easterners new to this city. We are the eyes and ears of a counterinsurgency, my good troupers. And as every play of politics and intrigue informs us, secrets are power."

Falcon continued, embellishing the glory of the task while using all his powers of reason and persuasion against opponents as skilled as he. While he spoke, Tal scanned the faces of the Dancing Feathers and saw most seemed to share Yelda's sentiments.

Can't say I blame them. Espionage was one thing, but in a foreign city among an unfriendly people, it was entirely another. And they had suffered tough times of late. They'd lost Jonn in Halenhol, then Mikael along the road. They were beleaguered and weary. Another dangerous favor was the last thing that he should have asked of them.

But this is a war, Tal reminded himself. *A war that has yet to remove its mask, perhaps. But all the more reason for it to be a troupers' war.*

For several long minutes, Falcon tried in vain to convince

them, before Wren, sitting in the back where he hadn't seen her, stood. Tal's stomach sank.

"What are we arguing about?" she demanded, anger edging her words. "We have to help, and you all know we do. Why else would you agree to come here? You knew it wasn't to perform before the Elf Queen or to see more of the World. We came here because Tal Harrenfel needed us to. Will you let him down now when he calls upon you?"

The troupers muttered, more than one resentful pair of eyes flickering up to Tal. For once, he kept his expression serious. If any people deserved not to be mocked right then, it was these.

"I won't," Wren continued, her gaze traveling over her fellows, daring them to challenge her. "I'll do as my father asks us. Because we're the only ones who can do this."

Where her father had failed, the lass succeeded. The troupers' muttering turned in a different direction. Yelda stood, her expression determined.

"That whip of a girl won't outdo me," she declared. "Yelda, too, can play the role of a common troubadour when she is called upon — and to perfection!"

The rest stood, shouting and singing their own intentions. Falcon looked over at Tal, and Tal held his gaze. In his friend's eyes was all the fear Tal harbored inside. When he'd asked the bard to help, he hadn't thought of what danger it would put his daughter in.

Garin will blame me for this, he realized. *He will think I roped her into it.* He wasn't sure the youth would be wrong. But it stung, knowing another dagger had thrust itself into the cold body of their friendship. Even if it was already dead.

"Mister Harrenfel?"

Tal turned and pasted a weary smile on his face. "Yes, Brother Nat?"

The two monks stood at his shoulder, both wearing their usual expressions of consternation and suspicion.

Brother Nat smiled wanly. "I know you're a busy man, fighting the Enemy and his own. But if you could spare a few minutes, Brother Causticus has some questions he'd like to ask you."

Tal glanced at the cantankerous monk, his smile growing sharper. "Well, let's hear them, Brother Causticus. What would you like to know?"

The monk's expression didn't shift, but he only continued to glare at Tal as if he were Yuldor himself.

Brother Nat cleared his throat. "Pardons, Mister Harrenfel. His vow of silence…"

"Yes, he keeps to it most religiously, doesn't he?" Letting his gaze linger on Causticus for a moment, Tal glanced back at the younger monk. "I suppose you'll have to be his translator."

Brother Nat gave a nervous laugh. "Oh, I can't hear his thoughts, Mister Harrenfel. He wrote them down beforehand."

Wondering why the Whispering Gods had inflicted their dull-minded devotees upon him, Tal outwardly gave a grave nod. "Ah, I see. Let's hear them, then."

Reaching into his pocket, the younger monk unfolded a piece of parchment and smoothed it in his hands. "First, he asks: 'What did you do to kill Heyl?'"

"Haven't you heard my legend? I believe I charged through his ring of fire and cut his head off. Though," Tal said pensively, "considering he's as tall as a kintree himself, I'm not sure how I managed it."

Brother Nat waited for Tal to continue, and when he only continued to smile at him, gave Causticus a nervous glance before looking down at the paper again. The old monk, meanwhile, never let his unblinking stare drift from Tal's face.

"He would also like to know what qualities the sword *Velori*, gifted to you by Queen Geminia Elendola the Third, possesses in an, um, unnatural sense."

"Oh, you know." Tal waved a hand vaguely. "It severs Nightborn enchantments and flesh alike. It resists rust and losing its edge. Very standard things for a magical blade."

"I see," Brother Nat said with a vague smile. "And the Thorn—"

Tal clapped the younger monk on the shoulder, startling him into glancing up from his piece of paper. "I'm sorry, Brother Nat, but I'm going to have to stop you there. All you have to do is look to Falcon's legend and you'll have all the answers you need."

With one last tilt of his head to Brother Causticus, who returned the gesture with a deeper scowl, Tal turned away and pushed through the busy room.

He kept his smile planted on his lips as he gave passing greetings to the troupers who would be his spies, but his good humor was quickly fading. He had to speak to Falcon to settle the logistics of their searching and spying. Somewhere, a vain hope remained lodged in him that he could prevent any harm to them if they only planned it well enough.

But this is a war. Even if it's a war of smiles and lies and poisons, it's still a war.

And to win it, he feared the cost would be far greater than he could comprehend.

As Garin entered the hall that the Dancing Feathers had claimed as their own, he paused in the doorway, stunned.

The chaos was absolute. Costumes had been flung over tables, instruments strewn across benches, their cases open and disregarded. Every actor and musician sang, spoke, or played, as if they were all holding their own separate performances.

A lot could change in one dancing lesson.

It had been his second, and it had gone slightly better than the first, though his skin was yet more chafed and blistered. Again, Ulen had started it by testing Garin's reflexes in the tub, then proceeded to training in the "forms," the sets of funda-mental stances and movements that underlay all elven dancing. The Dancing Master hadn't even given him a practice blade yet, explaining that it would be a distraction from the true lessons.

"The body is the weapon, not the sword," the Dancing Master had said, and so Garin tried his best to make it so.

But he forgot his pains and damp clothes as he wove his way through the din toward Wren. She had a wooden pipe in hand and was playing a tune that was unusually jaunty for her usual preferences. As she watched him approach, her eyebrows rose, as if daring him to comment. He contented himself with sitting and listening, wincing at the occasional shrill note.

As she finished the phrase and lowered the pipe, he clapped. "I didn't know you played the flute!" he called over the noise.

She shrugged with a coy smile. "I dabble."

"Why is everyone dabbling at once?"

She leaned closer and spoke in his ear. "Because we're to be spies."

Garin pulled away, trying to see if she was joking. "What?"

"Father asked us to earlier. Gave a big rousing speech calling us to help Tal find out all the rumors regarding East-erners in Low Elendol. I'll bet this has to do with the Thorn and the Silver Vines. It's what Tal hunted in Elendol last time."

Garin found his gaze wandering over the crowd, first catching on the scowling old monk in the room's corner, so out of place among the jubilant troupers, then settling on another corner where Tal bent his head in conference with Falcon. A fire burned in his belly. In a distant part of his mind, he felt the Singer's claws tighten briefly, as if Ilvuan, as the devil called itself, was roused by the sudden emotions.

Wren was speaking, but he ignored her as he rose and strode toward the pair of men. Tal saw him coming and flinched. The show of weakness only made Garin's anger flare hotter.

When he stopped before them, he kept it hidden behind a stony mask. "I need to speak with you."

Tal nodded, and with a shared glance at the Court Bard, turned and led Garin from the room.

On the platform outside, the air was chill and echoed with the clashing music from within. Garin found his head no cooler as he followed Tal to the railing, where he finally turned to face him.

"Wren told me," Garin said flatly. "What you asked them to do."

His former mentor looked aside. "She volunteered. There was nothing I or her father could say."

"Yes, there is." The rage bubbled up inside him, but he didn't let it out. He wouldn't give Tal the satisfaction of seeing him lose control. "You could say she can't go. You could say it's too dangerous, and that too many people care about her to let her get hurt!"

Tal met his eyes again, and the sympathy in them almost made Garin hit him.

"You can't protect her from her choices, lad," he said gently. "As much as you'd like to. Wren is her own woman, and she makes her own decisions. The best you can do is respect and help her."

Garin stepped closer, his voice dropping low. "You already killed my father. Do you have to kill her, too?"

Tal edged back, his expression going carefully blank. "I'll try my best not to. Though I always seem to bungle the things I attempt."

Before Garin could say another word, Tal turned and walked away.

He thought about charging and tackling him to the ground. He even thought about reaching for Ilvuan and drawing on the devil's power to attack. But as each idea occurred to him, they cooled the rashness of his anger. He wasn't so much of a fool as to ask for the Singer's help in this. No matter how much he might wish to.

"Garin?"

He turned. Wren stood just outside the door, uncharacteristic worry in her eyes. Somewhere in him, he found a smile and put it on.

"I'm fine," he said, and without considering what he was doing, he walked over to her, took her into his arms, and kissed her. She stiffened with surprise, then relaxed into it, her hands rising to touch his face.

As they pulled away, she rubbed his cheeks with a fond smile. "You need to shave; it's starting to get prickly. Should I ask Father to teach you how?"

Just like that, Garin's chest tightened again. "I'll ask," he muttered.

She took his hands. "I know you're thinking this is terrible, but it's not. And don't try talking me out of it."

"I wouldn't dream of it."

Wren grinned and brushed his face again. "Why don't you come stay with me some nights? I'm sure I'll appreciate the company. And maybe we'll get around to that thing we've been saving…"

As his face colored and butterflies took flight in his belly, she laughed, kissed him on the cheek, then pulled him back inside, his worries forgotten for the moment.

THE HUNT

TAL STARED AT THE INGREDIENTS AND IMPLEMENTS ARRAYED before him and wondered how, after all these years, he'd become no less a fool.

His room in the Venaliel kintree was not spacious nor well-illuminated, located further down the trunk than most. Round and a mere ten feet across in any direction, it seemed more suited for a servant than a guest. He supposed it had served that function before he'd come along. Yet though it barely fit the bed, desk, and chair, it suited his needs, and there was room enough in the bedside drawer to hide away the copied pages of *A Fable of Song and Blood,* locked by both key and sorcery.

At least, he thought, *if this fails, no one will be harmed. Probably.*

His eyes traced over the spellbook, open to a page over-flowing with words that writhed before his eyes like a nest of snakes. It had been long since he'd read the Reach dialect of the Worldtongue, much less the Gladelysh dialect he read now, and he was finding the transition difficult.

Strange, he thought, *that the Darktongue should be more familiar now.*

Yet more intimidating were the items he'd spread over his

bed. The feather of a silver eagle. A tuft of fur from a Gladelysh wolf. And the catalyst, a yellow powder the elves called *yethkeld,* which roughly translated to "hellfire."

A mocking smile tugged at his lips. He'd grown no wiser, indeed.

The spell was only three words long, but the spellbook had spent five pages in explanation of all the nuances and pitfalls in casting it. *Thest forl kaud* — "Hunt body place." If cast successfully, it would allow him to discover where someone he sought was within a limited range.

But though simple in concept, a thousand things could go wrong, even down to the Four Roots, the elven principles of casting magic. He had to keep in his mind a perfect image of the person he hunted, else the spell might mistakenly locate another. He had to transfer energy continuously from the catalyzing elements through his body to disperse in the seeking spell — but not too much, or he'd become "mind-charred," as the mages of the Chromatic Towers termed it. All of it required intense concentration, something Tal had never been much gifted in.

Knowing this, he'd sought aid. The unfortunate servant who'd been on the receiving end of Tal's sharp tongue was convinced to raid Ashelia's supplies and bring him a small pouch of a dried red herb. *Yinshi* was the only name Tal knew it by, but he understood its properties well enough. Ingesting even a pinch would cause the mind to latch onto the task before it with obsessive, and potentially fatal, focus. Measuring the proper dose and timing its ingestion were also key to the ritual's success.

Only a few things could go wrong, then.

But he had to make the attempt. When Garin had confronted him about Wren, he'd thought the youth would hit him, he was so furious. And he had every excuse to be. What right did Tal have, putting all of their lives in danger, when he hadn't tried every other avenue?

What right did he have to risk them before he risked himself?

And he was the only one who could perform this spell, as the Ilthasi captain Prendyn had inadvertently confirmed. No one else had seen a Silver Vines agent alive, nor the Thorn's face, and they couldn't attempt a seeking spell unless they had.

But Tal knew his enemy well.

He touched his side where, under his shirt, the old wound remained. Ashelia had sealed it securely, and it barely twinged through his morning exercises. Yet there was always the reminder that once, the Thorn and he had clashed, and Tal had nearly died from it.

His fist tightened over his shirt. He loosened it, then took in a deep breath and exhaled. *I must be focused and clear-headed. I must succeed.*

Tal reached for the mortar bowl, picked up a pestle, and started to grind.

They didn't blend well, the feather and fur and powder, but he did his best to incorporate them. When he could do no more, he opened the bag of *yinshi* and poured a small amount onto a scale he'd earlier uncovered. After some tinkering, satisfied he had the right dosage, he dusted the dry, red leaves into his hand. The peppery scent of the herb stung his nose as he lifted it to his mouth and, with a quick gesture, swallowed it.

Fire burned down his throat, and he coughed so violently he thought he'd choke the herb back up. But the fit quickly subsided. Eyes watering, he felt his mind quickly becoming rigid and firm. He focused back on the ingredients before him and said, "*Kald*," so that flames burst up from the bowl. The *yethkeld* quickly ignited. The fur and the feather wouldn't last long, he knew — nor might he, from the narrowing of the room in his vision.

Drawing in a breath, he pictured the hated face in his mind, then said, distinct and clear, "*Thest forl kaud.*"

He ripped free of his body.

Tal moved through the walls of the kintree and out above the forest floor. He kept his purpose fixed in his mind as Elendol passed by him in a rush of disconnected sounds and colors. The World seemed pale and drained as the magic bore him between and through trees, diving into the depths of the city — down into the Mire, where he'd suspected he would go.

The strangers, made more strange by the spell's effects, blurred beneath him as Tal flew like a phantom overhead. He tried to recognize the part of the city he traveled over, but concentrating on anything but his quarry made the World tilt and swirl, a warning of what would come if he persisted. So he clung like a flea to a hawk's feathers until the sorcery carried him straight toward the decaying, long-charred stump of a kintree.

Heyl's Fall — he knew the place well. When the fire demon came upon Elendol two decades before, it had cut down a kintree in its wake — one of the few truths Falcon had told of Tal's escapades in Elendol. This stump was all that remained now, a monument to the evils of the East.

But as Tal moved through the burned bark and into a lighted interior, he saw not all had abandoned it.

They moved in a hive around him, faces long and distorted as they cackled, like the depictions of demons in a puppet play. Somehow, they saw him, and he recoiled before their grasping hands. But though they tried to seize him, none touched him as he swept over their heads and back toward the deepest part of the stump.

He burst through another wall before jerking to an abrupt halt. His vision spun. Through it, Tal tried to study the chamber he'd entered. It was small, twenty feet wide at most and seven feet tall, and wreathed in a ghostly green light. Moss and mushrooms glowed as they grew along the walls. In the center, a man occupied a lone chair, his eyes burning with a feverish yellow as they stared up at Tal hovering above him.

"I knew you would come," the Thorn said. His voice was like

151

the rustling of the wind through night-shrouded leaves. *"You are clever, but far less than you believe. You have a failing, Skaldurak, a need to put yourself at risk if it means saving others from harm. Inevitably, as the danger became apparent, I knew you would come for me yourself."*

The Extinguished rose, his face barely a foot below where Tal, bodiless, hovered. He thought of escape, but made no attempt for it. Here was his prey, the one he sought, standing before him. He'd found the Thorn. He wouldn't let him go.

Even as he knew the *yinshi* chained him to the task, he had no power to release himself.

The Thorn looked just as he remembered. Unlike his ash-faced peer in the Ruins of Erlodan, he resembled an old, gnarled tree that had been overtaken by a swarm of parasitic vines. He smiled, and it felt as if Tal were once more a child peering into the dark hollow of a tree, fearfully wondering what might wait within.

"Soltor did not understand you, Skaldurak. He sought to trick you and ensnare you. But he need only have waited to let you trap yourself."

A vague memory bubbled up in his mind. *A dream* — had he seen this in his fever-dream? Tal tried to speak — out of defiance or to plead, he didn't know — but all powers of speech had been left behind with his body.

The Thorn came closer to where Tal's presence hovered. *"What is it?"* he whispered. *"What would you ask of me? To spare you? To spare your friends? But this is a war, Devil Killer, not a game. There will be casualties. And whatever knowledge you possess, I will rip it from your mind, not tease it out with bargains and bribes. Long ago, my knife robbed you of the will to defy me."*

One moment, the Extinguished looked up at him with those sickly yellow eyes; the next, his hands, brown and twisted like roots, grasped above him. And though he had no body, Tal felt himself seized as the Thorn chanted words that seethed in his mind, then burned.

As the incantation twisted him into knots, the Thorn paused and whispered, *"Should you survive, know that I will stop for only one thing. Bring me the Queen, and I will spare your friends' lives. Defy me, and I will slaughter them to the last."*

The World had disappeared in a torrent of movement. Not even the Thorn could hold him any longer. Tal felt himself falling far, far away, lost where no one could find him.

———

Garin jerked awake to a distant scream.

He listened into the silence that followed, his quickened pulse pounding in his ears. Beside him, Wren muttered incoherently and turned, then settled back into the blankets. He studied her face, limned in the faint werelight from outside his chamber's window. She'd always been a heavier sleeper than him.

But that scream…

Still, he heard nothing more. Had he dreamed it? He couldn't remember anything that had come before or after. Was he remembering a battle past? Was it all in his head?

Then, faintly, he heard something else. Despite himself, despite knowing what those sounds must mean, he strained to make them out. Pots clanging. Axes chopping. The creaking of a tree in a gust. The swishing of clothes being laundered.

Garin squeezed his eyes shut. He felt the faint pinpricks of the Singer's claws at the back of his mind. But Ilvuan — as he supposed he should start thinking of his devil — didn't appear to be causing the Nightsong.

Why now? he thought morosely.

Moving carefully, he peeled the blankets away from him and slipped from bed, then blindly stumbled around the room gathering clothes. He hoped some fresh, forest air would clear his head, and he ran less risk of waking Wren than staying there.

Dressed, he opened the door and slipped out. Elendol was dimly lit at this time of night, the werelights cooled to blues and violets. Garin moved across the small platform off of which his room was situated and leaned against the far railing, breathing in deeply. The rich scents of the woods filled him. A few birds chirped and sang, and other creatures croaked, hooted, and added their own sounds to the hushed chorus.

But the Nightsong didn't fade. Still, he heard the disparate sounds in his head. The sharpening of knives. The crunching of sand beneath boots. The cry of a newborn foal.

Perhaps I should have prayed more, Garin thought miserably. *Then a devil couldn't have worked its way into me.*

Do you still not hear its meaning?

Garin cringed as Ilvuan spoke into his mind. His voice, once whispering and distant, had deepened and become stronger since the attempted purging.

Ignoring the devil had never banished him before, so Garin answered aloud, "Hear what meaning?"

Derision that wasn't his own swept through his mind, very much as if Ilvuan had snorted at him. *For a Listener, you do not listen well. Someone you care for is in danger.*

He clutched the railing, trying to control the panic suddenly rising in him. *Who?* — the question rattled in his head. His first thought was for Wren, but he'd just left her sleeping peacefully. He cared for Falcon and the other troupers, but what trouble could they have found at this time of night?

But from the first, part of him suspected who it must be. *Who else, but the man who most often seeks peril?*

Garin clenched his jaw. "I don't care for Tal."

A low growl sounded through his mind. *You deafen yourself willingly. But I have claimed you — I cannot allow you to live in ignorance. Listen!*

Despite his resistance, Garin harkened again to the Nightsong. The crumbling of stone. Steam hissing from a pot.

He shook his head. The sounds made no sense. And besides, why should he listen to a devil?

"If you want me to know something, why don't you just tell me?"

A Listener must listen for himself. I will not always protect you, little one. Ilvuan's disdain flooded his mind.

Shivering under its weight, Garin tried to sort out his own feelings from the tangle of his thoughts. He pressed his hands to his temples, trying to ease the pressure in his head. *He wants me to listen, to act,* he thought. *If I humor him, maybe the sounds will go away.*

As much from desperation as reason, Garin turned and descended the stairs. He clutched his arms around himself, shivering in the chill forest air and wishing he'd thought to wear his cloak. But he pressed on, passing room after room, slowly realizing he didn't know exactly where Tal's was. Yet he'd come this far; he may as well see it through. And if he saw nothing strange, he'd return to bed.

But just as he'd resolved to turn around, he saw the faint glow of yellow light around the bend. Groaning softly, Garin continued until the windows and door came into view. Tal had drawn the curtains over the round openings, so he couldn't see within. All he could tell was that someone was still awake.

But the Nightsong had grown steadily louder. As he neared the door, it crescendoed to an almost painful volume before fading off. Wincing, Garin drew in a steadying breath, then firmly knocked.

No one answered.

He stepped back and examined the door and windows again. He didn't know for certain this was Tal's room. He didn't know that *anyone* occupied the room at all. Maybe the servants left empty rooms bright and cheery even when no one occupied them.

Another wave of derision poured over him. *Once more, you*

fail to listen, Ilvuan said lazily, as if he spared only a fraction of his attention.

Garin gritted his teeth. It was as good as confirmation that this was Tal's room. But what could threaten him here? A soulshade such as had assaulted him and Aelyn in the Coral Castle? Garin would be no use fighting that. He wasn't sure he could help against anything that might endanger Tal.

Besides, did he even want to save his old mentor?

He recoiled at the thought — and, as simple as that, he had his answer.

You're weak, part of him sneered, but he pushed the thought away and stepped up to the door again, trying the handle. The door didn't budge. Locked. He stared at it, frustration mounting, even as he wondered why he bothered.

"Ilvuan," he murmured. "Can you unlock the door for me?"

A spike of irritation drove painfully behind his eyes. *I will not. I am not your mule to do your work.*

Garin winced. "I can't quiet the Song until I enter. And didn't you claim me? Shouldn't you help me be a better Listener?"

Ilvuan rumbled, displeasure radiating from his presence in the back of Garin's mind. *Tread carefully, Listener. I am to be obeyed, not yoked in obedience. But this once, I will grant your request. Put your intention to unlock the door firmly in your mind. When you think of nothing but your intention, speak this word:* Uvthak.

Garin immediately recognized the word from the way it slithered between his thoughts. *Darktongue.* But with no other options, he nodded and set his mind to his task. *Unlock,* he told the door, staring intensely at it. *Open.*

Then he whispered, "*Uvthak.*"

The lock shattered.

Leaping back, Garin inspected himself for wounds and found his hands bleeding from several slivers. *Lucky.* A fist-sized hole had replaced the lock; he could have easily suffered worse.

Now, anyone or anything waiting in the room would know he was coming.

Ignoring the itching pain in his hands, Garin stepped slowly forward, straining all his senses toward the room. Easing the door open, he took it in by measures: the smell of fur and something acidic burning; the prone figure slumped over the bed, their knees to the floor; the book open next to their arm. As he saw only one person, and one he recognized immediately, Garin drew in a shaky breath and stepped inside.

Confirming no one waited around the edges of the room, he kneeled next to Tal and hesitantly placed a hand on his shoulder. "Wake up." He shook him roughly.

Tal didn't stir.

His gaze traveled over the items arrayed around him, but it was the book that caught his attention. *A book of spells,* he realized, as the unfamiliar figures convulsed before his eyes. He had a good guess what had happened now and understood enough to realize this was far beyond him.

Ashelia. She was the only one who might save him from whatever he'd done. Cursing his former mentor, Garin ran from the room and sprinted up the kintree steps.

He lay on the hearthstone, soaking in the warmth from the dying fire and trying to hide his shivers, as he watched his mother notch the end of an arrow shaft.

"But Markus knew the Clan Elders were lying to him," she said. Her voice was tired, but he could hear the effort she put into the storytelling still. "And so he decided that, instead of waiting for them to send in their warriors, he would flee first — but not toward the mine's entrance, where they'd be waiting, but deeper into the caverns below."

"Markus was brave," he murmured, tucking his arms tighter around his chest, hoping it would finally banish the chill lodged there, knowing it wouldn't. "I want to be brave," he added softly.

His mother didn't lift her eyes from her fletching, but continued to fit the arrowhead. "Are the town boys bothering you?" she asked quietly.

He hesitated. There was nothing she could do. As much as he knew she wanted to, she couldn't protect him.

"Bran," his mother said, a warning in her voice now.

Bran put on a smile. "No, Mema. It's not that. I meant I wish I was brave so I could be like Markus Bredley and have everyone tell stories about me around their hearths."

She finally looked up at him, and he found it hard to meet her gaze. Talania had been the beauty of the town, once; he'd overheard his neighbors bemoaning her fate on more than one occasion. *What happened to her?* they asked, though everyone knew.

He, Bran the Bastard, had happened to her.

"You cannot stay here."

Bran looked up. "Mema?"

He met her eyes, but they seemed different now. Her arrow lay limply in her hands, forgotten, and she sat unnaturally erect, staring at him.

"This place is not meant for you. Not yet."

Bran sat up, though it allowed the chill to claw in deeper. "I don't understand."

"All will come here one day. All will know their Mother's comfort. But you have much more to do before that day comes, Mother's Blood."

Talania stood, and Bran rose and backed away. He'd never feared his mother before; she'd never raised a hand against him, believing in the old ways of rearing a child. But now, with a stranger speaking frightening words with her mouth, he didn't know what to think.

"I don't want to leave," he said, unable to help a whimper creeping into his voice. "I want to stay with you."

"But she is dead," his mother said. "And you are alive."

She reached for him. Bran turned and ran, wrenching open the door to their shack and fleeing out into the icy darkness. But as he looked back, he didn't watch where he stepped. He slipped, and nothing was beneath him to catch his fall.

Tal jerked upright, gasping for breath.

"Easy," a soft, familiar voice murmured. A gentle hand pressed on his chest, easing him back down.

Mema, he thought, but the next moment he knew it wasn't she who had spoken.

Prying open his crusted eyes, he saw Ashelia leaning over him. Her hair was a mess, hastily bound back, and her eyes were shadowed from interrupted sleep.

He closed his eyes again, a slight smile creasing his lips. When he'd needed her, she'd come. She had always come.

"I was dreaming," he murmured. "Dreaming of my mother."

"You said her name while you slept."

He wanted to drift back into that place, but forced his mind to the present. With waking came the memories of what he'd attempted and what the Thorn had done to him.

Just a dream, he told himself. But he couldn't be sure it was true.

"You brought me back?"

"Yes. But only thanks to Garin."

"Garin?" He tried to rise again, hopeful excitement springing into his chest.

Ashelia pressed him down once more. "He's not here now. But somehow, he knew you were in danger, and he ran to fetch me. He saved your life, Tal."

He rubbed at his eyes, hoping she thought he only tried to wipe the sleep from his eyes. *He saved me,* he marveled. *There's still hope for us.*

"What were you doing, Tal? You were catatonic when I

came, and you only roused after a strong tincture. The book was open to a seeking spell. Don't tell me..."

She trailed off. He lowered his hands, trusting his eyes wouldn't betray him now.

"Yes," he murmured. "I was hunting him."

"That way? *Kolsk,* but that was foolish, Tal. Damned foolish, even for you."

He gave her a slack grin. "A fool may dare what a wise man would never chance."

She frowned in return. "And did your gamble pay off?"

"This time. I know where he hides — he and the rest of his weeds. I must tell the Queen immediately."

Ashelia held him down. "You're in no state to travel to House Elendola right now."

"We can't delay, Ashel. He may move now that I've seen him."

She didn't answer him for a moment, but stared at him, the gray in her eyes swirling.

"Don't call me that," she said quietly.

He couldn't hold down his despair any longer. "How long must we remain like this? Won't you talk to me?"

She rose abruptly. "You had your chance to talk two decades ago. Fine. If you want to kill yourself going to the Queen now, I'll have my guards escort your corpse."

Without another word, she turned on her heels, her silver nightgown swirling around her, and left his room. His door hung slightly ajar as she closed it roughly behind.

For a moment, his eyes caught on the jagged hole where his lock had been. Then he settled back into his blankets, pushing down all that had bubbled up and betrayed him.

Patience, he told himself. *Time heals all wounds.*

But time was something he had far too little of now.

PASSAGE II

If the Heart is sorcery itself, as I have so brazenly suggested, what does it mean to be the master of it?

I tremble even to ask this question — it comes too close to challenging our Lord's right to possess it. Yet, to understand the mysteries of the Founts, I must venture further still into heresy.

Long have we known there are limitations even to Yuldor's vast power. If it were not so, why would he not conquer the World and spread his paradise now? Many have put forth justifications: that we are unworthy; that we must prove our loyalty first; that, as Yuldor's hands, we must build Paradise ourselves. But I have found their arguments hold little sway. Either our god is capricious, or he cannot do and see all.

That I am alive still and writing these words is proof that he lacks omniscience.

Thus, the Heart, whatever it is, is not limitless power. Yet I believe it must enhance our Lord's magic so he may work his wonders across his Empire and spread Paradise.

I believe it is the reason, too, why the Peacebringer does not leave the peak of Ikvaldar — not, as others have suggested, because he is too holy to walk among the sinful lands. To access his full power, he must remain by the Heart, which suggests the Heart itself is immoveable.

Perhaps it is even what sustains his immortality.

No more — I must write no more. But I cannot stop myself. Even more than life, more than being a good adherent to the beliefs those around me hold, I need to know who and what our god is.

Even if it damns me.

- A Fable of Song and Blood, *by Hellexa Yoreseer of the Blue Moon Obelisk, translated by Tal Harrenfel*

BENEATH THE VEIL

Queen Geminia awaited Tal and the Venaliel guards when they reached the throne room.

Tal stared openly at her as he shuffled down the soft carpet and tried not to trip over his own feet. The journey there had been excruciating. Exhaustion pulled at his limbs, weighing them down like they'd been chained with balls of iron. His mind wandered, his focus drifting from one thing to another, unable to attach to anything — an aftereffect of the *yinshi*, he well knew. The guards, young men who were disgruntled at being woken to escort a human, had cast many a scornful look his way as they shortened their strides to keep pace beside him.

The Queen looked little better than he felt. Though her usual ethereal aura still hovered about her, as Tal squinted up at the throne, he could see how her eyes were heavy-lidded, and her posture less erect than before. He wondered if his coming, announced by Ilthasi scurrying ahead, had called her from sleep, or if she'd already been awake.

What's haunting your dreams, Geminia? he wondered.

The guards beside him gave deep gestures of respect, and Tal followed suit, mildly amused at the clumsiness of his movements. The Queen gave no sign of noticing, but only moved her hand in dismissal. The Venaliel guards turned and walked from the room. The Queen's own guards remained by her throne.

For a moment, doubt flickered through his mind as he faced the four hard-faced elves and Geminia's unsmiling countenance. Yuldor's reach had extended to one of the Westreach's monarchs; why not to another? But as he began to wish he hadn't relinquished his sword at the doors, the Elf Queen gestured again, and her guards followed Ashelia's out of the door. All gave him studying glances as they passed. No doubt they wondered how a *lenual* could be graced with a private audience this late at night. Tal just mustered the energy for a smirk.

Even after the door echoed shut behind them, Queen Geminia didn't speak, but watched him, a slight quirk to her mouth, tired eyes calm and considering. Tal endeavored to look as if his legs weren't plotting a mutiny.

"You have news for me?" the Queen asked finally.

"Yes, Your Eminence. My apologies for disturbing you so late, but it's urgent."

"No delays, then. Let us hear it."

"I know where the Thorn and the Silver Vines hide. Heyl's Fall — they've taken over the burned kintree."

Geminia didn't react to the news beyond a twitch of her eyelid. As the silence stretched on, Tal began to doubt. He hadn't questioned the validity of what he'd learned until that very moment; it had taken all of his scant energy and concentration just to reach the royal kintree. But now, he wondered how certain he could be in it. He'd rarely cast seeking spells and was far from a practiced hand. To make no mention of the Extinguished twisting his mind.

He'd sunk deep enough into his thoughts that he startled as the Queen rose from her throne and descended the dais to stand before him. Tal wanted to step back and hunch his shoulders. Though he had little respect for most of the leaders of the

Westreach, butchers and fools that they were, the Gem of Elendol was an altogether different creature. Before her, he felt the intimidation that others might before the King of Avendor.

He nearly stumbled back as she took his face in her hands. The skin of her palms was smooth. He winced at the thought of her touching the rough stubble of his jaw. The next moment, though, the uncomfortable feeling abruptly eased.

Geminia laughed softly, a throaty, mirthless sound. "I wear my glamour so often I forget what it is like to drop it. You should feel more comfortable now."

"As comfortable as one can while being touched by a queen," Tal murmured.

She laughed again, this time with a touch of true amusement. "I will not be long. Ease your mind, if you can. I feel his touch upon you, and I must see how deep it goes."

He wasn't a stranger to unusual situations, and the phrasing of her words made it easier to accede, for the Binding Ring on his finger required him to obey. He tried to ignore the odd, creeping feeling as Geminia's presence pressed against his being. His blood burned in response. She was like a fog rolling through his mind, leaving a chill feeling behind everywhere she touched, void of emotion and thought.

Some time later — how long, he could not say — he blinked and found the Queen's hands releasing him. He swayed in place before he could find his orientation again.

"You did well," she murmured, the pearlescent white in her eyes whirling. "Many of my subjects would have struggled with that request."

Tal kept his words neutral. "It was not a request, Your Eminence. And I am bound to your commands."

He studied her face, trying to find once again the reason she'd bade Aelyn to bind him with the artifact. But no guilt or shame crossed Geminia's countenance as she met his gaze.

"However it may seem, Aristhol, it is not about trust. I have watched you since you first came to my queendom, watched you throughout your darkest years and foulest deeds. But always, I knew you. You will do what you believe is best for the Westreach. Even at the price of your life. Even at the price of your happiness."

Tal couldn't hide his wince. Her words struck too close to the truth. "You watched me by sorcery? Why?"

"Do you not know? You are important to those who are dear to me."

He dared not hope what she meant, but waited, tense and expectant.

The Queen didn't elaborate, but said instead, "As I said, it is not about trust — it is about obedience. And neither of us have any choice in that now. You know as I do that you cannot remove the ring until you meet the terms of the oath, not even by my orders. Only by returning with Aelyn to Hunt's Hollow can you be done with it."

She sounded wistful, as if she wished for it to be otherwise. Tal longed for answers to all the questions she'd stirred up. But as her glamour pressed anew on his mind, he knew he wasn't likely to gain any.

You ask much, he thought as he stared at the Queen, anger flickering through him, *and give little in return.* But he knew it was better left unsaid.

"As I suspected," Geminia said without transition, "the Thorn meddled with your perception and memory. He was there in Heyl's Fall, I do not doubt. But his followers were but an illusion. Do you not remember them looking demonic and ill-formed?"

Tal frowned, pressing down his anger and focusing on the task at hand. "Yes, I suppose I do, now that you mention it. It didn't seem odd then."

"The *yinshi* tampered with your mind. It kept you concentrated on your quarry to the exclusion of many things that may have unveiled the trick." Her lips pursed in a disapproving frown. "You would do well not to rely upon an influencer."

He gestured respectfully to her reprimand. "No doubt you're right. But I'm long out of practice with sorcery. I feared the spell's consequences more."

"Be wary of both, Aristhol. We cannot lose you before the war breaks out in full."

Ghostly fingertips pressed down his spine. "Then you think it will come to that?"

Geminia smiled, and he'd never seen her look more sorrowful. "It is as inevitable as the sun's rising. The Named has shown he will stop at nothing to rule over the whole of the World."

For a moment, Tal sat with the finality of the statement. He felt as if he leaned over a precipice, toes scraping pebbles into an endless chasm below, the winds of fate kissing his face, urging him to leap.

A grin curled his lips. "If we're all to fall, we may as well brighten the way for those who come after."

He couldn't read the Queen's expression as sorrow was replaced by something else. Her usual mask of calm returned a moment later. "You are either very brave, Tal Harrenfel, or very foolish."

"With all due respect, Your Eminence, I may very well be both."

"Hold tight the reins of your rashness for now. Until we discover the Thorn's true lair, caution will serve you better than courage."

"Never fear, Queen Geminia. I am the most craven of cowards when occasion calls for it."

She smiled, and whether it was her glamour or the simple expression, Tal felt himself warmed through.

The joy was fleeting, and the next moment, her expression smoothed. "In the meantime, we will set our own trap. As Peer Balindi reminded me, the Winter Ball is due soon. I will announce it, and there, we can ensnare our enemies before we find ourselves trapped in their web."

"At a ball?"

"Where else would a game of courts be decided?"

Tal smiled his wolf's smile. "And I thought this was a war."

Geminia gestured wearily. "Every contest of power is a war, Aristhol. Make ready for it as if it were to the battlefield you rode."

Recognizing his dismissal, Tal made the sign of respect, turned, and strode from the throne room. The weight of his concerns should have been heavier, yet for all that they'd increased, he only felt lighter.

In a flash of insight, he saw their predicament as the traditional elven game of *Qorl*. The board was set, the pieces revealed one by one. And he saw his place, a Lowkin pawn in one corner, positioned to take down the enemy Peer — or die trying — by his Queen's edict.

You are *a fool,* he marveled, and shared a smile with the night.

THE MAGE'S LESSON

GARIN STARED AT THE CEILING IN HIS ROOM.

"You sure you're not ready to eat?" Wren asked him again, not hiding her annoyance. "I head down to the Mire soon. You may not see me for a while."

He knew what he should do. Silence, it was what he *wanted* to do. But he couldn't make himself rise.

"I'll be there in a moment, I promise. It was just a long night."

He listened to her shuffling about the room, gathering the last of her things. It was a chill feeling, her emptying his room, as if she never meant to return.

A pause. He waited, knowing the words that would follow it.

"You never explained how you knew Tal was in danger."

He kept his face carefully blank. "I told you, I don't understand either. I woke up and couldn't sleep, so I stepped outside. I must have heard something that I can't recall. Whatever it was, it was lucky for him, wasn't it?"

She didn't answer, but opened the door, allowing in the brightness of the morning werelights. "I'll be upstairs," she said flatly. "I can't be late for my dancing lesson with Ashelia."

She slammed the door shut behind her.

Garin winced, but didn't rise. Little point now; the damage was already done. Besides, what could he say to appease her? *I lied about the demon, Wren. It's not only still inside me, but has a firmer hold than before. And now I'm listening to it and taking its aid. Again.*

No. He couldn't tell the truth. The truth would never have gone down easily, and now that he'd lied, it would hit harder still. Though she must already suspect it — he couldn't see why else she would punish him for something he didn't say.

He sighed and slowly eased himself up to stare, bleary-eyed, at the faintly glowing curtains. He'd have to face the light eventually. *May as well do it while Wren is still here.*

Relenting, he rose, dressed, and headed up the stairs to the dining hall. He could already hear the merriment of the Dancing Feathers by the time he reached the top of the stairs. Though they'd agreed to risk their lives, they acted as if it were a feast day.

But then, executions are also often celebrations, he thought sourly.

For a moment, Garin hovered on the outside landing, preferring the morning chill, damp and clinging to his skin, to the warmth of company. Somehow, their exuberance made him feel even lonelier than before.

In the back of his mind, he felt Ilvuan's disdain radiating up like bubbles from a pond's surface. A bitter smile twisted his lips. The devil was right to disparage him.

"Something amusing this morning?"

Garin jerked around to see a pair of familiar bronze eyes staring at him. "Bleeding Silence, Aelyn, where did you come from?"

The mage studied him with narrowed eyes, his mouth contorting into a sour pucker. "I've been asked to teach you the Four Roots," he said without preamble. "So that you may be taught discipline."

"The Four Roots? For magic?"

"What else?" Aelyn snapped. "If you must eat, do so quickly. I have many other things to attend to beyond child-rearing."

Despite himself, anger flickered through him. Garin may have proven to himself that he was a man, but he still chafed at any implication of being a boy.

"I'll eat and return soon," he said coolly. Without waiting for a response, he strode over to the banquet hall.

Even though he braced himself, Garin still wasn't prepared for the onslaught of the troupers' greetings. Just as it always had, their cheerfulness only seemed to grow with the danger they faced. Ox pounded him on the back as Garin tried to serve himself a red-spiced sausage, nearly causing him to flip over the whole platter.

"A glorious day, the day we serve the Westreach!" the big man boomed. "Do you not agree, Gare?"

"I told you not to call me that," Garin muttered as he finally claimed a sausage.

"Oh-ho! But you did not sleep well, did you?" The Befal man grinned at him, his teeth bright against his earthy skin. "It is only natural before an endeavor such as ours!"

Garin's face flushed. Only then did he realize they expected him to come with them, down into the Mire, to do Tal's bidding. But then again, it meant the Dancing Feathers claimed him as one of theirs. A mixture of emotions swirled through him, and rather than untangle them, he hid them behind a grin.

"Right," he said genially.

Ox squeezed him on the shoulder and turned to rejoin the others at a table. Breathing out, Garin finished loading his plate and hurried to the opposite corner as the boisterous man.

He found no peace there, however. Wren scooted next to him, her expression hard.

"You didn't tell them you weren't coming," she said flatly.

Garin looked around quickly, but no one seemed to have overheard. "I didn't know they thought I was."

"Why wouldn't they? You traveled all this way with us. We've faced death together on several occasions. They think you're their friend. They thought you'd stick with us now."

The guilt that he'd repressed came back with a cutting vengeance. "I'll be down for visits," he muttered.

"But not to do your part."

"What do you want me to do, Wren? I'm supposed to do dancing lessons to maintain the facade of coming here. And Aelyn wants me to—" He stopped himself, realizing what he'd been about to admit, and pivoted to say, "I can't just disappear into Low Elendol and never come back."

Wren watched him with narrowed eyes. "I have dancing lessons, too, in case you forgot. And what was that about Aelyn?"

Garin's gaze betrayed him, and Wren followed it to see Aelyn waiting impatiently at the balcony. She looked back to him, gold swirling in her eyes.

"Aelyn doesn't willingly do things for others," she said slowly. "Which means if he's doing something for you, someone requested it of him. Or ordered him." She stared at Garin until he reluctantly met her gaze. "There's still something wrong with you, isn't there?"

His mind had been turning while she reasoned aloud, and he spoke the first plausible excuse he could think of. "Not wrong, necessarily. Ashelia just has a theory — that the Singer's influence might have left me able to wield magic."

"Magic?" That caught her off-guard. "So Aelyn is to instruct you?"

As he nodded, a thought occurred to him. "Maybe he could teach you, too. You've summoned fire before; why not learn to do it properly?"

He didn't recognize the fleeting emotion that crossed her face for a moment — but as he did, he nearly grinned with relief. If this scared Wren, he had every right to fear it himself.

He reached out and gripped her hand. "Your lesson isn't until later this morning, right?"

She nodded, seeming to have swallowed her tongue.

"Then it's settled. Finish up your breakfast — you know how impatient he gets." Garin found his mood significantly improved as he took up the *galli* and fumbled his way through his food.

Only halfway through his meal did his stomach drop as he realized what he'd done. *If Aelyn asks me about the Singer,* he thought, *what will I say now?*

He thought he'd been clever. But he found that being clever was a lot harder than some people made it seem.

Aelyn stopped in front of a door further down the Venaliel kintree.

"Enter here," he said impatiently, opening the door and following his own instructions.

Garin and Wren exchanged a glance, then followed him into the gloomy room.

The mage made a sharp gesture, and the room lit with a friendly, yellow glow as werelights rose from their lamps. He looked around the room and gathered it was a library or a study, for shelves of books were in neat rows to their right, while to their left, a stairway led up to a short balcony lined with yet more books. Tables and chairs filled the remaining spaces, while nearby, shelves supported a series of other items — tablets, parchments, quills, and ink, all that a student might need for their learning.

A deep sense of dread filled him. Garin liked to think he had discovered some courage along their journey, but at the sight of all those books, his bravery crumbled. Under Sister Pond's instruction back in Halenhol, he'd begun to learn his letters, and Wren had forced him to continue reading on the road to Elendol, pushing play after play upon him while the wagon rumbled on. But though letters had begun to form words, and words gathered into sentences, and sentences lined up to make stories, it all came so agonizingly slow he cringed before each new session, even as he enjoyed the stories themselves.

Wren had no such reservations, but walked before him, turning around with a slight curve to her lips. Her eyes were bright, the gold in them brought out by the diffused light, and he smiled as he watched her and felt his tension ease. If she could feel so at home here, perhaps he might, too. Eventually.

Aelyn had been busy at the shelves gathering materials, which he promptly placed on the table before him. "Each of you take an instruction tablet and follow me."

Without waiting for a reply, the mage turned and strode toward the back of the room, where he opened a door and disappeared beyond. Garin shared a look with Wren, then did as they'd been told, leading the way into the next room.

The chamber differed markedly from the room that had come before. No werelights lit it, the only illumination a fire burning in the hearth. By the flickering firelight, Garin could see that the room was much smaller, only two dozen feet long, and was bare of books and even shelves. All it held was a square table with four chairs in the center.

Aelyn stood by the fireplace and, when Garin and Wren stopped in the doorway, motioned irritably toward the table. "Set down your materials. Or do you think you'll use them while standing?"

His skepticism increased with each passing moment. But Garin followed Wren to the table, set down the tablet, and sat.

"Now," Aelyn said, "we will cover the Four Roots in far greater depth than Tal ever bothered to tell you."

And so they did. The mage spoke in long, intricate, and utterly dull monologues about each of the Four Roots. Garin found his attention quickly drifting. Not only could he never hope to make any meaningful notes while Aelyn lectured, but he could barely make sense of what he was hearing.

The Third Root, for example, was that magic required an energy transfer. But according to Aelyn, it wasn't the transfer of *energy*, but the transfer of *inherent* energy — or, by way of example, the potential for fire to set something aflame rather than actually burning it. Inherent energy supposedly existed even when it wasn't actualized, and it was, according to Aelyn, much more malleable and useful than energy itself.

But when Garin asked him what inherent energy truly was, the mage only snapped for him to pay closer attention and he would know.

Almost, he missed Tal as an instructor. Perhaps his former mentor had skimmed over the finer details, but within minutes, he'd had Wren conjuring flames in the forest surrounding the Ruins of Erlodan. Aelyn, meanwhile, had gone on for nearly an hour and only just reached the beginning of an explanation of the Fourth Root.

Aren't you a fine man? he taunted himself. *Missing the bastard you should want to kill. Wouldn't your brothers be proud?*

"Aelyn," Wren finally burst out, "are we just going to speak about sorcery, or will we actually practice it?"

The mage jerked his head around; he'd been staring into the flames as he spoke and not even facing them.

"Practice it?" Aelyn took several steps closer, and his eyes didn't need the light of the hearth to blaze. "*Practice* it? You don't know a fraction of what you must to *practice* it, girl! What Tal encouraged you to do before was irresponsible and rash, and I will not tolerate it under my instruction. If you are to learn sorcery, you will learn it properly, or not at all."

Wren bit her lip, though her own eyes swirled. Garin could practically feel the war raging inside her. But after several moments passed in silence, Aelyn smiled coldly.

"Perhaps that's enough for today. You can think on how seriously you wish to pursue the greatest of studies. It is not for the faint of heart, and I would not waste my time with flippant students."

Without a word, Wren stood, gathered her materials, and strode from the room.

Garin stood as well, but he hesitated. But he had to know the answer to the question that had hounded him all the lesson.

"How do you know I can do magic?"

Aelyn studied him for a long moment before responding. "I know what you wish. You wish to test your mettle and talent. Just like your mentor, just like your flame, you are rash and impulsive. But, as any half-wit scholar knows, we won't be able to deduce your ability until you're properly instructed in the fundamentals. So you must submit to my teachings, Garin Dunford, or I must find another way to do my Queen's bidding."

The Queen? Garin shivered, wondering how much Her Eminence knew of him.

"I'll learn," he muttered, then followed Wren out of the room.

He caught up with her on the landing outside, where she leaned against the railing, staring out with a forlorn expression.

"You alright?" he ventured.

She turned, eyes ablaze. "He's just doing it to torture us!"

Garin blinked. "Who? Aelyn?"

"Who else? He finally has us in a position where he can lord his power over us, so of course he does so at every opportunity!"

She turned back to the railing. Garin stared over the forest city as he thought. It was nearing midday, and the distant streets were bustling with people, though they appeared little more than ants at the great distance. He wondered if anyone had fallen from High Elendol to Low before, and he took a step back, his stomach queasy.

"I just think he might have a different style of instruction than you prefer," he finally ventured.

"What's that supposed to mean?"

He put up his hands in surrender. "Only that you're used to learning at your own pace. It's how you operate within the Dancing Feathers, and it's pretty much how Master Krador let you run our weapons training."

Wren glared at him a moment longer, then motioned him closer. As he stepped next to her, she wrapped her arms around him. Her head only came to his chest, and she rested it there, while he tucked his chin over her head. Contentment slowly filled him, like the warmth from a lit hearth on a winter's evening.

She broke the embrace and stepped away. "Do you want me to continue?"

"You think I'd prefer enduring these lessons alone?"

Wren grinned. "Fine. I'll tolerate his pig-headedness. But I want something in exchange."

Garin nodded, an uneasy feeling stirring in him. "Name your price."

"When we're not in lessons, you'll live down in the Mire with me."

His gut tightened. "And help Tal."

She gripped his arm. "No — we'll help the Westreach. What do you think we're all doing it for, as a personal favor to that self-important bellows? It's because we know that what happens here will have a rippling effect across the Reach Realms. We are the eyes and ears where no other can spy, and we'll learn things of our enemies that none thought possible."

The gold in her eyes was spinning fast. *She's in one of her stories,* he realized. *She finally gets to play the heroine.*

He'd be damned if he let her throw herself into a role that could get her killed.

He hid his concern behind a smile. "When you put it that way, how could I say no?"

She surprised him by seizing the back of his neck and pulling him down for a rough kiss. As they parted, she held him there for a moment longer. "And don't forget what else I promised down in the Mire," she said, her voice going low.

Garin swallowed and nearly stumbled as she released him, grabbed his hand, and pulled him along in her wake.

THE GROTTO

TAL STUDIED HER BACK AS THEY CROSSED YET ANOTHER ROPE bridge.

Ashelia had always walked with an effortless grace. Even before she'd trained in elven "dancing," she'd possessed a poise that spoke of every movement being intentional and confident. When she entered a room, it was not only her appearance that drew eyes, but an aura radiating from her that no magic could imitate.

Now, her beauty had matured and blossomed. He noticed subtle changes from her becoming a mother; a slight widening of the hips, a swelling of the breasts, a softening in her face. But where she'd been a carefully cultivated garden flower, now she was a wild bloom, with rough leaves and thorns, but even more splendid for it. He wondered if her training and time as a Warder had scarred her skin, remembering the soft feel of her under his hands.

Guiltily, he reined in his thoughts. *She's not yours to treasure*, he reminded himself.

But somehow, his restraint only made the feelings burn stronger still.

As if sensing his thoughts, Ashelia glanced back and met his eyes briefly as she mounted the next platform. Tal gained the landing himself and grinned weakly at her, but she was already looking ahead again.

Their route took them ever downward, closer to the swampy forest that waited below. The perfume of the canopy slowly gave way to the stink of the Mire, stagnant water and mud conspiring to foul the air. Tal breathed through his mouth and wondered how most of the city could live among it, and why the Highkin had never done anything about it. Once, he might have mentioned it to Ashelia, and perhaps he had. Now, though, he had to save what little credibility he had for other matters.

As they descended the last stretch of rope-threaded stairs, they reached a grassy knoll, and clean air circulated around them. Tal smiled as he recognized the small area. A patch of sunlight greeted them, and he held up his hands to it, soaking in the sun's heat. From the corner of his eye, he saw Ashelia doing the same, and he smiled at her. To his surprise, she smiled back. In that moment, he felt transported to two decades before, when they'd often walked this sunny stretch on the way to their secret rendezvous.

Her thoughts must have been traveling down the same lines, for the smile faded. "This is far enough," she said, letting her hands fall. "We can talk here."

"I wanted to see the grotto again." Tal paused, but when she didn't respond to his suggestion, he continued, "But I suppose here will do."

"You had something to say about Garin?"

Tal turned away, walking toward the brush to one side and gripping a branch. At the end of it was a long, white bloom. He lifted it to his nose and breathed in, and the honey-rich scent flowed through him. He grinned and plucked it, holding it out to Ashelia. "First, a gift for my hostess. You have been far more generous than I warrant, and certainly more than Falcon and his troupe of reprobates deserve."

Ashelia accepted the bloom with reluctance, but held it up to her nose all the same. Her eyes drifted closed as she breathed in. He watched, trying to catch the memory in his mind and hold it fast like a butterfly in sap.

Her eyelids fluttered open, and the stormy gray of her eyes swirled faster. "White mangrove blooms," she murmured.

"Do you remember how I once made you a crown of them? How the petals drooped in front of your eyes, and how you wore it long after the flowers had dried?"

A smile curled her lips, but it fled just as quickly. "You remember that. And yet..."

He winced. "It wasn't from forgetting that I failed to return."

Ashelia looked away, her hands falling to her sides again. The white flower hung limp in one hand. For a moment, he hovered in indecision. It felt as if he balanced on one of the support beams in High Elendol, a drop to either side, knowing he must plunge one way or the other.

He took a small step forward.

"Your son. I've been staying in your kintree, yet I haven't met him. I don't even know his name."

Ashelia looked up. "Yinin doesn't wish you to."

"And do you always obey him?"

Her eyes swirled suddenly. "Don't pretend to know our relationship, Tal."

"Do you love him?"

The words were out of his mouth before he'd even thought them. Yet Tal knew the question had long been simmering inside him.

Ashelia went rigid. "He's my bond."

"That's not the same thing."

She opened her mouth, then snapped it shut. Her hands unclenched, and the mangrove bloom fell to the ground. Tal followed its descent to the mud.

"Let's walk," Ashelia said curtly and led the way down the path.

He hesitated a moment, tempted to rescue the blossom, even as he knew it was too late. *As soon as you plucked it, it began to die,* he thought. *A fitting metaphor, wouldn't you think?*

As he caught up with Ashelia and walked by her side, she said in a level tone, "Let's keep our talk to Garin. What have you not told me?"

Tal sighed, realizing the battle was lost, if not the war. But he obliged her request.

"They're little more than suspicions and theories; I don't have proof of any of them. But they're based on a book I risked my life to retrieve, a book written by a sorceress branded a heretic by the Empire, and that Yuldor feared so much he destroyed a school of his own mages to hide it. Yet, as powerful as the Enemy is, he isn't omniscient. A copy of the sorceress' tome was hidden away in the tower's ruins, and with the aid of its custodian, I stole it from Yuldor's grasp and hid it away."

Ashelia stared at him with unabashed astonishment. Even now, all these years later, she didn't seem to take his unbelievable words with anything but trust. His chest warmed with gratification. They still kept that, at least.

"For five years," he continued, "I labored to translate it from the Darktongue. Perhaps I could have called upon your House-brother to expedite the process. But with Yuldor's eye no doubt watching for its reappearance — or mine — I feared to show my hand too soon. So I hid away until I was certain I had accurately uncovered its words."

"And?" Ashelia prompted when Tal fell into silence.

He sighed. "It's titled *A Fable of Song and Blood,* and the sorceress' ideas are little more than myth. But for how Garin's experiences have corroborated them, I might have thought them simply that. But Hellexa Yoreseer was no fool, and her ideas weren't condemned for nothing."

"What did she say?"

"Many things. That there is a great source of magic called the Worldheart. That Yuldor possesses it, and by its power, works the wonders and horrors of which he's capable. But also, she wrote that the Worldheart may have its own agenda — as if it possesses a sentience, of sorts — and that it's responsible for creating certain individuals that Hellexa called Founts, spread throughout the Empire and the Westreach. According to her, these Founts are the potential heirs to the Worldheart, seeded with its power so they may rule it in Yuldor's place. She saw it as a danger to him, and therefore heretical — for a god that can be replaced is less than a god."

Ashelia nodded slowly. "So you're saying Garin is one of these Founts. But how does it happen, this seeding of power?"

How indeed? he thought, fingers unconsciously tracing a vein in his arm until he stopped himself.

"Perhaps he was born with it. Perhaps it occurred when he picked up the cursed amulet in the Ruins of Erlodan. Either way, it does not change that Garin has to live with it now."

"So it seems. The devil gripped him tightly. So tightly I might wonder…"

She hesitated, darting a glance at Tal. He could guess the line of her thoughts. *Perhaps it never left.* He'd held the same suspicions when Garin went to learn sorcery with Aelyn.

Ashelia quickly pivoted. "I've never heard of Founts before, but the Worldheart you speak of is familiar. It mirrors our own tales among elves of the Mother's Womb."

"The Mother's Womb? I never heard mention of it when I was first here."

"It's more of a myth than history, and few lend it much credence these days, except among the elders. But according to the stories, the Mother's Womb was a gift given by Mother World to the Origins, the sole Bloodline that existed before the Severing. It held all the power of creation; every beast, every tree, everything that the Mother cradles in her palms came from the Womb, and anything that could be imagined might be manifested. It was a powerful gift, and one which flawed mortals would inevitably abuse.

"It's said that it brought peace to the Mother's domain for many centuries. But eventually, some sought to use its power for their own gain. Among my people, we call them the Betrayers — but your people name them the Whispering Gods."

"The Whispering Gods?" A crooked smile stretched his lips. "So you elves have secretly condemned the predominant religion of the Westreach for all these years?"

Ashelia shrugged. "Didn't you wonder why it was so little practiced here? But few recall the old tales. They don't remember why they despise your Creed, only that they do."

"Inherited hatred — the legacy of most cultures, in my experience."

"Still the philosopher, I see."

He gave her a small smile. "Only when I can dispense judgment with impunity. But all you have said of the Worldheart matches what I've heard."

"You mean read in that book of yours."

"Well, yes and no. I read of the Worldheart in Hellexa's forbidden tome. But some of what I know of it comes from what the Extinguished told me." At Ashelia's sharp look, he explained, "The one who impersonated Falcon."

"Oh." She frowned. "I've heard some of your adventures in Halenhol. But there were gaps in the story. Does that have to do with your bard's missing hand?"

Tal winced. "It does. Though the blame ultimately falls on me for that."

Before she could ask more, he hastily continued. "But according to the Extinguished, the Whispering Gods were not mortals, but deities at war with the Night. Out of desperation, they pulled the Worldheart from the core of the World and used it to imprison the Night above. Simultaneously, they enacted the Severing of the Bloodlines."

"There, our tales agree. For the Mother's Womb was said to possess all the powers of creation, and thus to remake the peoples of the World as its wielders saw fit."

Tal frowned. "But why? The molding of the Bloodlines has ever been a murky thing in the Creed. The best that the priests can explain it is that the Whispering Gods deemed it necessary for our survival. Why, though, they cannot say. Apparently, mortals can't understand the reasons of gods."

"So priests always like to say," Ashelia said drily. "But the Gladelysh version only ascribes it to an accident, a stray result of the struggle between the Whispering Gods and those who opposed them. Just as the Origins themselves were divided into Bloodlines, so were all beasts and plants that exist within the Mother's lands. It's why monsters walk among us, and we of the Bloodlines and our Eastern relatives share many traits, yet also vastly differ."

They walked for several moments in silence. Tal recognized the trail and knew they were drawing close to their destination. His pulse quickened in anticipation, but he kept his thoughts to the matter at hand.

"Whatever the tales say, the question remains: does the Worldheart or the Womb exist? And does Yuldor possess it, as the Extinguished claimed he does? Does it hold the powers of creation it's said to? Does it have a will of its own, and is it creating Founts to reclaim it from the Enemy's possession?"

Ashelia shook her head. "We cannot know. But do we have a better explanation?"

They fell into silence once more. Tal looked up to see the familiar grotto opening before them. A small cliff rose above the forest pool. The water was clear and a vibrant blue. They'd long ago discovered it held a hidden spring beneath its surface that refreshed the water and kept it clean of muck. Moss hung thickly down the cliff, providing a curtain of sorts across a shallow cave.

A smile curled Tal's lips. He had many fond memories of what had occurred between them behind that mossy curtain.

As he glanced at Ashelia, she seemed to be thinking of the same things, for her jaw had firmed and the color of her neck had darkened. He felt his hope drop away, but he couldn't let loose of it yet.

"I know things can never be the same between us, Ashelia." He longed to reach for her hand, but held himself in check. "I know I've muddled things in a way that apologies cannot hope to repair. But I'd be dishonest if I didn't say that I still care for you the same as when I left those long years before. And if you'd have me back, you'd bring me a joy that I haven't known since."

His hopes sunk further as the gray in her eyes swirled into a storm.

"So you wish to be my lover again?" she said in a low voice, her anger cutting through with every word. "You wish things to go back to the way they were before?"

"Not as before. But however you will have me, I will—"

"I can't believe you." She jabbed a finger in his chest. "You leave for two decades with a promise to return, then never do. Why didn't you come back, Tal? If you can't answer that, I don't know what else we have to discuss."

Tal grinned weakly, unable to help himself, though he knew she hated it when he smiled during their arguments. *What can I say?* he thought miserably. *What can I say that won't sound melodramatic and false?*

For a moment, he was tempted to give an excuse she might accept. He knew all too well that a lie might span a chasm over which the truth would fall short.

But he'd never knowingly told an untruth to Ashelia before, and he didn't intend to start now. The best he could do was remain silent.

Ashelia backed up a step and looked aside, her body as taut as a drawn bowstring. "Fine. That puts that to rest."

He knew he had to say something. "If I told you, would you believe me?"

"Not anymore."

His shoulders sagged, but he couldn't bring himself to stand straight. Always, she'd trusted him. And so quickly, through a moment of doubt, he'd broken it.

When she spoke a moment later, he dared to hope, but it died as soon as her words settled in.

"If the Mother's Womb is possessed by Yuldor, and the devil never left Garin, then he's in grave danger," she said coolly. "This Song and its Singer must be corrupted by the Named. And eventually, Garin will succumb to his will."

Tal nodded, then stared out over the forest grotto. *Once,* he mused, *we found our beginning here. Only fitting that it should die where it began.*

Without another word, Ashelia walked away. After a moment, Tal turned to follow.

IMPERIALS

GARIN STARTLED AWAKE AS SOMEONE YANKED OFF THE COVERS.

"What?" He sat upright and fumbled for his knife on the bedside table. "Attack?"

Wren snorted, fists on her hips. "Who's going to attack troubadours in a tavern? Half the patrons would tear them to pieces!"

Garin groaned and leaned back, his heart still racing. "Then what is it?"

"It's time you stop lazing around all afternoon. Come down to the tavern."

He stretched out his limbs. Already, they were sore from his dancing lesson earlier that afternoon, the pain compounded by all the previous lessons over the two weeks since they'd arrived in Elendol. "I told you, Wren, I'm not lazing around. Master Ulen says rest is very important for the body's health."

"And is Master Ulen here, or am I?"

He cracked open an eye. "You are."

"Right. Which means I'm the one who gets to tell you what to do."

Garin grinned, a little of his good humor returning. Wren let a smile crack through her tough veneer.

He sat up again, working his shoulders to loosen them. "So what is it you want? For me to watch you play and shower you with compliments?"

She raised an eyebrow. "When have I ever sought your approval?"

"You just seem very insistent suddenly."

"Well... there is something."

That piqued his interest enough to swing his legs over the side of their bed. "And that would be?"

"Not what, but who. There are some people you should meet. For... you know."

His gut tightened. *I should have known.* Working on Tal's behalf was the last thing he wanted to do after a long day of lessons. They'd had their second lesson with Aelyn that morning, and it had gone nearly as poorly as the first. In the week that had passed since that first lesson, the irritable mage had set them to reviewing the Four Roots yet again. He insisted that they must know them through and through before attempting sorcery, despite both of them having cast magic before. Privately, he and Wren plotted mutiny if the third lesson showed nothing different, though Garin had his reservations. He feared how Ilvuan might react to sorcery, and he had no desire to hear the Nightsong again.

"Who are they?" he asked.

She shrugged, but there was something practiced in the gesture. "Informed residents. You'll see what I mean. Just get dressed and follow."

Still muttering complaints, but knowing he'd get no farther with her mind decided, Garin dressed in his traveling clothes, more befitting the Mire than the fine garments Ashelia had gifted him, before following Wren downstairs.

The hum of the Whistling Thistle's commonroom could be heard from every chamber in the creaking inn, but as they descended, its sounds crescendoed into a melee. The clattering of mugs, the banging of tables, the loud voices laughing and shouting and arguing all across the room. The din made Garin tense and prone to clutch the dagger hidden under his shirt. In places like this, folks' smiles seemed as likely to hide malice as show friendliness, and he doubted the Ilthasi agents watching over them could prevent an errant knife from plunging into their backs.

Stranger still were the clientele who frequented the tavern. Not only Gladelysh elves were present, but every sort of Easterner, whose Bloodlines he'd finally learned: minotaurs, Nightelves, medusals, gnomes, and sylvans. Their foreign tongues hissed uncomfortably in his ears.

Though the Easterners and Gladelysh shared the room, they did little more than that. They'd divided it in two, and none crossed those boundaries. Just as the Mire was split between the Lowkin and the immigrants, so it was in the inn.

But as Wren grabbed his hand and pulled him through the warm, foul-smelling room, he saw there was one exception to the rule. On the Easterner side of the Whistling Thistle, Ox sat with a minotaur that rivaled even the big trouper's size, and a comically small gnome sat next to them. It was to this table that Wren brought them.

"Garin!" Ox said as he saw him, his voice booming even over the room's racket. The Befal trouper stood and, ignoring Garin's protests, crushed him in an embrace. "Good to see you, my young friend!"

As he released him, Garin staggered back and gave him a weak grin. The trouper's smile wasn't as wide as it had been before his partner and lover, Jonn, had been killed by the Extinguished in Halenhol. But, day by day, Ox had recovered with a remarkable tenacity, and Garin's respect for him had grown with it.

But his attention was pulled to the two foreigners who watched their exchange. "Hello," Garin greeted them, awkward with not knowing what to say.

The minotaur gave him a solemn nod. Her tunic sported

colorful feathers that resembled a quetzal's, but were far too large. Garin wondered uneasily what manner of Eastern monster they came from.

"My!" the gnome squeaked, the Reach words coming out nasal in her Eastern accent. "Aren't you a tall *lenual?* Almost as tall as one of those needle-nosed Mire elves!"

The gnome, who looked female, had her face painted extravagantly to resemble a large raptor, though her eyes were watery and kind amid the paint. She'd wrapped an orange robe around her child-like body that looked to have seen better days.

Garin saw Wren glance around, making sure none of the Gladelysh were close enough to hear. He smiled politely back. "My father was a tall man."

At the thought of his father, melancholy seeped back in. He wondered again what he was doing there on Tal's behalf.

"Sit down, both of you," Ox offered, drawing up a mismatched stool and a rickety chair. Garin, already self-conscious about how he loomed over the gnome, took the chair and its risks, while Wren perched on the stool.

She gestured to each of the Easterners. "Garin, meet Rozana and Temmy. They're frequent visitors to the Whistling Thistle."

Rozana the minotaur nodded her head respectfully. Though her features resembled a brown-and-white spotted cow, her eyes faced forward like the other Bloodlines.

"How do you do?" piped the gnome Temmy. She had a pleasant smile, even if her teeth were yellowed and strangely square, and her nervous hands fidgeted over a device unfamiliar to Garin. Her copper-hued hair was cropped short, though it was springy and lively atop her head, and stood in stark contrast to her sallow skin.

"What's new in the World today?" Wren asked the minotaur before Garin could reply.

Rozana folded her hands onto the table. Each hand was four-fingered, the fingers as thick around as Sendeshi sausages.

"I would consider us friends, Wren. But I cannot run a business without minding my coin."

Ox raised an eyebrow at her, and Garin watched with perplexity as Wren failed to hide her annoyance and flipped out a silver bit. The minotaur smoothly took it and hid it with more deftness than her heavy features would have implied.

"Are we better friends now?" Wren asked sarcastically.

"Of course." Rozana smiled, the expression looking strangely menacing on her bovine face. "What would you like to know?"

Wren exchanged a look with Ox. "Whatever you have to tell."

As the minotaur stared at them, as placid as the animal she resembled, Garin felt a glimmer of annoyance. *What am I doing here?* he asked himself. Wren didn't need him for these questions.

It wasn't Rozana who spoke first, but Temmy, who moved with such agitation that it made Garin nervous. "You know what to tell them about, Zana!"

Rozana frowned. "I told you not to call me that, Temmy. And haven't I counseled patience in the past?"

Temmy flushed, her eyes falling to her twitching hands.

The minotaur turned her gaze back on Wren. "I have hinted at this in our previous conversations. Now, I have gathered proof. Discontent rises in Elendol."

Wren looked far from impressed. "It doesn't cost a silver to know that. All I have to do is take a stroll."

Rozana shook her head. "Not as I speak of. Discontent pervades every…" She struggled to find the word. "…Surface — no, every stratum of society here."

"Meaning?"

The minotaur looked at Garin, and he tried not to flinch under her gaze as she seemed to speak to him. "You know how it is among the Lowkin elves. They believe their homes invaded, their lands trampled, their streets filled with too many bodies and unfamiliar customs. And discontent is just as present among Imperials."

Imperials — he'd never heard of Easterners referenced that way. He supposed it was how they thought of themselves.

"Why?" Wren demanded with her usual brashness. "Didn't you choose to come here?"

Rozana shook her head. "Not most of us. We are outlaws and outcasts in our lands, those who cannot or refuse to live under the Emperor's iron laws. But though we could not stay, that does not mean we wished to make this foreign soil our home. Many of us long for the mountains and plains and wide skies we left behind. The gloom and hostility, the grinding under the heels of the Highkin — they will drive our peoples into worse crimes still."

Wren exchanged a look with Garin. He guessed they were thinking the same thing.

Looking back at Rozana, she asked, "Are you implying some will rise against the Queen and Elendol? That they'll cause a civil war?"

Rozana stared at Wren for a long, unblinking moment. Wren's jaw only seemed to tighten as she stared back.

"Not them," the minotaur said softly. "It is Elendol's own nobility who will be responsible for that."

The Highkin? Garin wondered if it could be true.

"We have seen them among us, plotting, plying their contacts, weaving their webs." Rozana looked at each of them as she spoke, holding their gazes. "Not only among their lesser brothers and sisters but also my own peoples. They pass through by night, cloaked in shadows and sorcery, to hold their secret meetings and conspire their uprising."

Wren had leaned forward, and despite the din of the room drowning out their conversation, she spoke in a low voice. "If these meetings are secret, how do you know what they're plotting?"

"Because of whom they meet with. You may know them by the name the Silver Vines."

The Silver Vines, he thought. *The Cult of Yuldor.*

Rozana leaned back and crossed her arms over her chest, the placid expression returning. Wren's brow furrowed as she glanced at Garin.

He'd known that things were not right in Elendol. He'd heard of the Ingress and the conflicts surrounding it. He knew their traditions, for good or for ill, were crumbling, allowing women like Ashelia to take on roles previously denied them. King Aldric had even mentioned that Gladelyl was on the verge of civil war when they'd first arrived in Halenhol.

It should have come as no surprise that it was Yuldor's hand behind all that happened now.

He knew the stories of Tal's fight against the Silver Vines and the Thorn, the Extinguished who led them. It was said he'd killed his enemy and dismantled the Cult of Yuldor within Elendol, though it nearly cost him his life. Just as he and Wren had reasoned before, it made a certain sense that Tal had, once again, come to reenact the stories of his legend, like a poor parody of a well-worn play.

A bitter smile twisted Garin's lips. *Maybe this time,* he thought, *he won't be so lucky as the last.*

Tal stopped before the sign that led up to the building nestled under the roots of a kintree. A smile quirked his lips as he saw the glowing glyphs. "The Whistling Thistle," he read aloud. "So this is the place where you've holed yourself up?"

Falcon turned toward him, the weariness of his efforts showing in the blankness of his expressive face. "It doesn't look like much from the outside, 'tis true. But it's the best place to share a whisper with an Easterner. The inn is one of the few places in the Mire that caters to all. Any segregation is self-imposed."

"As you say."

Falcon led the way up to the inn's door on a natural stairway formed of roots. In front of the door, a pair of dour-looking male elves watched them, rapiers buckled at their hips.

"Cause no trouble, and we'll give you none," said one as he opened the door.

Tal gave him his wolf's smile. "Likewise."

Before either of the door guards could respond, he disappeared inside.

Contrary to his expectations, the commonroom of the Whistling Thistle was full nearly to bursting, and with every shape, color, and Bloodline imaginable. As Falcon had implied, it was largely segregated, with Gladelysh on the side of the room closer to the lit hearth, while the eclectic Easterners occupied the other side. On the Gladelysh half, one of the Dancing Feather troupers, a young human lass by the name of Melina, worked her fingers over a lute and sang a bawdy tune, filling the tavern with her sweet alto, to the light laughter of the elves.

The boundaries, however, seemed more fluid than first imagined, for he saw three humans along the line sharing a table with a minotaur and a gnome. A moment later, he realized who those three humans were.

"You've already set the others to work, I see?" he observed.

"Of course." Falcon smiled, but weariness seemed to drag at it. Tal could hardly blame him. Hunting down secrets, deciphering foreign accents, organizing his dispersed crew — it all had to take a toll, especially on a man still recovering from his not-so-distant experiences.

But as he followed Falcon's gaze to Melina, who had just received another polite chuckle from the elves — which amounted to uproarious laugh among other Bloodlines — he started to understand the true cause of his friend's melancholy.

"Have you been taking time for yourself?" Tal asked as they stepped further in to allow other patrons to pass by.

The minstrel snorted. "And what would I do? Strum a harp? Compose a new ballad for the Legend of Tal?"

Tal winced at the bitterness in his friend's voice. "Copious drinking and sleeping were more to my thinking."

Falcon's shoulders slumped as his eyes wandered over the room. "I cannot sleep, my old friend, and even wine has begun to lose its savor. I am a bard with one hand — which is to say, I'm no bard at all."

Fighting down his rising guilt, Tal gripped his friend's shoulder. "You've always been worth double any troubadour I've met. Now, you're just giving them a fair chance. And mistake me if I'm wrong, but I always thought there was more to being a trouper than playing an instrument."

"Oh? And are there many roles for one-handed men?"

"Not on the stage, perhaps," Tal conceded. "But behind it, most certainly. Only the most talented can write the lines and compose the songs that others recite."

Falcon snorted, but he appeared somewhat mollified. "I suppose I am the finest composer in the Westreach."

Tal laughed and drew him into an embrace. "That you are, my friend. Only the most shameless liars can be the greatest artists."

As a smile lit the bard's face, Falcon seemed to come back to himself. "Enough flattery — it starts to become cloying. And it seems our contacts have arrived."

Tal followed Falcon's gaze to see two Easterners — one a Nightelf, the other a medusal — enter and glance their way, then head for an open table in the far corner. Though their manner was suspicious, almost slinking, it was the silver monkey perched on the Nightelf's shoulder that drew his curiosity. As Tal watched them weave through the packed mess of tables, the monkey turned and glared right at him, its teeth bared in a snarl. Tal could have sworn that, for a moment, the monkey's mane shimmered a brilliant gold.

"Those two?" Tal asked skeptically.

Falcon sighed. "I've told Pylas not to bring that monkey around, but they seem rather… attached."

The bard led the way toward the pair of Easterners. As they moved around the tables, other foreigners gave them long stares, their eyes lingering on Falcon in particular. Tal could guess why. His friend had all the markings of an elf, and he knew there was little love lost between the immigrants and the native Gladelysh here in the Mire. He casually let a hand rest on a knife he'd secured at his waist and smiled at anyone who stared too long.

None accosted them, however, before they reached the Easterners' table. The medusal and the Nightelf broke off their quiet correspondence and looked up expectantly. After a moment, the medusal's lipless mouth curled in the approximation of a smile, her sharp teeth making the expression seem more menacing than welcoming.

"Falcon Sunstring," she greeted them. "Is this the friend you spoke of?" She spoke with almost a lisp, her words coming out half-annunciated.

Tal wore a congenial smile as he studied the Easterner. She had dusky violet skin ridged with the roughness of a reptile's. A bright blue fin on the top of her head identified her as female, for the males of her kind had manes of fins instead. Colorful feathers of green, red, and yellow came off of her head like hair, very much resembling a quetzal's. Despite having no nose or lips, her face was still strangely human. From the corner of his eye, he glimpsed her tail curled around the leg of the Nightelf's chair.

"Tal Harrenfel," Falcon introduced him with a broad grin. "My finest work."

The Nightelf, Pylas, looked up, eyes round and pink irises swirling. "*The* Tal Harrenfel?"

Tal turned his smile on him. His skin was the color of a twilit sky. His red robes were thick and intricately detailed with silver threads, but they looked to have seen better days. Likely he'd once been someone of means — perhaps a magician, if the monkey perched on his shoulder was any indication. He'd once heard that in the East, mages kept animals as "Namebound" to serve at their whim.

"Unfortunately so." Tal didn't know what to do in greeting, so he gave both a bow and the elven gesture of respect in a parody of both.

Pylas scarcely seemed to notice, for he continued to stare at him with undisguised interest. The monkey on his shoulder didn't hide his feelings either, but puffed itself up and leaned forward threateningly as it glared at Tal. He hadn't imagined the color-shifting before, for its mane turned once again from silver to gold.

"Pylas," the medusal said, the word ending in a hiss. "Your pet is misbehaving again."

The monkey chattered and turned its glare on the medusal. The sound seemed to rouse the Nightelf from his stupor.

"Uke Hesh, peace," Pylas said, holding a hand up to the monkey. For a moment, Tal thought it would bite him, but it placed both of its small hands around Pylas' fingers and seemed to calm. The suspicion in its glare, however, didn't diminish.

"What does his name mean?" Tal asked tentatively.

The Nightelf smiled. "Old Man. It describes him."

Not knowing what to make of that, Tal turned to the medusal. "My apologies, but I don't know your name either."

The medusal gave him another unnerving smile. "Yeshil."

At a gesture from Yeshil, he and Falcon sat. Tal was ill pleased to sit opposite of Pylas and Old Man, for the monkey still glared at him as if it would like nothing better than to gouge his eyes out.

An elven barmaid came by, and though her expression was

stiff, she took their orders without complaint before scurrying away.

"So," Falcon said with a friendly smile. "What do you have for us today?"

Tal watched intently as Pylas and Yeshil exchanged a look. Falcon had said little about the Easterners he wanted him to meet, only that they were well-informed individuals who might help in his hunt for the Silver Vines. But he'd had more than his fair share of shady individuals, and knew that anyone with that sort of knowledge was best watched carefully, lest they sell information to both sides.

Yeshil smiled again, her tongue flickering briefly up from her mouth. "There's to be a Winter Ball in High Elendol."

Falcon, surprised, looked at Tal, while Tal kept his face carefully neutral.

"Indeed?" he said disinterestedly.

"So they say," Yeshil said, studying both of their reactions, slitted pupils dilated with interest.

The serving elf returned and deposited their drinks without a word. A frown seemed permanently molded to her features.

After she left, Tal headed off any questions Falcon might have and turned the conversation. "I think you know we're not here for news about nobles' balls. Do you have anything more substantial?"

"I would not dismiss a ball so easily, friend!" Pylas flashed a smile, even as his eyes wandered up to the ceiling. "Gatherings of the most powerful in the city — nay, the nation! — must always be watched with the utmost care."

"Do you suspect something will be decided there?" Falcon interjected.

The Nightelf turned his smile on him, while Old Man silently fumed over the attention its master was bestowing on them. "Many things, I'm sure. *How* they will be determined shall be more interesting still."

Fear prickled down Tal's spine as he imagined all who

would attend the Winter Ball. *The Peers. The Queen. Aelyn. Ashelia.*

"What have you heard?" he asked with forced calm.

It was Yeshil who answered first. "Rumors, mere rumors. But what they speak of... it brings a chill to my skin not even the sun could relieve, if it would shine down in this swamp."

Falcon leaned forward with a conciliatory smile. "My dear informants, I'm sorry to ask this. But all the cloak-and-mist is obscuring your delicious point. Dispense with the formalities of your trade and answer, please: what's planned for the Winter Ball, and by whom?"

Pylas gave a laugh, and the monkey mimicked the sound a moment later. Gazes wandered over, and Tal forcibly kept his posture relaxed, though he felt several pairs of eyes linger on them.

"Very well!" The Nightelf leaned forward, his soiled sleeves dipping into his drink without his notice. "Our mutual friends have plans there, if the whispers speak true."

Mutual friends. No need to ask who those were — Falcon had been explicit about whom they wanted information about.

Falcon's smile faded. "And their intent?"

"To decide the feud," Yeshil said. "By whatever means necessary."

Tal leaned closer. "Do you know what they will attempt? What means they intend to use? Any information you might recover would be recompensed richly."

The medusal gave him a smile. "I'm sure it will be. But the *appropriate* form of compensation will be necessary."

Tal glanced at Falcon, wondering if he'd seen this coming. "And that would be?"

"Information!" Pylas spoke excitedly, but kept his voice soft. "And access!"

Misgivings swirled in his gut. But he'd dealt with far more ignobles than these and knew how to handle them. Promises were formed and broken as often as bread among men and women such as these, and unkept oaths were a trade in which Tal was well-versed.

"Anything you need, within reason, in relation to the value of the news." Tal held out his hand, intending to shake on it, but the Easterners stared at it as if it bore a contagion. Old Man looked ready to leap on him and tear his eyes out.

"They don't shake hands, Tal," Falcon said, pulling his arm back. "A bound word is enough for Imperials."

Tal settled back again, taking the reprimand in stride. "Very well. You have my word, and we have yours, then?"

"As we have said," Yeshil answered with a sly smile.

"Was there anything else today?" Falcon inquired, his posture already half-turned away.

When both Easterners shook their heads, the bard slid two silver coins across the table and rose, draining his mug as he stood. "Ah!" he said with a grin. "No finer cheap wine than in Elendol! Come, Tal. I trust we will see you both soon."

As they retreated to the Gladelysh side of the Whistling Thistle, Tal pulled him into an unoccupied corner. "What did you make of that?"

"I was less than impressed with your offer." Falcon raised an eyebrow. "You don't mean to uphold such a promise, do you?"

"Of course not. I mean to have just as much honor as any thief — as little as I can get away with."

"Be careful with those ones." He nodded at the table where Garin, Wren, and Ox had been sitting with the minotaur and gnome, now occupied by a trio of other Easterners. "They're in league with Rozana and Temmy, who you saw meeting with the others. And their confederation doesn't end there. Given enough time, I wouldn't be surprised to see them corrupt all the Mire, if not High Elendol itself."

"They seemed a striking pair, but I wouldn't go that far." Tal gestured at the divided room. "There's a long way to go before Elendol submits to Easterners gathering power."

"Perhaps not as long as you think, my friend. But the other

matter they spoke of, the Winter Ball. You knew it was happening."

"I did," Tal admitted. "Or at least, the Queen had told me of her intention to host it. I'd heard nothing since. Though Geminia doesn't seem a woman to say she'll do a thing and not follow through."

"I want to play it."

He tried to hide his dismay as he met his friend's gaze. It was nearly painful to hold. Falcon's eyes were filled with a determination and hopefulness that he couldn't refuse.

"I can request it," he hedged. "But why? You know they'll only disdain you as half-kin."

"*Why?* How can you ask why?" Falcon leaned in closer, the gold in his eyes swirling. "Tal, this is likely my last opportunity for a grand performance! To play before the Elf Queen — it's a dream I barely dared to harbor. But still, I have, for many long years. And now, when I am at hand to make good on it, you ask why I'd want to?"

"It's not your last opportunity, Falcon. You're not dying."

"But my troupe is! They're falling like flies! First Jonn, then Mikael… who will be next when the city erupts?"

Tal's stomach churned. He was likely right — everything they'd learned indicated that Elendol was close to boiling. And as much as he might need the eyes and ears of the Dancing Feathers, he didn't need them at any price.

He gripped his friend's shoulder tightly, and Falcon met his eyes. "You're right. Elendol will set aflame. And you and the others need not be here for it."

Falcon's eyes flickered to one side. "What are you saying?"

"Leave. Don't worry about playing the Winter Ball. Forget Garin's disguise. None of that will matter once Gladelyl is at war with itself."

"But it won't devolve before the ball! Surely, if things go wrong, it will still be months—"

"Maybe," Tal cut him off. "But maybe not. Please, Falcon,

leave, if only for my sake. I already took your hand. Don't make your life be on my conscience as well."

To his surprise, Falcon threw back his head and laughed, then pulled him into a quick embrace. "We came here of our own free wills, me and the Dancing Feathers. Partially for you, yes, and partially for the lad, but not entirely. Too long we'd been cooped up in the Coral Castle; too long had it been since we felt the road under our feet, or witnessed the tales we sang of with our very eyes. You think it's your fault we're here, but it's none but our own. If we die, we die in pursuit of that which none other has ever claimed. I couldn't wish to perish any other way."

As Tal tried to interrupt the diatribe, Falcon held up his hand. "If you must feel obligation toward us, feel obligated only to secure our place within the Winter Ball. I hold you responsible for attaining my apotheosis, my most glorious performance. Can you do that?"

He hesitated a moment longer. Some of his guilt had eased at his friend's words, but still it lingered, a hard pit in his gut. Yet he knew he had no chance of swaying him then and there.

Perhaps, he mused, *once he sees what he yearns for, he'll have the sense to run.*

"Fine. I'll ask for you. But don't fly your hopes too high. I serve at the Queen's leisure, not the other way around."

Falcon grinned and clapped Tal on the shoulder. "Ah, but if Tal Silvertongue cannot convince her, who might?"

"You gave me that name."

"And well-deserved it was! After all, who was it that sweet-talked the Clan Chiefs of the Hardrog Dwarves into releasing you from your cell?"

Tal sighed and resigned himself to Falcon's spewing of lies as they turned toward the commonroom's door. *An ear for a hand,* he thought with a crooked smile as they exited out into the cool forest.

THE DEVIL'S TONGUE

Aelyn was waiting at the Venaliel library when Garin and Wren arrived.

"Gather your materials and follow me." Without so much as a nod of greeting, the crotchety mage turned and strode toward the back room.

Garin exchanged a look with Wren. "I don't think he's going to be any better."

Her eyes swirled. "We've been waiting for *weeks*. This is our fourth lesson. If he drones on about the Roots one more time—"

"We'll just ask him if we can try our hand again," Garin cut her off hastily. He didn't want to think about Wren making good on her threat. As unpleasant as the lessons were, they'd be intolerable without Wren there to mock Aelyn behind his back.

After a moment, she just shook her head. Garin followed her by gathering their materials and making for the back room.

Closing the door behind them, the room once again fell into a gloom only partially remitted by the fire in the hearth. Garin sat down and stared into the flames. He'd asked two lessons ago why there were no werelights in the room, and Aelyn had responded — with contempt — that werelights could negatively interact with a budding sorcerer's flailing attempts to cast magic. A blazing hearth, however, might provide both an energy source and a receptacle for any excess energy.

But that doesn't matter if we never do anything, he mused.

"Open your books to Chapter Five," Aelyn instructed. He traced a finger along his copy of the text before slowly beginning to pace the room.

Garin shared a look with Wren before obeying. He was beginning to hate even the sight of *The Fundamentals of Sorcerous Bindings*, written by a long-dead elven sorcerer whose name he'd already forgotten. Aelyn had hinted they were lucky he'd provided them Reachtongue translations and not made them learn the original Gladelyshi. But to Garin, it was nearly as unreadable as if it were in another language. After months of practice, he could read from the Creed, but that was simple compared to the complex words and phrases used in *Fundamentals*. Only through Wren's help had he survived until Chapter Five, and then only barely.

As Aelyn drew breath to speak, Garin nearly interrupted him, but his courage faltered at the last moment. Ignoring Wren's smoldering glare, he listened as Aelyn lectured on the many effects of mispronouncing the Worldnames, as the individual words of the Worldtongue were called. Implosion of one's body came up several times, as did "mind-charred," which occurred when insufficient concentration was applied to an incantation, and "fragmented mind," which might occur when a sorcerer attempted and failed to maintain two spells at once.

But as he saw Wren squirming in her seat, silent only out of loyalty to him, he knew he couldn't torture either of them any longer.

"Peer Aelyn," he interjected as Aelyn paused for a breath. "If I could ask a question."

The mage halted mid-step, his eyes narrowed suspiciously. "Addressing me by my proper title... Do not believe me so easily manipulated by a show of respect. What do you want, Garin?"

He didn't shift his subservient expression, knowing that no matter what Aelyn said, deference put him in a more malleable mood. "I was only wondering if we could try applying what we've learned. Nothing complicated that would risk becoming mind-charred — just a simple, one-word cantrip."

Aelyn scowled at him. "Have I not told you this already? When I was first instructed in magic—"

"With all due respect, sir," Wren interrupted, "you were eleven when you began learning magic. And as I understand it, elves age slower than the other Bloodlines. Garin and I are both nearly sixteen."

"All the more reason to move slowly. You have not been properly principled to withstand the rigors of an education in the occult and are more prone to taking foolish risks."

Garin's patience was quickly thinning. "If you don't teach us something soon, we'll probably do something foolish."

Aelyn's scowl eased into a smile that was no more pleasant to bear. "Is that a threat, boy?"

"No, *sir*. A fact."

The mage looked back and forth between them. Garin could see he struggled to maintain the smile. *He knows he can't win*, he realized. *Failing to rein us in would be to fail his Queen.*

Aelyn's eyes blazed as he turned away. "Fine," he snapped. "Close your books and return them to their shelf, then return here."

Garin and Wren hurriedly did as he asked. His heart knocked at his ribs, and not just from standing up to Aelyn. *We're going to do it,* he marveled. He wasn't sure if his excitement or fear was stronger.

He'd summoned magic on several occasions, and two of those times had been without Ilvuan's aid. But always, it had been by the Darktongue, and always, the results had been unpleasant. Against his will, the memory of the big bandit by the Winegulch and what Garin had done to him came to mind. His skin prickled into gooseflesh.

Don't think of that. With an effort, he pushed the thoughts back down.

As they returned to the room and hovered behind their chairs, uncertain whether to sit again, Aelyn whirled and, with a resonant word, lifted a hand to the door. There was a sudden rush of air, and the door slammed closed, while the fire in the hearth danced wildly.

Garin glanced at Wren and found rapt attention on her face, her mouth slightly parted, her eyes whirling. A smile came to his own lips.

"Wipe away that grin," Aelyn commanded.

He immediately smoothed his expression to stillness.

Aelyn looked back and forth between them. "We are going to begin with a simple spell that will be difficult for even the most untrained novice to make dangerous: *fuln.* Do you remember what *fuln* does?"

"Light," Garin answered at once. "It summons a ball of werelight."

The mage gave him a sharp nod. "It collects light energy from the surrounding environment and coalesces it into a small area that a sorcerer might move by his or her will. Because light energy is so plentiful, this usually has little cost to either the environment or the user, making it a safe place to start. Now, recount the Four Roots."

Wren spoke up first. "Affinity, word, energy transfer, concentration and imagination."

"*Inherent* energy transfer," Aelyn corrected sharply. "But I suppose that must do. Wren, you'll begin. Remember your principles, hold them in your mind, and when your will is iron, say the Worldname exactly as I have: *fuln.*"

Garin's stomach fluttered as Wren lifted a hand and stared with narrowed eyes at it. He'd seen her summon fire before, even amid their fight against the draugars below the

Ruins of Erlodan. Yet somehow, this seemed their first real attempt.

Wren parted her mouth, then said with authority, "*Fuln!*"

Light blazed from her hand, so bright and sudden in the dreary room that Garin had to squeeze his eyes shut before it. Yet a grin stretched his lips as he squinted at Wren, and she grinned back, a ball of light hovering above her hand, the gold in her eyes more luminous than ever.

This is the woman who has chosen me, he marveled, and felt his chest warm with pride.

"Fine, fine." Aelyn waved a hand. "As you'll notice, it takes very little concentration to maintain a werelight — for once commanded, the sorcery molds the energy to its new form. To break the binding, you must actively force it back to its natural form."

Wren nodded, but stared at the werelight for several long moments before it dissipated.

"Garin, it is your turn. Remember all the same principles. Hold all of the Four Roots in your mind. Only when your concentration is unwavering must you speak the word, and with absolute precision: *fuln.*"

Garin nodded, swallowing hard. His nervousness clawed up from his belly into his throat so he wondered if he'd be able to speak. In the back of his mind, he felt a glimmer of amusement from Ilvuan and shivered at the Singer's unexpected touch.

Focus. He lifted his hand, palm up, and stared at it. In accordance with the Fourth Root, he pushed all other thoughts from his head but the light that would form there and imagined every detail he could. The gentle, white-gold glow. The pulse and slow bob as it hovered over his hand. The hint of warmth, like the kiss of the sun, on his skin.

He opened his mouth and spoke the word. "*Fuln.*"

He stared, breathless for a long moment. Then another. He blinked, unsure if he was imagining the light or not — then he realized he was. Nothing had appeared.

"*Fuln*," he said again, and when nothing happened, spoke louder, "*Fuln!*"

"Enough!" Aelyn snapped. "You are growing impatient, and impatience is a magician's worst enemy."

"Then how did you get this far?" Wren muttered.

Either Aelyn didn't hear her or pretended not to, for he continued to stare at Garin. "Your pronunciation was correct, the first time at least. Were you focused?"

"Yes."

"And vividly imagining the light?"

"Yes!"

Aelyn frowned and began to pace. Misery bubbled up inside Garin, only made worse when he felt Ilvuan's amusement radiating stronger than before. *This is your fault, isn't it?* he thought furiously at the Singer. He received no reply but another glimmer of feeling, this time of contempt.

"Perhaps we will attempt another word," Aelyn said at length, stopping before him. "*Kald*. It is slightly more dangerous, but most novices find it easier to control than *lisk* or *mord*. You remember what *kald* means?"

"Yes," Garin replied sharply, his irritation getting the better of him. "It's fire."

"Fine. Now, ready yourself and make your attempt. Leave no Root unattended!"

Ignoring him, Garin raised his hand again and set his concentration to it. *Fire*, he thought, willing it to be. He could almost feel the heat pouring down his arm to rise in a burning column from his hand. *Fire*. The lit hearth was in his vision and served as inspiration. He mimicked the images of the flickering flames in his mind, dancing and twirling and ever-rising from the logs. *Fire, damn you.*

"*Kald!*" he cried out with as much command as he could muster.

A moment passed. Two.

Not even a wisp of smoke rose from his palm.

Garin let his hand fall as it clenched into a fist. From the corner of his eye, he saw Wren's pitying frown and Aelyn's cruel smile.

"That will be enough for you today, Wren," he said without taking his eyes from Garin.

Garin didn't like the spark of interest in the mage's eyes, but was glad to mutter farewell to Wren. If the elf had further embarrassment in mind for him, it was better that she didn't witness it.

After the door sealed shut behind her, Aelyn spoke softly. "Let's try a little experiment."

He tried not to shift his feet. "What experiment?"

Aelyn took a step closer. "You've cast magic before — I've seen it. Something moved through you when you killed the Extinguished, and I witnessed what you did to the bandit in the woods. You possess the Eldritch Blood, Garin, or something near to it. And I mean to awaken it."

Ilvuan stirred in Garin's mind, interested by the mage's words. He didn't like to think of why.

Yet as much as he feared the Singer's influence, he feared never harnessing his magic more. It was nothing to do with his devil. As much as their travels had crushed his naivety, he still felt the same fire burning in him that his sister Lenora had once spoken of. His many whispered promises to the night, promises that he would earn his stars, still echoed faintly inside his chest, pulling him ever onward. No matter the danger or cost.

Tal has his demons, he thought. *If a man like that can make a name for himself, can't I?*

Aelyn watched him in silence, his gaze resembling a butcher deciding how to carve a carcass. Steeling himself, Garin nodded. "I want to learn magic. However we do it."

The mage's smile grew sharp. "Very well. Then we will try summoning werelight once more. Only this time, you must say the word '*fashk.*'"

Garin winced as the word whipped through his mind, burning like an afterimage of the sun. Ilvuan's claws, ever tenderly on his mind, deepened their grip, as if the Singer leaned closer to watch.

"Is that... the Darktongue?"

"Yes. It is what you've spoken before when you've cast magic, is it not?"

He'd almost forgotten his confessions in Kaleras' tower back in the Coral Castle, and couldn't help a sliver of regret at how much he'd revealed then. "Yes," he muttered.

Aelyn gave him a broad smile. "Well then, we must build on what foundation we have. Remember — articulate the word, all Four Roots attended to with rigorous attention. All the same principles apply."

Garin nodded and raised his hand once more. He tried pushing his doubts from his mind and dampening his awareness of Ilvuan's interest as he pictured the werelight hovering over his hand.

"*Fashk*," he said, his voice barely above a whisper, speaking the word like he was a child saying an adult's curse.

At once, he felt something move through him. Discordant noises surged in his ears, out of place and time. The protest of wooden stairs underfoot. The swish of a fishing line cast out. The light from the hearth distorted, and he blinked.

A ball of werelight hovered above his hand, the same pale yellow as Wren's had been.

Aelyn's smile widened, and his eyes swirled furiously. "Well, boy, you have it in you after all."

Garin stared at the light, studying the slow rotation and pulse of it. The Nightsong faded to a murmur. *I did it. Without any help.*

Ilvuan's amusement radiated down stronger. *Of course. Every Listener can.*

Garin ignored the Singer and willed the werelight to dissipate. It shredded into increasingly smaller threads of light until it disappeared.

The mage had stopped smiling and seemed lost in thought, his brow scrunched up in nearly a scowl. "I will think on this," he announced. "For now, do not attempt any castings on your own. There may be additional dangers for you."

"I'm not afraid," Garin said, and immediately wished he'd kept his mouth shut.

Aelyn gazed at him with scornful amusement. "No? Then you are as much a fool as your mentor. The Night is not a power to be trifled with."

"He's not my mentor."

Without a word of farewell, he strode to the door, jerked it open, then slammed it shut behind him.

I forget how much Listeners feel, Ilvuan opined lazily.

Even in his anger, Garin knew the best he could do was ignore the Singer. Already, his anger was turning into a wallowing despair. Not for the first time, he wished he could tell someone about the devil still haunting him.

But who? he thought miserably. He didn't want Wren to worry. He didn't want to disappoint Ashelia and admit he'd lied to her. Aelyn wasn't the type to confess to, and Garin was worried what he might do with that knowledge.

Despite himself, he knew whom he wanted to confide in. Tal had carried his fair share of demons, literal or not. He'd been possessed by one of the Extinguished and made to slaughter dozens of warlocks. If anyone might have counsel for a curse, it would be him.

If my blessing is a burden, it is not one you can share, Ilvuan spoke, reprimand plain in his words. *Some burdens are best borne alone.*

Garin hunched his shoulders and left the library, wishing it weren't true, knowing it had to be.

THE NOBLE TRAITOR

TAL STARED AT THE RUNES SWIMMING BEFORE HIS EYES AND murmured, "*Nyns kor.*"

At once, his vision blurred, and his stomach pitched like a ship in a storm. Fighting down the wave of nausea, Tal leaned closer to the book. As his face hovered within inches of the parchment, the tome came alive in ways it never had before.

He could see every flaw in the paper, every dust speck settled in the crease, every edge of the inked glyphs. Looking deeper, he could picture the pen that had written the book, then the hand attached to it, though the writer and their face fell into shadow beyond it. He turned his sight back to the pages and found they were not dead as he'd imagined, but swimming with things too small for the ordinary eye to see. Seeing the book writhe with unseen organisms gave him another bout of queasiness. They made it seem as if the tome itself had come alive.

Tal squeezed his eyes shut and drew in slow, deep breaths. But even with his eyes closed, he could see the back of his eyelids in excruciating detail. The gentle light emanating from the drawn curtains of his room and the lit hearth; the veins criss-crossing the skin in blue and red; even the particles forming the skin itself.

"Yuldor's prick," he groaned. "Which masochistic warlock invented this spell?"

A knock came at his door, and his eyes flew open. His blood, already burning with the magic, turned hotter still. Relaxing his focus, Tal dismissed the spell, and his vision resolved back to normal, the room reorienting itself.

The knock came again. "Quickly, Tal!" Falcon's strained voice came through.

Tal staggered over to the door and wrenched it open to see the bard standing amid the blue werelights of dusk. Falcon's hair was wind blown, his clothes ruffled, and sweat dripped down his face. He felt a prickle of misgiving at the base of his neck.

"What's happened?"

"No time," Falcon gasped between breaths. "The Highkin traitor, Tal — they're in the Mire now!"

He followed the thread to its logical conclusion. "Highkin have no business being in Low Elendol. They must be meeting with the Silver Vines."

"What'd you think they'd be doing? Follow me — or do you want to waste more time?"

"Just a moment."

He quickly gathered what necessities were within easy access. *Velori* belted at his hip. Boots pulled on. Travel leathers thrown over the simple tunic and trousers he'd been wearing, and a cloak over the rest. Hair bound back securely. At the door, Tal hesitated, ignoring Falcon's barbed comments about the time it took him to prepare. If there was trouble, it might be worth preparing a few catalysts for spells. But after a particularly ribald remark from the bard, he settled for stashing away a few small pouches. He always had cantrips, the minor spells he'd just been practicing, his sword, and the knives always hidden on his person.

"Finally," Falcon said as Tal emerged. "You take longer to primp than a princess before her bridal night."

"Or a bard before a show."

They shared a grin as they turned down the stairs, heading for the lift near the lowest rooms of the kintree.

"Now," Tal said, taking the stairs two at a time, "tell me what we know."

"Little enough," Falcon huffed, less used to exercise. "Rozana approached me in the Whistling Thistle and told me of the meeting. I didn't stay to ask questions, but ran to come fetch you. Do you know, but the lift operator wouldn't allow me up! I had to run all the way around to the main bridges."

Tal shook his head. "Probably didn't trust a half-elf."

Falcon shrugged, the movement awkward from their dash down the stairs. "He won't deny me passage with you around."

Though he wasn't certain of that, Tal nodded.

They passed the last of the Venaliel rooms, which served as storehouses, and reached the lifts. The lifts were typically used to transport goods, such as foods and furniture, up to the kintrees. Each kintree had its own set of lifts to be used at their Highkin's discretion. Tal just hoped that included allowing the passage of guests.

The lift operator had his legs crossed and propped up on a small desk, his head bent close to a book. As he noticed their approach, he closed the book slowly. Tal blinked. He wasn't sure if his vision was still fuzzy, or if he'd seen drawings of nudes in the elf's book.

"The Peer needs something dropped?" the lift operator asked, his voice dripping with contempt.

"Yes." Tal flashed him a smile. "Us."

He looked them both over and scowled. "I doubt that."

"Would you like us to bring her down here to inform you otherwise?"

The lift operator only stared stonily back.

"Please, good sir," Falcon interjected. "We're in a great hurry."

As he spoke, the bard produced a crystal marked with the Venaliel sigil, the same outline of a stor as was tattooed onto Helnor's face. The Venaliel glyph-seal — it was a rich gift by Ashelia, as it lent the power of her House to whoever bore it. Tal himself hadn't received one. He tried to push away the hurt of the slight.

But for all its import, the operator barely glanced at it. "Oh? And why should I be concerned about that, *kolfash?*"

Sudden anger rushed through Tal, but he reined it in and remained silent as Falcon spoke for himself.

The bard closed his fist around the glyph-seal. "Because if you don't take us down the lift, we'll turn you and your little book in. I don't suppose the Peer knows how you occupy your time, does she?"

The lift operator stood, his cheeks flushing. Tal noted that, like the Highkin, he wore a rapier at his hip, on which he now placed a hand.

"You'd threaten us?" Tal shook his head as if in wonder. "Lad, you have much to learn."

"Lad?" the elf hissed. "I'm far older than you, Aristhol!"

"So you know who I am. Then you also know that Peer Venaliel will hear of this unless you swiftly obey."

The lift operator held out a moment longer, then exhaled noisily. "Get on," he said gruffly.

They complied warily. The contraption was a system of ropes and pulleys, and Tal hadn't the faintest idea how it worked. He felt no easier as he stepped onto the platform and felt it shift underfoot. His only consolation was that the operator wouldn't be able to drop them without dropping himself, for the levers to make the machine function were on the lift itself.

As the lift operator stepped on, closed the gate behind him, and moved to his station, Tal asked in what he hoped was a conciliatory tone, "So, how does the lift work?"

The elf met his gaze with a blank stare. "Magic."

Tal half-smiled, unsure whether it was a jest. He accepted silence as the only explanation he'd receive and watched closely as the operator shifted levers. The lift began to descend. Tal fixed the levers' positions in his mind, but he still didn't know why any of it would make the machine operate.

Another thought distracted him. "This Highkin traitor — they used their lifts to descend, didn't they?" Tal muttered. "So they wouldn't be seen?"

Falcon nodded. "That was my guess."

He considered the implications as they sank below the lowest branches of the kintree. Low Elendol came into full view. They could see the entire stretch of the winding city between the roots of the great kintrees, thanks to the hovering werelights. But if anyone were watching them, they might see the lift descending.

Likely, that is how our Easterner friends detected the Highkin cultists, he thought. *Why wouldn't the Silver Vines be watching us as well?*

He pushed the unease from his mind. There was nothing he could do about it but to keep moving forward.

"Did you speak with the Queen about the Winter Ball?" Falcon asked him softly.

Tal winced. He didn't meet his friend's eyes. "I haven't had the chance."

For a long moment, the creaking of the lift replaced all conversation.

He finally looked over and saw uncharacteristic anger crossing Falcon's face. He looked away again.

"I'm sorry," Tal muttered. "I'll do it at the first opportunity."

"I told you what it meant to me."

"I know you did. It's just that I have little clout with Geminia as it is, Falcon. And I know it's been over a week since you asked, but I'm not lying — I *have* been busy. Scouting, training, practicing — the days go by quicker than I can track."

"We're risking our lives for you, Tal, seeking the information you requested!" Falcon hissed back. "Besides, would you have me disappoint the others? We've already begun practicing the play. No *Kingmakers and Queenslayers* for the Elf Queen — we're performing *The Fall of Narkeska*."

Tal stared at him, astonished. "Truly? Can you pull it off?"

"Of course," Falcon said grimly. "Perhaps you forget that we're the finest troupe in all the Westreach. All we need is the opportunity to remind everyone of it."

Guilt prodded deeper into him. "You're right. Tomorrow, I promise that I'll ask."

The bard nodded, but the hurt didn't leave his expression. Tal sighed, wishing he'd done as he'd pledged earlier — or even better, that he didn't have to ask at all. But, as his old commander in the army had always said, *When hoping for rain, wishing's no better than pissing.*

He'd make it right with his old friend, and that was that.

The ground grew nearer, as did the constant hum of the Mire. Even during the night, Low Elendol never slept. The cool tones of the werelights brightened near the forest floor. Tal was never so glad to smell the foul mud as when the platform settled against the ground with a jolt.

The lift operator opened the gate, and Tal donned a crooked smile. "Here," he said to the elf. "For your troubles."

He flipped a copper to the operator, intentionally shooting it short. The elf scowled and didn't bend to pick it up. Falcon openly grinned.

The night seemed to brighten as they hurried away from the Venaliel kintree and its sour servant.

The Whistling Thistle wasn't far, and soon Falcon was leading Tal through the door and into the bustling interior. Almost immediately, a familiar person was at their elbows and escorting them back outside, to the scowls of the guards by the door.

"You took your time," Rozana said, her irritation plain.

She acted very familiar toward him for someone he'd met only once before, so Tal resolved to return the courtesy. "Never mind that. What do you know?"

The Easterner gave him a flat look, though most minotaurs' expressions came out flat. "Little, but enough. House Heilinis' lift lowered earlier, and the elves who exited were not servants."

"You saw this yourself?"

She shook her head and gestured behind her. Following her sign, Tal nearly jumped when Yeshil emerged from the shadows, her yellow eyes glimmering in the low light.

"*I* saw them," she hissed softly.

Tal smoothed his face, hiding his alarm. "And could you identify them?"

"No. They were too far away."

"How do you know where they are if you're here?"

Yeshil gave that eerie smile of hers. "Pylas was with me, and he followed them. Old Man will lead us back to him."

Yet again, Tal found himself surprised as the sonku monkey swung down from a root to perch on the roof. He gave a quiet screech, his mane turning gold for a moment.

"Nice to see you, too," Tal muttered.

"If you want to catch your quarry, you must go now," Rozana advised.

Tal exchanged a look with Falcon. They'd barely known these Easterners for a week. Now, they were to follow them blindly into the night-shrouded Mire. Even with the Ilthasi tailing them, the thought didn't make him comfortable. And he noticed that the Nightelf wasn't the only one missing — the gnome, Temmy, wasn't around either. A suspicious man might wonder why.

But this is what you hired them for, he reminded himself. *And remember what happened with your own attempts to discover the*

Thorn.

Falcon looked even more frightened, but he gave a slight nod. And Tal knew if the bard was fool enough to go along with it, he certainly was.

"Lead the way, Old Man," Tal told the monkey.

Old Man set a punishing pace as he leaped from the rooftop of the inn to a nearby root, then more roofs and roots beyond. When Tal and Falcon tarried, trying not to shove past the crowds still thronging the streets, the sonku monkey would turn and shriek at them in a tone that left no room for interpretation as to his disapproval. Tal kept his smile plastered on. He'd once heard that for beasts like monkeys, baring one's teeth was seen as a threat, and hoped it was true. Yeshil had an easier time keeping pace, her thin, sinuous body easing her through gaps that wouldn't fit Falcon and Tal. He only kept sight of her by the colorful feathers rising off her head.

Low Elendol was as much alive at night as during the day, though its populace grew seedier as midnight drew nearer. Vendors harked their wares from carts, the scents of spices both Gladelysh and foreign filling the air. Other characters sold less savory goods, muttering as they approached Tal and Falcon's party, cloaks pulled tightly about their bodies to hide their wares. Streetwalkers did just the opposite, wearing barely enough fabric to call clothing as they called slurred invitations after them.

But there were other things to be wary of. More than once, Tal had to seize hands scrabbling about his belt, only just stopping himself from breaking the fingers before growling at the pickpocket to scram. In the alleyways off of the main street, fights and screaming proliferated.

His shoulders bunched tight about his neck.

"How much further?" he asked the medusal after they caught up. It had taken them nearly an hour to do so, and the crowds had thinned. The houses surrounding them had also grown shabbier, a sign that they neared the edge of the Mire.

This was dangerous territory, he'd learned from experience. Not even Elendol's city guard dared venture here after dark.

"We are nearly there." Yeshil watched Old Man as he leaped to the opposite side of the street, then scowled back at them. "Come. Best not keep our impatient friend waiting."

As he and Falcon followed, Tal risked a glance back and glimpsed a shadow slipping into an alley. He hoped his smile was warranted. With luck, it was the Ilthasi who followed them rather than someone more nefarious.

He loosened *Velori* in its scabbard as Old Man took them down a dark alley. Glancing back at Falcon, he saw the bard openly held a knife in hand, his eyes wide, the gold in his irises tangling into a hazy cloud as he watched warily about him. Tal tightened his jaw as he turned his eyes forward again. *The protection of many over the safety of one,* he told himself. It was one of the more serious mantras his soldiering days had taught him. Though noble in sentiment, he and his compatriots had rarely acted upon it.

Yeshil stopped ahead and held up a clawed hand. "Old Man has descended into the alley opposite us," she hissed.

Tal eased past her, sweat trickling down his back, to peer out of the alley onto the street beyond. He was all too aware how easily Yeshil could drive a knife into his gut if she felt so inclined, and how little he knew whether she might be liable to do so.

Confirming no one walked up or down the street, he led the way forward. As he crossed, he glimpsed a shadow slipping into an alley further down the road.

Silence, Solemnity, and Serenity, he thought, *if you're real, now's a damn good time to prove it.*

Ignoring their pursuer, he entered the alley beyond to see the silver-haired monkey perched on the shoulder of someone waiting within. Pylas watched them approach, his pink eyes seeming more threatening as they glimmered in the darkness.

For once, Old Man restrained his disgust with them to a stare of silent contempt.

"They have been meeting for half an hour now," the Nightelf reported softly as Tal and the others gathered around him. "From this distance, you cannot hear their conversation, but I dared not approach closer."

Tal hesitated at asking the question needling him, but time pressed harder. "You're a Nightelf. Couldn't you use sorcery to listen in?"

Old Man's mane grew gold once more as the monkey bristled, but Pylas held up a soothing hand. "I could, but it would not help. I long ago learned your common speech, but Gladelyshi is beyond my knowledge."

"Allow me, then." Tal navigated past him and peered over a pile of rotten lumber and other debris that had accumulated in the alley ahead. It rose nearly to his eyes, allowing him to approach undetected.

If he were an ignorant onlooker, he might have thought the meeting little more than a dealing between merchants, albeit one with uneven power dynamics. The Highkin, identifiable by the two guards flanking them, had their back to him, while the other cultist faced him.

But who are you? Tal squinted, hoping to make out a telling detail, but the conference was over fifty feet away. Without aid, he didn't stand a chance of seeing or hearing anything of significance at that distance.

But he knew exactly the spell for the job.

Tal turned back to his companions. "I'm going to try something, but I'll need everyone to remain as silent as they can."

The others nodded, while Old Man scowled. Tal smiled and turned back to the far-off scene.

Focus. Drawing in a steadying breath, he breathed out and said, softly but firmly, "*Nyns kas.*"

Just as with the spell cast in his room, the World blurred — only now his vision expanded. The details that eluded his ordinary sight became so sharp that he could see the stray, golden hairs peeking out from beneath the Highkin's hood, and the beads of sweat lining the brow of one of the guards. The woman who he assumed was the Silver Vines agent looked far too kindly to belong to the Cult of Yuldor, with lips that naturally curled up at the corners like a cat's smile, and a heart-shaped face uncommon among elves.

But seeing was not enough. Even as held his focus for the first spell, Tal split his mind and braced himself for the second. *"Sols kas."*

The transition was even more disorienting than the first. Except for the shuffling of his companions and the soft, disapproving grunts of Old Man, the Mire had been quiet. But as the spell expanded his hearing, it felt as if the World were suddenly trying to crawl into his ears, a multitude of noises competing for attention. The night was filled with sounds: the whispering of a mother to her child; the chopping of a knife against a wooden board; the distant shouts of two men arguing; the buzzing wings of insects. As he squeezed his eyes shut against the onslaught, some part of him sympathized with what Garin endured every time the Nightsong marched through his head.

Focus, he told himself again, and tugged his thoughts back to the task at hand. It wasn't only that time was short and their quarry so near. Even a moment of lapsed concentration might fragment his mind and leave him a drooling husk of a man.

As the melee filled his ears, Tal opened his eyes. His stomach turned at the distortion of his vision, but he narrowed his eyes and honed his mind to a sharp point, directing all his attention and magic toward the conversation ahead of him. Bit by bit, as if he pulled slivers from his skin, the noises faded, his focus winnowing the sorcery down so it only threaded ahead. Amid the falling quiet, the voices emerged, and he sorted out their words.

"...That it is, perhaps, dramatic?" the unidentified noble

said. It was a woman's voice, and not one he knew, though her annunciated speech confirmed her as Highkin.

"No, Peer. Only necessary," the Silver Vines agent replied. He was surprised to hear the Lowkin lilt in her voice, for she held herself as if they were equals.

"You'll start a war!" The Peer's voice raised for a moment, then she looked around, as if fearful of being overheard. Tal didn't move, trusting the night to hide him, and strained to make out her features. He still didn't recognize her. Her cheeks were high and hollow, her lips thin, and her eyes smoldered with silver.

The cultist seemed unfazed. "Our Lord will do what he must to save this land. You should not question that."

"You will address me with respect! You may have the trust of the Peacebringer for now, but you are nothing but a tool to him. *I* am irreplaceable. What you do down here means nothing without my support."

"And your support means nothing without Peer Lathniel's."

Tal's pulse quickened. *There it is — the chimera's final head.* There could be no greater indictment than to hear of the Lathnieli's guilt from one of the Silver Vines themselves. *If only they could be bothered to admit it before the Queen.*

The Peer took a step closer and held up a finger in the cultist's face, while her guards flanked her. "You are nothing," the noblewoman hissed, "*nothing* to speak to me that way!"

The Silver Vines agent didn't flinch, nor did her voice waver. "But you forget our Lord's lessons. We are all equal on the Path to Peace, Sister. All chains will be broken — even the ones you have draped over me and the people of Low Elendol."

Silence fell between them. Tal trembled with the exertion of maintaining both spells, but he didn't dare release them. His blood ran boiling hot through his veins. His skin felt clammy and cold. He walked along the edge of a precipice now, but he didn't back down.

"Of course, *Sister*. But some must inevitably die in their chains."

The cultist nodded slightly. "Some must. Do as you're commanded, and you may not be one of them. Gain us admittance to the Winter Ball, Peer Heilinis. Do not disappoint our Lord or my master."

"No doubt one of us will disappoint before this is over." Peer Heilinis turned and strode away, her guards tailing her.

Though he wanted to throw both off at once, Tal forced himself to release first the listening spell, then the farseeing one. He gasped as his senses returned to their usual dullness, then bent over double and closed his eyes to the alley spinning around him. His head pounded.

He felt a hand on his arm and knew he should be wary, but couldn't force himself to look up.

"Tal? Are you alright?" Falcon's voice was low and urgent. "I don't think we should delay any longer."

Tal didn't dare open his mouth, for his stomach pitched like a tree in high winds. He held up a hand, pleading for a moment.

Behind him, Old Man gave an annoyed grunt, and Pylas spoke in soothing tones. Yeshil made no noise. *Probably watching with that supercilious smile of hers,* he thought.

After several long moments, he felt well enough to stand again, even if his vision swam before his eyes.

"I'm fine," he forced out. "Give me a moment. I have something that should help."

Falcon kept hold of his arm as he rummaged in an interior pocket of his cloak, then drew out a small pouch. Opening it, a foul stench resembling urine greeted him. His gut gave another jerk.

The bard scrunched up his face as he peered into the pouch. "What is that?"

"*Gildoil* — or pissleaf, as some inventive soul once called it. It's an analgesic."

"So long as its name doesn't imply the method of application, take it quickly — it's rather increased my own pain."

Tal managed a sickly smile as he took a pinch of the green powder and arranged it on the back of his gloved hand, then hesitated.

"I should warn you," he said to Falcon, "*gildoil* has its drawbacks. I'll have lowered inhibitions and lack focus for hours afterward."

The bard frowned. "Are you sure you should take it then?"

"At this point, I have little choice."

Though Falcon didn't look convinced, Tal lowered his nose to the powder and inhaled sharply. It hit the inside of his head with stinging force. Even as he flinched at the overwhelming stench, the throbbing instantly diminished, and the pitching in his stomach abated.

Coming upright and relinquishing himself from Falcon's grip, he looked around to see the others watching him with a mixture of bemusement and disgust. Old Man seemed the most repulsed among them. Tal met their expressions with a grin.

"Right as rain now, I reckon. Shall we return?"

"Your voice," Falcon said softly, his voice tinged with panic. "You're speaking too loudly, Tal."

He barely restrained a laugh. *Yuldor's prick, when was the last time I felt this good?* His nose stank of urine, true, but he felt as if he could start dancing and never cease. It had been over a decade since he'd taken a pinch of *gildoil*. Now, he was wondering why he'd gone so long without it.

Falcon pulled his arm and led him down the alley. "Come on," his friend muttered. "And keep quiet."

"As you wish." Part of him realized his voice was probably louder than Falcon wanted, so he repeated in a whisper, "I'll be quiet."

The bard managed a small smile, but his eyes never stopped darting from side to side.

Tal's gaze wandered. The night truly was beautiful in Elendol. *Werelights hovering above like stars recovered from the Night,* he thought. *The trees are our great mothers, sheltering us like sleeping children under their protective arms.*

"Perhaps I missed my calling," he said to Falcon, lowering his voice halfway through the sentence as he remembered to keep quiet. "I think I should have stayed with the Dancing Feathers through the Red Years, Kaleras and his Circle be damned."

"How about we discuss it later?" Falcon suggested in a low voice.

Tal didn't see why they should, so he kept talking. "I think it would have made me happy, or as happy as a man like me can be. It would have been a damn sight better than becoming the Red Reaver and butchering men for sport."

"Tal. Leave it."

He tried to heed his friend's fear, but it was like trying to keep hold of a handful of sand. As he felt empathy slipping away, he abandoned all efforts toward it.

"When I was a boy, sitting on the hearth at my mother's feet and listening to her stories as she fletched by the firelight, I could dream of nothing but the adventures of those mythic men — Markus Bredley and the like. But you know what? They were probably as miserable as I was through every step of my journey. Dwarven mines are cold, dark places, filled with horrors beyond even Yuldor's imagination. I don't like to think of the traitorous deeds that the old treasure hunter had to perform to steal the dwarven treasure — if he didn't make the whole thing up."

"Tal," Falcon said through clenched teeth, "for the love of all you don't hold holy, shut up."

A glimmer of shame breaking through, Tal forced himself to silence. His gaze, however, still wandered over the street. Suddenly, the World felt too empty, and not only for his ceasing to speak. He pulled Falcon to a stop as he squinted around him, a realization slowly sinking in.

"What is it?" Falcon hissed with annoyance.

"The Ilthasi aren't following us," he said, dread seeping in through the haze of the *gildoil*.

A shriek sounded behind them — an animal's scream. Tal whirled and saw Old Man topple from a rooftop to thud to the street below. Pylas' wail rose in its place as he took several tottering steps toward the silver-haired monkey, then shrank back from the street ahead.

Velori was already drawn and in his hand by the time the silhouetted figure dropped from the rooftop. The fall was a dozen feet down, yet the man showed no hesitation as he stepped off and tucked into a roll, then sprang back to his feet. Tal's blood burned again, filling him with heat like he'd stepped into a long-burning forge. Yet even with sorcery filtering through him, his thoughts strayed, refusing to latch onto the danger before them for long, even with the Nightelf's pained pleas rising.

As the man stepped into the light, revealing a masked face, Tal stuck his free hand into his cloak and dug out a second pouch, then attempted to yank its ties free. "Falcon!" he hissed when he failed. "Help me get this open!"

The bard's eyes were wide as he reached forward, his hand-less wrist supporting the bag as his deft fingers loosened the strings. "Another powder?" he said, fear making his voice shrill.

"No choice. Help me take it!"

"*Yinshi?*" The bard became shriller still.

Ignoring Falcon's twitching, Tal worked his fingers inside the pouch and came up with a pinch of the crushed red leaf within.

In the corner of his vision, he saw the shrouded man close in on the Nightelf. Pylas threw up his hands, and fire blazed toward his assailant — but a moment later, his scream cut through the night.

Tal grimaced and lowered his gaze. It was too late for Pylas — but he could still save Falcon.

Dropping the bag, he put the pinch of herb on his tongue, worked it around his mouth, and swallowed. It would take a moment to settle in, but already, he felt as if his mind was settling to the task at hand, his thoughts whirling down a dozen direct paths.

"Run, Falcon." His voice sounded distant to his own ears. "Send help if you can. But don't you dare die here."

"Are you going to—?"

Tal roughly shoved away the bard, then stepped out from the shelter of the building to stand in the middle of the street. The masked figure waited, watching him. At his feet, both the body of the sonku monkey and its master were still. Pylas' dull eyes staring toward him left no doubt to his fate. Of his companion medusal, there was no sign.

Hoping to draw the assassin's attention to himself and away from his fleeing friend, Tal shouted, "What? Why not attack me? Don't want to try your hand at a man who will fight you back?"

The assassin didn't move for a moment, so still Tal might have not noticed him if he'd been casually passing in the street. The self-possession of the man grated on him, sharpening his fear. Confidence such as that could only be backed by skill. He held a bloody rapier loosely at his side and tucked the other hand inside his black jerkin.

The stranger moved, jerking his hidden hand free of his tunic so quickly Tal could barely follow it. The werelights gleamed on something metal.

The assassin positioned the knife between his fingers for a moment, then snapped his arm forward, and a blade whirled through the air — straight for Tal's chest.

AMONG THE ALLEYS

GARIN LEAPED TO HIS FEET AS WREN BURST INTO THE ROOM.

"Quick!" she said between breaths, her cheeks flushed and her eyes bright. "Come with me!"

He covertly pulled the blankets over the items on the bed. "What's got you in a tiff?"

Her gold whorled in a way that told him he walked a fine line. "Rozana found me. She says that Tal and Falcon went with two of their fellow Easterners to follow a Highkin in the Mire. They might be spying on the traitor right now!"

He slowly wrapped his mind around her words. "Alright — that's good then. But why are you in such a rush?"

She stared at him for a moment. Then her eyes wandered over the rumpled blankets. "What were you doing?"

"Nothing."

She was already striding toward him, gaze set on the bed. A childish impulse to stop her rose in him, but he forced his hands to remain by his sides as she wrenched the covers away and revealed what lay beneath.

Wren stared for a moment, her brow knitting. "*The Fundamentals of Sorcerous Bindings?* Doesn't Aelyn give us enough of that drivel?"

Irritation spiking through him, Garin reached over and closed the book. "Sorcery doesn't come to all of us so easily."

At least not the right kind, he amended in his head.

Her expression shifted, and he quickly turned away, putting the book back inside the drawer beside the bed.

Wren's next words were gentler. "Never mind; that doesn't matter. What *does* matter is that we need to follow Father and the others."

"Follow them? Why in Yuldor's black name would we follow them? We'll only get in their way."

Though he believed that to be true, it wasn't the real reason he didn't want to go. *I'm helping that bastard enough. No need to stick my neck out further for him.*

Wren stared at him in disbelief. "What's wrong with you? How can you not want to know?"

He stood. "I do want to know — but this isn't a game, Wren. It's dangerous to wander the streets at night, especially down here. Tal can take care of himself. He doesn't need our help."

"Dangerous?" Her eyes narrowed in disgust as she turned away. "Fine. Stay here."

She kneeled to retrieve something from her possessions next to the bed — her sword.

"You're still going?"

"Yes, I am!" she shot back over her shoulder. "I'm not a coward like you, Garin. If there's something I can do to help, no matter how small, I'll do it. I won't just bury my head in the dirt and say it's too big for me."

It is too big for you, and for me. He wanted to say the words aloud, but her accusation stung him to silence. He'd always wondered if he was a coward; now, he realized that she'd always wondered, too.

Tightening his jaw, he bent and began pulling on his boots.

"Oh, *now* you come," she said acidly.

"If you're foolish enough to go, I have to." Locating his sword, he belted it on along with a knife, ignoring the foolishness he felt at arming himself. How proficient was he, really, at either weapon?

You are never unarmed, Ilvuan suddenly spoke in his mind.

Garin repressed the shiver that often came with the devil's unannounced arrival. *Not now,* he thought back with irritation.

Wren had said something and seemed to wait for an answer. When he gave none, she exhaled noisily, turned on her heels, and strode from the room.

Ilvuan's amusement drifted through his mind.

Pulling on his cloak, he followed Wren out, walking down the hall and stairs to enter the bustling room below. Cringing at the din, he scanned the room until he found Wren standing next to Rozana. The full extent of the minotaur's bulk was now apparent, particularly with her gnome companion, Temmy, next to her, who watched Garin's approach with wide eyes.

Pushing through the Thistle's patrons, he caught the end of Rozana's words. "—A half-hour ago."

"A half-hour?" Wren's brow furrowed. "We might still catch them."

Rozana seemed to frown, though it was hard to tell on her bovine face. "You might. If we knew where they'd gone."

"You don't know?"

Rozana shook her horned head slowly.

"And there's no way to find out?"

The minotaur shrugged and glanced down at the gnome. Wren followed her gaze. "Do you have a way?" she asked Temmy.

The gnome cringed as Wren addressed her. "I don't know where Old Man took them. But if I cast a seeking spell..."

Rozana shook her head again. "Too great a risk." She looked back up at them. "Gnome magic is different from elven. Every spell comes at a cost. A seeking spell might be beyond her."

Wren looked ready to argue again when Ilvuan spoke again.

I will lead you. The Singer sounded resigned.

How do you know where to go?

A glimmer of amusement. *You have barely glimpsed what I am, little Listener. I know.*

"I can lead us," he interrupted Wren's protests.

All three of them looked around at him.

"You can?" Wren asked incredulously. "How?"

"No time to explain — you'll just have to trust me."

She hesitated for a long moment, then nodded.

Rozana exchanged a look with Temmy before looking back at Garin. "We'll go with you."

Distrust stirred in his gut. How much did they really know about these Easterners? They'd acted as their informants for the past week, but he didn't know who they were or what motivated them. But short of breaking ties, he wasn't sure how to turn them down.

Wren answered for them, nodding and striding toward the door. "Come on!" she called over the clamor of the commonroom.

Hurrying after her, they walked out into the cool night of the Mire. At the bottom of the stair-like roots, she turned, and the others faced him.

"Which way?" she asked, her flat tone betraying what she thought of his guidance.

Garin hesitated. *You got me into this,* he thought to the Singer. *Don't let me flounder now.*

He lies to the northeast.

That's it?

The warmth of irritation accompanied the glow of amusement. *I can sense where he is, not the paths to reach him.*

He chewed his bottom lip for a moment as he studied the streets. He'd oriented himself to the cardinal points when they'd first reached Elendol, so he knew the direction at least. *But which streets must I take?* he thought desperately.

"You don't know, do you?" Wren's annoyance simmered over a deeper anger.

"He's to the northeast." He spoke with as much confidence as he could muster.

Wren frowned, while Rozana stared at him, her expression lost within her foreign features. "I can lead us northeast," the minotaur said.

Having no better plan, Garin nodded.

They followed Rozana as she led them through the ever-thinning crowds. Garin's shoulders rose toward his ears, and his hand strayed to his sword. He'd had over half a dozen dancing lessons now with Master Ulen, but they'd only just touched upon actually using a sword. Most of it was about movement and often used metaphors of the elements. He was to sway like fire and react like water; be firm like earth, but light like wind. It was fine in principle, but Garin found it harder to move "light like air" when his muscles were aching and iron-heavy.

Still, as they progressed through the Mire, he felt the changes that had worked their way into his body. The way he composed himself was different, holding his weight ready to face any direction at a moment's notice. His feet were light and didn't plant into the ground as they once had. He was alert, and even if his habitual layer of anxiety simmered beneath the surface, he was confident in how he'd react.

Now I just need to know how to wield a sword like a Dancer, and I might actually be a threat.

Ilvuan interrupted his thoughts. *Enough — you must concentrate on your surroundings now. Travel east. You are not far.*

Garin shivered. He doubted he'd ever grow used to the devil speaking to his thoughts. He wondered if he could ever hide from him.

The spark of amusement told him otherwise.

"We need to orient toward the east," he told Rozana. "They're close."

The minotaur nodded and turned down an alleyway. It stank even worse than the rest of Low Elendol did, excrement and waste adding to the perfume. Garin studiously ignored Wren's continued stare. He'd resolved to come clean to her, but it would have to wait until later.

If we make it out of here alive, he thought morosely.

"Stop there!"

Garin whirled around at the shout, heart hammering, and instinctively began to draw his sword. A male Nightelf walked toward them down the alley. He was slight, but tall, and wore a confident sneer. In his hand, he held a bared rapier such as a Highkin might wear, which Garin guessed he must have stolen.

Garin pulled his sword free of its scabbard as chuckles sounded from all around them. He risked a glimpse behind them to see three Nightelf youths approaching from the alley entrance. When he looked forward, two more had materialized. All had a similarly thin stature and carried a weapon of some sort, some stolen, others shoddily manufactured.

"Let us walk free!" Wren snarled at the one who had first spoken.

The Nightelf youth laughed, the sound sharp with bitterness. "Shouldn't have walked here," he said, as if they might have known better.

Rozana stepped forward. Though shorter than the Nightelves, her considerable bulk and calmness drew every eye.

"I am Rozana of Haudden," she said calmly. "You have heard of me."

The Nightelf flinched, but covered it with a sneer. "You're lying."

"You know I am not."

"What of it?" one of the other Easterners said. "Much good you did! Your entire herd massacred, and what did we gain from it? We're still exiled!"

Rozana bowed her head. "Perhaps it made little difference. But I did what I could."

Though Temmy looked as if her heart would stop, she took a step forward and piped up, "She saved you. All of you!"

The two who had spoken remained defiant, but the other Nightelves exchanged glances. Garin wondered what Rozana had done, and who she truly was. But most desperately of all, he wondered if she could save them now.

"Doesn't matter," the first youth said. His voice was slightly husky, but his eyes were hard. "Look what you got us now! No food, no home, no family. Now we have to take what we need." He held up the stolen rapier. "Starting with you."

Rozana bowed her head. "Do as you must."

Garin gritted his teeth. It was the wrong answer. He subtly shifted into a balanced, but firm, position — the Form of Stone.

The Nightelves lifted their weapons and closed in.

Tal dodged the knife, but he couldn't turn out of the way of the slash that followed.

Twisting *Velori* around, he caught the assassin's rapier with a glancing blow, but it nicked his side. Hissing with pain, he used the longer reach of his bastard sword to keep the assassin at bay as he danced away.

The man was quick. His dark eyes, visible through the mask, spun with a silvery-blue light, marking him as an elf. The assassin gave him a moment, stalking carefully around him like one of the large cats said to roam the southern jungles of Gladelyl. He'd taken Tal's measure and didn't seem the least bit threatened.

But I always did enjoy enemies underestimating me.

Lips spreading in a grin, Tal edged forward, feinted, and dodged to the left. The assassin didn't take the bait, but carefully kept him just within striking distance.

"Come, friend." The last word came out sharply as the

shallow wound in his side throbbed. "I'm sure we can sort this out another way."

Still, the assassin didn't attack. A moment later, Tal realized why. *Poison.* As any good assassin would, he'd treated his blade. But with what? A paralytic? Or something worse?

With time pressing ever shorter, Tal lifted his hand and muttered, "*Mord.*"

The street fell into blackness.

Tal crouched and, hunched over, scurried toward the edge of the dark orb he'd summoned. Uneven cobblestones endeavored to trip him, and he cursed silently at the noise of the pebbles under his boots. But remaining still wasn't a strategy he could afford.

Repositioned, Tal rose and lifted the darkness, then quickly took in the scene. The gloom of night-shrouded Elendol seemed bright as the spell dissipated, and so the assassin stood out starkly, his back to Tal. But no sooner had Tal seen him than the assassin pivoted and saw him. He charged, savagely stabbing toward him. *Velori* curved around the blade, pushing it away, and Tal spun closer to hack at the back of his opponent's knees. Too slow — the assassin leaped out of the way in an impossible dodge.

He's more skilled than me. Once, Tal had been declared the best duelist in the Westreach. Unfortunately, it had been an unscrupulous bard who had deemed it so.

But he hadn't survived all his trials by giving up on long odds.

Flicking a knife into his hand, Tal aimed and threw it forward. The assassin instantly reacted, flicking his blade around and bending to one side, and Tal watched in disbelief as he parried his dagger midair. He'd seen men try such a move often on Avendor's training grounds for sport, but most had failed, and no one had succeeded consistently. But his adversary had managed to. Every move of his looked intentional. It hadn't been an accident.

The assassin rushed forward, quicker than blinking.

"*Fuln!*" Tal cried, spinning away from the flash of light and only opening his eyes after he'd dismissed it. If it had blinded the assassin, though, he quickly recovered. His earlier tactic of waiting abandoned, the elf slashed at him twice in quick succession, and Tal managed to block and dodge the blows.

But he couldn't avoid the third.

It caught Tal in the leg, and his weight collapsed under the injury. Tal turned it into an awkward roll, but as he tried to gain his feet, he found his leg uncooperative and weak.

"Damn," he breathed as he blinked through the pain. "Damn."

The assassin slowed again, taking his measure, or perhaps waiting for Tal to bleed out. The last possibility, at least, was unlikely for the moment. The wound was deep, but it had avoided the major arteries in his thigh. *The gods are not that fickle, at least,* he thought with a pained smile.

He couldn't beat him. Even as the *yinshi* ravaged his mind with a near-fanatical desire to overcome the man before him, he knew it was a drug-born delusion. His only hope was to escape.

But with the deep cut to his leg, he doubted he'd be winning any races.

Why brandish your sword? Ilvuan seemed both amused and scornful. *Magic is deadlier than metal claws.*

I can't use magic!

You attempted it earlier.

Garin didn't respond, for the Nightelves were within a dozen feet of them now. His heart hammered in his chest. Rozana made no move to protect herself, only stood with her arms crossed and a placid expression on her elongated face. Temmy trembled by Rozana's side. Wren backed up to him, and he had a feeling they were the only two who would fight for all of their lives.

He couldn't let her die.

A thought came back to him, a memory from the beginning of their journey. Tal, when he'd still gone by Bran, had turned away the bandits without harming anyone through a few tricks of sorcery. Perhaps Garin could do the same.

Is there a spell that could drive them away? Garin thought desperately to Ilvuan.

The Singer's presence hummed for a moment, as if thinking. *Yes.*

Will you tell me?

The warmth of approval radiated through him, dampening his fear even as the Nightelves neared. *Speak the words:* Keld vorv alak.

And what do I imagine?

The Song knows.

There was no more time. The Nightelves rushed forward, weapons held aloft. Even as Garin made to parry and dodge, he cried, "*Keld vorv alak!*"

The Nightsong burst into his head, a discordant melody streaming through him. He felt torn from his body for a moment. As if from a distance, he saw the Nightelf before him stumble to a halt, his eyes wide as he stared at his hands. Smoke rose from his skin.

The youth erupted into flames.

The other Nightelves scattered, but not soon enough. As the youth wreathed in fire screamed and flailed, he ran down the alley past Garin and the others and came close enough to one of his companions for the fire to catch him. The second Nightelf went up in flames as quickly as the first.

As if it were some demonic chasing game, the second blazing Nightelf ran after the others fleeing before him. But a third Easterner was too slow and was caught by the consuming flames.

Garin pulled Wren back, sickened by what he'd done, while Ilvuan's approval hummed as a harmony to the Nightsong that continued to pour through Garin's mind.

Well cast, little Listener.

He could only stare dumbly as their assailants fled or fell to the ground, the fire eating away too much flesh for the Nightelves to keep going.

I'm a monster, he thought. Ilvuan didn't bother to reply.

Rozana and Temmy stared at him. Wren pulled away from his grasp and looked at him as if he was a stranger. Her lips moved, but no words came out.

"Our sorcerous tongue," Rozana said slowly. "That is what he spoke, was it not, Temmy?"

The gnome, trembling so much that speech had been robbed from her, nodded three times. Her eyes never left Garin.

"Come on," he said, his words deadened by the Nightsong still marching victoriously through his head. "We still have to find the others."

Walking forward on heavy feet, he led them on.

As the assassin paced around him, a wolf waiting for its prey to fall, Tal tried to stay upright and sort through the spells at his disposal. His cantrips had been of little use. Perhaps the assassin was skilled enough that they could not hamper him, or maybe he wielded his own sorcery in protection.

Tal's grin stretched like a hide over a tanning frame as his enemy stalked him. As he sought for an option, any option, he cursed himself for not gathering catalysts before leaving his room. What he could have done with *yethkeld!*

But he'd been through enough fights to know wishing was likely to get you steel in the gut and little more. He had one choice, even if it wasn't much of a choice at all.

"*Mord,*" he whispered, and darkness fell around him again. As soon as his vision disappeared, Tal turned and limped the other way, mumbling, "*Fisk kord ferd,*" as he went.

Nothing changed to his own ears with the second spell, but he knew that outside a range of ten paces, all sounds would be silenced, like a smaller form of the Mute monks' Quietude. As he held both the darkness and circle of silence in place, he felt his mind pulling in two directions. But between the *yinshi* and the *gildoil*, the strain remained just manageable.

He stepped out of the orb of darkness and found himself once again exposed. Glancing around quickly, he didn't see the assassin waiting for him and continued limping forward as fast as he could. Blood poured down his leg despite the hand he held to it, but he knew it was the least of his concerns.

The cramps settled in as he reached the entrance to the alley. *A paralytic, then*, he thought, and was relieved marginally. Gasping, he tried to quiet his panicked breaths as he turned into it, and with an effort almost beyond him, he released the spells from his *yinshi*-obsession.

Time ran short now. His legs had already become numb and foreign, like he walked on two wooden pegs. He sheathed *Velori* before his trembling hand could accidentally drop it. His muscles seized, but he forced them to keep moving. He only hoped to hide long enough that Falcon could bring back help.

He didn't fool himself into thinking it would arrive in time.

A stray root tripped him, and Tal fell to the alley floor. The fall didn't hurt; his body was too numb to feel it. He forced his arms, little more use to him now than a marionette's, to reach forward and drag him across the mud, inch by inch. The assassin was coming. He had to hide.

But his neck had lost its strength. His face fell half into the mud. His breathing became labored as the muck smothered him. He struggled to keep an eye open, but even that required too much effort.

Falcon, he thought in vain. *Ashelia. Aelyn. Garin. Someone, please. Anyone.*

But no one could hear him. No one was coming.

Tal clung to consciousness for a moment longer before his grip slipped, and he fell far away.

BARROWS

He fades.

An uncharacteristic agitation tinged Ilvuan's thought as he spoke in Garin's mind.

Garin tried to pay attention to the Singer's words. His every sense was filled with what he'd done. The smoke. The heat of the flames. The dying shrieks.

His stomach wrenched.

You will soon lose him, the devil insisted.

He didn't have to ask whom he meant. *Then tell me where he is.*

All he received back was a mental tug in the same general direction as they'd been walking.

"I think Tal's in trouble," Garin said. Though he was already breathing hard, he pushed their pace faster, as if he could outrun the memories circling through his head.

"What?" Wren demanded, though she kept her voice soft. "How do you know?"

"Trust me. We have to hurry."

To his surprise, she followed. Somehow, even after all she'd seen, he kept some measure of her trust.

They emerged from the alley onto a wider road. Garin took

them down another side street. The stench of burning meat still coated the inside of his nose, nauseating him, but he fought his sickness down and kept up their pace.

Though he hadn't used it before, his sword was still in hand. A glance back showed Wren still carried hers. Rozana's face was as expressionless as ever, while Temmy's was pitted with worried wrinkles. Garin set his jaw and kept his anger in check. He wondered if it had been a setup and the informants had been in league with the Nightelves. If they had been, he didn't like their chances of surviving the night.

Ilvuan tugged again in his mind, this time to the left. Garin wondered if Tal had moved or if their path had veered off course. They didn't have time to spare, if the Singer's concern was any sign.

No time to wonder why a devil would care about Tal Harrenfel.

He emerged onto a street and stopped. The Mire was gloomy at night, but he could still see that, huddled next to an alley entrance, lay two bodies — one large, one small. He could barely breathe around the lump in his throat as he stared at them, unmoving.

Wren muttered something as she came up next to him. At the sight of the bodies, she brought up her sword and glanced around. Seeing no one, her gaze came to rest on the shadows again. "Are they dead?"

Garin, having no answer, edged forward.

As they came to stand over the bodies, he flinched, expecting someone or something to descend from the rooftops or hanging roots above them. Wren, meanwhile, kneeled next to them, holding a hand out as she looked them over.

"A Nightelf and a monkey," she said flatly as she rose. "Dead, if their wounds say anything."

"Pylas!" Tears ran down Temmy's face as she fell next to the Nightelf's body, her limbs shaking. "Pylas, g-get up!"

"Temmy," Rozana murmured, her big hands resting on the gnome's small shoulders. "He's gone. Old Man, too."

Temmy folded in on herself, an impossibly tiny ball. Garin looked away, his teeth clenched. *The killer could still be here,* he reminded himself, and looked around to be sure no one approached.

But despite the situation weighing on him, he couldn't help but ask, "You knew him?"

Rozana nodded slowly. "He was one of us. And he was leading your friends to the traitor's meeting."

Garin repressed a shiver as he looked around with renewed unease. "I'm sorry," he muttered. He wondered if his old mentor was still alive, and where he'd gone if he was.

He wondered if Tal had killed the two at his feet.

Wren touched his arm. "We have to keep going. Father and Tal are still out there."

"Right." Garin looked back at Rozana. "Will you stay with him? With… Pylas?"

The minotaur nodded again. "It is the least we can do for him now."

His gut tightened further, but he only nodded. *Only two of us now, a man and woman barely grown,* he thought numbly.

And a devil. Ilvuan's thought rolled lazily through his mind, like a cat uncurling.

Ignoring the Singer, Garin cast one last look back at the mourning Easterners, then continued down the street, Wren by his side. *Where are you, Tal Harrenfel?* he thought. *And what have you roped Wren's father into now?*

He was drunk, but far less than he wanted to be.

Gerald Barrows grinned as he leaned back in his chair, but there was no humor behind it. Smiling was like drinking ale to him — sometimes pleasant, sometimes not, but always a necessity.

The few others in the backwater tavern studiously ignored him. Those who hadn't been on the receiving end of that smile knew what lay behind it and wanted no part of it.

Wise, Barrows thought, then realized he'd spoken the thought aloud. He barked a laugh and ignored the subtle glance from the bartender.

The door to the tavern banged open. Like a sail's line had been pulled taut, his awareness sharpened. His blood surged through him, churning like a river in a narrow channel, and he grew warm with anticipation.

The smile returned as he watched the men charge into the commonroom and surround him, weapons held at the ready. His hand went to the sword's hilt at his side, ever waiting to be drawn, to hum the song of blood and glory.

He'd been waiting a long time for this.

No.

He twitched, and the scene distorted for a moment. Hostility was plain on all the faces looking down at him — all except the last man to enter. When his gaze fell upon the captain's face, he was suddenly no longer Barrows, no longer the monster who wanted to butcher other men to slay his own demons. He was someone else.

I am Tal, he thought. *Not Brannen Cairn. Not Gerald Barrows. I'm Tal Harrenfel.*

He clung to the thought as he stared through the greasy locks of his unkempt hair at Jindol Dunford, captain to His Majesty King Aldric Rexall the Fourth. The man whose king had commanded him to seek Gerald Barrows, more commonly known as the Red Reaver.

His childhood friend, come to capture or kill him.

I don't want to see this. I don't want to do this again. He couldn't tell if he was in control or not. The hatred that he'd shed with the identity Gerald Barrows still burned inside him. His hand clenched *Velori's* hilt, and his eyes scanned the scene, taking the measure of the disguised soldiers surrounding him.

He already knew how this would play out. It had already happened.

He forced his lips to move. "I'm not Gerald Barrows."

Jin looked down at him. He wore the same stricken expression he had in his memories, torn between duty to his King and obligations to an old friend. In those early years in Hunt's Hollow, Jin had been his only ally. And though he hadn't always stood up for Tal when they called him "whore's get" and "demon's bastard," he'd always been there afterward to bind the cuts and tend the bruises. He'd been as good of a friend as he could have been.

A far better friend than Tal ended up.

"No," Jin said, but his voice sounded different from how Tal remembered it. "You are not Gerald Barrows. Not anymore."

Tal forced his eyes shut. His heart still pounded with the danger surrounding him, but he kept them closed. "This is another one of those dreams. The twisted memories. And you're the puppet master."

"Yes."

"Why? Why I am reliving this?"

His voice cracked, and he swallowed hard as he opened his eyes again. His old friend's face was blurry through sudden tears, but he could tell his expression had shifted. All of his indecision had smoothed away like the surface of an undisturbed pool.

"As before, this is a moment that shaped your life, just as the wind and water shapes the stone. Just as you have and will shape the Mother's World."

"This?" Tal laughed, low and hollow. "Listening to stories while shivering in the winter and seeing my mother waste away before me? Those aren't the high moments of my life. Haven't you heard my legend?"

"I did not say triumphant moments. Only the important ones."

Tal stood, shifting the stool back. Even as the surrounding soldiers grew tight with caution, he ignored them, but stared at the creature who wore the face of the friend he'd betrayed. "What is it to you? Who are you, and why are you here?"

Jin didn't smile nor scowl. He might have been made of stone for all he reacted. "I am one who came before, and one who comes after. I am familiar and foreign. I am a servant and a master."

"You're a riddler and a pompous ass."

If his insults roused the creature, Jin's face didn't show it. "You come here, again and again, as if you seek death's escape. But you will not find it yet."

Tal swayed. At the prompting, memories of falling in the alley, of crawling, of growing still, flooded through his mind.

He chuckled mirthlessly. "My memories say otherwise."

Jin raised his hand. "You come here for solace, for your final resting. But death is not your fate, Thalkunaras."

He didn't ask how the creature knew his Heartname. *More likely than not, I'm imagining this as I drift off to the final sleep,* he thought. *No Quiet Havens for Tal Harrenfel. Just a collection of ugly memories.*

He stepped around the table, coming so near to one of the soldiers his shoulder brushed against the edge of his axe. But the soldier didn't strike.

"No?" he taunted as he stood just a few feet before Jin. "What's keeping me from dying? Destiny? A fable about Founts formed by a mythical, sorcerous heart?"

Flecks of spit had leaped from Tal's lips, but Jin didn't flinch.

"No," Jin said slowly. "Destiny, for good or for ill, has been broken throughout the long, dark ages. No, Thalkunaras. It is the sliver of the Heartstone within you, the same that has cursed you all these years, that protects you now."

"A sliver of Heartstone?"

Jin's hand pointed to his side. "From a wound you took long ago. One that never healed."

His thoughts tumbled about as if a storm had blown in. *The devil wants to confuse you,* he thought, pushing half-formed ideas away. *And everyone knows you shouldn't listen to a devil.*

"Just as it has dulled your connection to the Motherblood," the demon continued, "so it has protected you from foreign influence."

Tal forced a sneer. "You think I'll believe that?"

"Believe what you will. Soon, you will wake and see the truth."

"I doubt that. But even if I do, it proves nothing."

The first hint of an expression showed, little more than the twitch of Jin's eyebrow. "Remove it. Then we will see."

Tal took a step forward, his hand grinding into *Velori's* hilt. But the ground lurched beneath him, pitching him to one side as the tavern dimmed and swirled into mist around him.

"Wake, Thalkunaras. The poison is lifting."

Tal opened his eyes.

The ground was moving beneath him — or he was moving over it. Something had grabbed hold of him and was dragging him through the mud. At first, he thought a jungle cat had seized him and brought him back to its den. But even as reason banished the thought, he held himself still. Best to play dead until he knew what manner of creature had hold of him.

Rolling his eyes around, he recognized the silhouette of a man against the gloomy werelights hovering above.

The assassin. Fear surged through him. The assassin had found him. And now, instead of killing him, he was bringing him... somewhere.

Tal's groggy mind tried to sort through it. *He wants to capture me, not kill me. He believes the soporific still affects me.* He tried not to wonder if it truly had lifted. He hadn't attempted to move, and wouldn't unless he had a death wish. Only long hours spent pretending to be unconscious on the stage, enforced by a merciless Falcon, restrained him from twitching.

The assassin's face was upturned, not looking down at him as he pulled him along. Tal could see from the line of the rooftops they were nearing the end of an alley. Whether it was the alley he had fallen in or another, he couldn't say.

One chance. That was it — one strike to even the vast odds. He didn't have much hope for it. Yet he rehearsed the movement in his mind, again and again, while keeping his body carefully limp. *Grab the knife, stab, speak... grab the knife, stab, speak...* A simple sequence lasting less than a second, but one on which his life balanced.

Tal made his move.

His hand darted to his side, seizing the knife, and his arm twisted up and forward as he cried out, "*Kald!*"

As the burning knife entered his flesh, the assassin released him at once, leaping away and dragging Tal's dagger free from his hand as he staggered back. A scream escaped the elf's pressed lips as the flames licked up his leg.

A smile worked free from Tal as he stood upright, drew *Velori*, and limped forward.

The assassin, after a panicked moment, thrust a hand down at this leg and hissed out a word. The flames that had licked up his body died down, then disappeared in a vapor of smoke.

Tal didn't wait for him to recover, but lunged at his exposed side. A clumsy move — the assassin, even preoccupied with the burns up his leg, easily turned it aside.

But Tal hadn't been hoping to hit the lunge. Turning with the parry, he moved around the assassin, barely refrained from falling as weight went on his bad leg, and pivoted around to strike at his back — a strike that couldn't miss.

Yet it did. With impossible acrobatics, the assassin snapped forward into a half-roll that put no weight on his injured leg, then stood up again, sword at the ready. But he made no advance.

Tal breathed in deeply and tried to blink away the stars in his vision. He'd gained his footing, but he was far from fighting-ready. The stench of pissleaf lingered in his nose, and the bitter taste of *yinshi* sat on his tongue. His muscles spasmed and twitched as they struggled to throw off the vestiges of the paralytic. His head throbbed, and pains announced themselves across his body despite the dulling properties of the influencer.

Yet he'd be damned if he let any of it put him in the mud.

Still, he didn't know what move to make next. The assassin seemed as much at a loss. *Perhaps we're both waiting for aid,* he thought grimly. He hoped Falcon hadn't been waylaid. If he somehow survived this, he couldn't stand the thought that he'd put his friend to yet greater harm. He could see the sky-blue swirl of the assassin's eyes, calm in his contemplation. *The gaze of a hunter,* he realized. *He doesn't wait in fear. He's taking my measure.*

He feared the assassin wouldn't see much. Which meant it was time for a different tactic.

"Neither of us has to end here," he called across the space between them. "You need to take me in alive. Leave, and you can fight me another day. What do you say, my bastard of a friend?"

The assassin didn't speak, but only continued to watch. Tal didn't bother trying again. He was too well-acquainted with Aelyn to know a lost cause when he saw one.

He backed down the street, his sword held before him, trying hard not to fall every time he put weight on his injured leg. Despite his hopes otherwise, the assassin trailed slowly after him, keeping pace, but not closing the distance. Tal clenched his teeth into a smile, trying to exude the confidence he so sorely lacked at that moment. His mind whirled through empty possibilities. None were even remotely feasible.

Then the assassin froze and turned. A moment later, Tal understood why. Footsteps, running footsteps, sounded closer with each moment.

His pulse fluttering in his throat, Tal edged his eyes toward the alleyway they'd emerged from, now situated behind the assassin. The assassin was edging away, backing toward the opposite buildings. Tal took his opportunity and limped away faster. *Are they your friends or mine?* he wondered, eyes straining to see the oncoming figures.

Two lithe people, one as tall as an elf, the other half a foot shorter, emerged, their weapons glinting in the dim werelights. Squinting, Tal's hopes lifted even as his stomach sunk with recognition. He stopped backing away, but instead shuffled forward again.

"Tal!" Wren recognized him, but her eyes were hard as they slid from him to the assassin. "Where's my father?"

He didn't like the implications of the question. "I thought he fetched you. Though why he'd have sent you two—"

"We came on our own," Garin interrupted. The youth didn't look at him as he spoke, but at the assassin rapidly backing away. Even the two youths seemed to outweigh the odds for him.

"Did he do this to you?" Wren demanded as she watched the assassin escape.

"Yes. But let him go — even injured, he's far too dangerous for you to try."

"Too dangerous for you, too, old man." She approached him and looked him over critically before stepping up next to him and wrapping an arm around his waist.

Tal winced. "Watch the ribs. The cut's shallow, but enough to sting."

She shifted her grip and grabbed ahold of his belt. Awkwardly, he allowed her, knowing that, no matter his shame, he'd probably need the assistance before long.

Garin watched the assassin until he disappeared down the street, then turned to them. His eyes were oddly flat as he watched them walk forward. Wren's help was dubious for the first few steps, but it grew easier as they found a rhythm.

"So you're alive," the lad muttered as they came to stand before him.

Tal gave a weak smile. No matter Garin's distance toward him, he'd come. Even if it was for Falcon, he was grateful that he didn't spite him now. "So far. But let's worry more about my companions. I think one of the Easterners I was with fell."

"The Nightelf with the monkey? We saw them on our way over." Wren frowned toward the alleyway. "I suppose we should check on them before heading back."

"No sign of the medusal?"

Garin had turned to the alley entrance, but said over his shoulder, "They'd be hard to miss, wouldn't they?"

Tal tried to ease his worry as they turned into the alley. *It doesn't mean she's a traitor. Perhaps she just fled.* He knew he would have in her position. Yet he couldn't help a creeping suspicion. He didn't like to think what Yeshil's betrayal might mean for Falcon. If she showed her sharp smile again, he'd have more than words ready for her.

"Thank you," he said when they were halfway through the alley. "Part of me wishes you hadn't been so foolish as to come. But mostly, I'm grateful you did."

"Don't be grateful yet," Wren warned. "If we don't find my father soon, you'll be a lot more regretful."

"I'd expect nothing less."

"Less talk," Garin said from ahead. "We're not safe yet."

Tal couldn't quite repress his smile. No matter the hesitancies the boy had shown in the past, he couldn't deny there was iron in him.

But at what cost? he wondered as he limped through the night.

PASSAGE III

THE HEART SEEKS A NEW MASTER.

This is the premise I began my treatise with and that threatens my life and soul. Though I am convinced of its likelihood, the evidence for my assertion remains elusive.

For one, I am uncertain there is any sentience to the Heart. Though all assume the World is alive in some respect, few believe it is in the way that those of the Bloodlines and animals are awake. Perhaps it is more like the liveliness of the plants and the rivers and the mountains. In the same way, the Heart, a mound of stone, might bear some sliver of consciousness. But could it be enough to act upon the World as we do?

The Gladelysh elves of the Westreach tell tales of the "Mother's Heart" that was stolen — the Mother being the World itself.

The Reach Creed is founded on ancient tales of their deities, the Whispering Gods, taking the Heart from within the World to defeat their enemy, the Night.

Here in the Empire, our stories speak of the World as one being; day and night not separate, but a cycle; and all of us are part of the ground on which we walk. To us, Yuldor is the caretaker of the World's Heart, and uses its power and his wisdom to rule over us.

Perhaps each of these stories carry a sliver of truth, and none are complete. Perhaps, if I could discover how the pieces fit together, I would understand the deepest secrets of the World. But I do not have that knowledge. I can only guess, as I incessantly have, and I will continue to.

Thus, with little support beyond supposition, I put forth my theory:

Long ago, someone ripped the Heart from the World and used its power to their own ends. But power breeds greed, and greed always finds a way to its desire. Others rose to claim the Heart themselves. Perhaps they destroyed each other in the struggle. Or perhaps our Lord was only the latest to take its power for his own.

Is that all it takes to make a god? If the Heart seeks a new master, will the World bow before another man or woman bent on domination?

May the World strike me down now if I write untruths. But my fears compel me to dig deeper still.

- A Fable of Song and Blood, *by Hellexa Yoreseer of the Blue Moon Obelisk, translated by Tal Harrenfel*

CHANCES

GARIN STARED AT THE CEILING AS WREN STRIPPED OFF THE LAST of her travel leathers. A single thought whirled through his head.

She knows.

Neither of them had voiced it. Yet it hovered over them, a brewing storm that could break open at any moment, lingering as they'd found their way back to the Venaliel kintree and entered the room they'd occupied before.

She knows. And soon, she'll reject you. No woman could love a man with a devil nested in his head.

Love. Is that what had happened between them? He had trouble imagining his life without Wren now, to be true. Yet as he lay there, still dressed, his mud-splattered boots hanging off the bottom of the bed, he knew he had to accept the possibility. In her position, he couldn't imagine staying. He was tainted, unclean, untrustworthy. He'd spoken the Darktongue and burned youths, lads younger than himself, to their deaths.

He was a murderer. He was an abomination.

He clung to one consolation — that they'd found her father. As Wren had assisted Tal back to the Venaliel kintree, the Court Bard had met them coming down the lift, accompanied by Ashelia and a small contingent of guards. Ashelia had looked much as she had when Garin had met her, dressed in Warder armor and a grim expression on her face. He wasn't sure exactly what lay between her and Tal, but she'd been ready to fight and risk dying for him.

Even Tal deserves better loyalty than you, he thought bitterly.

Ilvuan's disdain radiated from the back of his mind, caustic and biting. Garin wearily pushed at him, and the Singer relented, his presence ebbing again.

Though Garin hadn't wanted to ascend the kintree, they'd gone up to see Tal to his bed, then taken their former room at Ashelia's offer. If she had offered two rooms, Garin was sure Wren would have taken her own. As it was, she'd stiffly accepted the offer, not bothering to consult Garin and ignoring her father's rueful expression.

"Aren't you going to undress?" Wren asked softly. She didn't look at him.

She can't even stand the sight of me now. But the self-directed barb was half-hearted; even deserved self-loathing grew tiresome after too long. With a sigh, Garin rose and pried off one boot, then the other, before laying back down.

Wren came and sat on the bed next to him. He stared at the back of her head and her short, black hair. Part of him longed to reach out and run a hand through it, to feel the coarse fibers between his fingers. Yet he refrained, waiting. This was the moment. She'd condemn him now.

And he'd accept it.

"Why didn't you tell me?" She didn't look around as she spoke.

"I don't know. I didn't want you to worry. But also... I wanted him to go away. Acknowledging him to you made him more real. More... permanent."

"Him? Not it?"

Garin winced. "Yes. He's named himself to me."

Ilvuan stirred, and he sensed he might be crossing a line. It only made him forge ahead faster.

"Ilvuan, he calls himself. That's the name he gives to mortals, anyway."

He'd scared her off. It sounded ridiculous when he said it aloud — a devil naming itself. Yet he didn't explain further, but gnawed at his bottom lip, waiting for her response. He felt Ilvuan's presence fully now. The devil was listening.

"Does he want something?"

Garin glanced at her back, brow furrowed. "I don't know. The day Ashelia tried to cleanse me, he resisted and claimed me as his own. That's when he gave me his name."

He couldn't tell whether Ilvuan approved of his confessions. Perhaps the Singer would try to punish him. Ever since he'd stabbed the Extinguished in the courtyard of the Ruins of Erlodan, the Singer hadn't tried to possess his body. But he remembered all too well when he had. His hand had driven the knife into Kaleras' side, and he'd been glad to do it. He'd never forget what the devil was capable of.

Wren turned back toward him, the gold in her eyes slowly swirling. Garin reluctantly held her gaze.

Her hand slowly reached across the bed. Her fingers intertwined with his.

"You should have told me," she chastised softly.

His pulse quickened. Garin leaned up on one elbow, careful not to let go of her hand. "How could I?" He tried not to let all of his fearful desperation show. "Knowing I'm still tainted by the Night, how could you...?"

The unspoken question hung between them.

She turned further toward him, her hip pressing against his leg, and took his hand in both of hers. "You're a fool of a man, Garin Dunford. Don't you see? I thought you were weak and capricious. But this shows you're stronger than anyone knows."

Even as he tried to decide how he should feel about her blunt confession, she leaned down and kissed him.

He didn't dare move, not believing it even as her lips pressed first softly against his, then hard. One of her hands touched his neck, running along the back of it to twist tightly into his hair. She pulled away then, holding him in her grip. As he opened his eyes, her golden tendrils were shining bright.

"Don't lie to me again," she said softly. "From now on, only tell the truth. No matter how hard."

He nodded, the lump in his throat barring words.

Wren's lips curled into a coy smile as she released him. Garin drew in a shaky breath, trying to ward away the disappointment that the moment was over, until he realized it wasn't.

Her gaze holding his, Wren drew off her tunic, then unwound the bindings around her breasts. When the cloth spooled on the floor, she sat, bare-chested, before him. He found his gaze wandering over her body before self-consciously flitting back up to her eyes.

Wren had gathered an almost feral look as she pulled one leg over to straddle him, then leaned down, her lips on his neck. Garin felt his worries draining away.

Maybe she does love me, he thought in a dizzy whirl. *Somehow. Despite everything else.*

His arms came up and embraced her. He held her close as they tumbled into the blankets.

Tal watched her back, gently illuminated by the soft werelights from the lamps, as he lay prone in his bed.

At another time, such a scene might have led to an intimate moment. He was half-clothed under the blankets, his shirt and trousers removed so she could tend to his wounds. But if Ashelia's stiffness and Warder garb hadn't dispelled the delusion, the stink of urine lingering in his nostrils, the acid at the back of his throat, and the roaring ache in his head put things into perspective.

She turned back around. "And that's all?"

He nodded. He'd told her all he'd learned for his pains. Of House Heilinis being in league with the Silver Vines, and House Lathniel being named their collaborators. That the Silver Vines meant to do something at the Winter Ball, something that could start a war. That there were tensions between High and Lowkin, even within Yuldor's Cult, divisions that might be exploited.

Ashelia had been quiet for a long time, considering the implications of his words, before she'd spoken again. What her conclusions were, she didn't reveal, and he didn't ask.

"I'll speak to the Queen of this." Her gaze wandering to stare into a shadowy corner. "She must know immediately. If the Winter Ball is to take place in two weeks, we have to begin preparations against it."

"So it will proceed?"

Her gaze found his. "It must. We must resolve the tensions between the Peers of the Realm. Better we do it where the Royalists have the advantage."

Tal shrugged, seeing the sense in it. He knew she must often be in harm's way when she served as a Warder. But it didn't help it sit any easier.

"Just be careful."

She smiled, but it fled as quick as it came. "You act as if you care. And yet you never came back."

Tal stiffened. He wanted to look away, look anywhere but at her, but he couldn't tear his gaze away. Ashelia watched, waiting, her eyes like a storm cloud brightened by lightning.

And though he'd sworn never to tell her, he'd broken enough oaths not to be surprised when he spoke.

"Though I try not to be, Ashelia, I'm a jealous man. I couldn't bear sharing you with Yinin any longer. If I returned, I knew I'd ask you to break your bond to him, and thus the oath between your Houses."

"But you didn't."

He couldn't bear the accusation in her eyes; her words were sharp enough. He dropped his gaze to the floor, staring at the whorls in the seamless wood. "You know what that would have meant."

"So a rift would have formed between our Houses — our marriage has done little to prevent one. He's a Lathniel, Tal, and he shares his sister's sensibilities. We stand on opposite sides of Elendol's widening chasm."

"I did what I thought was right. What was best for you."

"And that was where you went wrong." Her voice trembled, not with weakness, but with the feelings behind it. "You decided what was best for us — for *me* — without letting me decide. You denied me that choice."

He wanted to approach her, to stand before her and embrace her if she'd let him. But his wounds were still mending, the runes she'd painted on his skin working their magic beneath the bandages. He sat up instead.

"It wasn't just about politics. Your own family would have disowned you. You know there can be no reconciliation after breaking a bond-promise. You would have never seen your mother and father before they passed, never seen your brother again. Ashel, don't you see? I would have barred you from all of Elendol society."

"And what would I have cared?" Her voice was soft, and her eyes shone with unshed tears. "I would have lived the life I'd wanted to live. That I *chose* to live."

Tal clenched his jaw, fighting to hold back all he wished he could share with her. *It would not have been a life you wanted to live, Ashel. No one should walk the paths I have. You would have hated me by now. You would have cursed my name.*

"I didn't want to tear you away from your world."

"Do you think this way was less painful?"

261

She turned away, walking a few halting steps toward the door before stopping. He'd been afraid she would leave; now, he was afraid for her to stay. Afraid of what he couldn't help but say.

The words came out of him, inevitable as the rising moon, though hushed with hesitancy. "The greater part of me wishes I had come back."

She turned back, the corner of one eye visible. A wet streak glimmered in the soft werelights down her cheek. "The greater part of me wishes that as well."

Before he could respond, Ashelia wrenched open the door, stepped out, and closed it roughly behind her.

Tal found his hand raised toward her and lowered it to his other hand. Freed of the gloves, he felt at the place where the Ring of Falkuun had been cut from his hand, then at the Binding Ring on his other. He clenched his hands together.

"It's for the best," he muttered to the shadowed room. "For both of us."

He leaned back and tried to ease his tight muscles into relaxation. It was a long time before he slept.

WHERE THE VINE BLOOMS

THE SUN FAINTLY GLOWED THROUGH THE HIGH CANOPY BY THE time Tal stood, his wounds barely sealed and his head still pounding, before the Queen's throne chamber.

After the guards at the door had taken *Velori,* they admitted him. The opulence of the room dazzled him again for a moment, but he steeled himself and, trying not to limp, walked down the long, mossy carpet toward the silver throne at the end. A strange resonance hung in the air. Only as he neared did he understand why. The chanting of a lone Mute monk, standing at the base of the throne, permeated the air with Quietude, hiding the conversations near him. Yet for all the sanctity such a ritual implied, Brother Causticus' eyes found Tal's, and they held anything but heavenly devotion.

Looking aside, Tal studied the others who surrounded Queen Geminia. They'd dressed in even finer robes than hers. He quickly realized that these were many of the Peers of the Realm, the women leading the noble Houses of Gladelyl, gathered for a formal enclave, by their appearances.

To Geminia's right, Ashelia stood in a long gown of red that accentuated the shape of her body. In all his time in Elendol, he hadn't seen her in such a luxurious garb. He swallowed the sudden lump in his throat. Her hair, typically braided or bound back in an untidy bun, was intricately arranged atop her head. The paints for which elves were widely known adorned her face — though with her stern expression, it seemed more paint for war than civility. Next to her stood several other elven women that Tal didn't know, except for his fellow conspirator, Balindi Aldinare, the only one who wore a bright smile.

On the Queen's left stood yet more elven women, all staring with hard expressions at those opposite to them. Though they all seemed unfamiliar at first glance, Tal recognized one of them with a start. Peer Heilinis, the woman he'd seen speaking with the Silver Vines agent the night before, stood now before the Queen. Despite himself, a moment of paranoia came over him. He glanced over his shoulder, as if he might see the assassin approaching to finish the job he'd started.

You're safe, he told himself irritably. *Nowhere is safer than in the presence of the Queen.*

Yet he couldn't help but yearn for *Velori* as he approached. He was witnessing the rift in Elendol before his very eyes, the Sympathists against the Royalists. But as to the topic of their present disagreement, he could only tell as he came near enough to enter the bubble of Quietude and hear their words.

"...And he was attacked!" One of the Sympathists spoke, her pale skin flushed. "All the goods he meant to lift to our House were stolen, and the lift was damaged. He was lucky to escape with his life!"

"The protection of your House's lift is not a concern for Her Eminence," Ashelia responded sharply. "As was long ago decreed, each kintree must provide for the defense of their own, and damages to their property are their own responsibility. It is the price for the power we gain through the Peers' House. Perhaps you'd remember if you'd listened to your tutor rather than flirted with him."

The Sympathist began an angry retort, but the tallest of the Sympathists, a woman with skin an even deeper shade than

Ashelia, held up her hand. She was beautiful in a severe way, like a tree worn smooth by many storms and rain. "Let us not devolve into insults, Peer Venaliel, but maintain a veneer of civility. We all remember the Eternal Laws — and so we also remember that the harming of persons, no matter where it occurred, is under the purview of the Queen to judge."

"A matter for the lower courts, perhaps," Ashelia said, her words no less combative. "Not for Her Eminence herself. Must we bother her with every trifle?"

Queen Geminia lifted her gaze from the Peers to where Tal waited a dozen feet beyond. An unspoken weariness seemed to pass from her to him, an understanding that went beyond words. He gave her a small sympathetic smile. *I'd have beheaded the lot if I had to listen to them prattle all day,* he thought.

The Queen's lips quirked at the edges, so briefly he wondered if he'd imagined it.

Ashelia half-turned to acknowledge him, her expression stiff. The other Peers turned to stare. Balindi was once more the only one with an even vaguely warm expression, though hers was filled with the glee of a gossip gathering a new tale to spread.

Queen Geminia nodded slowly to him. "Aristhol. I was told you wished to speak to me." She cast her gaze over the Peers gathered around her. "Good Peers, if you would pardon me. I'm afraid I must meet with this man now."

Before the Sympathists could give voice to the outrage written across their faces, Geminia had risen and gracefully descended the stairs. Her dress, white and flowing with her movements, shimmered faintly with the full spectrum of colors, as if a rainbow had been sewn into the silky fabric. Hoping he hadn't been staring, Tal eased his eyes over to Ashelia, and found her watching with a yet harder look. His eyes darted away, but Brother Causticus' gaze behind her held no relief.

"We will continue our discussion later," the tall Sympathist said as Queen Geminia slowly strode across the room, Tal in tow.

The Queen didn't deign to respond, but walked over to a door on the side of the chamber. Tal quickly took the hint and opened it for her, then gladly fled within after her.

As the door closed behind, Tal took in the fresh sights. He'd expected to exit onto the platform. Instead, they stood in a wild, lush garden still within the kintree. The walls glowed a pale yellow. He couldn't tell if they were made of wood or not. Flowers of every color and variety flourished, and slender-limbed, white-barked trees held the yellow-green leaves of spring. Vines swarmed every available surface, green laced with red, and they sprouted the occasional flower along their lengths. The far end of the gardens curved away out of sight.

The Queen continued along the path before stopping to bend over a patch of tall, bulbous violet flowers. She closed her eyes and breathed in deeply, and Tal watched her, trying to push away the discomfort she felt. He didn't know why, but her allure seemed stronger in that garden than it ever had before.

After several long moments, she opened her eyes and straightened, then met his gaze. "Well, Aristhol. What do you think of my private gardens?"

"They're as luscious and ornamented as I'd have expected."

She awarded him a soft smile as she looked over them again. "They are my solace. During the long hours of the day, I often come here for refuge, to stroll among the plants and breathe in their scents."

He nodded. "Your pardons, Your Eminence. But I didn't come here to see flowers."

She didn't look over at him. "No, you didn't. You came because you have news of your exploits last night."

"You already know?"

"Peer Venaliel was already attending me, was she not? Do you suppose she would withhold such information from me?" The Queen turned toward him again. "According to her, at least two of the women standing in my throne room are traitors. Peer Lathniel and Peer Heilinis, I believe?"

"Was the tall woman Peer Lathniel?"

Geminia nodded. "The old blood runs strong in her, of that there is little doubt."

She seemed to leave something unspoken, but Tal didn't try teasing it out. "There's little else I can supply. Perhaps only that they had a skilled assassin at their disposal who seemed intent on killing everyone but me."

"They wish to take you as a prisoner. I wonder why." The Queen took several steps closer to him until she stood barely a foot away. It felt odd to look down at her; somehow, it made her seem less of a queen and almost ordinary.

He tried to remain at ease. He had informed the Queen of much, but not all. No doubt Ashelia had filled in the gaps with what she knew. But not even she knew everything of Yuldor's desire to possess him.

A lie is best mixed with nine parts truth. He decided it was time to put his own axiom to the test.

"There's a book I've brought with me, or the copied pages of one. The Named wishes to possess it and the knowledge within it."

"So Peer Venaliel has informed me. At least of the book's importance." The Queen waited, as if knowing more remained unspoken.

"But that's not my first concern. The Winter Ball — Ashelia must have told you they mean to threaten it."

"Yes, she did. And she told me that laying our own traps is better rather than fleeing any they set for us. Do you concur?"

He bought himself time by studying the broad leaves of a fern next to the path. "To an extent. As long as we protect those who neglect protecting themselves."

"And whom would you be referring to, Thorn Puller?"

Tal met her eyes. "Very little escapes you, Your Eminence. So I'm sure you know my feelings for Peer Venaliel haven't

267

changed or faded, not in all the long years since they first began."

"Long years for a human, perhaps; two decades is little to an elf. I would not be surprised if her feelings had not changed either. And with the many recent changes to our society, perhaps all kinds of rules can withstand bending."

He struggled to speak around the sudden lump in his throat. He couldn't hold to that hope. Once held, he was afraid he'd cling to it, Silence take the consequences.

"Nevertheless. If you protect her at the Winter Ball, I swear I'll do anything necessary to bring the Silver Vines to justice."

The Queen took a step closer, and his blood, already warm from the sorcery surrounding him, grew hotter still as her aura pressed against him. It dizzied him and scrambled his thoughts.

"You will do as I command, Tal Harrenfel. No matter the cost, no matter who might pay it — you will obey me."

Anger brought clarity to his thoughts. "Not any cost."

Geminia smiled sadly. "Do you so little trust me? I would not ask you to sacrifice Ashelia Venaliel; I am not the Thorn to play games designed to goad and hurt."

"Then why ensorcel me? Why bind me with a ring? Why speak in riddles and not plainly as allies should? I don't believe you serve the Night. But I'm not sure you stand with the Westreach, either."

"Perhaps the lines are not drawn as firmly as you think."

"How so?"

The Queen turned away from him, and he felt her sorcery ease, allowing him to take a deep, steadying breath.

"There are things you should know," she said softly. "Things I must tell you. Of the Named, Yuldor. Of his beginnings and his banishment. And of his possession of the Mother's Womb."

As Tal's mind raced ahead, Geminia motioned, and they continued their walk through the gardens.

"Yuldor was born far before my time," she began, "but was contemporary with my *helgimini* — my great-grandmother.

Queen Geminia the First was sovereign of Gladelyl in her day, and she ruled with a hard hand. There were no female Warders then — all remained to the roles demanded of them, for this was how she perceived the Mother was best pleased. After all, she reasoned, why else would the Mother have set up our society in such a way?"

The Elf Queen shook her head before continuing.

"Then Yuldor came into prominence. He was the opposite of my *helgimini* in everything. Where she held the traditions as sacrosanct, he spat upon them. One of the Lowkin, he'd raised himself through talent and tenacity from the mud of Low Elendol to join with the Obsidian Tower, one of the Chromatic Towers of that time. He could have selected any of the towers he'd wished, for he showed an aptitude for every discipline, and one did not have to be a practitioner of the Diamond Tower to divine that he was destined for greatness.

"Geminia the First did not approve of him from the start. He was too ambitious, too disregarding of the hierarchy and rules. She quickly sought to restrain his ascension. But Yuldor's talents were not only in sorcery. Through persuasion and perhaps even coercion, he became a Master of the Obsidian Tower within five years of beginning his studies, when decades might not have seen another to such esteem."

The Queen's hands drifted along a pair of orange and yellow blossoms hanging down from a vine, and she paused to breathe in their scent. Tal looked away. There was something desperate and sensual in the way she took in the flowers, as if they were the last she would ever smell.

A few moments later, she straightened and continued their circuit. "By thirty, a young age by elven standards, Yuldor had free rein over his studies. He made liberal use of it. Within another five years, he'd boasted creations beyond anything his fellow masters could conceive of. He summoned spirits regularly, using his and others' bodies as channels, and claimed to have won secret knowledge from them. Not long after that, he claimed to be 'the Night's Heir.' Though the Creed was still not widely practiced in Gladelyl then, all knew of the adversary of the Whispering Gods.

"It was the leaf that broke the bridge, as my people say. My *helgimini* was wroth at his proclamation. Summoning Yuldor before her, she banished him from Gladelyl, accusing him of consorting with devils and meddling in black arts. Yuldor, it is said, did not deny the charges, nor put up any defense at all, but only smiled back and said his parting words: 'One day, I will repay your kindness in full.' Then he turned from the throne hall."

"If she feared him," Tal interrupted, "and feared the depths he delved, why did she let him go free? If she'd acted with an iron fist, perhaps all this could have been avoided."

Geminia nodded slowly. "I have often wondered that. In some ways, it seems out of character from what I know of the woman. But I believe you have guessed it correctly: she *did* fear him. Perhaps she feared him so much she did not wish for a confrontation, lest he overcome those she set against him. Including herself."

Tal's chest weighed heavy. "So, even as a mortal, he was too powerful to contend with."

"We shall never know. Yuldor went quietly, taking only some supplies from the Obsidian Tower and four of his most loyal apprentices. These would, in time, become the Nameless — his Soulstealers, his Extinguished. After he had gone, Geminia the First disbanded the school of sorcery and formed in its place the Onyx Tower, which was to study the same dark workings as had attracted Yuldor, but with the intention of defying and defeating them rather than plumbing their depths."

"And Yuldor?"

The Queen traced a hand along a leaf. "No one knows what happened next. But he must have done or found something in those fell mountains. It was only thirty springs later that the first of the endless monsters came down into the forests.

Perhaps he began something he could not stop, opened some rift to another plane beyond mortals. Perhaps he intentionally beset the world with a legacy of demons, fulfilling his promise to my *helgimini*. Or perhaps he found the Mother's Womb and has sustained himself through its power, plotting and chipping away at the Westreach just as he did the East for centuries before."

Tal let out a deep sigh. "He must have discovered something. All have heard of the resurrections of the Extinguished. I killed the Thorn once, two decades ago. Yet here he is again, plaguing your city. If his servants are undying, how much greater power has Yuldor claimed for himself?"

"Yes," Geminia said, almost in a whisper. "I have come to the same conclusion. But it is only part of the story. Someone must discover the truth, the unmitigated truth. And put an end to whatever remains of the Named."

The Queen of Gladelyl looked at him then, and he had to take a steadying step back under the brute force of her aura. *Not much mystery whom she means,* he thought bitterly.

"Why me?" he demanded. Anger fueled by helplessness spiked through him. "Why did you bind me to you?"

She turned away, and he felt her sorcery ease. "You of all people must know, Aristhol — the game is already lost once you reveal your hand. Even to your allies."

"If you use your sorcery to dazzle and confuse your allies, you may find few of them remain."

Geminia turned with a sad smile. For a moment, he glimpsed the woman beneath the glamour, and again saw her plain, fatigued features. "I know you speak truth. But this is what it is to be a queen. You mistrust all those around you. You test and prod them, forcing them to prove their loyalty, over and over again. Never is there a place you are not the monarch. No one can ease your burden, not for the whole of your life's length. And an elf's life is long."

As she stared across the garden, weariness etched into her

every part, Tal wondered how long Geminia had lived. Two centuries? Three? The years didn't show in her skin, but in that moment, they'd all caught up with her.

Even if this was her continued manipulation, he couldn't harden himself to it. His anger slipped away. "You need not test my loyalty again, Your Eminence. Ring or not, I won't betray you."

"No," she said softly. "You *will* betray me, Tal Harrenfel. But only when I ask it."

He furrowed his brow. Geminia had trained in the Diamond Tower and was said to be strong with the gift of prescience, able to see what events may come to pass. He didn't like to think what she'd seen of him.

But if it's a choice between Ashelia and the Queen, or any of my companions, would I hesitate to choose?

He forced the thought down, down where not even the Queen's sorcery could reach it.

Geminia looked back at him, and a shadow of her aura returned. "We will hold the Winter Ball. And there we will endeavor to trap our enemies. We will reveal the Sympathists for their true loyalties. And perhaps, if we play our hand cleverly, we will prevent Elendol from tearing itself apart."

He made the gesture of respect. There was no arguing with the Queen now that she'd decided. "I have only one other request, Your Eminence."

"Speak. You have not restrained before."

Tal flashed her a shameless grin. "The troupe I traveled here with, the Dancing Feathers. I would ask that they perform the Winter Ball."

It gratified him to see her eyelids flicker, the barest hint of surprise. "That would be ill-received."

"It would. But wouldn't it be an insult to King Aldric to turn away Falcon Sunstring, Court Bard to His Majesty of Avendor, at one of your own events?"

A smile briefly quirked Geminia's lips. "Very well, Aristhol.

It might serve as a much-needed distraction. You may tell your friend I grant his wish."

Tal made the gesture of respect again, wondering if he'd truly gained a victory. It was what Falcon desired, but if the Winter Ball was to be the trap for the Sympathists, blood was promised.

But that's what it is to be a friend, he thought. *You let them make their mistakes, then try your best to save them.*

"They will not be the only surprise guests of the evening," the Queen continued. "There is another you will not expect."

Just when I thought we'd dispensed with secrets. "And who would that be?"

Her eyes curved with amusement. "Allow me my diversion where I may find it. You will see soon enough."

She made the sign of dismissal, and Tal had no choice but to leave. At even his hesitation to obey, the Binding Ring turned faintly cool.

Let her keep her secrets, he thought as he exited the garden and went back to the throne-room. *I still have some precious few of my own.*

The Peers, having given up hope of the Queen's prompt return, had departed from around the throne — all except Ashelia. As he reappeared, she strode toward him, her manner that of a Warder despite her voluptuous dress.

"What were you talking about in there?" she demanded in a low voice.

He smiled at her. "She'll hold the Winter Ball."

The familiar crease between her eyebrows appeared. For a moment, he wished he could trace it, pretending to smooth it, as he had all those years ago.

"That was already decided," she said. "Your conversation went much longer than that warranted."

He shrugged. "She treated me to an old tale. And she wasn't at first well-pleased at my suggestion that the Dancing Feathers play the occasion. But she came around."

273

"A half-kin bard serenading the Winter Ball." Ashelia shook her head. "Elendol changes faster than I can keep track of some days."

His pulse quickened slightly. "Perhaps it changes fast enough."

She eyed him curiously, then looked away. "Come. There are many preparations we must make in these next two weeks, and you'd do well to be informed of them."

Ashelia turned to lead him from the throne room, and Tal kept pace by her side. His thoughts raced over all that time they'd be together, even if they spent it preparing a trap.

Perhaps all kinds of rules can withstand bending, the Queen had said. And despite his best efforts, that hope had found roots inside him.

You're a fool, Tal Harrenfel, he told himself. *But then again, I've always known — a fool can do what a wise man never could.*

He smiled, not caring how it looked to the guards as they passed. For the first time in a long time, he saw a glimmer of light in his future.

If only he could survive the Winter Ball.

A DEADLY DANCE

Garin felt like a new man.

A smile played upon his lips, provoked by the smallest of things. A butterfly landing on the railing. The fresh forest scents stirred by a breeze. A monkey cackling at him from the canopy. A stray memory of Wren and himself, tangled together in the blankets.

The World was a wondrous place, and Garin was glad to be in it.

There'd been moments of awkwardness. They were both inexperienced, and he'd heard from the older men in Hunt's Hollow, with much elbowing and winking, that was how it started. But at the core of their experience the night before was something he felt he'd only just glimpsed, and he was eager for another look.

Then he stepped foot onto the Dancing Plaza, and the smile slipped away.

Ulen stood, waiting for him. Before him, standing within the circle of the carved tree of Gladelyl, was a young, male elf. Though Garin was tall, this lad was taller still, and beneath his shirt, he appeared lithe and well-muscled. His hair was shaved close on the sides of his head, but left long on top in a style similar to Ulen's. His eyes were a dark green laced with a band of lighter emerald. The elf watched him approach imperiously, his eyes swirling slowly. A practice rapier hung loosely in one hand.

A new pupil? he wondered, though the lad held himself with far too much surety to be new to dancing.

Garin repressed his unease as he walked between the scaffolding, crowded with more than the usual number of Highkin. With no other choice, he ignored them and approached his Dancing Master.

"Finally," Ulen said as Garin entered the circle. As was his habit, Ulen didn't meet Garin's eyes, but stared somewhere beyond his right shoulder. "We must test your limits. Pick a sword from the rack and take your place opposite of Tendil."

Obeying, Garin walked before the rack of weapons. Most were rapiers, though it also bore similar longswords and short blades as he'd practiced with in Halenhol. Sensing a test, Garin selected a standard Gladelysh rapier and tested the edge, then pulled his thumb away in surprise. Blood trickled down his skin. Expecting a dulled blade, he'd pressed harder than he should have.

He looked up at Ulen. "Master? These blades aren't dulled for practice."

The Dancing Master stared at the top of his head. "A test of your limitations," he said, the familiar edge of impatience coming into his voice. "You must walk the blade's edge to discover how far you can stretch."

Garin hesitated. Ulen hadn't voiced his intentions, but they were slowly becoming clear. *A contest. He means to pit me against the youth.* Though his pride demanded that he rise to the occasion, his fear and practicality were stronger.

"I don't feel comfortable sparring with sharpened blades, Master."

For an instant, Ulen's eyes met his, then flitted away. "You will obey me, Garin Dunford. Or you will learn no more from me."

Indecision paralyzed him. Dancing, according to what they'd told King Aldric, was his and his fellow Avendorans' reason for coming to Elendol. If he abandoned it, their true goals — both his and Tal's — might come to light.

Even as dread numbed his limbs, he knew what he had to do.

Garin walked to the edge of the circle where all dances began. A faint ringing sounded in his ears. *Maybe this is only a test,* he thought. *He wouldn't make us do this. He only wishes to see if we're brave enough to face the possibility. Elves don't get killed in practice sessions — there's too few of them to risk that.*

But then again, he wasn't an elf.

The youth, Tendil, took the spot opposite of Garin, standing in the canopy of the carved tree. Garin occupied the roots. He'd learned enough to see the lad's form was fine: his weight was balanced, and he was light on the balls of his feet. He wore dancing slippers, the same as Garin wore for his practice sessions. As he took his stance, his muscles were relaxed but ready, set in the Form of Water, prepared for anything that might come.

Garin held himself in a similar position and felt it a pathetic mockery. The scar on his arm seemed stiffer than ever before. The sounds of the crowd hushed as they stared at them, waiting for the signal. All hope that this was a pretense fled.

"Begin," Ulen said.

The elven lad darted across the circle, but skidded to a stop just short of striking distance. Garin quickly sidestepped, keeping his body facing Tendil and holding his sword slightly higher before him.

Tendil wore a mocking smile as he darted forward, feinted a jab left and down, then tried for a swipe at his right. Garin saw the feints and mostly blocked the last attempt — but not entirely. A red line blossomed on his arm, burning where the torn pieces of cloth clung to it.

"A touch to Tendil," Ulen said. His eyes were on them now, following every movement with the attention of a hawk to two hares.

Tendil didn't slow, but kept up his assault, whirling and launching two more attacks. Garin ducked one and awkwardly jumped back from the other, then thrust forward just to ward off another attack. To his surprise, the tip of his rapier grazed Tendil's right forearm.

"A touch to Garin."

The elf backed away, his olive skin flushing a darker shade. He didn't like being embarrassed — Garin wondered if he could use that to his advantage. But with the cut still burning along his arm, he knew who still had the upper-hand here. As Ashelia had once said, elves trained in dancing since they could walk. Tendil had much more experience and a longer reach. If Garin had managed a touch, it was only because of his opponent's overconfidence.

But all I need is three touches. In a standard duel, three touches was a round, and the winner of two out of three rounds was declared the victor. But Garin wasn't sure he would last three; he had to hope they'd stop after one.

There was still a chance he could survive, perhaps even win. All he had to do was let Tendil do his work for him.

The elf came forward again, and instead of assaulting with the Form of Fire, Garin recognized the Form of Air, which used light attacks to wear out an opponent and confuse them. Even knowing the tricks, Garin found it difficult to know which blows to parry, dodge, and ignore. Every time the blade came flickering within inches of his face, he couldn't help but jerk back, even though he knew he should use the Form of Stone to stand his ground and break the assault. But each time, he imagined the tip of the blade piercing his eye, and his body made its own conclusions.

Ilvuan's anger suddenly flared in the back of his mind.

Cede me control, Listener. I will strike down this insolent youth.

A different fear chilled Garin as he skirted along the edge of the circle, trying to gain some room to breathe. *No, Ilvuan. I can't.*

He will kill you. And then you cannot come to me.

Before Garin could think of a response, Tendil charged again, this time employing the Form of Stone, but in an offensive way Garin had never seen before. Adopting the Form of Air, Garin kept light on his feet, but he felt like a bird against the woodsman's axe as Tendil chopped at him again and again, narrowly missing each time.

As their swords locked, the guards grinding against each other, Tendil came close, and to Garin's surprise, his fist came up. Garin's head rocked back, pain exploding through his head, half of his vision blurry. As Ilvuan's fury burned through him, he felt their swords come untwisted and Tendil turning. He tried to intercept and missed.

Pain exploded from his hip.

He collapsed on the injured leg, half his body going boneless. It was all he could do to keep his blade up and eyes on his enemy as he collapsed to the ground. For all the good it did — Tendil stood by his legs and tapped the tip of his sword to his foot, just hard enough to pierce the soft fabric of the shoes. The elf lad didn't bother to hide his sneer.

Knowing it was over, Garin let the rapier fall from his grasp and stared down at his hip. Blood poured down his leg, more blood than he knew he could lose. He stared at it blankly, then put his hand over it, not sure if he was trying to stem the bleeding or just hide it from sight. Only the Singer's rage radiating in his mind broke through the shock. As the devil rose in him, his hands twitched of their own accord.

Gritting his teeth, he rallied himself and kept Ilvuan at bay. *No,* he thought, all other words beyond him.

Ulen stood over him. His voice was flat as he said, "Three touches. The round goes to Tendil."

"I'm bleeding." His tongue felt thick in his mouth, his head strangely disconnected from his body.

Through his hazy vision, he saw Tendil's expression shift, and the youth stepped away as he looked to Ulen. But the Dancing Master only stood over him, his eyes looking up and away past Garin.

"Ulen Yulnaed!"

Garin tried to look around at the familiar voice, but even sitting, he lost his balance and fell back. His hands slipped away from the bloody wound. He heard shouting and tried to follow it, but darkness crept up at the edges of his vision. Only an anger that wasn't his own kept him from slipping away, claws digging in painfully and holding him in place.

Take vengeance, little Listener! Ilvuan demanded. *This was a contest, but only between youths. Such a blow should not have been dealt!*

"*No.*" Garin couldn't tell if he said it or just thought it. He tried to slip between his claws.

Ilvuan held him fast. *Wake, Listener, and rise, or I will force it upon you!*

Only the Singer's threat could have provoked him to rally. With the last scraps of willpower, Garin forced himself upright and his eyes wide. The World spun dizzily around him, but he kept his eyes open. His lips pulled back in a snarl of their own accord, and his fingers clawed at the wooden grooves.

Approval radiated through his mind, like a wash of sunlight after a long time in shadow.

Then someone pressed on the wound in his hip. Garin roared his pain and outrage and tried pushing them away, but his arms had lost their strength. He vaguely saw his hands smear blood across a shoulder before one tangled in the light brown curls cascading down their back.

"Garin!" the person snapped. "Let go of my hair!"

He obeyed as recognition settled in. *Ashelia.* It was all he could make of the situation. He clung to consciousness, ever mindful of Ilvuan's waiting claws and threat should he fail to.

Pain pulsed from the wound — then a cleansing, stinging feeling burned up and down the veins in his body. Garin thought he might have screamed, though only the pounding of his heart filled his ears.

Then it was over, and he gasped for air. The pain faded. His head cleared, and though his body was still shaky, he felt the limpness dissipating.

Blinking rapidly, he found Ashelia's angry gaze on him and flinched. He muttered, "Thank you."

She blinked, as if realizing what she'd seen, and nodded before looking back around. There, Ulen stood over them, his expression as stony as ever.

"You could have killed him," Ashelia said in an icy voice.

"His limits had to be discovered." The Dancing Master's gaze wandered across the forest behind them. "I believe I have found them."

Ashelia stared at him a moment longer before turning back to Garin. "Can you stand?"

He nodded, though he was far from sure he could. His eyes wandered down to his hip. Ashelia had lifted her hands away, and he could see where his flesh had torn apart, but was now a fine seam amid the dried blood.

"You healed me," he said in wonder.

"I *am* a healer," she answered wearily before standing and extending a hand.

In vain, he tried to wipe his hands clean, then took Ashelia's hand to come to his feet.

He looked back at Ulen, a mixture of feelings running through him. Had he meant for this to happen? Why had he let things go so far? The whole contest seemed even more foolish from this side of things, Garin's participation in it the stupidest of all.

"Don't bother," Ashelia said as she turned him away, keeping an arm around his middle and draping his arm over her shoulders. "Let me take you back to your room."

Reluctantly, he turned his gaze forward and left the Dancing Plaza behind.

The bridges endeavored to trip his clumsy feet, but Garin managed to cross them all the way to House Venaliel. Though his hip had split open only minutes before, now it functioned just as it always had, with only the slightest pull where his flesh had mended back together. He still felt far from himself, but after the last bridge, he carefully removed Ashelia's arm and stood swaying on his own.

"Are you sure you're strong enough?" A crease appeared in her brow as she looked him up and down.

He shrugged and tried to smile, wondering how bad he looked. "I'll make it."

"Still, I'll walk you down."

Knowing she wouldn't take no for an answer, and mindful that it was her home anyway, Garin led the way down the stairs. The railing around the edge had never seemed so inadequate to prevent a fall, and he clung to it at every step.

When he reached his and Wren's room, however, he paused. A vague remembrance stirred in his mind. Garin grimaced, wanting nothing more than to fall into bed and sleep. But this couldn't wait.

"You're not thinking of still being up and about, are you?" Ashelia wore a severe look as he turned back to her.

"I have to tell Tal something. Something I noticed."

"He's not in right now. But tell me — I'll be sure he hears."

Garin wavered. It wasn't that he didn't want to tell Ashelia, he realized — somehow, he'd wanted the excuse to speak to his old mentor. Disgust and anger mingled inside him, defeating his will for anything else.

"Fine," he said, unable to keep the sullenness from his voice. "I thought it odd that Ulen didn't spar himself, as he usually does. But when he approached me as I lay on the ground, I saw he had a limp."

Ashelia frowned. "And?"

Garin hesitated, realizing how large a leap of logic he was about to propose. But having admitted this much, he took the plunge. "The assassin that almost killed Tal? He was burned up his left leg. The same leg that Ulen was limping on."

For a moment, he thought she would deny his inevitable conclusion. But she only looked sad as she nodded. "Maybe you're right. I'll let Tal know. Now, stop worrying about anything but rest — I don't want your death on my record."

Giving her a wan smile, he tottered over to his door, went inside, and barely stripped off his clothes before he collapsed on the bed.

THE THREE-FACED ROGUE

TAL HAD JUST OPENED HIS ROOM'S DOOR WHEN ASHELIA CAME
down the stairs.

She stopped as she caught sight of him. "Where have you
been?"

Confusion and delight warred within him. It wasn't often
that she found the occasion to visit — and though her expression was serious, he treated her with a devilish grin. "About."

"About." She stepped closer, her eyes swirling. "While you
were about, your apprentice almost died."

As quickly as it had come, the smile fled.

"Almost died?" He imagined Garin's face, pale and bloodied.
"How? Where is he?"

"He's fine now. Fortunately, I caught wind of what Ulen was
planning from Balindi. When I arrived, I found Garin severely
wounded. The fool!" she interrupted herself suddenly, and Tal
wasn't sure whom she was railing against.

"How did he get hurt? An accident?"

"If only." She glanced around, then motioned him toward
the door. "Best continue this inside, where prying ears will
have more trouble overhearing."

Banishing boyish notions of what her visiting his chamber

might portend, Tal led the way inside and sealed the door behind them. Ashelia activated one of the werelight lamps so the room filled with a friendly, yellow glow.

Tal crossed his arms and leaned against the wall. "Well?"

Ashelia seemed to steel herself before raising her gaze to meet his. "Ulen set Garin against Tendil, one of the Gladelysh youths under his tutelage. With undulled blades."

His blood warmed, and Tal suspected it wasn't because of nearby magic. A smile tugged at his lips. "Surely a Dancing Master would know better than to do that."

She turned, a hand absently tucking a stray curl behind her ear. "That's the thing. Not only is it suspicious, it's more than foolish. Ulen would never hold such a contest between two of my people — it would be enough to cause a rift between Houses."

"Perhaps he intended just that. He's a Sympathist, isn't he?"

Ashelia nodded reluctantly. "I thought him honorable enough to put politics aside. But it seems I've been the fool here, not seeing this for what it is."

"Which is?"

As she met his eyes again, he winced at the sorrow and pain swirling in them.

"This is a war. A war between brothers and sisters over power and greed. How did it come to this, Tal? How could anything be worth the pain and death that's coming?"

He'd taken several strides toward her before he caught himself. Yet as she looked up at him, eyes brimming with misery, he threw caution to the wind.

Slowly, gently, he took her into his arms.

She was stiff for a long moment. Then her arms curled around him and held him tightly.

He closed his eyes and didn't smile. A smile couldn't convey the contentment he felt in the circle of her embrace, so long denied. For two decades, he'd imagined this — yet his imagination paled in comparison with the moment.

They held each other for long enough that the seconds slowed and their breathing matched and the World seemed suspended in a drop of amber. Then Ashelia pulled away, and he felt as if she tugged roots out from his skin. The lack of her touch cut deeper than a blade ever had.

She didn't look at him, but tucked her arms tightly under her breasts, seeming a different woman than the proud Peer or the independent Warder. Now she resembled the lonely healer he'd met as he hung over death's precipice, the one who had pulled him back and saved him.

His Ashelia.

"You should go to Garin," she said, staring at the window as if to look outside, though the curtains were drawn. "While you were out, he tried to visit you."

Little could have jolted Tal from the moment. That revelation managed it. "He did?"

She gave him a small smile. "Nearly killed himself just making it back to his room, but he wanted to tell you his suspicions as soon as he could. There's hope for you two, you know."

"Hope is too strong of a word for it."

"If you say so."

Not daring to harbor the thought, he asked, "What did he want to tell me?"

"That he believes Ulen was the assassin in the Mire."

His mind worked through that for a moment. *No matter how clever you think yourself, Tal Harrenfel, you're still a fool.* "The way he moved, his training, his skill — I thought the assassin an exceptionally experienced dancer. It only fits that he'd be the finest among them."

"It was because of his wounds that Garin guessed it. He says you burned the assassin's left leg, and Ulen was limping today at the match."

"He was taking vengeance on me. And sending a warning." Anger stirred in his chest, even hotter than before. "He might have killed him."

"Don't try hunting him down, Tal. You're still recovering yourself, and no good can come of it. Say you kill him — what then? You'll be branded a murderer, and with Elendol as it is, it might be the spark to set the city aflame. The Queen won't be able to protect you. And I..."

She hesitated. He could guess the line of her thoughts. *How much would she sacrifice to protect me, her former lover? Her House? Her son? Or nothing at all?*

He wasn't sure he wanted to hear the answer.

Ashelia pivoted the conversation. "What I mean is, don't let this chance slip away with Garin. Talk to him — or try, at least. Even if he rejects you, at least you gave him the chance."

Tal sensed there was more behind her words than she let on. But he only nodded. "You're right. He deserves that much."

He didn't move immediately toward the door, though, but continued to stare at her. She shifted her gaze first, but remained standing where she was.

Waiting, he thought. He hoped.

"You deserved that chance as well," Tal said quietly. "I'm sorry I never gave it to you."

She didn't look at him, nor react. Yet he waited. He'd waited long years for a chance such as this. He wouldn't rush it now.

Finally, her eyes met his. The stormy gray of the irises glimmered with silvery light. "You're an honorable man, Tal. *Thalkunaras.*"

She whispered his Heartname, and he felt a shiver run through him that went beyond his body. His voice was hoarse as he responded with hers.

"*Neshenia.*"

He couldn't tell if her smile held joy or sorrow. After a long moment, she looked aside. "You should go to him."

He nodded. "I should."

A heartbeat passed. Two.

Then she took the final steps to the door and opened it.

As he followed her from his room, the werelights of Elendol had never felt so harsh.

Awaken.

Garin started. Halfway sitting up, he stared at the door, partially cracked open. His groggy mind tried to work through why it hung ajar. A moment later, he saw the silhouetted man next to it reach over and close it.

"Hey!" Garin croaked, grappling for his sword, though he wasn't sure where it was. He could scarcely remember where *he* was, and the darkness didn't help.

All he knew was that he was in danger.

"Peace, Garin. It's only me."

The werelight lamp glowed as the man activated it, and Garin recognized him. Relief washed over him before apprehension settled back in, self-loathing following quickly on its heels.

Always relieved to see your father's murderer, aren't you? part of him taunted.

But somehow, the thought's teeth were dull, the pain less than it once had been. He wasn't sure what to make of that.

Tal dragged a chair from the wall, moved it closer to the bed, and sat on it backwards. "I heard you had a rough morning."

Garin shrugged. "Nearly died, that's all."

His one-time mentor grinned, and Garin felt a smile tug at his lips before he squelched it.

"Ashelia said you wanted to tell me about Ulen. That you think he's the assassin."

He shrugged, trying not to show the anxiety stirring inside him. *I can't do this. I'm not ready. I only wanted to warn him, not make amends.*

Yet another part of him silenced the words that might send

him away. A doubt, always there, had spread its roots and ground itself firmly in his mind. And he knew he couldn't banish it without knowing the truth.

He tried maintaining the pretense. "I did. But something doesn't seem right."

"Oh? And what's that?"

"If he was the assassin, he hid his face before. Why would he reveal himself by doing this now?"

Tal frowned, his eyes downcast. "Perhaps the game has changed. Or, as one tactic failed, he is attempting another. But it's a good question, Garin. I hadn't thought of it."

As his praise warmed Garin's chest, he abruptly couldn't stand it any longer. "Tell me what happened."

Tal's head jerked up. His eyes, shadowed with the lamp at his back, seemed to hold an animal's wariness, like a dog that had scented a wolf. "What do you mean? With the assassin?"

"With my father."

The muscles in Tal's jaw twitched. But he didn't look away as he asked quietly, "What do you want to know?"

"Why don't you start with why you killed him?" He said it with acid, anger finally seizing hold of his tongue.

Tal winced, his gaze flickering to the side. "To explain, there's more you should know. About what led up to that day."

Garin stiffened his jaw, and his body tensed as if expecting a blow to the gut. He didn't look away from Tal's scarred face. *I need to know,* he thought as he studied every reaction and emotion that crossed the man's expression. *I need to know the truth.*

Tal was silent for several long moments, then began in a low voice. "At that time, I went by the name of Gerald Barrows. Do you know it?"

Garin held himself still for a moment. Then he slowly shook his head.

"It didn't make it into Falcon's song, even if the first title attached to it did — the Three-Faced Rogue. I took that third name when I fled from the Circle, for this was after the Extinguished had made his use of me. As Gerald Barrows, I quickly became a man no one could venerate. The little good that he did — if it can be called 'good' — Falcon assigned instead to the name of Tal Harrenfel, while the bad was swept away and forgotten."

Fury, never far from the surface, stirred again. *Not forgotten,* Garin promised him silently.

"But when I first became Gerald Barrows, I joined with the Dancing Feathers — first as a bodyguard, then afterward as an actor. Falcon and I grew to know and care for one another. We had some good times in those years.

"But it wasn't to last. During what would be my last performance on the stage, Kaleras recognized me, and I knew I had to flee further from civilization. Hunted by the Magisters, haunted by my slaughter of their brothers, I had only just started to mend before they drove me into the wilds once more. So, as Gerald Barrows, I gave up on the high ideals I'd once held and became more a beast than a man."

Tal's gaze had fallen to the floor, and his eyes were lidded for a moment. Just as Garin wondered if he'd fallen asleep, he raised his head again. There was a slight shimmer about his eyes.

"I can't tell you all the things I've done, Garin. I suppose I held to a low code at least, never harming an unarmed woman or any child, but... I slaughtered men like they were sheep. Even before the Yraldi arrived on the Sendeshi shores, I sought fights in seedy taverns and alleyways and left bodies cold behind me. Always, there was a reason for it — the other man threatened me, or he'd recognized my face from a bounty posted by the warlocks. But the truth was I wanted an outlet for my fury at all my life had become. Or, barring that, a way to escape it all.

"Then the Black Ships came, and I had a better excuse to kill. I went with the local militias to meet the invaders and, town by town, we drove them back. Though they could tell I was Avendoran, the Sendeshi locals grew to admire me, praising my courage and battle prowess. Even my sorcery, wielded to defeat the Yraldi, could not abate their praise. I became a hero to them — the Red Reaver, savior of the Northern Coast."

A bitter smile twisted Tal's lips. Garin shared his sentiments. *You're no hero,* he thought. *And we both know it.*

"But once the ships had burned and the few remaining Yraldi had fled back across the Crimson Sea, the battles were gone — but the fury still lived in Gerald Barrows. He — I — hadn't sated the bloodlust as I'd hoped. Yet even as I longed for the summer's war, I'd grown sick to the bones with what I'd become. I tried to drown myself in indulgence — liquor, influencers, and other vices. I didn't deserve to live, I well knew. Yet I couldn't find the courage to put myself down like the feral beast I was."

Despite all he'd heard, Garin felt a stirring of horror. *He wanted to kill himself — he hated himself that much.* Part of him wondered if Tal should have, if things wouldn't have been better that way.

But the greater part only pitied him.

Tal's gaze lingered on the door as if he wished he could flee rather than finish his tale. But he continued, his voice hoarse. "Your father found me then, in a backwater tavern in Sendesh. He came with a dozen Avendoran soldiers, all disguised to travel through the foreign lands unmolested. Jindol had the tavern surrounded, and then he and half his men came inside to arrest me."

Garin found he was shaking, but he tried to keep his voice firm. "Why? Why was my father there?"

Tal shrugged. "Politics. I had done Sendesh a great service by rallying the shore-side militias and leading the charges against the marauders. Many more people would have suffered had they not taken heart at the Red Reaver's resistance. But aid to Sendesh was a blow against Avendor, especially when King Aldric was only just establishing himself in his reign. He deemed it an insult to Avendor that I aided our 'enemies,' and sought to undermine Sendeshi morale by having me executed. Or converted to his cause, perhaps — I don't know if that idea had occurred to him yet."

Garin closed his eyes against his spinning vision. *A pawn. My father was just a pawn.* It made him see his father differently somehow, and he didn't like the view.

Opening his eyes again, he found Tal watching him. "What happened then?" Garin asked quietly.

His former mentor looked away. "You know the rest, more or less. I had too much hot blood in me to yield — but even then, I had no desire to fight your father. So I appealed to Jin, asking him to remember our childhood, plucking at his conscience and loyalty. It worked for a moment. But when Jin didn't issue the orders to capture me, his second took charge. What happened afterward is... murky."

"Tell me anyway."

Tal nodded slowly, still not meeting his eyes. "I used the cantrip for darkness, *mord*. Even though they knew my reputation, it's not something you can prepare for, becoming blind in a room bright just a moment before. I used the chaos to my advantage. I had noted where Jin stood and moved around him as I fought. Yet when I lifted the darkness, he..."

He stopped and bowed his head further. Garin kept his eyes on him, silent, waiting.

"I don't know if it was a strike from my blade that killed him or not. But it doesn't matter, does it? I'm still responsible for his death. If I'd only gone with him..."

"Maybe he'd still be alive."

Garin only stopped speaking because his throat had closed up. He clenched his teeth and looked away, trying to hold back the tears and lashing anger.

But he couldn't restrain them any longer.

"He was my father, Tal. My father! And you killed him. You took him away from me! It doesn't matter if it was an accident. It doesn't matter if King Aldric would have had you executed. My father was your friend. And when he hesitated to capture you, you took advantage of it."

Tal watched him now, but made no response. His calm acceptance only spurred Garin on, even if he couldn't meet his eyes.

"You always have an excuse for why the blame doesn't lie with you. You think politics killed my father? You think Aldric did it, sitting on his throne? You think the Extinguished did it when he made you the Magebutcher?"

Even as he spoke, doubt seeded itself through his fury. Garin shook his head violently and struggled on.

"How could I ever forgive you when you can't even own up to what you did? You can't even admit you killed him!"

"You're right."

Tal's words were quiet, but Garin stopped regardless. His eyes had never looked darker as he stared back at him.

"You're right," Tal repeated. "I killed him. I killed Jindol Dunford."

Garin felt as light-headed as he had when he'd been bleeding out on the Dancing Plaza. This was what he'd wanted: an admittance of his guilt.

Wasn't it?

He ground his teeth together and looked aside. *If it's what I wanted,* he thought, *how can I not even believe it?*

Tal slowly rose from his chair. "I think I should go now," he muttered.

Part of Garin wanted to goad him. *Run, coward. Just like you always do.* The words were on the tip of his tongue.

Instead, he only looked aside.

He felt Tal's gaze linger for a long moment. Then the old hero turned and pushed out into the afternoon light.

Garin stared at the door after it closed, his head buzzing.

He settled back into his bed, suddenly exhausted. He was tired to the bone of being angry.

And with all that was going on in Elendol, he had a feeling he and Tal would need each other for everyone to get out of this alive.

He expected to stew for a while longer, doubting his words and actions. But no sooner had he closed his eyes than he was carried down into a quiet darkness.

Tal walked aimlessly across the rope bridges. He recalled the conversation, again and again. Garin's accusations. His admittance.

I killed him.

Despite his weariness, his feet carried him far. When he raised his head, Tal looked out over the forest to the roaring Ildinfor. He watched the mist breaking off from the frothy white water, full of power and awe. Where an errant beam of sunlight hit the water, a glimpse of a rainbow barely shown through.

At another time, such beauty might have made him smile, or wax poetic if he had an audience. Instead, he only watched the colors flicker in the churning mist and felt the numb ache that had claimed his body.

He'd killed Garin's father. And there was nothing he could do to change that.

At least that's one thing Garin and I agree on. A small, joyless smile found his lips.

It was a long time before he found the will to turn away — but inevitably, he did. No matter how he might wish to let his despair drag him down, he couldn't allow it to. The Thorn still pulled his strings from the shadows. The Silver Vines and the Sympathist Peers still plotted. People were relying on him.

He, Tal Harrenfel, still had a role to play in whatever was coming to pass.

And so, even though it cost him an effort, he donned a smirk as he made his way back to the Venaliel kintree, flashing it at every Highkin he passed. They gave him frowns or looks of open disgust in return and continued past.

Tal kept smiling. He carried on.

BEGINNINGS

Garin was already awake when Wren slipped into the room.

He watched her walk quietly through the gloomy chamber, her eyes faintly glimmering with gold, and place a gentle hand on his shoulder. "You up?"

He nodded, yawned, and stretched. "Lively as a draugar."

Wren wrinkled her nose. "And you smell like one, too."

Grinning, he pulled her down onto the bed and kissed her, and she let him, though she pretended to be annoyed.

But before long, she pushed him away. "None of that. I can't interfere with your recovery."

"It's been a week. I'm only still in bed because Ashelia insists on it."

"Or is it because you're afraid of being ambushed on the bridges?" she countered.

He had to admit that he'd had the thought more than once. Again and again, the shame of falling to Tendil's sword suffused him. It didn't matter how he rationalized it to himself — that the elf had years of experience over him, or that he'd never been the most gifted fighter. It still made him burn to remember how easily he'd been overcome.

Sometimes, in his dreams, it wasn't Tendil he fought, but Ulen himself. During those nightmares, the Dancing Master didn't have a limp, and he would flow around his flailing attacks, leaving cut after shallow cut along Garin's body until he bled from a hundred wounds. He was as helpless before the elf as he would be in reality.

Worse still was when Garin didn't dream of being helpless. He dreamed that Ilvuan reached out to help him, and this time, he accepted it. Fire blossomed from his hands, enveloping and consuming both the Dancing Master and his pupil. And Garin would grin and delight in their screams, their writhing, and finally the stilling of their ashen corpses.

But nightmares and sleepless nights weren't Garin's reason for his recent reclusion. It was a different encounter that he feared.

Wren's gaze softened as if she guessed his thoughts. "You haven't seen him since, have you?"

Garin shook his head. "He stopped by once, a couple days after we spoke, but I pretended to be sleeping. He hasn't been back."

"Of course not. He's giving you space."

Wren fell silent for a moment. Garin reached out and took her hand, and she gave him a fleeting smile. But her eyes still creased with concern.

"Do you... want to talk about it?"

It was only the second time she'd asked about it, after he'd turned her down the first time. Though the thought of discussing it made his chest almost too tight to breathe, he murmured, "I guess."

"What did he say?"

He explained it to her as best as he could — who Tal had been then, and why King Aldric had commanded his father to capture him. He tried to keep his voice even as he explained how his father had died, and Tal didn't know if he'd been the one to strike the killing blow.

When he'd finished, Wren's face was set hard. He quickly said, "I know how it sounds. I felt like Father's blood was on his hands. But the more I think about it..." He shrugged. "Things aren't cut as straight as I thought."

The gold in her eyes whirled. "I don't see how they're not."

Garin sighed. "Remember how, when Ilvuan possessed me, I did things I didn't mean?"

"But you were possessed. Stabbing Kaleras wasn't your fault."

"But I convinced Tal and Aelyn to let me enter the Ruins of Erlodan. I didn't heed their warning to stay close, but wandered off and discovered the amulet that let the Singer speak to me. If I hadn't done those things, I never would have stabbed Kaleras."

Wren frowned and withdrew her hand from his to cross her arms. "So what are you saying?"

Garin hunched over, staring at the floor. "I'm saying that maybe it's the same for Tal, but the opposite. There were events that led to that confrontation between him and my father, events beyond his control, like the Extinguished possessing him and forcing him to slaughter most of the Warlocks' Circle. If that hadn't happened, he wouldn't have fled to Sendesh and fought the Yraldi. And King Aldric might not have sent my father to capture him."

Wren shook her head. "I don't know, Garin. We may not have control over our pasts. But each new choice we face — that's on us to decide. No matter how messed up Tal was then, he made the wrong decision."

"Did he?"

Garin felt as surprised at his words as she looked. But he couldn't deny the ring of truth in them.

"He was being wrongfully captured and condemned to death over politics and mistakes that weren't his. Would you have gone quietly in his place?"

Wren opened her mouth, then shut it. Her eyes blazed as she stared at the wall.

"Your father was his friend," she said at last.

"He was." Garin suddenly felt so weary he wanted to lie back down. "And my father was his. But circumstances put them against each other. There was no good choice."

He thought of his childhood, the days spent waiting at the edge of the fields and staring down the road into Hunt's Hollow. He'd dreamed of his father riding up it, returned at last. His eyes misted with the memories, and he took deep breaths until he calmed.

Wren looked at him from the corner of her eyes, then placed a hand on his shoulder and squeezed it.

They both jumped when a knock sounded at the door. Wiping his eyes, Garin exchanged a look with Wren, then called, "Who is it?"

"Ashelia," came the answer. "I wanted to check how you are."

He looked down at himself, still in the silken clothes that had been in his wardrobe for sleeping. But having tended to his wounds, Ashelia had seen him in worse conditions. "Come in."

She opened the door, but Garin was dismayed to see she wasn't alone. Aelyn entered after her, a small smirk playing over his lips at the sight of Garin's clothes.

Ashelia gestured toward the werelight lamp, and light filled the room. "Are you feeling well?"

"Never better."

She eyed him critically. "Your color is good. Perhaps you can return to your normal routine now."

"And wear some proper clothes, perhaps," Aelyn added, his eyes gleaming.

"His normal routine," Wren said with a sly smile. "Does that mean magic lessons as well?"

That wiped away Aelyn's amusement. He turned to his House-sister. "So that's why you brought me here."

299

"Of course," she said dismissively. "They can't go to the Winter Ball defenseless, can they?"

"A cantrip or two won't change that."

Garin exchanged a glance with Wren. Her spinning eyes told him she suspected the same thing as he did.

"Yes," Ashelia confirmed with a smile. "At my insistence, Aelyn is going to give you a useful lesson."

"Reckless," Aelyn muttered. But Garin noticed he didn't contradict her, nor appear as sulky as he might.

Garin hid a smile. Despite his apprehension, he said, "Good. I'm ready for it. And I know Wren has been waiting a long time."

"I'm sure you are. If I know Aelyn, he's been preparing you far longer than you needed."

The mage began to protest. "A sound instruction in the fundamentals of sorcery is imperative to proper—"

Ashelia quieted him with a hand on his shoulder. "I know, *Belosi*. But we don't have time for that anymore. We all have to make sacrifices. We all have to do things we've long put off, but know we must."

Her expression grew solemn. Garin wondered what else she meant.

Aelyn seemed to guess, for his expression grew tender. "It's for the best," he said in a low voice. "Those bastards never deserved you."

She gave him a small smile. Then, plainly not wishing to say more in front of Garin and Wren, she turned away from her House-brother. "One more thing. Since you've lost your dancing master, Garin, I wanted to offer myself in Ulen's place."

The proposal caught him off guard for a moment — then Garin smiled. "Thank you, Ashelia. I'd be honored to be your pupil."

"The honor is mine." A ghost of a smile graced her lips, then she set a hand to the door handle. "I'll see you later this afternoon. Now, since that's settled, I'm sure you two will want to break your fasts, and I know better than to stand in your way."

"Our lesson will be tomorrow at noon," Aelyn said over his shoulder as he and his House-sister left. "Do not be late!"

The mage slammed the door shut.

"Is he never in a good mood?" Wren muttered.

"He wouldn't be Aelyn if he was." To his surprise, a bit of the weight of the past week had lifted. "But Ashelia's right — I'm starving."

She glanced back at him, a dangerous look in her eyes. "You sure you wouldn't rather occupy ourselves some other way first?"

He needed no further convincing. A grin finding his lips, he pulled her close.

As Tal ascended the stairs, intending to fetch lunch from the Venaliel dining hall, an elven boy came flying around the corner.

"Whoa there, lad!" Tal caught the boy just before he crashed into him, barely avoiding a rough jab from what he carried. "You just about knocked me off the tree!"

The boy grinned and backed up a stair. "Sorry, sir! I was trying to stop Mistress Shelan from taking Crawg away."

"Is that so?"

As he took a second look, the boy looked very much like a child on the run. Under one arm he carried a miniature lute, and while it was finely polished and crafted, a multitude of scratches spoke of frequent use. In his other hand, the lad held a bright, orange frog who looked rather resigned to its fate, its legs hanging long and limp. *Or perhaps it's dead*, he reflected.

"Your mistress doesn't allow tree frogs in your nursery, does she?"

"I'm not in a nursery!" The boy seemed affronted. "But no,

she doesn't. She says they're slimy, disgusting creatures and I should never play with them. But who else am I supposed to play to?"

"Your lute, you mean?"

The boy looked up with disgust for a moment, but he quickly disguised it. "Yes, sir."

The longer they spoke, the more Tal's suspicions grew. The lad had a nursemaid. His clothes were plain, but tailored to fit him well, which spoke a lot for a growing boy. And while he looked seven, he guessed his age to be around ten or eleven, as elves aged slower than humans. His manners and speech spoke of High Elendol.

He studied his features. He had pale skin and limp, black hair that swayed like a curtain around his face. His features were petite with his age, yet held the promise of developing to be strong and handsome. But his eyes — as he stared up at him, they swirled with a familiar, stormy gray.

"What's your name, lad?"

"Rolan Venaliel, sir."

"Your mother wouldn't be Peer Venaliel, would it, Rolan?"

The boy cocked his head to one side. "Who else, sir?"

Before Tal could respond, a shout cascaded down the stairs.

"Master Rolan! I see you, you disobedient boy!"

The lad glanced over his shoulder with a panicked expression, then thrust the tree frog at Tal. "Quick! Take Crawg!"

With a conspiratorial wink, Tal accepted the frog and held it firmly as he stuck it beneath his jerkin. "Crawg" too late sensed his opportunity for escape and struggled belatedly, dispelling the notion at least that the boy's music had overcome it entirely.

An elven woman with a severe expression came bustling down the steps. She gave the briefest sign of respect toward Tal before lowering her eyes to the lad.

"You were told not to leave your chambers, remember? Your father's orders were explicit."

Rolan cast a rebellious glance toward Tal. "I remember."

"And animals are forbidden in your room — especially poisonous frogs! Is that not so?"

Tal felt much less certain about continuing to hold the wriggling Crawg. But loyalty kept him from letting it go.

Rolan seemed to struggle for a moment before the words burst out of him. "But what else am I supposed to do? I'm tired of playing the lute to an empty room. I require an audience!"

"I recall that *I* have been your audience these past weeks, young master," the nursemaid Shelan said drily. "Now come along and leave Mister Harrenfel alone."

"Harrenfel?" Rolan glanced back at Tal, his eyes swirling faster. "You mean *Tal* Harrenfel, The Man of a Thousand Names?"

Tal grinned. "As accused."

As a wide smile broke out over Rolan's face, though, Shelan gripped his arm in one bony hand. "That is enough, Master Rolan. Come along now."

"But Shelan! He's *Tal Harrenfel.* There are songs about him! He saved Elendol from the demon Heyl! The Queen gave him—"

"Haven't I told you not to believe stories, Master Rolan? Now come along, or your *pepua* will be angry."

Tal's smile slid away as the nursemaid towed Rolan back up the stairs. The lad glanced back and gave him a farewell wave, his eyes shining with disappointment. Tal waved back.

When they were out of sight, he withdrew the unfortunate Crawg from his jerkin and raised him to eye level. "I suspect you're better off without him. But I'm sure he'll miss you."

With that, he set the frog carefully on the railing, then slowly ascended after the boy and his maid.

Tal kept his distance, but saw the door closing to Rolan's chambers as he came around the bend. As he ghosted by, he heard the click of a bolt falling into place. A glimmer of pity ran through him, followed by anger. *A prisoner in his own home.*

And all because Yinin can't stand the thought of his meeting me. He wondered why Ashelia went along with it. Did she not want him to meet Rolan, either?

Sighing, he continued up the stairs, his belly announcing its needs once more. The dining hall was close at hand. But he hadn't gone far before muted shouting drew him to a halt.

It came from Ashelia's chambers, the location of which he knew from his frequent visits two decades before — though now, he supposed, they belonged to both Ashelia and Yinin. Tal crept closer, careful not to let his footfalls make a sound, and hovered outside their door. He could almost make out the exchanged words, but the door was thick enough to distort the exact words. Guilt stirred through him, but his curiosity was stronger.

"*Sols kas,*" he whispered as he braced himself.

The increase in his sense of hearing was disorienting, but not as much as before. He heard monkeys fighting somewhere in the branches above, and other animals scuffled through the leaves. An insect buzzed near his ear and nearly drowned out all other noises. Waving a hand by his ear — the swish of the air annoyingly loud — he banished the bug and honed his focus in on the muffled words now made audible.

"—You live in my House, Yinin. Don't pretend otherwise."

"*Our* House, you mean. I'm as much Venaliel as you!"

"No. Not anymore."

Ashelia's denial nearly took the wind out of Tal. A small smile curled his lips.

Her voice shook slightly as she continued, but her words were firm. "You wear my glyph, have slept in my bed, fathered my son. But you're not loyal to our Queen. I've ignored it for years, your courting of the Sympathists and aiding in their schemes. I ignored it for the sake of our son and my House. But I won't anymore."

"Will you shame yourself and House Venaliel, then? Will you break your oath?"

"A promise to a snake is no promise. Return to the Lath-nieli, Yinin. You belong among your own kind."

Yinin exhaled with obvious anger, and his pacing footsteps sounded.

"Rolan — I'm taking him with me."

A deadly silence exuded from the room.

"You won't have my son."

"*Our* son. And I will. I must protect him."

"Try to take him, and I will have you thrown from this tree. I mean it, Yinin. Don't you dare touch a hair on his head."

Tal could almost hear the clicking of Yinin's jaw as it worked for words.

"And that's it?" he said at last, the words coming out in a choked whisper.

"Yes."

Tal released the spell and backed away from the door, fearing Yinin might leave the chamber that very moment and find him there. As the spell dissipated, though, he noticed someone ascending the stairs.

As Aelyn came into view, he paused. He'd tucked a satchel under his arm, by which Tal guessed the mage had again been looting the Venalieli's stores of magical implements, as he'd done frequently before. His eyes flickered from Tal to the door. Slowly, his brow creased into a scowl.

Tal could only shrug.

At the mage's impatient gesture, Tal followed him, glancing back one last time at the door. Despite the dubiousness of his spying, he couldn't help the seed of hope growing in his chest, nor the smile that sprung out of him.

When they were out of earshot of the door, Aelyn glanced back at him, bronze eyes whirling. "What," he said in measured tones, "do you think you were doing back there?"

"Eavesdropping, as you well know."

"That is low, Harrenfel, even for you. Though I suppose that bard's song does name you the 'Three-Faced Rogue.'"

"It does." He thought he might agree to any insult Aelyn threw at him. At that moment, nothing could bring down his buoyant mood.

Aelyn surprised him when he looked back with a wry smile. "I suppose they had it out?"

"From the sound of it, our dear minister will pack his chests and move back home momentarily."

The mage made a scoffing noise. "About time. She was always far too good for those *kolfash* Lathnieli."

Tal's smile slipped away, and not just from the crass word. "You won't do anything... rash, will you, Aelyn?"

"What, kill him?"

"The suspicion crossed my mind."

They ascended in silence for a few moments. Tal tried to picture what the other man was going through. *Would I be able to stop myself in his position?*

They reached the top of the stairs, where they opened out to the dining hall. Aelyn turned back to face him, his eyes not quite meeting his.

"No," he said in little more than a whisper. "I won't kill him or his kin. Ashelia would not want me to. Nor would my Queen."

If Aelyn had been another man, Tal would have reached out to him, showing him through a touch what words poorly conveyed. As it was, he only nodded and made the attempt.

"You're a good man, Aelyn. Underneath all those layers of sarcasm and pessimism, you have a good heart."

The mage snorted. "And the bard calls you 'Pearltongue.' Leave sentimentality to the poets, Harrenfel."

"Fair enough." Tal grinned — then, because he *was* Aelyn, he gripped his shoulder and gave him a friendly shake. "I'll fill my mouth with food instead. Share a meal with me?"

Aelyn scowled as he shrugged him off. "Fine. But only because I already intended to eat."

"Tell yourself whatever you please, my sour friend."

The mage spoke over his shoulder, already heading toward the long buffet tables. "If, indeed, we *are* friends."

THE NATURE OF EVIL

AELYN SWEPT INTO THE LIBRARY'S TRAINING ROOM, HIS SCOWL even more pronounced than usual.

As Garin exchanged a glance with Wren, the elven mage glared at them. "As you may recall, with the Winter Ball a week away, my dear sister has informed me I must abandon all sense to teach you cantrips."

Though pleased they wouldn't spend interminable hours reciting passages from archaic books, Garin shifted nervously in his chair. He remembered all too well what dialect of the Worldtongue he had to speak to summon magic. And though Wren had accepted it, he felt no easier about flaunting it in front of her.

"But I will not neglect my duty." Aelyn gestured impatiently at the tablets laying before them, gathered prior to the lesson by Garin and Wren. "To ensure that you do not mispronounce the words — as much as can be ensured for you two — we will utilize the rune tablets."

Though Aelyn had largely kept them from casting magic, he'd already led them through learning their runes. It was like reading, yet somehow, understanding the runes came quicker to Garin than to Wren. For him, it felt like remembering something he'd forgotten, and once reminded, it fixed itself in his mind. For Wren, each rune felt foreign, and only through many scowls and hours did she reproduce them by memory.

But I won't use any of those runes, he realized. *I have to speak the devil's tongue.*

Ilvuan's amusement bubbled up from the recesses of his mind.

"Wren, speak the word for fire," the mage instructed.

Wren obeyed, and the familiar rune for *kald* formed in spindly lines of red light across the front of her tablet.

Garin forced himself to meet Aelyn's gaze as he looked at him.

"Garin. You will speak its Darktongue equivalent, *keld.*"

Keld. He saw again the Nightelf youths swallowed by flames, their clothes blackening and stripping off to reveal the fire-eaten flesh beneath. Wren's eyes flickered toward him, then away.

Fixing his gaze on the tablet, he forced out the word. "*Keld.*"

A faint jingle of bells, the first toll of the Nightsong, sounded as lines formed on his tablet. The symbol that appeared differed from the one displayed on Wren's. Just like the glyphs in the Ruins of Erlodan, the lines seemed to possess a life of their own, twisting and coiling like a nest of serpents. Yet, as he forced himself to look at it, he found it took but a glance for the symbol to burn itself into his mind.

Wren still had her head bent to her tablet, her eyes working over the lines. Aelyn scowled as he saw Garin's head raise, but he'd seen enough of his quick memory not to disbelieve it. "Very well, Garin. If you already think you know it, by all means, demonstrate your fire."

At Aelyn's prompting, he stood and moved closer to the blazing hearth behind the mage. He didn't try tricking himself into believing the sweat running down his back was from the heat. Holding up his hand, he banished his fears of Wren watching him and pictured the flames rising from his palm.

The shape of the rune flared in his mind, and for a moment, all thoughts but it fled.

"*Keld.*"

Flames soared up from his hand, so sudden and intense that he jumped. It was only with a force of will that he prevented what Aelyn called "magical externalities" — burns up his arms, if not within his very veins.

Heart knocking on his ribs, he quickly dismissed the flames.

Aelyn nodded his grudging approval. "A bit enthusiastic, but you managed it. Wren, are you prepared?"

They continued practicing in a similar fashion for several more cantrips, first speaking the word to their tablets, then memorizing the rune, and finally summoning it. Sometimes, the words were similar between the Darktongue and the Worldtongue — *kald* and *keld* for fire, *lisk* and *bisk* for ice. More often, they were completely different — "gust" was *wuld* for Wren, but *jolsh* for Garin. Yet though they spoke different words, the effects remained the same. There was no hint that the language Garin used to summon his magic was of devils and demons, at least not from the light, wind, or fire that he produced.

But all the while, the Nightsong marched through his head with its discordant rhythm.

After Wren dismissed the orb of darkness that had swallowed the room, Garin couldn't repress his question any longer. "Why are they the same?" he asked Aelyn without preamble.

To Garin's surprise, a rare smile appeared on the mage's lips. "The effects of the two tongues? Because, boy, for our purposes, the words are the same."

Garin glanced at Wren and found her incredulity mirrored. He knew Aelyn had once studied the Darktongue in the Onyx Tower, but it made what he said no easier to believe.

"How can they be the same words?" Wren demanded.

"When I say *mord* for darkness, Garin says — well, something different."

Usually so bold, Wren had shown reticence about speaking the Darktongue. Garin could hardly blame her.

Aelyn's eyes were swirling fast as he stepped closer. "You are missing the obvious point. The Worldtongue and the Dark-tongue — they share the same origin language. All differences between them are mere differences in dialect. Time and location have distorted their pronunciations, but the things they represent — those have never changed."

Instead of alleviating Garin's confusion, Aelyn's explanations only expanded it. "But you've always said we must be very precise with the pronunciation," he interjected. "Now you're saying the words have changed. How does that make sense?"

Aelyn, for a wonder, seemed to be enjoying himself. "Let me put it a different way. When I say 'Uleni' in Gladelyshi, I mean 'Hello' in the Reachtongue."

Wren's brow was still furrowed, but Garin nodded, a hint of comprehension dawning. "They sound different, and they're different words, but they mean the same thing. They're both a greeting."

"Precisely! The languages comprise unique words, but the meanings are essentially the same, often word for word. But though, as a principle, this is largely accurate, mortal languages have some variations across each other in their exact meanings and syntaxes.

"But variants of the Worldtongue do not. What we call the Worldtongue in the Westreach is a dialect of an older language, the same as the Darktongue is. But the words mean precisely the same thing, because that which they refer to are elements of the world. Fire is fire, no matter if it's named *kald* or *keld* — and in the dialects of the Worldtongue, the words speak to fire's very nature, symbols so true they allow those with sorcery in their blood to speak its name and control it."

Garin felt his mind floundering to track the reason even as

the words resonated in a deeper part of him. The part of him that seemed to recognize the glyphs understood, too, the nature of the Worldtongue — and the Darktongue. To that part of him, their interchangeability was a fact. But to his conscious mind, Aelyn's logic seemed too circular to be true.

Wren leaned back in her chair and crossed her arms over her chest. "That's ridiculous."

"Ridiculous, is it?" Aelyn moved to stand over her. "So you, a half-trained, fifteen-year-old girl, claim to know more than me, an accomplished scholar, on the etymology of sorcerous languages?"

Her jaw tightened, and she didn't look away — but neither did she respond.

One last question niggled at Garin. "But if they're essentially the same, the Worldtongue and the Darktongue... can one really be good, and the other evil?"

Another smile blossomed across the mage's face, and he looked like a different man. "Precisely the question I sought to answer with my studies. And I believe I did. No, Garin, they cannot — neither speech is good or evil. Others might dispute it, but I have proven that, despite the biases attached as to who is speaking it, there is no inherent morality to any dialect of the Worldtongue."

Garin leaned back, staring at the blank wall opposite of him. He could feel Ilvuan stir for a moment and probe his emotions, then grow disinterested and recede once more. Evil and good, he imagined, were not things a devil would concern themselves with.

But if the Darktongue isn't evil, does that mean he's not a devil? Does it mean I'm not a monster?

Ilvuan roused again, impatience flickering through Garin's mind. *A tool is not good or evil,* he noted. *Nor can a language be. You'd do better to learn it, Listener, and use it as you must.*

Garin didn't respond, but let his thoughts drift tentatively over the conclusion. He wasn't sure he believed it. He desperately wished he could.

Aelyn turned away, calling back his attention. "But that is enough amateurish scholarship for now, and a good place to end this lesson. You've learned all the basic cantrips. I will not risk you learning two-word spells while you have not mastered one word. Practice those, for they shall have to be enough."

Wren's eyes were still bright with her elven gold. But at their dismissal, she stood with Garin and led the way out of the practice room. As they walked between the bookshelves of the library, Garin's thoughts turned back to all he'd learned and the unspoken question that had plagued him for long months.

When they'd stepped outside the library door and onto the platform, Wren looked up and down the stairs, then pulled him close to the railing. He didn't like to stand too near the edge of High Elendol's terraces if he could help it, and he edged around her, while Wren brashly leaned against the balustrade.

She stared at him, and he withstood her scrutiny for as long as he could. "What?"

"You're not evil."

Though he'd been marveling over the possibility in his own mind, the words stirred a flicker of anger in him. "Did you think I was?"

She shrugged. "Not you. But with a devil in you... I didn't know what to think."

"Yet you still laid with me."

Unflappable as she usually was, Wren's eyes darted to the library door behind Garin, as if afraid Aelyn might overhear. But her voice was unconcerned as she retorted, "You didn't object."

"No. And I still don't." He grinned, the anger dampening as soon as it had come. That she didn't think he was Night-touched or tainted was the important thing. He couldn't hold it against her for wondering when he'd been uncertain himself.

Wren didn't return his smile. "But even if speaking the

Darktongue doesn't make you evil, you still don't know the first thing about that thing inside you. And I don't see how it *can't* be a demon."

Ilvuan's presence was a whisper in his mind, passing by like a brush of tall grass against his skin. Garin wondered what might happen if he was offended by their conversation. Though, considering the Singer's earlier words, he doubted morality mattered to him.

"I don't know," he murmured, looking out over the forest and the sprawling city below. "I know Ilvuan controlled me on behalf of the Extinguished before, but—"

"Ilvuan?"

Garin felt heat blossom across his face. "His name, remember?"

Her expression had gone graver than he'd seen since her father's slow recovery. "I remember. But with the devil naming itself to you, that makes finding out what we can even more urgent. Garin, speak to Tal about it."

He couldn't help but flinch. Maybe he'd told Wren he wasn't sure his father's death was all Tal's fault. Maybe he'd meant it. But he hadn't forgiven him yet, and in the aftermath of Tal's confession, his thoughts and feelings had grown more muddled than before.

Wren took his silence for resistance. "Before we rode to the Ruins of Erlodan, he spoke something of what the devil was. A Singer, he called it — and it had something to do with a 'Worldheart' and a 'Song'?"

He nodded. "That's how I understood it. When I cast magic, there are sounds that accompany it, ones that make little sense to be hearing. The clanging of a spoon against a bowl, water lapping against a boat's hull, the whinny of a horse..." He shrugged. "That's the Nightsong."

Her brow furrowed. "But if the Darktongue isn't evil, what if... what if the Song *isn't* of the Night? What if the devil isn't a devil at all, but something else entirely? It was allied with the

Extinguished, but it turned against him. That doesn't make it good, but maybe..."

She trailed off, mulling over the implications. Garin had as much trouble deciding. Yet, devil or no, ever since Ilvuan had given him his name, a trust had built between them. In his times of need, the Singer had been there for him. He'd sent Garin to Tal's room when the man had endangered himself. He'd put the curse on Garin's lips that had saved him and Wren from the Nightelf youths. He'd held Garin to the World as he'd slipped away after Ulen's deadly match.

I have claimed you, little Listener, Ilvuan spoke softly in his mind. *Until you have fulfilled your purpose, I cannot release you.*

Garin repressed a shiver. Good or evil, the Singer had him in his grasp. And he meant to use him.

He looked aside from Wren's imploring stare. "I'll talk to him."

She reached out and gripped his hand tightly. "Good. But if you think it can wait, I have one thing in mind that could keep us occupied for the afternoon."

His pulse suddenly racing, all worries of the moment before forgotten, Garin grinned as Wren pulled him down the stairs and back to their room.

LOST KEY

Tal entered the Whistling Thistle and repressed a wince at the sight of Rozana sitting alone.

He'd been avoiding this confrontation. Though it had been the assassin who killed Pylas and his monkey, he felt that part of the blame fell on him. He hadn't known the Nightelf well, nor did he know much of the minotaur.

But for all the blood on his hands, Tal had never been much good at coping with death.

He steeled his resolve and slipped into the empty seat opposite of the minotaur. Slowly, she looked up and met his eyes with her usual placid stare.

"I'm sorry I didn't come sooner," he began with an apologetic smile. "I've been—"

"Elendol grows more dangerous by the day," Rozana interrupted. "There are many things to report, so long as you remember the price."

She held out a thick-fingered hand. Tal's smile slipped away. He wondered if she'd ever cared about her compatriots. *Perhaps the skepticism of Easterners is for good reason,* he mused, though he'd had enough experience to know such biases rarely held much water.

Producing a pair of silver coins, Tal set them in her palm. Rozana swiftly secured them inside a pouch under her shirt before leaning forward. "The Silver Vines are stirring. They have spread throughout the city, taking up abandoned houses, hiding in plain sight."

He clenched a fist underneath the table, but kept his expression relaxed. "Are they doing anything?"

"Many things. The lifts of Sympathist Houses move incessantly. Crates and barrels are being carted to their new locations. What they contain, I cannot say. Many of the cultists also look familiar with battle, with scars and calloused hands, and weapons belted at their hips. Some are of the Empire, but many more are Gladelysh."

"Can you show me these places?"

Rozana stared at him for a long moment. "I would have to show you myself," she said slowly. "Yeshil has not returned to me since... the incident. And Temmy has not been well."

Tal winced and silently repented his earlier thoughts against the minotaur. "Did Yeshil sell us out then?"

"Likely."

It didn't speak well of the solidity of Rozana's operations, though Tal had to admire her character for admitting it. "Nothing for it now, I suppose. Can you show me yourself?"

She leaned back, her great head turning as she scanned the room. He saw several pairs of eyes glance at them from both the Easterner and Gladelysh sides of the commonroom, and he realized her concern. The minotaur didn't exactly make for a subtle figure.

Rozana's gaze settled on the door, and she nodded toward it. "I do not think I need to."

Tal followed her eyes and hid his surprise. Condur, the Ilthasi he'd encountered when first venturing into the Mire, stood waiting by the door, his face just visible.

He turned back to her. "I'm not sure I know what you mean."

"I am the overseer of a spy network, Tal Harrenfel. Do you think I do not know the Ilthasi who wander the Mire?"

Tal shrugged. "Better to pretend you don't until you say otherwise."

"Yes, it is. Perhaps you had best speak to him before he grows impatient. I hear the Ilthasi are not pleasant when they are made to wait."

He ignored her hint. "That's all I get for two silvers? Surely, I've paid for more."

The minotaur stood, her wide bulk bumping the table, but she lost no composure for it. "Only a piece of advice. Leave the Mire and do not return. Dark times are coming for all who live here."

Doesn't that include you? But Tal stood as well and, despite being short-changed, he made the elvish gestures of respect toward her. "If we don't meet again, I just want to say, I appreciate what you've done and sacrificed for us."

She studied him for a long moment, her dark eyes moving back and forth between his. "It was business, nothing more."

Then she turned and walked slowly up the stairs to the rooms above, the wood creaking with each heavy hoof-fall.

Tal watched her disappear up the stairs. He didn't resent her anger. Inadvertently or not, he'd gotten one of her friends killed, driven away another, and crippled the last through grief.

Yet another broken family left behind, he thought as he turned away.

He hid the melancholy behind a wide grin as he strode toward Condur, who waited by the door. The Ilthasi didn't return it, but turned from the tavern and stepped back outside. The smile slipping a little, Tal followed him.

The afternoon werelights in the Mire seemed subdued, like sunlight before a storm passed overhead. Tal followed Condur around to the back of the inn, then stopped as he turned to face him.

"Where have you been hiding?" He said it half-teasingly, but a sharp edge lingered behind the words.

Condur either didn't take the hint or didn't care to. "I have been commanded to move all of my operatives out of the Mire."

"I had a strange feeling you might say that. Does this have something to do with your lapse the other night?"

The Ilthasi captain stared at him for a long moment. "That assassin killed three Ilthasi. One by one, he cut them down. The Queen believes it is too risky to continue our operations here with such menaces loose."

"So you'll abandon Low Elendol altogether."

A flicker of anger swirled in Condur's eyes. "I do as my Queen directs."

Tal's lips twisted in a wry smile. "As do I, Condur. But I cannot help but wonder if she is as omniscient as everyone seems to believe."

The Ilthasi twitched. "Do not criticize the Queen in front of me again," he said quietly. "I may not be so forgiving next time."

Tal inclined his head, hiding the thrill that pulsed through his veins. "As you wish," he acceded, then pivoted, "Will you attend the Winter Ball? I hear that's where our true concerns lie."

"Yes. I am not unknown, so I must go in disguise. But we will not let any harm befall the Queen."

Though he noticed that Condur didn't extend his protection to Tal himself this time, he nodded. "As it should be. Farewell for now, Condur. And thank you for watching my back when you could."

As he returned to the Venaliel kintree by its lift, the same operator as before sullenly perusing his book of nudes in the corner, Tal stared out over Low Elendol and wondered what would become of it. So many of them were innocent of wrongdoing, yet they suffered from the games of the Highkin. And still more was to come.

How has your great nation come to this, Geminia?

A somber mood had seized him by the time the lift arrived at the top, so much so that he left a silver for the operator on his small desk and didn't say a word against him.

Ascending the stairs, he wondered what he should do. How could he prepare for a menace whose face he didn't know? Though he'd had many such encounters in the past, and he'd never felt much fear then, he recognized it hadn't been bravery, but foolishness that made him so rash.

Age was making him far too sage.

Yet he knew of one fool still clinging to his old ways. So, without knowing what else to do, he sought Falcon out.

Continuing past his room, he found the Court Bard and the Dancing Feathers where he'd expected: the secondary hall designed to host diversions other than feasts and dancing. Upon the stage, a maudlin scene played out. The princess, played by the human girl Melina, leaned out over a parapet erected at the edge of the stage. She wore a look so forlorn that Tal was seized with both amusement and pity. On the right side of the stage, several actors dressed as elven nobility were seated around a table, laughing and pointedly ignoring the sorrowful girl.

Falcon glanced over at Tal's entrance, but held up a finger. Lips quirking, Tal watched as the girl stepped onto the wall's embrasure and, her balance swaying, looked down at what was supposed to be the sea, shown by the cut-outs of waves.

"O, capricious fate," Melina said, her voice hiccuping slightly. "If thou will seize my heart, spare not my soul's vessel. Less than a speck am I with Palinor's love bereft! The sea is better company than all the royals of Isinel. Swallow my tears in your salty embrace — *take me for yours!*"

With a final, whimpering scream, Melina threw herself forward to her watery death. In the shadows below, Ox, clothed all in black, gently caught her and cradled her safely to the floor.

As the troupers erupted into applause, Melina stood and, face flushed, gave a low bow. Tal glanced over to find Wren standing next to him, her hands propped on her hips and her mouth puckered.

"She's very good, isn't she?" he said innocently.

She looked up at him with a raised eyebrow. "People think so."

"Wren, Wren. As our playwright Rominia Soulsight wrote, 'Is it the glimmer of green I see in your eye?'"

"Jealous?" Falcon's daughter scoffed. "Of Melina? Your eyesight's failing you, old man."

"As you say."

His grin faded, however, as he contemplated what he must ask next. "Garin... has he mentioned me to you?"

Wren gave him a flat look. "What do you think?"

"What I mean is, since my — well, confession. Has he spoken of it to you?"

"We *do* sleep in the same bed."

Tal looked away. "Forget I asked."

She sighed. "Yes, he's mentioned it. You two will be fine, Tal. He just needs time."

He wondered how much Garin had said, and if Wren herself held it against him. She wasn't one to take grudges lightly.

"Thank you," he murmured. "I have to speak with your father now."

She waved a hand. "By all means. But be careful — you know how he gets right before performances."

True to her warning, Falcon had undergone a transformation. His usual jovial manner had been replaced by an almost manic energy, sharpened by impatience aimed at anyone who stood in his way. Despite the apprehension it filled him with, Tal pressed forward, knowing he had to speak his mind.

"Old friend. I know you're busy, but can you spare a moment?"

"Of course, Tal, of course. Yelda! Run the scene through again! I'll be back in a moment."

As the dwarven actress projected her shrill voice over the rest of the babbling troupe, Falcon led Tal outside to the platform.

"Well?" the Court Bard asked brusquely, his good hand tapping on his leg. "What's on your mind?"

Tal couldn't help a flicker of annoyance. Here he was, worrying about ambushes and civil war, and Falcon was acting as if he inconvenienced him.

But considering Tal still owed him a hand, he let it slide.

He explained, as succinctly as he could, all he'd learned and feared of the Winter Ball. Though Falcon's eyes darted around, Tal could tell he listened with the focus only a trouper had for the moment.

Before he'd finished, the bard interrupted, "I know where this is going, Tal, and the answer is no."

Tal blinked. "To what question?"

"To the Dancing Feathers walking away from the Winter Ball! That's what you came here to talk me out of, isn't it?"

A smile found Tal's lips. "No, my old friend, it's not. As much as I might wish I could, I won't ask you to back away from your dream now."

Falcon seemed taken aback. "Then what do you want?"

"Your advice. What should I do? How can we prepare for an ambush we know is coming and that the Queen has invited, but I fear we cannot stop?"

The bard stared at him for a long moment, eyes finally still but for the gold swirling through them. "You go, and you keep watch, and you obey the Queen's commands. That's all you can do."

He hadn't known what to expect from Falcon, only that he'd hoped for more. "Is that it?"

Sympathy shone in his friend's eyes as he clasped Tal's shoulder. "I know you wish to save all you can. It's that very quality of yours that makes you such material for songs. But sometimes, there are things too great for one man to solve. There's nothing else you can do, old friend, but play the game as its been laid."

Tal turned to the railing and leaned on it, staring out across the forested city. "I'm afraid, Falcon. Afraid for you, and your daughter, and your troupe. I'm afraid for Garin and Ashelia and the Queen who has bound me to her service. I'm even afraid for Aelyn. All of you are in danger, and there's nothing I can do to stop it. Even though I'm the one who has brought it upon us."

He flinched at Falcon's laugh.

"You brought it? Oh, Tal, you silly fool. What did you do to cause this?"

Tal met the bard's smile with a somber look. "Yuldor wants me and what's in my head — *The Fable of Song and Blood.* I think that's why, after months of simmering tension, things are coming to a head now."

"So maybe you're the spark to set the barn on fire. But if it wasn't you, another ember would have blown along. Honestly, Tal, sometimes I think you *believe* your legend."

To his surprise, Tal felt a weight lift from his chest. He gave a low chuckle. "Perhaps you're right. I never did claim to be more than a man."

"As well you shouldn't."

"But," Tal added, "it doesn't change the way things stand. You'll be careful, won't you?"

Falcon gripped his hand tightly. "I believe it is I who should secure that promise from you."

Tal gave him a crooked smile. "You know me. I'm as careful as a chicken in a griffin's den."

With a last embrace, they parted ways. Falcon hurried back to his rehearsal, while Tal turned down the stairs to his room.

He'd taken heart from his friend's words. But with each step he descended, the comfort faded, and the bleak truth remained.

He was the Man of a Thousand Names, the Devil Killer, the Thorn Puller — yet underneath the legend, he *was* only a man. He couldn't stop a war, nor much sway it. He might not even be able to defend those he loved.

A thought stopped him mid-step. *We could run. Gather them — Garin, Wren, Falcon, the Dancing Feathers — gather them all and flee.* This wasn't their fight; they didn't have to die for Gladelysh feuds and politics. And it wouldn't be the first time Tal had run from a fight he couldn't win.

But as soon as it occurred to him, he knew it as a vain hope. Ashelia would never leave Gladelyl — she loved her Queen and country, to make no mention of her son and Helnor. And Aelyn — he wouldn't abandon Geminia in her darkest hour. Falcon had already insisted he would play the Winter Ball as his crowning performance. Wren wouldn't leave her father, and Garin wouldn't leave Wren.

You could still run. You alone.

The thought was more tempting than he wanted to admit. Despite Falcon's reassurances, Tal knew Yuldor reached for him especially, and that a war in Elendol might be a price the Prince of Devils considered worth paying for his capture. If he fled, Yuldor might pursue him and forgo his plans for Elendol.

But again, Falcon's logic defeated him. If Tal was significant, it was as the final spark. The Enemy had many goals; possessing Tal was only one of them. Elendol was far too fine a prize to relinquish in place of Tal alone.

His hand held tightly to his sword's hilt. *So I will stay and fight.* Imagining the faceless enemies, he felt a cold dread grip his heart. Once, he'd been fearless. As Gerald Barrows, as the Red Reaver, he'd faced down dozens of flint-eyed killers and never flinched.

But that was before he'd again found something worth living for.

As if his thoughts had summoned her, Ashelia appeared around the bend of the stairs, stopping him in his tracks.

"Ashelia." He tried to smile, but his concerns dragged at the corners of his lips.

"Tal."

They stood, facing each other, several steps apart. The leaves rustled overhead. A monkey shrieked.

He'd seen her but occasionally since she broke her bond-oath to Yinin a week before. Though he'd longed to go to her immediately afterward, reason had prevailed. The best thing he could do was give her space.

Ashelia didn't smile now, but he could feel satisfaction radiating from her like morning fog off of a pond. His interest stirred in response.

"I believe you."

"Believe me?" His voice fell to a whisper. Hope, rising despite his earlier despair, now squeezed his chest tight.

"Yes. I believe that you left to protect me. I believe that you never returned because you were ashamed of who you'd become. I believe that no matter what you've done and what you claim to have been, you are the same man I once loved. And love still."

The kintree was full of people — yet in that moment, Tal felt they were the only two people in the World. The words he hadn't dared to imagine, could hardly believe now — she'd spoken them.

"Why? Why do you... love me?"

Ashelia ascended the stairs until they were within arms' reach. At her closeness, his fragile restraint cracked further.

"Why does anyone love anyone else?" she murmured. "You balance my scales. You challenge me and never let me settle for less. You help me remember what it is to desire and be desired. You are mine."

Tal closed his eyes and tilted his head back. He knew what he had to say, knew it at his core. But he didn't know that he had the strength to say it.

"Why now?" he said instead.

"We don't know what will happen with this conflict, Tal." An edge had crept into her voice. "Elendol could be in ruins before the sun rises. I hope it will survive. But if it has to end, I want things to end the right way. With the right person."

He lowered his chin and met her gaze again. A tear escaped one eye to trickle down his cheek.

"Elendol might burn tomorrow," he said quietly. "But it might not. You can't throw away the life you've built here on the chance that we lose. I won't let you."

"Throw it away?" Laughing softly, Ashelia seized his hands in hers. "For the first time in a long time, I've taken my life back."

He didn't have the heart to pull away, even as his tongue fumbled over the damning words. "You have a son, Ashelia. Rolan — I met him, here, on the stairs, with his lute and his frog."

"I know. He told me. And soon, I'll properly introduce you."

"You have to look after him."

"I will. I always have."

"But that's why you must refuse me. I'm a hunted man, Ashel. The Thorn and his master don't yet know about me, but I can't hide the truth from them forever. And he and all those who follow him will never stop pursuing me."

"Know about you? What do you mean?" She released him and stared at him with sudden wariness.

Tal looked over the darkening forest and the twinkling werelights. "You know what I said about Garin? About him being a Fount of Song, and what that means?"

Ashelia waited in silence.

"I'm the other side of that coin — a Fount of Blood. It's how I'm a sorcerer without possessing elven blood or a patron god. And it means that, like Garin, I can inherit the Worldheart from Yuldor. In theory."

She stared at him for a long moment. He wanted her to

speak, to say anything, just so long as she didn't look at him with that accusing stare.

Then she stepped closer, took his face in her hands, and kissed him.

For a moment, he couldn't move for shock — then all his doubts fell away. His lips softened to hers, and he drew her in, his hand cradling the nape of her neck, his fingers tangling in her hair. She held him so tightly he couldn't have pulled away if he'd wanted to. Moisture touched his cheek, and he wasn't sure if it was from her tears or his.

Finally, she released him, and he caught his breath. His head felt light and dizzy, and his blood was pleasantly warm. Her hand still captured his, and she kept him close, her lips slightly parted, her eyes whirling with the storm inside her.

"What was...?" he tried to ask, but his thoughts were too scattered for words.

"You idiotic fool." She wore a wide smile such as he hadn't seen in two decades. "Haven't you learned by now? You don't get to run away and make my decisions for me. You were never a safe man — I knew it when I first claimed you, and I haven't forgotten it. But nowhere is safe, and the Mother take me if we're not safer together than apart."

Tal worked his sluggish mind through her logic. "I don't know, Ashel. The risks—"

"Damn the risks!" she said with a short laugh. "What's life without the spark of risk — isn't that what you used to say?"

"I can't let you—"

"You can't control that. I'll do what I think is best."

"And your son—"

"Will finally look up to a man of honor rather than the father he's had."

She drew his lips down to hers again, and Tal couldn't hold himself back from her any longer.

Some time later, with the hour of the ball quickly arriving, Ashelia left him there on the stairs and ascended back to her chambers, a promise in her smile. Tal returned to his own room, his mind in a blur. Entering, he threw himself on the bed and stared up at the ceiling.

A slow smile spread across his face as he remembered every detail of their moment on the stairs. The slow kisses. The press of her body against his, familiar and exciting from their long separation.

But he knew he couldn't savor the memory now. There was a ball to prepare for.

By compulsion, he first reached for the drawer next to the bed and, with a muttered word, unlocked it. He always checked that Hellexa's tome was safe when he came home.

But as he reached inside, he felt nothing.

Bolting upright, he peered inside, but it only confirmed what he already knew. The drawer was empty.

He didn't move for a long moment. Then he jumped to his feet and mindlessly searched the room. He opened the few other drawers, looked under the bed, peered into the wardrobe, sifted through his scattered books. But even as he searched every nook and cranny in the small space, he knew he'd find nothing.

The copied pages of *A Fable of Song and Blood* were gone.

Tal sat heavily on the bed, his head spinning. Only now did he realize what a fool he'd been. He'd counted on secrecy and subtlety to keep the duplicate book from the Thorn's notice. He'd assumed that, with the first copy burned, the Extinguished wouldn't even know to look for it.

Someone told him. He felt sick even considering it, but he couldn't help but think someone must have. He ticked off the names of those who'd known of its existence in his head. *Aelyn. Kaleras. Garin. Falcon. Wren.* Had he told Ashelia? It didn't matter — he'd never consider her betrayal.

Just as you never considered Falcon's before?

He stubbornly shook the thought away. It had to have been someone else. But how many others might they have told? Members of the Dancing Feathers? The two Mute monks who traveled with them? Even a passing mention to a stranger?

But it could be even simpler. Anyone who tried hard enough could access his room, whether by magic, a key, or clever lock picking. And though he had sealed the drawer with sorcery, it wouldn't take much of a guess to figure out something protected was worth stealing.

Yinin.

The minister had left House Venaliel, but he could still have contacts within the kintree. Some, at least, might keep some loyalty to him rather than Ashelia. And Yinin's alignment with the Sympathists and House Lathniel made its final destination obvious.

The Thorn has it.

He held his head in his hands and closed his eyes. All that Tal knew, the Extinguished — and consequently, Yuldor — would soon know, if they didn't already. About the Worldheart. The Founts. The Song and the Blood. About what Tal was.

About Garin.

Garin. He had to warn him. Soon, the Thorn and his master would know of their significance. Then they'd kill them, just as they'd slain Hellexa and the sorcerers who'd followed her.

But with the pages recently stolen, they had a little time before that occurred, and the Winter Ball was nearly upon them. Though it seemed a meaningless gesture, he had to prepare and dress. Once he'd done so, he could find Garin and prepare him for what was coming.

And tell him what? part of him mocked. *That, just as you killed his father, you've surely killed him?*

Tal clenched his fists. He could do nothing for the past and his mistakes. But he could do his best to correct them.

Exhaling raggedly, Tal eased his body and stood, then began to dress for the feast.

THE WINTER BALL

"Do I have to wear this?"

Garin pulled at the collar of his elven robe. It seemed designed to choke him, so tight it dug into his neck every time he turned his head.

"No," Wren said with a wry smile. She herself wore a dark tunic and trousers, plain but finely made. "Or you wouldn't have to if you were performing with the troupe instead of attending as an honored guest."

"Don't start with that again."

But as he considered himself in the small, round mirror in their room, he couldn't help but wish he'd tried harder to join in the play. His robe was the deep blue of East Marsh robins and twilled with lace and silver threading. It wasn't feminine, but it also wasn't comfortable.

And it wouldn't be practical if a civil war erupted during the Winter Ball.

In the mirror's reflection, he saw Wren standing by the door, her hand resting on the handle. "Ready?"

Garin sighed and turned away. "As ready as I'll ever be."

They ascended the stairs to the highest platform of House Venaliel and saw High Elendol was busier than they'd ever witnessed before. As they neared the royal kintree, the plat-forms and bridges became almost crowded. People milled about or stood in lines, all dressed in robes or dresses. *At least I won't stand out.* He tugged at his collar until Wren cast him a look.

Every color was represented in the flurry of fashion, but blues, silvers, and whites dominated, the season determining the palette. The hair of both men and women were arrayed in complicated patterns, from intricate braids to tall stacks that seemed impossibly balanced. Paints were in liberal use, with purple shadows under eyes and scrawling shapes on cheeks and necks. Some of the symbols on their skin Garin identified as Worldtongue glyphs. He wondered if they had any power to act as charms. Jewelry shone with a sorcerous light like glim-mering shards of ice.

Interspersed among the crowd were draped palanquins, each held up by six straining men and decorated with extrava-gant ornaments in the shapes of animals and trees. He guessed that they held Peers who thought themselves too good to walk. Garin wondered if Ulen was one of them, but quickly dismissed the thought. Whatever else his Dancing Master had shown himself to be, Ulen Windlofted wasn't lazy.

After they'd filtered down the stairs, the royal feast hall came into view. Garin had dined in the Venaliel hall many times, and the Lathniel's provincial kintree once, so he thought he'd known what to expect. But as he and Wren turned the corner, he discovered what a kintree hall truly could be.

The entrance to the hall was huge, soaring a hundred feet or more above their heads in an archway adorned every foot of its length. Werelights crowded the air, and despite their cool tones, they lent a bright and cheery atmosphere to the event. The crowd was sparse below, but only because the chamber was so large — a hundred had already accumulated, and a thousand more could join them without bumping elbows.

Throughout the hall had been placed sculptures made of

what looked to be ice, despite the air being warm enough to melt it. Some were in the shapes of familiar creatures, like monkeys and birds and bears, but there were also unfamiliar ones. A cat-like beast, as large as Garin himself, reared over his head, snarling with its claws extended. Next to the royal dais, on which the Queen sat, a large, serpentine creature with wings dominated the view. Garin recognized it as a dragon, though it didn't fully resemble the illusion of the one that the Extinguished had summoned in the Ruins of Erlodan.

"Do you want a drink?" he asked Wren, turning back to her.

"Sorry, can't. I have to get the others ready for the background music and set the stage. But I'll see you afterward, alright?"

"Right." He tried not to let his spike of anxiety show. "Stay safe back there."

Wren flashed him a coy smile. "No need to worry about me."

Pressing his hand, she slipped into the crowd.

Garin sighed and looked around for a gray-robed servant when his gaze caught on a familiar face. Aelyn was almost unrecognizable without his usual pointed hat and his traveler's clothes, but even with combed hair and silken, sky-blue robes, his eyes still burned the same bronze as he stared at the people surrounding him.

For once, Aelyn's scowl wasn't directed at Garin. Several other elves stood around the mage, all of them women, and all so ostentatiously dressed that he suspected they were Peers. As Garin came within earshot, he stopped at a small unoccupied table close to them and pretended to watch the goings-on as he eavesdropped.

"Now really, Aelyn, you cannot be serious," one of the women said. "You have no intentions for anyone?"

"I am a Peer, Peer Heilinis, the same as you," Aelyn reminded her stiffly. "And my duties keep me well occupied. I have no time for courtships and coupling."

The women laughed, but there was a mocking edge to it.

"You are a Peer — for now," the same woman as before, Peer Heilinis, said with a slight smile. "Until you find a woman who can properly handle the role you leave so woefully unoccupied. What is it you fear about women, *Peer* Belnuure? Are you afraid we have teeth between our legs, waiting for an unsuspecting man?"

The women tittered laughter again, shriller than before. Garin found his fists clenched until he forced himself to relax. He accepted a drink from a passing servant and took a long drink.

Aelyn can take care of himself, he told himself. *He wouldn't want me to intervene.*

"Your behavior ill-befits you," the mage merely replied.

To Garin's surprise, instead of Aelyn flaring up in anger, he seemed to wilt before the women's assault. It made him wonder if there was any truth in their needling.

"You need not pretend before friends, Peer Belnuure!" Peer Heilinis leaned toward him, but spoke no softer. "We know your little secret. It would be one thing if you preferred males to females. But to prefer no company but your own? That is a shameful thing."

Even as Garin puzzled over what she meant, he found himself turning. Aelyn's feelings be damned — the man had tutored him and fought by him; he wouldn't leave him alone against enemies, even if they only wielded barbed words.

But before he could march toward them, he found a firm hand on his shoulder. "Wait, Garin. I can handle this."

Garin flinched at the touch, believing it at first to be Tal. But as he turned, he was just as surprised to find it was Helnor who stood at his shoulder. The Prime Warder had donned clothes that seemed equally suited for his duties as a scout and the ornate feast. Unlike most of the other guests, his were in the hues of the forest, greens and coppers dominating with a lining of silver.

"I didn't know you'd be here." Garin wasn't sure what else to say. He'd spoken little to Ashelia's brother, for the Prime had most often camped with Tal on the ride in.

"Others guard Elendol's borders tonight. I'm to watch within." The handsome elf smiled grimly down at Garin. His white scars and inked glyphs stood out against his skin, making Helnor seem stranger and more dangerous than he'd ever appeared before.

"Then it will happen tonight." He suddenly felt foolish in his robes. Helnor wore trousers, as did Wren. Had he insisted, perhaps he might have won himself a pair as well and been prepared.

"Perhaps. Do not stray out of sight; better yet, stay close to myself, Aelyn, or Tal. Or Ashelia," he added grudgingly. "I suppose my sister can take care of herself."

Another laugh sounded from the mocking group. Glancing back guiltily, Garin saw Aelyn's face had gone white.

"But don't worry about this battle," Helnor continued. "He is my House-brother. It's a familiar fight, and one I know how to handle."

With a nod, the Prime Warder moved toward the group and gave a raucous greeting, his arms spread wide. Peer Heilinis and the other women looked around, greedy smiles appearing. With a start, Garin remembered the rumors he'd heard from the troupers about relationships among the Highkin — that women could have whatever relations they desired with unmarried men. He wondered if that was what was behind their eager greeting for Helnor, and why that made him feel uneasy.

Aelyn's face had turned pale as he watched his House-brother first charm, then propel the women away from him with offers of drinks and insinuations of other things. Even after Helnor had drawn them away with little more than a greeting for Aelyn, the mage stared after them, the bronze in his eyes spinning rapidly.

Garin hesitantly approached and stood next to him, awkward with not knowing what to say.

Aelyn seemed to have plenty of words. "He calls me 'brother,'" he sneered softly. "But what brother acts the way he does? Every woman fawning over him like human princesses over a prince!"

Garin ignored the insult to his Bloodline. "What are you talking about? Helnor just saved you."

The elf whirled on him, and Garin realized, too late, that he should have kept his mouth shut.

"Saved me?" Aelyn hissed. "So I'm some poor, helpless foundling in need of rescue, am I?"

Garin blinked. "I don't think that's it at all, Aelyn. They were needling you — I don't understand how, but it's plain that they were. And because he's your brother, he couldn't stand for it. It doesn't matter that you don't share blood — Helnor cares for you. I'll bet he finds those women revolting, but he still volunteered himself to their company to draw them away."

Several times, Aelyn had snapped open his mouth to speak during Garin's explanation, but had paused each time. He turned his gaze after his brother, who had receded to the other side of the room. His face was set in a grimace that told Garin he was brooding.

"It doesn't change the past," Aelyn noted sourly.

"Maybe not." Garin's eyes had wandered over the feast and caught on a figure seated next to the Queen at the far end of the room. His chest squeezed tighter at the sight of Tal, particularly in a spot of such honor, but he exhaled deeply and felt it ease.

"But even if it doesn't," Garin said at length, "it changes something."

Aelyn finally drew out of his reverie and noticed where his gaze lay. "Ah, that reminds me. The Queen would like to greet you and the bard's girl before the night is through. Best gather

her up before she's dressed in one of those ridiculous costumes."

"The Queen wants to see us? Why?"

The mage's mouth twisted into a mocking smile. "Why, indeed? But I don't question the requests of Her Eminence. Go — fetch Wren."

Nodding, Garin made off through the crowd, glad to be given a purpose. Though he wondered what the Queen had in store for them.

"Look at how they divide themselves."

Tal pulled his gaze from Garin, who crossed the grand hall, and looked at the Queen. Geminia appeared more radiant than ever, and not just in her garb. Her gown was still relatively simple compared to the peacockery of some of the guests, though it spared no expense of fabric or frill. Silvery lace ran along every edge, and fold upon fold of silken fabric wrapped around her form. Her hair was elegantly curled, but wasn't piled in the tedious stack that more than one woman in the crowd had adopted. Her silver crown glittered with diamonds.

But the effect of her appearance was not in her clothes, but in the aura that diffused from her. Her glamour was as thick as fog that night, exuding from her to film the room. As close as he was to her, Tal found his mind cloudy when he didn't actively fight against it. His blood ran hot through his veins.

He absently fingered the Binding Ring beneath his silk gloves. How she maintained her aura, he'd never known. He doubted it was an artifact, for it seemed to ebb and flow with her moods, nor a spell cast by the Worldtongue, for she maintained it as effortlessly as breathing. No — he guessed that this power was inherent to her, running through her blood since birth.

Just as the World's blood runs through you.

He roused himself to respond to her earlier words. "Sympathists on the left, Royalists on the right, from what I can tell."

Geminia inclined her head slightly. "None even attempt to maintain the veneer of civility. We are a fractured nation, Aristhol. Broken beyond mending."

Tal's eyes wandered over people other than Elendol's nobility, however. It was the servants he watched, moving unseen among the guests as they delivered food and wine. He wondered which of them might wear the twisting silver serpents upon their skin underneath their gray robes.

How simple it would be to kill all the Highkin this night. He hoped Prendyn, Condur, and the other Ilthasi were keeping their vigilance. He was glad to have *Velori* belted at his hip.

He turned back to see the Queen's eyes watching him. Fighting against her allure, Tal kept his words calm and measured. "You speak in despair, yet I didn't think you a woman easily beaten. Yes, there's a rift in your nation — but how can you say it can't be repaired? Yuldor breeds this sickness that grips Elendol, and his servant is at the root of the corruption. Pull the Thorn — all the rest will heal in time."

Geminia stared in silence for several long moments. Tal had to force himself not to look away.

"You have always been faithful to me and to Gladelyl, Tal Harrenfel," she said softly. "You 'pulled the Thorn' once for Elendol, and I am grateful for all you have done, then and now. I am sorry that you never found the happiness you deserved. But even now, it is not too late."

His chest tightened, and he inadvertently found his eyes scanning the room. Before he could find Ashelia, though, he forced himself to look back at the Queen.

"Thank you, Your Eminence. But there are still two mysteries you have yet to explain."

One fine eyebrow arched. "And those are?"

He leaned toward her and pitched his voice lower so that

the servants passing behind them wouldn't hear. "First, you know that I'm loyal. So why did you say I'll betray you?"

The pearly cloud in her eyes danced, and a small smile tweaked a corner of her mouth. "You know that glimpses of the future sometimes come to me, Aristhol. They are phantoms of events, uncertain possibilities, almost dreams. But enough have come to pass that I trust them, and the Masters of the Diamond Tower confirmed my prescience. I know you are a good man, and that you will do your best to do what is right. And that is how I know, with more certainty than most, that my vision will come to pass."

"My betrayal?"

She looked out over the room. "Yours, and mine, and all of Elendol's. That is how I know it is lost."

"No."

Geminia looked back, her eyebrows lifted. Tal found his hands had tightened over the arms of his chair and forced himself to relax.

"No," he repeated. "You say you know it's certain. But it's only so once you've resigned yourself to it. You're the Gem of Elendol. You've ruled your queendom for hundreds of years and should rule for hundreds more. Maybe you're tired of protecting your realm — I wouldn't blame you if you were. But to give in — what kind of ruler would do that to her people?"

"Your own." Reprimand was hard in her voice. "King Aldric Rexall the Fourth is less than faithful to the Reach Realms these days, or so my emissary reports."

Tal inclined his head. "So I also suspect. But to compare him to yourself is to set a serpent against a hawk."

"You flatter me, Aristhol. But it is not from resignation that I speak of these dark tidings. Do you know how visions work?"

He shrugged, wondering what answer she was fishing for. "They're readings of what may pass. Interpretations of future events, should the present play out as expected."

"For most oracles, that would be true. But with my gift,

strong as it is, the prophecies are more certain. I know how these events will occur, how they must occur. And I know at what cost the end will come." She turned her head aside. "But to fulfill my vision, all must be as I've seen. To stray even a little might cause even greater harm."

Despite the morbidness of her words, Tal thought something of her old resolve had returned to her. Now, though, the sight of it filled him with unease.

"And your second question?" the Queen prompted him after a long moment.

He was glad for the change of topic. "You spoke of another who'd attend the ball, someone I wouldn't expect. Yet I've seen no one out of place."

A slight frown creased her lips. "I had hoped he would have arrived by now. His message implied he would be in Elendol this evening. But the High Road is dangerous these days, even for him."

"Who—?"

But he cut off as Geminia looked past him. Following her gaze, he fought down a boyish grin at the sight of those who stood next to them.

"Peer Venaliel," the Queen said with a smile of her own. "A pleasure to see you this evening."

"And you, Your Eminence."

Ashelia's brow was knitted, her mouth halfway between a smile and a grimace. Yet for all her conflicted emotions, the sight of her made his breath catch in his throat. She wore a dress the color of a clear sky, cut along the sides to reveal her moss-dark skin. Once smooth, her sides were now puckered with scars that made him wince to imagine how she'd gained them, accompanied by the smaller stretch marks from pregnancy. But none of the flaws diminished her beauty — it only grounded it. Even now, arrayed in a courtly garb, she brimmed with an almost feral energy.

As his gaze traveled down her arm to where her hand rested, he suddenly understood why.

Her son stood with her. For a moment, he admired the pair they made. In place of the simple clothes the boy had sported at House Venaliel, he now wore robes that matched his mother's. The glyphs of House Venaliel were painted in violet across his forehead, complementing Ashelia's tattoo. His black hair had been braided and adorned with beads, and his face scrubbed clean. He truly looked the son of a Peer now.

Tal gave him a smile, and though his wide eyes showed uncertainty, Rolan returned it.

Raising his gaze, Tal found Ashelia watching him. He wondered if she'd ever imagined what their child might have looked like, just as he did when he looked upon her boy.

"Tal," she said, "I'd like you to meet my son officially. Rolan, pay your respects to the Queen and greet Tal."

Obeying his mother, the boy made the gesture of respect correctly, then shifted his eyes back to Tal. "Hi. Did you keep Crawg?"

A grin split Tal's face. He slid from his chair to kneel before Rolan. "I'm sorry, lad. He slipped away from me."

The boy only shrugged. "Oh. That's okay. I'll sneak one of his friends in when Mistress Shelan isn't looking."

"Rolan." But Ashelia sounded more exasperated than chastising.

Standing, Tal met her eyes. "Thank you for introducing us."

She smiled, and though it was small, he found it a welcome sight. "I'm glad you two properly met."

He leaned in closer to speak in her ear. "Are you sure he'll be safe here?"

"No," she murmured back. "But it's better that he's with me. And you won't let anything happen to him, will you?"

Tal pulled away to give her a wry smile. "You already know the answer to that."

Her eyes were like pools he would have gladly drowned in. Her hand took his.

"I do," she said softly.

Tal glanced at the boy and saw the Queen had occupied him, directing his attention to several of the ice sculptures depicting dangerous animals. Rolan's mouth had dropped slightly open as he listened to her regale on the dangers each beast represented. He remembered how he'd listened to his own mother's stories during winter evenings, and how his imagination had soared with the tales.

Then he recalled where they were, and all the soft feelings of reunion fell away. He squeezed Ashelia's hand and pulled free, fully alert once more. Ashelia sensed the change in him and didn't seem to resent it, but scanned the room again, her eyes spinning faster.

Something he'd intended to tell her came to him then. "Do you remember the book I told you about before, *A Fable of Song and Blood?*"

"Of course."

"Someone stole the pages from my room this evening."

Her eyes darted to meet his. "Does that mean...?"

"I think so. It's what the Thorn has been searching for. And if he has it, none of us are safe."

The muscles worked in Ashelia's jaw. Her gaze wandered to her son.

"It must have been Yinin," she said slowly. "I find it hard to believe he would willingly help the Nameless. Perhaps he only thought it aided the Sympathist cause..." She shook her head. "Regardless. I know there are some in my House that retain more loyalty to him than me. I suspect one of them acted on those feelings."

Anger flared in him. Though he'd believed the same of Yinin, he couldn't comprehend how the man could betray the mother of his child and all she stood for.

But before he could say anything, movement distracted him

341

at the end of the dais. His stomach gave a slight lurch as he saw Garin, dressed in elvish robes, approaching with Wren, who wore the simple dark clothes of a backstage trouper. Garin's eyes flickered away from Tal at his look.

Time to own up to another mistake, he thought with a bitter smile.

As he and Wren ascended the dais past the royal guards, Garin quickly picked out Tal. He stood near the silver chair belonging to the Queen, Ashelia next to him. An elvish boy hovered by Queen Geminia's side, watching intently as she pointed at the ice sculptures arrayed across the room.

Like Helnor, his former mentor had managed to secure trousers, and his clothes were even cut in Avendoran fashion. His colors at least matched the season, his jacket a deep sapphire and his trousers the purest white. Silken gloves hid the Binding Ring from view.

As he stared, Tal's gaze found his. Garin pretended to be distracted by the troupers. The Dancing Feathers, who were set up on a different stage, had begun to play accompanying music, swelling the festive air of the vast chamber.

It's almost as if a civil war isn't brewing, he thought wryly.

Wren led the way past several other guests seated upon the dais. No doubt they were Peers and ministers to the Queen to be so privileged. But as they glanced around, Garin kept his gaze forward. Only after he'd passed half of them did he wonder if ignoring them was rude. *Too late now,* he thought, and continued after Wren.

They reached Tal and Ashelia first. For a moment, they stood in uncertain silence. Wren donned a sardonic grin.

"We're a merry company, aren't we?" she noted.

Ashelia returned the smile. "All of our minds weigh heavy this evening. I assume the Queen summoned you?"

Wren nodded. "Anything we should know?"

"Just be honest — she can often sense when someone with-holds from her. But she's kind. Pay your respects, as is her due, and she'll handle the rest."

Tal, meanwhile, stared at Garin. Reluctantly, he met his gaze.

"Garin," Tal said quietly. "I need to talk to you."

Though it was the last thing he wanted, he nodded. Some part of him had expected it. Though he wondered why Tal had to dredge up the past at the Winter Ball, of all places.

The dais boasted significant space behind the table, through which servants moved as they brought drinks and dishes to the guests. Standing between their paths, Tal faced Garin and drew in a deep breath. Apprehension filled Garin, but he tried to ready himself for whatever was coming.

"I'm sorry to ambush you like this, lad," his former mentor said. "But he knows."

Garin blinked. "Who knows?"

Tal leaned in closer, and Garin barely refrained from pulling back.

"The Thorn. He stole the copied pages of the old book I translated from my room. Soon, he'll know about you."

Garin's mind buzzed with anxiety. "About the Singer?"

His old mentor nodded slowly.

"How? Has anyone spoken of it?" He tried remembering everyone to whom he'd mentioned his devil or his magic. It was a short list — Ilvuan and the Nightsong weren't often subjects he sought to broach.

"They don't have to. You underwent a cleansing. You've been learning sorcery, though you display no signs of elvish blood. Yinin knows all of this, and he's a Sympathist." Tal gave him a small smile. "I'm sorry, lad, to put you into danger once more."

Despite the warmth of the room, a shiver ran through

Garin that made his muscles go weak. "How? Will he try to make Ilvuan — I mean, the Singer control me?"

Ilvuan displayed a flicker of annoyance at that, then settled back into the dim recesses of his mind.

If Tal had noticed his devil had a name, he didn't show it. "I don't know, lad. But he may consider you a danger. I thought I'd best warn you."

"Garin. We shouldn't keep the Queen waiting."

Wren stood next to them. Part of Garin was glad for the excuse to leave and longed to flee with her immediately. But still, he lingered.

Slowly, his eyes rose to meet Tal's, and words he hadn't been sure he could say burst free from him.

"I don't know if I can forgive you for what you did, Tal. I don't know that anyone could. But just know that… I want to."

Tal stared at him. He resembled a man who hadn't drunk for days and had stumbled upon a cup of water.

"I…" the man started, but seemed unable to continue.

Garin's lips twisted in a bitter smile. *For once,* he thought, *Tal Harrenfel is out of words.*

He turned away before his old mentor could speak, then followed Wren to the silver chair. He only glanced back once to see Tal's eyes shining, a small smile pulling at his lips. Garin turned back and hid a grudging smile of his own.

It quickly faded as Queen Geminia the Third looked around at their approach. She was seated in the middle of the dais, the chairs spaced so that only the one where Tal had been seated was near her. A boy now occupied the chair, and as he glanced back at them, Garin recognized him as Ashelia's son. His stormy eyes were unmistakable.

Wren cleared her throat, reminding him to make the gesture of respect, and he clumsily did so. For all his time in Elendol, he'd grown little better at navigating its formalities.

"You may look at me."

The Queen's voice was gentle, and as Garin met her eyes, he

found her features mirrored her voice. Her individual aspects were not striking, but somehow, the sum of them added up to far more. A radiance clung to her like a sunset glow to the horizon. After a moment, he realized how long he'd been staring at her and turned his gaze aside.

"Wren Sunstring and Garin Dunford. Thank you for coming to me." The Queen gave each of them lingering looks, her gaze growing distant.

"Of course, Your Eminence," Wren said smoothly. "We're happy to serve, however you see fit." Whether it was her long acquaintance with nobility in the Coral Castle or her trouper's training, she was much less awkward than him before the Elf Queen.

"You are gracious and kind." Queen Geminia seemed distracted, her brow creasing as she looked back and forth between them.

"Hello," the boy piped up beside her. "I'm Rolan."

The shadow passed from her face as she turned to the lad. "This is Peer Venaliel's son. I understand he has been kept apart from you, despite staying as guests in her House."

"Yes, Your Eminence," Garin responded. He wondered if he should explain more.

"Folly," she murmured. Her eyes had strayed from his face to look somewhere above his head. "You must grow to trust one another if…" She closed her eyes and shook her head. "But we must attend to one crisis at a time."

Wren gave him a skeptical look that Garin didn't dare return. He was starting to wonder if he wasn't the only mad one in Elendol.

Ashelia appeared from behind them, striding to her son's chair. "My apologies, Your Eminence, for forcing Rolan on you. I'll take him back now."

"No need for apologies," the Queen said without looking around.

If Ashelia took it remiss, she didn't show it, but only

gestured respectfully and escorted her son away — to find some food, if the boy's supplications were any indication. As they departed, Tal emerged from further down the dais, and the three of them left together. Garin wondered if something had changed between them that he'd missed.

After they'd departed, the Elf Queen spoke softly again. "I should have arranged this meeting before. You must know what I am about to tell you. Only... I would not wish this knowledge upon anyone. Least of all two youths just beginning their lives."

She lapsed again, and they stood in silence for several moments longer. Garin wondered uneasily what she could mean.

Finally, Wren ventured, "Are you well, Your Eminence?"

Queen Geminia's eyes snapped fully open. Pearly white tendrils lanced furiously through her lavender irises as she stared hard at Wren.

"You have a bright future, Wren Sunstring, by your present reckoning." Her voice was low, but every word came out crisp and sharp. "You will endure many hardships and learn more of your own heart than you wish. But you will also gain what it is you believe you desire — so long as you stay true to yourself and those who surround you."

Wren seemed enraptured, her mouth falling slightly ajar as she stared into the Elf Queen's eyes.

Then Geminia's gaze turned to Garin, and he felt himself swept into it.

"But you, Garin Dunford," she said, her words falling even softer, "you have a black path to walk. You will lose all that is precious to you and gain little that you value. Yet it is the trade that must be made. Careful you do not give too much of yourself, lest you cannot return from the precipice."

He was lost like a man in a fog, clawing through it to reach the murky shadows of her meaning. "I don't understand," he said faintly.

Queen Geminia smiled, but there seemed a deep well of sadness behind those swirling eyes. "You will, my poor lad. You will."

A sudden shout jerked Garin's attention away. He was almost glad for the distraction as he looked around to behold the man who had screeched. He stood in the middle of the ball-room, people moving away from him to leave an open circle around him. But the elf didn't seem to notice as he stood facing one side of the ballroom.

Then he recognized who the man was, and his stomach sank.

"Tal Harrenfel!" Yinin shrieked.

The Dancing Feathers stopped playing on their stage, the instruments coming to a clattering halt. The crowd parted, revealing Tal along the side of the room.

The minister stood, his arm extended and trembling, his finger pointing. "Aristhol!" he spoke again, his voice curling the title into an accusation. "You have smeared my honor, and I demand the satisfaction of a challenge!"

THE QUEEN'S CRIMES

As Garin watched, everyone in the feast hall turned from Yinin to Tal.

The extravagantly dressed elves wore as wide a variety of expressions as their clothes — anger, fear, pity, resentment. Yet none intervened as his former mentor moved within the empty space around Yinin to stand a dozen paces before him.

"I'm here, Yinin," Tal said, his voice carrying throughout the grand hall, now filled with whispers. "To what insult do you issue this challenge?"

"What insult?" the minister sneered. He looked triumphant, though Garin could see little reason for it. "Which of the many, you mean!"

"Name them all, if it pleases you. I'm sure all our friends here would love to know."

Tal looked around with a raised eyebrow, and several chuckles sounded throughout the hall. Garin had to hand that much to the man — he knew how to play a crowd.

Yinin's face was splotchy with rage, but his voice was measured as he declared, "I will not burden them with a complete list, but detail the greatest offense among them. You have come between my bond and me and divided our House.

Through your manipulation, Ashelia Venaliel has tried to renege on her bond-oath to me and send me back to my House of birth. She would take away my son!"

Fresh mutters started up at this. Garin spotted Peer Heilinis appearing to be shocked, though her smirk ruined the effect.

To Garin's wonder, Tal didn't seem the least bit affected by the accusation. He only met Yinin's trembling stare and waited for the hall to grow quiet.

But before it could, a tall woman stepped out from the others, a man one step behind her. Garin recognized him as Houselord Lathniel, their host on the way into Elendol. He assumed that made the woman his bond and Peer of their House.

"Such an offense to my brother cannot go unnoticed by House Lathniel," Peer Maone Lathniel said in a carrying voice, turning to speak to all those gathered rather than just the pair at their center. "Nor is it the first crime of Tal Harrenfel's since his return to Elendol."

Tal turned his gaze slowly to meet hers. "And what harm have I done you?"

"It is not to me, but to our dear city and country. Did you think we would not notice your sins in Low Elendol? You have been seen fighting in the lower streets. And near where you brawled, the bodies of five burned Imperial immigrant youths were discovered. I wonder who would be so devilish as to do that."

The mutters started up again, louder than before. Garin's blood pounded in his ears. *Five.* He hadn't known it had been so many. *Five dead by my hand.*

He turned to reel off the dais, but Wren grabbed his arm. "Don't!" she hissed. "You'll only make it worse!"

He let her hold him in place. In the distance, below the growing outrage of the royal feast hall, discordant sounds had started up. The screech of an eagle. The whisk of metal against cloth. A trickle of water.

Calm. Ilvuan suddenly filled his mind, pushing away the Nightsong and the scene. *You cannot lose control, little Listener. You will not.*

Vaguely, he noticed Tal speaking, and tried to focus on his words through the tumbling noises in his head.

"I've been a devil many times in my life, Peer Lathniel. And I've sent many offenses your way, Minister Yinin, though most of them were uttered when your back was turned. But I've killed no one within Elendol."

"And he didn't come between you and me, Yinin. You did that all yourself."

The crowd rippled as they turned to see Ashelia entering the empty circle in the crowd. Her bearing was upright and proud, and she possessed all the confidence and control of both a Warder and a Peer of the Realm. Her son held her hand, his eyes wide, but his chin upright and proud.

Yinin was staring at her, his mouth working. "Ashelia, please," he said hoarsely. "You cannot mean that!"

"You will address me as Peer Venaliel now, Minister. And I do mean it. You have been unfaithful to my House and our son."

"Unfaithful! You say *I* am the one who has been unfaithful, when you've been sneaking off with that — that *ragamuffin* every moment you could spare!"

"Tal and I have not continued our liaisons, if that is what you mean," Ashelia said calmly through the reawakened mutters. "But even if we had, within the sight of the Realm, such is permitted to me as a Peer and is not grounds for a duel."

To Garin's eye, Peer Lathniel seemed to regret her involvement more with each passing moment. Yet as she turned to face Queen Geminia, her expression was no less determined. "We cannot know the truth of these personal matters, Your Eminence. But the evidence of Tal Harrenfel's guilt in the Mire is certain. Detain him and bring him to justice."

"Then you and your House should be brought to justice as well!"

Another figure emerged into the space — Aelyn, his face twisted into uncontrolled fury. Garin had never seen him so wrought. His rage dowsed Garin's own turmoil as he feared what the mage might do.

Peer Lathniel seemed reluctant to turn and face him as her moment was stolen. "Do not interrupt, Peer Belnuure," she said dismissively. "Everyone knows of your complaints."

"*Complaints*." Even at the distance, Aelyn's eyes smoldered as he stood six feet before the Peer. "Is that what they are, when your entire House is slaughtered? I have known what you did for many years, Maone. I have known why you did it. They say they caught the men who killed my kin. But the one who hired them has walked free all these long years, reaping the rewards of House Belnuure's downfall!"

"Aelyn, don't—" Ashelia began.

The mage cut her off, his voice trembling with emotion. "I was bound by loyalty to my sister to refrain from taking vengeance. But now, she has broken ties with your House. So I say to you, Maone: I swear, by the Mother, you will suffer as I did, whether by Elendol law or my hand. You will know what my pain has been all my life."

"Emissary Belnuure, that is enough."

The Elf Queen had stood. Her face seemed to hold all the sorrows of the World as she gazed upon Aelyn.

He crumpled for a moment before her reprimand, then rallied. "Your Eminence, I—"

"I have heard your words, and I will attend to them. But now is not the time. Please, allow me to speak."

Aelyn bowed his head and gestured respect. Though Garin could still see him shaking, and his fists clenched at his sides, he took several steps back away from the woman who had killed his family. A wave of mixed feelings rose in Garin. He'd never respected or pitied his tutor as much as in that moment.

Queen Geminia briefly smiled at him, then turned her gaze to Peer Lathniel. Maone had boldly turned her back on her accuser. For a long moment, silence filled the great hall once more.

"As to your demands, Peer Lathniel — I will never detain Tal Harrenfel. Not now. Not ever."

The hall burst into excited murmurs. Yinin's fury almost matched Aelyn's, while Peer Lathniel looked strangely triumphant.

"Then you would deny the Realm justice?" she called above the din.

"I deny only you and your satisfaction." The Queen gazed at her subjects until they quieted, then looked back to Tal. "Aristhol, please remove your glove."

Tal looked stricken for a moment. Then, slowly, he pulled the glove free from his right hand to reveal the milky-white crystal band resting on his middle finger.

Garin had known that he wore the ring. But amid his fury with Tal and the other goings-on, he'd stopped wondering who had bound him. Unease stirred in his gut.

"A Binding Ring," Queen Geminia confirmed to a fresh round of whispers. "You all know that an oath made through such a ring cannot be broken. When I sent Emissary Belnuure to King Aldric, I entrusted to him this artifact with the intent that he use it. And so it was that when the King of Avendor sent Aelyn onward to fetch Tal Harrenfel, to ensure his complete obedience, Emissary Belnuure used it to bind him to me."

Garin exchanged a look with Wren. Both of them knew that wasn't the complete story. But they only knew half of the truth, he realized now.

"Thus it remained when Aristhol came here to Elendol, and so it has been in all of his time here. And so, Peer Lathniel, he could not have committed any act against Gladelyl. For he is under my command."

It was the nail in the coffin. The crowd seemed to behold Tal with fresh eyes. Yinin looked around wildly, his support rapidly dissipating. But Peer Lathniel only wore a small smile as she looked to the left side of the room and spoke.

"You see, my fellow Peers? Tal Harrenfel was under her command this whole time. Which means every crime committed by his hand is her crime. But what is an Imperial lad to the Queen of Gladelyl? We all now know."

Peer Lathniel turned to face the Queen, her eyes nearly glowing with her triumph. "Time and again, Queen Geminia has shown no sympathy for the Easterner refugees. Only by the demands of the Peers' House did the Sun Gate open! But for us, all those seeking to escape the tyranny of the Empire of the Rising Sun would be slaughtered, down to the last babe. And you, Your Eminence, by closing them out of this haven, would have had their blood on your hands — but for us, the Peers of the Realm."

Garin glanced at the Queen, hoping she would respond. But the Gem of Elendol, calm and radiant in the face of the accusations, remained silent and watching. The crowd was anything but quiet; some of the gathered nobility even shouted. All shifted uneasily, feeling the current coursing through the room.

"Perhaps," Peer Lathniel continued, strolling around the open circle as she turned to face those gathered around her, "the Peers might rule Gladelyl better alone. Perhaps the age of queens is past. Perhaps it is time, Geminia the Third, that you abdicate the throne."

Gasps rippled through the room. Garin felt his chest tighten so it was difficult to breathe. *A coup.* His eyes flickered to either side of the dais. Though royal guards blocked the stairs, he couldn't help but imagine assassins, hidden in the crowd, sneaking up on the Queen.

Then he felt an anger that wasn't his own flicker through him. At first, it was as gentle as the sun's kiss; but quickly, it turned uncomfortably hot, like he'd sat too close to a roaring hearth. For a moment, he thought it was Ilvuan who spawned the emotions. Then he turned toward Queen Geminia, and the full force of her aura rolled over him, nearly overwhelming his mind.

"A queen does not take orders, Peer Lathniel — a queen gives them. You wish me to surrender the crown. Why? So that half of Elendol may tyrannize the other? I will not pretend that I have always been right. Long-lived as I am, as carefully as I consider every decision, I am still mortal and subject to mortal failings. But Mother take me if I commit a crime so great as giving over the care of Gladelyl to you."

Peer Lathniel thrust an accusing finger back up at the Queen as she spoke to those gathered. "She would repress us! The Tyrant Queen would silence even the Peers of the Realm!"

"Only you, Peer Lathniel! For all know the master whom you serve!"

The muttering erupted into objections and assents. Garin saw the two sides of the room split further, the Royalists and the Sympathists marshaling to their respective sides. Peer Lathniel once again faced the Queen, triumph and fury breaking through her calm, while Yinin shrunk behind her. Tal, Ashelia, and Rolan stood close together, Tal's hand clutching to his sword's hilt.

"House Lathniel will not stand for these accusations!" Peer Lathniel called above the din. "Nor will it back away from the demands of it and its allied Houses. You have until dawn to yield, Geminia. Do not cause more bloodshed than you already have."

With that, Peer Lathniel turned away and began striding from the feast hall, gesturing at Yinin as she passed him. The minister gave Ashelia one last lingering look before outrage overtook his sorrow. He turned and followed his sister.

The two sides of the crowd shifted, the Sympathists trailing after Peer Lathniel, while the Royalists gathered around the dais. Ashelia and Tal pushed through the others toward the dais. Rolan was lost from sight.

"That's it," Wren said next to him. She sounded dazed — except that when she looked at him, it was awe in her expression. "Elendol is at war."

Garin nodded and stared at the Queen. She still looked out over the emptying hall. He wondered if she regretted what she'd said. He wondered if this could have been avoided.

But it doesn't matter. Just like with the Singer, there was no regretting past actions. All they could do was move forward.

Ilvuan's approval threaded through his mind. *Now you are thinking as you should, little Listener.*

Somehow, the devil's approval made Garin feel no better.

Tal walked silently by Ashelia across another platform. Her son walked on her other side, clutching to his mother's hand as he looked around, wide-eyed, at the people surrounding them.

Tal kept a wary eye on them himself. Soldiers, clad in the royal regalia, served as their escort back to House Venaliel. Though he trusted Geminia now — as much as he could trust her — her guards were a different matter. Yet their protection had seemed preferable to risking ambush out in the city.

Not that any signs of ambush were apparent. High Elendol was deserted, its platforms empty and its bridges unmoving but for their passage. Even the canopy was nearly silent, the birds and monkeys seeming to sense the mood of the city. Before they had departed House Elendola, other bands of soldiers had marched Royalist Peers back to their respective Houses, while the Sympathists had made do with their own guards for protection. Everyone hunkered down within their homes, waiting for the storm to break out, for it was clear neither faction intended to yield.

Tal was thankful, at least, that all of their companions had agreed to shelter in the Venaliel kintree: Garin, Wren, Aelyn, Helnor, Falcon, and the Dancing Feathers. He didn't even mind the two monks of the Creed coming along. Altogether, they numbered more than the guards. Tal hoped it would be enough to prevail against assailants from any quarter.

After they crossed the third-to-last bridge, Falcon slipped up next to Tal on the platform. "Couldn't you have waited to have your big moment until I'd had mine?"

Tal looked over at his friend, disbelieving. "A civil war is breaking out, and you're making japes?"

There was a mischievous gleam to his eyes. "You think I'm joking? I worked hard to prepare *The Fall of Narkeska!* It's an elven classic and damned difficult to pull off. But you couldn't even make it until dinner, much less the dessert entertainment, before you implode the whole feast!"

Despite himself, Tal grinned. "I'll find some way to make it up to you, my friend. Someday."

"Promises are empty when spoken from a pearly tongue." The Court Bard of Avendor returned the smile.

"Aristhol! Tal Harrenfel!"

"I'm growing tired of people shouting my name," Tal muttered to Falcon as he turned to face the man calling behind them.

Their company parted to reveal the portly Prendyn. Sweat filmed the Ilthasi captain's brow as he bustled up to him.

"Aristhol!" he panted. "Queen Geminia summons you — you must come with me immediately!"

"What is it?" Ashelia demanded. "Is the Queen under attack?"

"No, Your Grace. But she requires Tal Harrenfel's presence at once." His eyes flitted back to Tal. "Will you come?"

Tal glanced at Ashelia. He loathed leaving her side, especially now of all times. But though the Queen had revealed his bindings, it didn't change his obligation.

A bitter smile crept onto his lips. "I must do as my Queen commands. Lead the way, Prendyn."

He met the eyes of his companions as they passed. Aelyn, his eyebrows cocked with disdainful interest. Helnor, questioning if he should come, too, and Prendyn turning him away. Garin and Wren, silently watching, anxious curiosity in both of their eyes.

Then they'd passed through them, and he left them behind to walk across the shaky bridge back toward House Elendola.

Tal kept a watchful gaze around them. Though he didn't doubt the Ilthasi could handle himself, they were vulnerable traveling as only a pair. An ambush wouldn't be difficult to achieve. Though the platforms and bridges were exposed, any number of assailants could hide within the carved rooms of the supporting trees along the way. His hand ground against *Velori's* grip as he wished he could have stayed with his companions. *At least they're close to House Venaliel. Soon, they'll be safe.*

"What does the Queen want?" Tal asked aloud.

The Ilthasi captain faced forward as he responded. "Ah, she didn't precisely say. But civil war is nearly upon us, is it not?"

Tal frowned as he stared at Prendyn's back. He hadn't caught it before, but there was a nervous edge to his words.

"You know this conflict isn't about me, don't you? The Sympathists would have found an excuse if Yinin hadn't started things."

The Ilthasi captain didn't answer for a long moment. "Perhaps you're right. Nevertheless, Aristhol, you were the spark to start the flame."

Tal frowned and hesitated as Prendyn stepped onto another bridge. With every exchanged word, his unease grew. He glanced around the platform behind him and saw no one. Yet his veins itched with the warming of his blood.

Prendyn had taken several steps before he halted and turned back. His face still wore the same vague smile, but something else smoldered in his eyes. "Come on," he said. "The Queen awaits."

Tal didn't follow.

"Prendyn," he asked quietly. "Was it truly the Queen who sent you?"

The Ilthasi captain's expression became carefully guarded. "In a way."

Tal thought through the implications of his behavior. It didn't take him long to realize the logic behind his avoidance. The Ilthasi were branded with the Elendola sigil, a tattoo that couldn't be forged, and that tied them to the Queen as surely as any Binding Ring. A hard pit formed in his stomach.

"How?"

Prendyn seemed to see in Tal's eyes that he'd guessed the truth. And before he looked away, Tal saw the shame in the captain's.

"It was over before I arrived, Aristhol," he said softly. "And she commanded me. I have no choice but to obey."

With a heavy sigh, Tal drew *Velori* from its scabbard.

"I'm sorry, Prendyn. But you know I can't go willingly into the Thorn's arms. Not with someone who might easily put a knife in my back."

Prendyn glanced up at him. Then daggers appeared in each of his hands. "No choice," he whispered again.

Tal fell into a ready position at the end of the bridge, his feet light and shifting across the terraces, while his eyes scanned around him for waylayers. No one emerged from the shadows. They were alone — for the moment, at least.

"Is there anyone else?" he asked as the Ilthasi slowly crossed the bridge, closing the gap between them. "Anyone to ensure you don't fail?"

The Ilthasi seemed to consider his words. "Yes. I think I can safely say that without consequences. They'll be coming soon."

"Then you don't need to do their work for them, do you?"

A glimmer of hope appeared in the Ilthasi's eyes. "As long as I make an effort, I should be abiding by my oath."

Tal flashed him his wolf's smile. If Prendyn worked with him, they might pull off their ruse and allow Tal to escape both Prendyn and his approaching assailants. Then Tal could assist the Queen.

"Good," he said. "Now follow my lead, and we'll give them a show."

PASSAGE IV

REGARDING FOUNTS, THERE IS ANOTHER IDEA I HAVE YET TO propose: that it is not the Heart itself that seeks the new master, but the Singers who have made their nest within it.

The Song and the Heart are connected — of that I am sure. How, I cannot know. But from all the evidence I have gathered, I will put forth what possibilities I have conceived.

First, the Song may be generated by the Heart as a manifestation, or even a source, of its power. It is said the Song is formed of all the sounds of the World. Perhaps this is the language with which it speaks, though ordinary men and women cannot understand its words.

The second possibility is that the Song is sung by the Singers who roost on the Heart. It would not be the World's Song then, but the music of these creatures, whatever they are. From the destruction they have wreaked across the Empire, they seem to be devils, and perhaps they are — parasites of the Heart, or another spawn of it, like the beasts that roam the mountains surrounding Paradise.

But they might be its guardians, the true caretakers of the World, who seek to right the wrongs of its predecessors. Yuldor has not stopped the monsters from coming down from the mountains. I have long suspected he does not wish to.

Perhaps it would not be wrong to seek a new god.

- A Fable of Song and Blood, *by Hellexa Yoreseer of the Blue Moon Obelisk, translated by Tal Harrenfel*

ELENDOL IN FLAMES

Tal watched Prendyn and waited for his signal, his sword held at the ready.

From the corner of his eye, he examined the bridge before him. The ropes holding it in place were as thick as his wrists. Six of them strung across the expanse. He'd be hard-pressed to cut it down and cover his escape.

But that's not the only way to break a bridge. The ropes, he knew, were treated with an oily bonding to resist the frequent rains and prevent rot.

A bonding that happened to be flammable.

The Ilthasi made the slightest movement with one of his knives, little more than a twist of his wrist. But it was enough to tell Tal their audience had arrived.

"*Kald!*" he yelled, then swung *Velori* as it ignited with sorcerous flames. He chopped into one rope, then another, then a third. As the blade sank into each rope, the fibers began to burn, flames racing down their lengths.

But the Ilthasi captain had to also play his part. As Tal pulled his blade back in from a fourth swing, Prendyn threw his arm forward, a knife shimmering through the air.

As they'd agreed, Tal pitched himself backward so that the knife flew harmlessly past.

Rolling to his feet, Tal turned to see Prendyn sprint onto the platform and draw a rapier with his free hand. To their watchers, wherever they were, it would look as if Prendyn had gained the advantage, and perhaps dissuade them from joining in.

But that was as far as they'd agreed upon their rushed choreography. From here on, he'd have to trust that the Ilthasi's training would be enough to prevent Tal from killing him. *Or him killing me.*

Tal launched an attack, feinting a stab, then turning it into a slice. Prendyn didn't fall for it, but parried the blow and positioned himself for retaliation. Tal worked *Velori* around just in time to knock aside the rapier, and again as it darted forward a second time. Tal's bastard sword had better reach, but an elf's rapier was quicker, and Prendyn didn't seem to be pulling his strikes.

Then he noticed a pattern to Prendyn's attacks: each of his movements seemed designed to push Tal back toward the burning bridge. Not bothering to hide his smile, he yielded to his herding, slowly losing ground before him.

As he grew near enough to the flames for them to warm his back through his cloak, he finally caught sight of their onlookers. Three bridges led to their platform, one of which burned behind him. The other two now danced with the footsteps of advancing figures.

Prendyn finally stepped back, panting and dripping sweat, as half a dozen men and women, all with their faces masked except for their eyes, formed an arc around Tal. One of the masked figures stepped forward, and Tal recognized him by his fluid movements alone.

The assassin.

The man removed the wrapping over his face and tossed it to the ground, and Tal had to repress a groan.

The man's eyes seemed to look just past Tal's shoulder. "You know me."

The way the assassin spoke the words, Tal couldn't tell if he was stating it or asking a question.

"In a way," Tal said. "It's not the first time we've danced."

"That is not what I mean. You know my name."

Tal gave him a grim smile. "I do at that, Ulen Windlofted. How's your leg?"

Ulen's face was blank, not betraying any sign that he'd noticed the gibe. "I rarely fail."

"It's a feeling every man and woman should be familiar with. I certainly am."

With every moment he bought, Tal sized up his adversaries. Rapiers were in most of their hands, while knives and crossbows occupied the rest. His knees went weak at the odds. He'd struggled to survive Ulen alone in the Mire on open ground. Here on a platform, with his back to a burning bridge, six other opponents surrounding him, and Prendyn unable to provide aid, he had no hope of survival.

Only one desperate escape occurred to him. He tucked it away, knowing the moment wasn't long until he had to choose.

"I do not fail." Ulen spoke as if he hadn't heard Tal. The Dancing Master's rapier rose, and the people he'd brought with him readied their own weapons. "You will die."

Tal hesitated a moment longer. *Fight or flee — death or death.* It was barely a choice.

He made it anyway.

"*Mord!*"

Inky blackness unfolded around him. Ducking, he threw himself back onto the bridge. Blistering heat surrounded him, instantly scorching his skin and desiccating his throat and eyes. Gasping for air, Tal stumbled to his feet and over the planks, tripping in the near-darkness. The flames that had engulfed the bridge were still visible, but nothing else was. He could barely keep his feet under him. All feeling but pain had left him, and though subtlety could make the difference between life and death, he couldn't help the grunts escaping him, interspersing them with cries of *lisk* to dampen the killing flames.

Then the bouncing planks of the bridge disappeared beneath him, and the heat pressing against his skin was replaced by the coolness of the night. Tal realized he'd closed his eyes and opened them to see another platform around him. He coughed and gulped in fresh air. *I made it. I'm still alive.*

He looked back toward the other side. During his dash across the bridge, he'd released his focus on the orb of darkness. Now he could see the figures scattering to circle around by other paths. Only Ulen remained, his eyes wide as he stared at the burning bridge.

Tal grinned. For all the pain and burned flesh it had cost him, at least he'd put the fear of fire in the Dancing Master.

He turned and began lurching away from his pursuers, heading across another bridge. As he crossed, he lit the ropes aflame. Only the bridges would burn, he guessed; following the debacle with Heyl, the elves had treated the structures of High Elendol with a fire retardant.

He hoped it would be enough.

Crossing the next bridge, Tal realized he'd come to a crossroads. Did he continue on to the royal kintree, to spring whatever trap lay in wait, and protect the Queen? Or return to the Venaliel kintree to protect his companions? A glance back told him he didn't have much time — already, his pursuers were only one platform away.

"Damn you, Geminia," he muttered under his breath, and made for House Elendola.

Garin mulled over their changes in fortune as Ashelia led them across the last bridge to the Venaliel kintree.

In one night, Elendol had fractured, the Sympathists and Royalists making their allegiances clear.

And his actions had been at the center of it all.

He remembered the burning corpses of the Nightelf youths and swallowed hard. His limbs trembled beneath him. His vision blurred.

The Queen, a woman gifted in prescience, had seen his dark future. Considering his past, he could hardly dispute it.

None can see what path you may take, Ilvuan opined. Garin could feel only a small part of his attention with him, yet the Singer still felt the need to say his piece. *Do not worry for the future, little Listener. I will take care of that for you.*

"Why doesn't that reassure me?" Garin muttered.

Wren jerked her head around. "What did you say?"

"Nothing."

Ashelia held up the hand that didn't clutch her son's hand and stopped. The rest of the company halted behind her. With the Queen's guards having left them at the last bridge, they were on their own. She was several feet ahead of them, so as she turned to speak to Aelyn and Helnor, Garin couldn't overhear what she said. He chewed his bottom lip as he looked ahead, trying to see what she had.

Wren, however, had edged closer, so he followed.

"...Should be here," Ashelia said, a crease between her eyebrows as she studied the kintree.

"It's a festival night. Perhaps they retreated to grab a moment of revelry. It wouldn't be the first time men skirted their duty for a drink." Helnor didn't sound convinced by his own suggestion.

"We can't wait out here for fear," Aelyn said irritably. "We must simply remain wary."

Ashelia looked between them, then down at her son, before raising her head again. "Everyone stay together," she called back, "and keep quiet."

She motioned their company forward again.

"No guards," Wren muttered to him as they descended the stairs after Aelyn and the Venalieli. "That's why they're worried."

"But no bodies either. Though I suppose they could have pushed them over the railing."

She gave him a wry look. "Isn't that a cheery thought?"

Garin wished he'd been permitted to bring a weapon to the festival. As ill-proficient as he was at dancing, he trusted it more than his fledgling sorcery. At the thought, Ilvuan stirred again in his mind, oozing with condescending amusement. Garin once more ignored him.

Ashelia led them past several doors, listening carefully at each and checking inside before continuing down. In his mind, Garin rehearsed the cantrips Aelyn had taught them, knowing he couldn't hesitate when the time came to use them. *Keld. Bisk. Jolsh. Vuud. Fashk. Multh. Korfel. Korfisk.* He pictured their effects in his mind and wondered how any of it could help when half the Houses of Elendol were pitched against them.

They stopped again, and Garin peered ahead, his throat squeezed tight. Ashelia stepped back while Helnor, his saber raised, pushed inside a door. Shouting came from within, and Garin cringed at the noise. Yet as Ashelia, Aelyn, and Wren darted inside, he followed.

Inside, Garin stumbled to a halt and stared blankly around. It looked to have been a guardhouse. Mugs, some still filled with a golden liquid, were arrayed on the upright tables. A small buffet hovered invitingly in the corner. Mugs and plates and *galli* were scattered across the floor. Benches and tables were flipped on their sides.

And amid the overturned furniture and shattered crockery lay a dozen hacked-apart bodies.

Helnor's face was a mask of anger and grief as he stalked among the fallen. He turned over the bodies to peer at their bloody faces, all the while muttering their names to himself.

Ashelia pulled young Rolan back out, the elf child staring

367

wide-eyed at the bodies as she dragged him away. Garin longed to flee himself. The bodies reeked as he'd never imagined they would, the metallic, sharp scent of blood mixed with the stink of piss and excrement. He'd heard once from an old veteran in Hunt's Hollow that some men couldn't hold their bowels when they faced the end, and he'd seen glimpses of it after the Ravagers had attacked their caravan. But he'd never fully comprehended the reality of violence until then.

He glanced at Wren and found her nostrils flared. She didn't look away from the dead, but stared at them, anger visible in every tensed muscle. Falcon approached hesitantly behind her and placed his intact hand on her shoulder, but she immediately shrugged it off.

"You don't need to see this," her father pleaded. His eyes flickered up to meet Garin's, begging for his help, but Garin couldn't find it in him to speak.

"I do." Wren didn't look away. "I won't look away from devilish work just because it's ugly. Someone will pay for this. And I intend them to remember every bit of pain they inflicted on these guards when I find them."

Ilvuan stirred with interest at her words, as if the threat were a tasty morsel. Garin couldn't stand it any longer. He fled from the room and went to the railing outside, gulping in the fresh air.

"Bad in there?" Ox muttered next to him. The big Befal man placed a hand on his shoulder. "Worse than the attack on the High Road?"

Garin could only shrug, not daring to open his mouth lest he lose control of his stomach. He glanced over and found Rolan watching him. He wondered what the boy's eyes saw, and whether he understood the butchery and the hate behind it.

At length, the others exited. Helnor looked to have aged decades, lines wrinkling the green tattoos on his face and deepening his scars into furrows. "Either this was a message," he rumbled, "or it's a trap."

Ashelia gripped her son's hand. "We must find somewhere safe. Either we can attempt to secure our House, or we must retreat to the Queen's kintree. The war has already started," she added, almost as an afterthought.

"Abandon our kintree?" Helnor shook his head. "I loathe saying it, but we don't have the strength to keep it. We will retreat and hope the same fate hasn't befallen Her Eminence."

A shock ran through Garin. *Tal.* He'd been called back to the Queen. As much in a hurry as they'd been, he hadn't given it more than a passing thought. But now, he realized how strange an occurrence that had been. Why call him back so soon?

We'll find out soon enough, he thought grimly.

"We need weapons," Wren spoke up. "We can't just rely on Helnor and Aelyn to protect us. We all need to be prepared."

Garin glanced around to see the younger monk, Brother Nat, staring wide-eyed at Wren's suggestion. Brother Causticus, meanwhile, clutched a bag to his middle and seemed to be folding in around it. Their fear somehow gave him a little more courage.

Helnor nodded heavily after a moment. "We can take them from within."

"I'll go with you," Wren said firmly, and turned back inside the guardhouse with Helnor.

Though he little wanted to follow, Garin knew she spoke sense. He wouldn't force her to gather his weapon. Drawing in a breath, he went back in.

As quickly as he could, he unbelted a sheath and took a saber to match. Suddenly, he couldn't hold down his revulsion any longer. When he'd emptied his stomach in a corner, Garin rose, legs shaking, and stumbled into a back room, where Helnor had said clean uniforms and armor would be. The stench had permeated back there, and he trembled as he stripped off his formal robes and garbed himself in the unfamiliar clothes and armor. Even when Ashelia joined him and matter-of-factly disrobed to put on armor, he found nothing could distract him from the pitching of his stomach and senses.

Finally, several excruciating minutes later, he'd dressed and tottered out of the room. Wren and Helnor somehow bore the macabre scene long enough to gather weapons for all the Dancing Feathers. As strange as it felt to wear elven armor, it was a stranger sight still for the troupers to belt on blood-splattered swords over their costumes, still worn in preparation for *The Fall of Narkeska.* Even Ox, big man that he was, looked ill-suited to the glaive he took in hand.

"We'd best ascend now," Ashelia instructed. "In case they come back." Wearing a Venaliel guard's armor, she looked much like the Warder she'd been when they'd first met, and her bearing was upright and confident. Though, even as she held a bared rapier in one hand, she clutched her son's hand in the other.

The Dancing Feathers and the two monks parted to allow Ashelia, Helnor, and Aelyn to go first, while Garin and Wren stayed at the rear. He watched the troupers, clutching awkwardly at their weapons, and felt a pit of guilt settle into his empty stomach.

They're here because of me. None of this would have ever happened if I hadn't touched that damned amulet.

Ilvuan spoke softly in response. *Had you not, I would not have claimed you. And had I not claimed you, you would have perished before Yuldor's servant.*

Aren't you his servant as well?

A bubble of amusement. *Can a predator ever be a pet?*

A cry of alarm jerked Garin back to the moment. Exchanging a look with Wren, he followed her as she pushed through the troupers to see what lay ahead.

The bridges leading away from the Venaliel kintree burned.

"Back down!" Helnor barked. "To the lift! They mean to trap us here!"

Garin glimpsed the silhouetted figures on the other side of the bridges before turning away. He pushed down the stairs with the others, barely avoiding being impaled by the weapons the troupers held at dangerous angles. He grabbed ahold of Brother Causticus as the old monk nearly took a tumble. But even as the Mute scowled and yanked his satchel back into his hands, he continued to descend at their deadly pace. Garin's heart thumped with every step, his breath coming quick. He imagined what it would be like to burn alive and didn't relish the thought.

The feast hall passed, littered with more bodies — then his and Wren's room — and finally Tal's. He didn't dare stop to retrieve anything, but pressed on with the others. None of his possessions were worth dying over.

Finally, they reached the bottom of House Venaliel. Helnor and Aelyn pushed to the front of the company. The mage's mouth twisted into a bitter smile at the sight of the dead lift operator, slumped in his chair, and the cut cords next to it. "Dismantled," he announced.

Helnor stared at the lift, then at his adopted brother. "Can you make it operate another way? Sorcery of some kind?"

Aelyn met his gaze. "I can try."

Garin watched the mage fret over the cords and peered down at the lift far below until he couldn't stand it any longer. He moved to the railing, and despite his aversion to heights, looked out at the lower city. Elendol was never dark, but it was brighter than usual that night. The orange glows of fire were interspersed throughout the Mire, and even in parts of High Elendol above them.

"Elendol burns," he muttered.

"It seems to do that every time Tal is here."

Garin glanced over to find Falcon next to him. "You mean Heyl?"

The bard nodded. "Tal had been here for months, and for all that time, he'd been trying to gain an audience with the Queen.

His warlock mentor, you see, had been murdered by the Silver Vines, and Tal had gathered enough clues to follow the trail to Elendol. At that time, he had no renown, and as gracious as Her Eminence is, her steward saw no reason to admit him before her. Only when Heyl suddenly rose from the Mire as if from nowhere did he discover his chance. Recklessly, foolishly, he charged at the devil. And despite all expectations to the contrary, he smote it, a feat all the mages of Elendol couldn't accomplish."

Garin was hardly in the mood for a story. Yet his curiosity, ever close to the surface, got the best of him. "How did he do it?"

Falcon shrugged. "He could never explain it to me. Or perhaps he neglected to. But from what I understand, the Tal Harrenfel you know is but a shadow of what he was. When he faced Heyl, twenty years old and unimpeded by injury or guilt, I'm told he was fearless and rash with both life and sorcery. But that changed after his encounter with the Thorn."

Garin glanced back up the stairs, expecting at any moment to hear the pounding of enemy soldiers coming down. "What changed?" he asked, as much for a distraction as to know.

The bard smiled sadly. "The Thorn dealt him a wound that would never heal — the wound in his side, you remember. Tal only said that the Extinguished stabbed him with a knife just as he dealt the killing blow, and that it seemed to tear the World asunder. Perhaps, had he not received that wound, he might never have fallen under the influence of the second Extinguished he encountered — for, in his prime, he had the power to match even those fell sorcerers. And then he'd never have become the Magebutcher, or the Red Reaver, or Death's Hand, as the dwarves call him."

He might never have killed my father. A pain lodged in Garin's chest. Though he pressed at it, it wouldn't go away.

A triumphant shout sounded by the lift. Garin and Falcon

turned to see Helnor grinning as Aelyn, his arms outstretched, overlooked the lift hovering in midair.

Garin edged closer to Wren and Ashelia, the Dancing Feathers coming after. The Venaliel Peer examined the lift with skepticism, then shook her head.

"It's as stable as we can manage," she said. "Everyone, get on."

The lift barely fit them all. Garin was one of the last to board. As he stepped over the gap between the platform and the hovering lift, he felt his stomach lurch at the imagined fall. He shuddered and was glad when Wren gripped his arm and held him against her. Only Aelyn and Helnor remained. Helnor had to guide his adopted brother onto the platform. The mage's eyes were faraway, his limbs stiff in the position he'd left them, the whole of his concentration on maintaining whatever spells allowed him to levitate the lift.

As soon as Helnor had crossed, the lift began to lower.

Garin closed his eyes, feeling he'd pitch forward if he dared to look. But closing his eyes seemed just as dangerous. He opened them again and stared at a single branch as they descended, directing all of his focus toward it slowly moving above them.

"Attraction," Wren spoke excitedly in his ear. "Aelyn's using a more complicated form of the metal attraction cantrips we learned — magnetism, or whatever he called it."

Garin nodded, but could manage no more response.

Finally, after what felt like ages, the lift settled with a final lurch on the ground. By the speed with which the others exited, Garin knew he wasn't alone in his discomfort. Yet though he wanted nothing more than to double over and gasp for air, he forced himself to remain upright and survey the surrounding streets.

The Mire had never felt like a safe place, but never had it looked so dangerous. The streets were deserted, but echoing screams told of violence not far away. One building nestled into the roots of a kintree opposite of them burned, the flames not yet spreading to the majestic tree. Garin wondered if fires would spread in this wooden city, and how much of Elendol would burn this night.

"We have to make for the bridges to High Elendol!" Ashelia called back, then led them away from the lift and into the Mire.

But before they'd gone more than a dozen steps, two figures stepped out from a shadowed alleyway. All of their company's weapons rose, and the figures halted, their faces barely illuminated.

But Garin had suspected by their forms who they were, and as they stepped into the light, he cried out, "Wait! We know them!"

"Who are they, Garin?" Helnor demanded. He didn't take his eyes off of the pair.

"Rozana and Temmy," Wren supplied. "They've been acting as contacts for us here in the Mire."

Ashelia lowered her sword, though she looked no less wary. "Tal mentioned you. What are you doing here, Rozana and Temmy?"

The minotaur took a step closer, and Garin saw that she hadn't escaped the night unscathed. A dark cut ran down one shoulder, its binding dark with blood. Yet her face was no less determined than before.

"Low Elendol revolts," she announced, her dark eyes meeting each of theirs. "The Cult of Yuldor began it, but the people, Imperials and Lowkin alike, have taken up the fight themselves. They've burned all the bridges that lead up to High Elendol and most of the lifts that were left unprotected."

Garin listened to her words and felt dread hollow him out. *Nowhere to run,* he thought numbly. *We're trapped.*

"But some lifts are intact?" Ashelia pressed.

Rozana nodded. "At my last report, there is one still in Royalist hands, Peer Venaliel. The Queen's kintree still stands. Though, were I you, I would not venture near it."

Hope, which had so quickly died, flared up in him again.

"Why are you assisting us?" Helnor demanded, his suspicion unabated. "What's in it for you?"

That much was clear to Garin. "Rozana and Temmy are just as adrift as the rest of us. We might be their only chance of coming through this alive."

Temmy gave a muffled shriek, and Rozana placed a large hand on the gnome's trembling shoulder. "Garin is right," she said. "Aiding you may aid ourselves."

"Fine." Casting them one last look, Helnor waved their party down the street. "No time to delay! Head for the royal kintree!"

As Garin set off with the others at a jog, Wren by his side, one fact hadn't escaped his notice. The road to the Queen's kintree led toward the screaming, not away from it. Glancing back, he saw Rozana and Temmy following behind slowly, as if reluctant to go that way.

But what choice do we have? He ran with the others toward the fires and the fighting.

THE CHOKING VINES

Only once the Elendola kintree towered above him did Tal stop running.

He slowed, gasping for breath, his side cramping around his old wound. Yet though he'd lost his pursuers some time ago by burning the bridges he crossed, he knew it wouldn't take them long to catch up.

The bridges weren't the only thing to burn in Elendol that night. Far below in the Mire, the sounds of violence echoed up to the canopy. As he'd crossed the final bridge, he'd glimpsed a sea of people — Easterners, common Lowkin, and Gladelysh guards — coming together like waves crashing against a rocky shore. Fires dotted the streets and quickly spread from one thatched roof to another.

But High Elendol held its own conflicts. In the distance, people fled across bridges, their aggressors trailing their heels. Whether the Royalists pursued the Sympathists or the other way around, he couldn't tell. All he could do was hope that his friends had the sense to hole themselves up in House Venaliel this night.

He held *Velori* tight in his aching grip as he quieted his breath and walked cautiously around the kintree. First, he'd check the throne room, for the Queen had told him before it was where she was safest. With peril thick in the air, he suspected it would be her bastion.

But as he neared, no sounds of struggle joined the battle noise from the Mire. The doors came into sight — as did the splayed bodies of the four guards outside of them. The doors were cracked open. Heart pumping, blood burning, Tal crept forward, trying to see within the chamber. Was he too late? Was Geminia dying, even now, under the Thorn's knife?

He reached the doors and peered within just as a voice called out.

"Do not be shy, *Skaldurak*. Come — join us."

Tal's gaze found the speaker immediately, but he already knew him. His voice echoed back to him from recent dreams and old memories. A voice as rough as a kintree's bark and as commanding as a whip, with all the menace of a wasp's hum behind it.

Tal stared at the Thorn and knew they'd lost before they'd begun.

The Extinguished stood next to Geminia on her throne, one hand resting on her shoulder. Blood drenched her white dress, and her ever-present aura had disappeared. For a moment, he feared she was already dead. But even at the distance across the throne room, he saw her chest heaving with breath.

She's alive. For now.

He couldn't say the same for her loyal servants. The corpses of royal guards littered the room, as did half a dozen enrobed figures Tal recognized as mages of the Towers. Other figures, clad in dark clothes, also lay still. He recognized one of their faces and understood who they were. *Condur.* Most of the Ilthasi seemed to have died for their Queen.

Blood pooled on the floor. The intricate and pristine tapestries were charred beyond recognition or repair. The high windows were shattered, their glass layering the ground. The mossy carpet leading to the throne had turned from green to

J.D.L. ROSELL

brown. The room smelled of a battlefield, of the newly dead and the sulfuric stench of sorcery.

Four figures still stood below the dais, all wearing the dark gray robes of the Onyx Tower. Medallions, displaying the insignia of the chimera, glinted on their necks. Though one of them leaned on an injured leg, and another clutched a bloody arm to their chest, they all wore determined expressions as they watched him. A bitter smile twisted his lips.

As Yuldor gathered four apprentices to him, so does his servant.

Ignoring the Thorn's command, Tal didn't come any nearer. His blood nearly boiled with the magic hanging in the air. The moment balanced on a blade's edge, and a shift the wrong way would bring it to a sharp and painful end.

The Thorn stared at him, his feverish yellow eyes visible even at the distance. "I see our guest does not wish to accept our hospitality. Geminia, if you would convince him."

He only managed a step backward before her words arrested him.

"Tal Harrenfel," the Elf Queen's voice called faintly. "Come to me."

Though he knew it was futile, Tal resisted and tried to take another step back. The next that he knew, he was on his knees, feeling as if sharp icicles were stabbing through his body. Gasping, he crawled forward. The cold pain eased, leaving him shivering in its wake.

"That will not do, *Skaldurak*. You know the futility in resisting a Binding Ring. Spare us all and come to me. Now."

Velori had fallen from his numb grasp. Though he knew it would do him no good, Tal picked it up, rose to his feet, and walked slowly toward the throne.

When he was two dozen paces away, he stopped and braced himself for the pain again. But the command seemed to have been fulfilled, for this time, he was spared.

"That is close enough." The Thorn looked down on him. His face appeared the same as in his fever-dreams, brown and

378

pocketed like dead vines. Brambles punctured his skin in places, as if a rose bush grew inside him, and green veins curled through his eyes.

Tal turned his gaze to Geminia, and the Queen of Gladelyl met it. Despite the Thorn's hand clutching her shoulder, his coarse nails digging into her flesh so that blood trickled from the punctures, she didn't wince or show any signs of pain, but stared with an unfamiliar desperation into Tal's eyes.

He examined the four elven mages arrayed before him. One of them was female, and all were young. Their expressions were parodies of the Thorn's own derision. *Power-starved,* he thought, *and foolish for it.* After the slaughter they'd carried out in the Thorn's service, he knew he'd find no aid there.

Tal looked back to the Thorn. Time and the odds were against him. His only hope now, vain as it appeared, was to talk.

"You're looking better since the last time I saw you," he said with a smile that was an effort to stretch. "But I suppose I'd killed you then."

The Thorn didn't return the smile. "A mistake I will not repeat. My comrades and I have underestimated you in the past, *Skaldurak*, that I will admit. But though Soltor did not learn his lesson, I have."

"Then why not kill me?" He almost mentioned Hellexa's tome, the copied pages stolen from his bedside table. Caution held his tongue. Thin as it was, the chance that it hadn't been the Thorn behind the theft could make all the difference now.

A moment passed, and the Onyx mages surrounding Tal shifted. To a one, they looked like wolves stalking a lamb, waiting for the moment their leader commanded them to strike.

"It is as I said, *Skaldurak*. I have learned my lesson." The Thorn turned his face down to Geminia, whose eyes hadn't left Tal. "When you struck me down before, I could not comprehend how you had done it. The power that radiated from you, enough to deny mine! I had only known such sorcery once before, and feeling it again, doubt made me hesitate. You did not waste your chance."

Tal barked a laugh. "Since you're bothering to explain, speak plainly. Men on their deathbeds rarely relish riddles."

"Very well; I will tell you what I know. And when I am finished, you will tell me the rest."

The threat rang loud in Tal's ears. "I expect I will."

The Thorn turned his fevered eyes back to Tal. "Our Master's power runs through your veins — I knew it the moment you faced me. All these years — the decade during which he reformed me, and the years after — I have wondered how it could be. I begged our Master to tell me. But he is deaf to our pleas, deaf to all but the voices that ravage his head."

Tal strained to understand what his words meant, but he kept his tongue still. *Give a man rope, and he just might hang himself,* he thought, and hoped his axiom was true.

"It still burns in you now, that power, straining to escape. Can you feel it, the World's own lifeblood singing within you? But something holds it back. I thought, perhaps, you had locked it away, repulsed or afraid of your own strength. But then, when I was reborn, I discovered Soltor had pulled you under his sway. It was impossible! I had felt the brunt of your sorcery, and untamed as it was, it was too much for me. I knew my comrade, and as high of himself as he thinks, he could never have done such a thing unless something had shifted. And then it came to me."

The Thorn removed his hand from Geminia's shoulder, and Tal's eyes lingered on the bloody pinpricks in her flesh before he saw what he reached for. From within the robe tucked around his emaciated body, the Extinguished pulled into view a knife unlike any other. It was made of black stone veined with red and white, and was so crudely formed it had no hilt or blade, but seemed little more than a sharpened shard.

Tal's side suddenly ached, and he winced. For a moment, a

phantom pain spiked through the old wound, as if the knife that had inflicted it were stabbing into him again.

The Thorn watched Tal's reaction and only spoke after he'd smoothed his expression again. "You recognize it," he said in a harsh whisper. "You still bear the wound to this day, do you not? Did you not wonder why it never closed? Perhaps you told yourself it was some devilish sorcery that could not be undone. Or perhaps you feared what you would become if you truly tried to heal it."

"I don't know what you're saying." He forced the words past numb lips.

"This dagger is forged from a piece of the Heartstone. The Worldheart, I believe my comrade told you it was called."

His thoughts tumbled around his skull, trying to fit together all the scraps of information into something that made sense. "So you wounded me with a piece of the Worldheart."

"Yes. In some ways, it is sorcery itself, petrified into a form that can be touched, even wielded. Or perhaps its power comes from those who formed it. Either way, by the wound I dealt you, I inadvertently restrained your power."

Cold clarity struck through him. Tal could have laughed for the realizations that poured through him, one after the other. *Too late. Once again, I understand too late.*

"Now you see," the Thorn said softly. "You see what a sorcerer with the Heartstone's blood running through him could accomplish. And you understand why Yuldor has been seeking you."

"Yes, I understand — I understand it all, Thorn. Far more than you think." Tal gestured with *Velori* toward the mages standing to one side. The closest flinched, his hand half-rising to cast a spell in defense. Even now, they were frightened of him. It brought a bitter smile to his lips.

"You have gathered four disciples to you, just as Yuldor once did," he continued. "You have reined me in, a man whose power might eclipse your own, were it unchained. You intend to use me to unseat your Master and take his place as the Prince of Devils, the Peacebringer, the Night Puppeteer. And you believe Yuldor suspects your plans to use me and thus wishes to capture me for himself first."

The Thorn's eyes blazed with a yellow light, the pupils lost within it. "You speak as if you know our Master's mind. But you do not know a fraction of what you believe you do, *Skaldurak*."

"And what of you, Thorn?" Tal mocked, taking a step closer. "Have I guessed your mind?"

"In part. But you missed one critical piece."

The Extinguished gestured to his disciples, and Tal braced himself, expecting them to close in around him. Instead, they carefully avoided his reach as they climbed the dais' stairs. Two of them grasped Geminia's arms to lift her to her feet. The Elf Queen's head lolled on her shoulders, revealing her to be far weaker even than he'd suspected. Sorrow, sharp as a sickle, cut through him.

"Geminia," the Thorn said. "You thought to bind *Skaldurak* to yourself to ensure his loyalty. But even with your prescience, you neglected to see this." His eyes flickered back to Tal. "Command him to obey me in every respect, from now until we meet our Master again."

Fear overwhelmed him. Tal stared, wide-eyed, at the Elf Queen. Only one thought remained, the words she'd uttered to him in her gardens: *You will betray me, Tal Harrenfel. But only when I ask it.*

Only now he understood.

He watched her lips part. *She knew. All this time, she knew how this would end.* The thought of how that must feel, to know her end was coming and do nothing to avoid it — he didn't know how she could have stood it. Had she known the pain the Thorn would inflict upon her? Had she known all she'd have to do? All she would betray?

"Tal," she said, her voice so weak now he could barely hear her words. "Obey the one we know as the Thorn in every way until you stand before Yuldor. This is your Queen's final command."

A shiver passed over his skin, and his last hope of escape died.

———

They reached the clamor and chaos.

It had been a breathless dash through the muddy streets of the Mire. As they'd progressed, Garin had looked away from bodies tucked into alleyways and gutters, then openly left in the streets. He'd felt that the glassy eyes followed him, staring accusingly at his back. Guilt seeded through his mind. He ran faster still.

But now, as they turned the corner and the melee came into full view, Garin stopped and stared.

Men and women fought in a seething mass. Gladelysh and Easterners struggled against each other, fury twisting their faces. In places, they only shouted, pots and pans raised alongside rusted swords and kitchen knives and wood-axes. But in others, the hatred had devolved into violence, and the two factions battered each other until one side pulled away, bruised and bloody. In the spaces between them, bodies, some crawling, some still, remained in the mud.

Every instinct in him screamed to flee and never look back. But Helnor shouted something in his booming voice, and Garin followed his waving arm to look at the base of the royal kintree only a couple hundred feet beyond. The mechanisms of the lifts led down to where two other factions fought with much deadlier intent. Gladelysh guards — some royal guards, some city guards, and some even appearing to be Warders — fought against Easterners wielding deadly weapons and piece-meal armor. But as a minotaur caught a guard on the chest with a warhammer and sent him flying back, Garin suspected it was an even match.

He felt his stomach pitch again and swallowed hard.

Wren pulled him close and shouted in his ear. "Who are they?"

He'd already puzzled it out. "Ravagers! Like the ones who attacked the caravan!"

Wren's eyes blazed with wrath, no doubt remembering Mikael's stiff body. Garin kept a firm hold on her, fearing she'd lose her senses and charge into the fray.

The others had gathered in closer, Helnor gesturing them toward an outcropping roof. Aelyn stood nearby, a disdainful sneer carved into his face. Several Easterners had noticed them and lingered on the other side of the street, calling out taunts that were swallowed in the crashing din.

Ashelia, still clutching Rolan's hand, had gathered Rozana to her. Temmy trembled close by the minotaur's side. Garin and Wren closed in next to them.

"You were right! We can't go this way!" Ashelia had to shout to be heard. "Is there another way up?"

Rozana gestured back the way they'd come. "Yes! Back around, several hours walk!"

The Peer shook her head and glanced back toward the royal kintree for a moment.

Garin guessed what she intended. "We can't go up there!"

The others looked around at him.

"What are you talking about?" Wren asked, eyes narrowed.

"You want to go to House Elendola. But it'd be suicide! Can't you see the Ravagers are gaining ground? Even if we broke through, they'll ascend. Where will that leave us? We can't fight that many of them!"

Fear pumped through him. Fear for himself. Fear for Wren and the others. But stronger than the fear of their deaths was what he might become once the fighting began.

Temmy's wide eyes spoke her agreement, and Rozana didn't

seem opposed. But Wren stared at him like he'd turned into a stranger before her eyes, and Ashelia's gaze was full of hard judgment.

"You're not a coward!" Wren shouted, as if the statement might make it true.

"Do what you must!" Ashelia waved to catch Aelyn and Helnor's attention, and the men backed toward them.

Garin's breath came so fast he thought he'd faint. "I'm *not* a coward," he muttered.

Ilvuan's amusement radiated through him. *Survival is not the highest ideal, little Listener. But you are right. There is a greater purpose waiting for you than death here. You must come to me, as you swore. Come.*

"No."

You will come.

"No!"

Even as Ilvuan's amusement turned to anger, he couldn't hold it back any longer. All the fear, all the rage — it clawed out of his throat and ripped free.

"NO! I WON'T HURT THEM! I WON'T—!"

His vision blurred. Garin stumbled, reeling as something knocked him off balance. Heat washed over him in rippling waves. A howling wind blasted from somewhere just ahead.

The World erupted into fire and smoke.

"Kneel."

At the Thorn's order, Tal tried to stand straighter. Only as icy pain pierced through him did he fall to his knees, gasping.

"Good." Satisfaction dripped from the word. "Now take her outside. *Skaldurak*, follow, and do not harm me or my disciples."

Tal stumbled to his feet as they passed by him. Though it would be useless against the enchantment of the Binding Ring, he still clung to *Velori* as he dragged his feet in their wake. The mossy rug endeavored to trip him.

Tal...

He almost stopped as a thought not his own intruded upon his mind. The voice was familiar.

Geminia, he thought in return, not knowing if she could hear him as he could hear her.

Remember...

Remember what? He stared at her back as he trudged after the Thorn and the disciples. He wished she would turn and tell him what she was trying to say. He guessed she was too weak to say more. But what could he remember now that would help them?

Free...

Free what? Please, Geminia. Tell me what to do. I don't know how to fight this.

Yourself...

Two of the Onyx mages wrenched open the doors to exit the throne room while the other two dragged the Elf Queen through. The Thorn glanced back once, as if to reassure himself that the binding stayed true, then turned as his disciples carried Geminia to the railing. The Thorn lifted a hand, and a sudden, sharp gust blasted the wood to splinters, leaving behind a precipitous drop.

Tal stared at her hair, once golden, now limp and bloodied. Slowly, he understood. He glanced down at the knife tucked in his belt. *Can I do it?* Even the thought of what she proposed brought up revulsion. The acid of bile bit at the back of his throat. *Am I strong enough?*

Is the power of a god not enough for you, Tal Harrenfel? another part of him mocked. *Take it back. What you once had. What you lost and feared to regain. Take it.*

"Geminia." The Thorn stood by the Elf Queen's side as his apostles held her next to the edge. "You remember how your bond died, don't you?"

Tal couldn't see her face, but for a moment, he felt her aura flash to life again, her anger lancing across his mind.

"Yes," the Thorn said softly, his rough voice just cutting through the noises echoing up from below. "You remember. And you remember what his death, the sacrifice of such a powerful sorcerer, enabled me to summon."

Tal slowly set down *Velori* while his other hand reached inside his cloak. He silently withdrew two pouches and wrenched them open. A green powder lay in one, while the other contained a red dried herb.

He didn't look up, didn't hesitate, but put a pinch of *yinshi* on his tongue, and as he swallowed, he poured out a smattering of *gildoil* and bent his head to it. Breathing it in sharply through his nose, his left hand felt for his knife and drew it. He was still on his knees as he raised his right hand and stared at the crystal band glimmering on his finger.

"But your demon," the Thorn whispered, "will be far greater than his."

Out of the corner of his eye, Tal saw the Thorn suddenly move. Geminia's body jerked in response. Pushing away the horror that threatened to drown him, he stared at the band on his finger, then placed his hand against the smooth wood of the platform. Slowly, he set the knife's tip against the skin just below the Binding Ring. The *yinshi* gripped his mind, firming his resolve, while his body grew numb to its pains.

"Free yourself," he whispered.

And as Geminia's body tumbled forward, flames beginning to eat her flesh, he stabbed down the knife.

INFERNO

GARIN STARED AT THE TOWER THAT ROSE ABOVE THEM, BLAZING with the light of the sun and boiling with heat.

As he watched, the tower split, and four legs stepped apart, while twice as many arms reached for the branches of the kintrees above. A head, with burning coils of flame lashing away from it, opened wide as a mouth formed, and two tails curled around its body.

Though he'd never seen it before, he knew its name.

Heyl.

The demon threw back its head and roared, a sound like stone breaking and forests burning. Vaguely, Garin noticed all the fighting had stopped as people turned and stared at the devilry incarnate looming above them. Heyl stood near the base of the royal kintree, the flames curling off its head nearly reaching the highest platform. It had no eyes, yet Garin felt it could see them all as it turned its torso around unnaturally, no bones or muscles binding its movement. For a moment, it only stood, examining Elendol, for long enough that Garin began to hope they were all mistaken, that it wasn't the evil it was reputed to be.

Heyl raised one molten hand to the trunk of the royal kintree, and the bark caught flame.

The mobs were scattering, running past Garin and his companions and shoving them roughly to the side as they fled the demon. Those too injured to rise were left in the streets, hands raised, mouths whispering unheard pleas. At the base of the royal kintree, the Ravagers fought harder than ever with the Gladelysh guards and appeared to be winning.

Aelyn shouted something at them and pointed frantically back toward Heyl. Through the ringing in his ears, Garin tried to heed his words.

"The mages!" Aelyn was screaming. "We have to protect the mages!"

Garin followed the elf's gestures to see figures standing atop the rooftops below Heyl. Though they were minuscule compared to the demon, as he watched, they raised their hands, and sorcerous light shot forth in brilliant beams at Heyl's flaming body.

But if the demon took notice, it gave no sign of it. Another of its great arms moved to touch a second kintree. This one, too, erupted into flames that splashed up and down the massive tree.

Then he saw why the sorcerers needed protection. One of them, light beginning to glow from their hands, suddenly stumbled and fell. Garin glimpsed the dark shafts erupting from their chest before they fell out of sight. Beyond them, Easterner archers had mounted a different roof, setting arrows and taking aim at their next target.

Helnor and Aelyn had already started running toward the hapless mages. Ashelia looked after them, her eyes telling of her inner conflict. But with her son clinging to her leg, she didn't move.

Wren shook him roughly, bringing him back to himself.

"Are you coming with?" she snarled in his ear. "Or are you too much a coward?"

He wanted to say the brave words — that he would fight by her side, through thick and thin, no matter the odds. He wanted to want to throw away his life in noble sacrifice.

But his doubts had hold of his tongue now. Though he opened his mouth to speak, nothing came out.

Don't you see? he begged her silently, willing her to hear his thoughts. *Don't you see that I don't wish to become the devil inside of me?*

Wren's expression twisted, then went hard. She released him and began running after the other two men.

Survival is not the highest ideal, Ilvuan rumbled in his mind. *But often, it is the needed one.*

Garin couldn't respond, but only watched as his friends went to battle while he cowered behind.

A blaze, hotter than the scorching air rising from the devil beneath the platform, coursed through his hand.

Tal strangled his scream to a gasp as he stared at the bloody gap between his fingers. It pulsed, and with each throb, more blood spurted from the gap. Pain shot up from his hand and arm into the base of his skull. Only the *gildoil* kept the agony from overwhelming him.

The *yinshi's* obsessive focus had already latched onto the finger he'd cut off, and it took all his strength to lift his head to the mages scattered around him. To his surprise, none of them had noticed him, absorbed as they were with peering over the edge of the platform, all watching the devil the Thorn had brought back into the World through Geminia's sacrifice.

Get up! he raged at himself. *Don't let her die for nothing!*

Grasping for his knife and *Velori*, both dropped during the amputation, he tried gripping their hilts and failed. The blood on his hands made them too slippery. Cursing silently, Tal fumbled for the silk gloves he'd earlier put away and dragged them on. They helped a bit, if only for a moment; his right glove quickly became saturated. But having no better solution, he stood on shaky legs and braced himself against the pain.

His focus narrowed to the five figures standing against the railing. The twin influencers pumping through his veins pushed away all of his other concerns — the pain, the fury, the fear. Only his purpose, cold and clear, remained at the fore.

He danced forward.

The rightmost mage turned almost immediately, his eyes widening and his hands raising. Tal cut him down, whipping *Velori* across his neck. He nearly lost his grip on the sword as it jarred against cartilage and bone.

As the first fell, the other Onyx mages spun around. The Thorn continued to stare below, lost in the adulation of his creation. Taking his opportunity while it lasted, Tal threw his knife and missed, but the toss sent the furthest two disciples scattering. The closest shouted in the Darktongue until he suddenly broke off. His eyes bulged, and he looked down in disbelief as he crumpled over Tal's blade sticking through his stomach.

Tal kicked his sword free and charged at the last two. The platform seemed to lurch beneath his feet, the World reeling and tumbling as his overtaxed senses rebelled. The last two mages released hurried spells, and Tal threw himself into a dive just as flames and a gale burst from their hands, buffeting and burning him.

But he'd closed the gap. He surged to his feet and swung his sword in a wide, upward arc. The first sorcerer spun away, a slash opening up his gut. *Velori* jarred midway through the torso of the female mage, the blade catching between her ribs. The hilt slipping free of his hands, the momentum of the swing carried Tal to the railing, and he sprawled against it. For one terrifying moment, as it buckled under his weight, he thought it would break. But it held, and Tal glimpsed the scene playing out below.

The Thorn had summoned Heyl, as he'd known he would. He recognized the whipping flames atop its head, the many arms and legs that burned all they touched. Flames licked up the royal kintree, less than fifty feet below them. The heat blazing up from the devil dried his eyes and made his skin feel feverish and paper-rough.

Tal pushed himself away, gasping for fresh air. He bent for *Velori* and, prying it loose, clasped it with blood-slick hands as he rose and faced his last opponent.

The Thorn still ignored him — how, he didn't know. Did all his focus go to controlling the devil below? Was he so confident in Tal's obedience through the Binding Ring and Geminia's lingering command? He pushed all doubts aside and forced his quivering legs to take one step forward, then another, staggering into a dash. A feral grin found his lips. He positioned his blade, ready to skewer the Extinguished.

A shadow darted forward, impossibly quick, and turned *Velori* aside.

Tal tried to recover, twisting around mid-charge to face his new assailant, but it was too late. The Thorn, moving faster than any mortal could, darted toward him and struck. He only glimpsed the marbled black shard in his enemy's hand before it thudded into his side.

Pain flared through him. His senses boiled away. Tal felt himself falling, but there was no floor.

Darkness devoured him.

Follow them! Garin screamed at himself as he watched Wren's back retreat, chasing after Helnor and Aelyn. *For once, don't be a gods-damned coward!*

He gripped his saber so tightly it felt like the bones in his hand would crack. Every muscle was taut with fear and anger. Yet he couldn't force his legs to move. Around him, the members of the Dancing Feathers muttered, some voicing the very thing that Garin wished to do, while it shone in the wide eyes of the monks and in Brother Nat's feverish prayers.

Flee.

"Garin."

He didn't meet Ashelia's gaze. She knew how craven he was now. He couldn't bear to see that knowledge reflected in her eyes.

"Garin. Look at me."

Despite his resolution, he found his eyes rising to meet hers. Rolan's wide-eyed stare was on him, too, as he pressed against his mother's legs, but it was Ashelia that held his gaze. Somehow, he didn't see the condemnation he'd known would be there. Something else took its place.

She spoke slowly and deliberately. "I know you want to protect your fellow troupers, and that's a noble thing to do. But I must stay to protect my son — so I'll protect them for you. Go after the others. I know you won't leave our friends to fight alone."

He turned his head aside. "It's not that."

"Then what is it?"

Understanding had lit her eyes, and that more than anything drew the truth out of him. "I'm scared to die — I'm not ashamed to admit that. But it's the devil inside me I fear more. I'm afraid if I let it out, it won't ever go back in. I'm afraid of what it will make me do."

Ashelia didn't flinch away as he'd expected. He wondered if she knew he'd been the murderer of the Nightelf youths. He bowed his head once more.

"You could never be a devil, Garin. That you're worrying you could only shows your true character. Sometimes, we must do a lesser evil to save a greater good. That's all I ask of you right now. Go to my brothers and to Wren. Protect them. Even if it means letting the devil out for a time."

Hesitantly, Garin nodded. Though he felt far from certain, somewhere in him, he knew it was the only thing he could do.

Yet he still asked, "And if I don't come back as myself?"

Ashelia reached forward and gripped his shoulder. "You will. You must."

He lowered his gaze. But he knew no words could make this right. It was his choice, a decision only he could make. To risk damnation, or damn himself by fearing it.

"I must," he muttered. Then he turned in the direction that Wren and the men had gone and set off at a jog.

As his run turned into a dash, Ilvuan twined through his mind. *You have harder scales than I believed, little Listener. But you must not die here. You have a higher purpose to fulfill.*

"I'm helping my friends," he said between gasps. "Or dying with them."

He ignored Ilvuan's annoyance and pushed his pace faster, fear propelling his limbs. They'd disappeared in an alley ahead, but before he'd lost sight of them, they'd passed the rooftops where the mages had been fighting against Heyl, moving toward where the Ravager archers had set up. His attention kept drifting to the demon slowly moving through the forest city, the screams of pain and the clashing of weapons growing nearer with every step.

Then the fighting came into view. Ravagers, their foreign faces snarling and spitting, chopped at the elven guards. The Gladelysh were outnumbered and losing more quickly. Fear rasping in his throat, Garin turned into the alley where he thought his companions had gone, then skidded to a halt. It was an empty dead end. There was no sign of where they'd gone.

Then he saw it: a ladder, set against the giant kintree root at the end. Hurrying over to it, Garin sheathed his borrowed sword and began climbing. He pushed away the images of arrows puncturing the mage, pushed away the fear of Heyl turning and seeing him. Elendol was bright around them now with the fires the demon had started. The smoke thickened by the second, filling the air with a gray haze.

He reached the top of the ladder and pulled himself onto the rough root where it angled against a roof and raised his gaze. Four figures were silhouetted against a fire above him. As he watched, a blade flashed, and one of the figures tumbled toward him. Garin flinched away as he strained to identify them, his heart choking his throat. Only as he recognized the falling body as medusal was he able to breathe again.

As the shadows disappeared on the other side of the roof, Garin scrambled after them, cursing every noise his feet made against the shingles. Reaching the top, he slowly peered over and finally recognized Helnor, Aelyn, and Wren on a house one further away. Just above them, two Ravagers had their backs turned to them as they aimed at several mages three rooftops further on. Not letting his doubts catch up, Garin clambered down the slating after them, hoping the noise would be lost in the battle's clamor.

By the time he leaped across the narrow gap and moved up the next roof, the Ravagers were falling, Helnor and Wren's blades exiting their bodies. Wren glanced back, and her eyes widened in surprise at seeing him, then narrowed. He quelled the fear of what that meant and came up next to them.

"About time you caught up!" Helnor boomed, grinning over at Garin as he reached the top with them. "We've already taken care of all the marksmen, but I'm sure there will be more entertainment to come!"

"I must do what I can against the demon!" Aelyn shouted. "But I'll be vulnerable during the incantation. Try to not let me die."

With a grimace, the mage sat on the ridge of the roof and began ruffling through his robes, producing various small bags that he balanced on his lap. Garin raised his gaze to scan the surrounding rooftops. He felt horribly exposed, and though he knew Aelyn needed an unobstructed view of the demon, he wished they could hunch down in the alley and out of sight.

"So. You finally came."

Garin reluctantly glanced at Wren. She wasn't looking at him, her eyes narrowed and scanning around them, her body braced still for a fight.

"I'm sorry I didn't come sooner."

"What changed your mind?"

"I didn't want to lose you."

Wren snorted and turned away. Anger surged through him. *Not now,* he told himself, and tried to let it go as he continued to scan the area.

His eyes fell on the ladder just as a hand, broad and lined with fur, pulled a horned head into view.

"Down there!" he shouted.

The minotaur hauled itself up and charged up the roof. Garin nearly lost his footing as he shinnied over to meet it. The Ravager wore armor over its chest, but none on its shoulders. A big, double-headed axe was clutched in its hands as it surged toward him, hooves gouging the wooden shingles. Garin couldn't see if anyone stood with him, but he heard their shouts behind him. Fear lanced through him. *We're surrounded,* he realized. They were coming up on all sides. Soon, they'd overwhelm them.

But he couldn't die here. He couldn't let Wren die.

He saw the blow coming long before it arrived, and as he had the higher ground, he jumped clear of it. The minotaur stumbled, off-balance, from the momentum of its swing. Garin almost felt as if Ulen himself pointed out the opening in its right flank. Skidding over shingles, he jabbed at the Easterner, scoring a deep wound in its side.

But he'd lost height and stood on the same level as the minotaur. Despite its wound, the Ravager seemed no slower. Roaring, it swung its axe again, chopping into the rooftop and narrowly missing Garin's foot. Before he could counterstrike, the axe had torn loose and swung upward, then around to hiss through the air where Garin had been a moment before. He could do nothing but scrabble up the rooftop and not fall, whereas the minotaur's hooves seemed to break in footholds for it to swing from.

Provoke it into climbing, he thought, and gained the top of the roof again. The Ravager glanced back toward the ladder just as a second one crested the top. From the corner of his eye, he saw another fall before Helnor's stroke, while Wren faced a sure-footed medusal, its clawed feet allowing it to grip the shingles and dodge around her to jab forward at all angles. He gritted his teeth. No one was going to help him but himself.

He couldn't hold in the devil any longer.

"*Keld!*" he shouted, and the Nightsong surged in his mind as flames licked up his blade.

The minotaur, having just taken a step up, slipped, its dark eyes wide with surprise. Garin took the advantage, running along the top of the roof to stand directly over it, then waving the blazing sword forward. The Ravager seemed to want nothing to do with the sorcery, for it nearly lost its balance and fell into the alley below trying to avoid it. Ignoring the blistering heat seeping through his gloves, Garin shouted and drove forward, and though his swing fell short, it dislodged the minotaur. The Easterner went tumbling over the edge, bellowing as it fell.

Releasing the flames, Garin stared down to see not one Ravager had mounted the ladder, but two, a sylvan and a Nightelf. The Nightelf wore a grim smile and extended her hand toward him, while the sylvan, wearing little in the way of armor but for some hardened leather, ascended to the apex of the roof.

The Nightsong swelled in his ears. Yet Garin had a feeling even sorcery would be hard-pressed to save him now.

THE WORLD'S BLOOD

HE DROVE HIS BLADE THROUGH HIS ENEMY'S BODY, THEN FELT A burning pain in his side. A chill followed, cutting into the deepest parts of him.

Tal gasped and fell to his knees. *Velori* slipped from his hand as he felt at his side. The knife stuck in him seared with a cold such as he'd never experienced before. He'd had his fair share of wounds in the Avendoran army and as a warlock's apprentice, but none had burned with a pain like winter's touch.

The Thorn gasped around the sword sticking through his lungs, jerked once more, then lay still.

He's supposed to dissolve into ashes.

The thought intruded as if from someone else, yet Tal felt it to be true. The pain, though still present, suddenly felt as if it were no danger, but an echo of an event long past.

The Thorn's head jerked toward him, and he flinched. The yellow eyes were still dull and empty, yet his mouth moved.

"Do you remember now?"

Tal looked slowly down. The knife lay at his knees, its tip broken. Red and slick with his blood, the veined black stone was still visible beneath. *Heartstone,* his enemy had called it — not then, but later.

Time knotted.

Tal's vision blurred, and he felt his balance tipping. Then the Thorn spoke again, and his words stuck in him and held him there in the memory.

"Do you remember how you overcame him?"

I drove my sword through him. That's all. But even as he thought it, the rest of their battle came back through the haze. The Extinguished hurling every ounce of his sorcery at him. Tal laughing as his blood surged and he dispelled his enemy's attacks. Had he even spoken the Worldtongue then? Had he needed to?

His head bowed forward. A different pain drove into his head, making him sick and nauseous. "Yes," he whispered.

"You do not die here," the Thorn rasped. "The Mother remembers her own. Rise, *Thalkunaras.* Yuldor's servant awaits."

No, he wanted to say. *I can't fight any longer. I'm done. He's already killed me, don't you see?*

But his vision blurred, then slowly went white as if he stared into the sun. Tal cried out as pain blazed through his head. He was blind and mute — he was lost and drowned, never to rise to the surface—

Tal gasped, and his body screamed against the cold, foreign object stuck inside him.

His head jerked up as his vision returned, dark around the edges, but painted in the flickering orange light of Elendol ablaze. Someone held him, but he shivered as his gaze found the fevered eyes staring down at him.

The Thorn's expression, stiff with the dead vines threaded through it, had somehow shifted. Now, he looked like the viper about to catch and swallow its prey. At his shoulder, Ulen Yulnaed looked down with even less emotion.

"What did you see?" The voice of the Extinguished rasped like scales brushing against a branch. "I know that look. I have seen it before, jealously longed for it. The Stone has shown you a dream, has it not?"

Tal couldn't have answered if he tried. His lungs fluttered in his chest, as if trying to escape the knife stuck midway through his body. Even before the fiery pain, the wound seemed to chill around the Heartstone dagger like he was turning to ice.

He closed his eyes. Even through the pounding in his head, he heard the screams of battle and the roar of fire swallowing the city. *The dream.* It had been like the dreams before, visions that showed him glimpses of his past, but twisted with an unknown speaker. They'd spoken truth before.

But no matter what they'd said of his fate, he was dying.

"It's too late," his enemy spoke from a great distance. "You're wasted to me."

The Thorn released him, and the knife slid out of his wound. Tal nearly fainted as he folded onto the ground. His body pumped out more of his life's blood from the wound in his side and the missing finger on his hand. He didn't have long.

Not long, he reveled. *Not long before it's all over. The pain. The worry. The struggle. The guilt.*

Ashelia.

Her name, her imagined face, drew him back from the darkness. The others he conjured tethered him there.

Her child, Rolan. Garin. Falcon. Wren. How can I rest when they're dead or dying below?

But for all his storied past, he couldn't stop death.

The Thorn spoke again above him, but his thoughts strayed back to the dream. *Remember.* He'd remembered, remembered everything of the first time he'd slain the Thorn. But could he do it again, do what had to be done? He was a man, just a man, a horribly flawed man. How could he perform an impossible task?

Yet, whatever else he was, he was also a fool.

Tal breathed in deeply, deep so that the pain boiled through him in fresh waves. Fighting the clawing darkness, he moved his hand, the fingers clumsy and deadened, around to the fresh wound in his side. It was the old wound tore anew; the glyphs Ashelia had inked around it hummed against his fingers. Not daring to think, Tal hissed in another breath, then thrust his hand in.

He screamed as pain swallowed him. He fought his instincts of self-preservation to dig his fingers in further, probing and searching the tortured flesh. Even with the *yinshi* and *gildoil* he'd earlier ingested, the pain dragged him down.

Then his fingers touched something hard and cold.

A whimper escaped his lips as he drew it out. Then his hand was free, and the Heartstone sliver slipped from it. He went limp, barely flailing above unconsciousness. He'd done what he could. Now, he could only pray to the Whispering Gods he wasn't wrong.

The change bubbled up inside him.

His body had been both feverish and chilled. Now, it grew warmer. Slowly at first, then quickening, the heat grew within him, like sparks stoked to a fire. Tal's eyes eased back open as the fire blazed like a blacksmith's forge, then swelled into an inferno. Lava burned in his veins. The pain fell away before it.

The sorcery poured through him, becoming him, consuming him.

"Garin!"

He narrowly dodged the sylvan's thrusted knife and couldn't find the breath to respond to Wren's shout. It was all he could do to stay alive.

He feinted retaliation, and the sylvan flinched back, distinctly aware of the longer reach of his sword. Instead, he raised a hand and screamed, "*Jolsh!*"

The Nightsong screeched as a gale burst from his hand,

buffeting his enemy into losing his balance. He tumbled backward and rolled off the rooftop.

His victory was short-lived. The Nightelf had been content to cast magic from afar while the sylvan faced him. Now, however, she was unrestrained with her sorcery and threw flame and ice up the slope. Having no way to stop it, Garin instinctively stepped back.

And over the other side of the roof.

His foot slipped over the shingles, and Garin grabbed at the ridge of the roof, but he'd grabbed where it had grown icy from the Nightelf's spells. His fingers slipping free, shingles tore at exposed skin. But the guard's armor he wore slowed his slide as it caught at their rough edges, just enough that as he reached the edge below, he could anchor his feet against the lip and stop his descent.

He balanced at the edge of the rooftop. His saber had fallen to the alley below, but he still had a knife at his belt. Above him, Helnor and Wren had dispatched their opponents, and Garin saw Helnor go skidding down the other side after the Nightelf.

Wren whipped her head down toward him, and he was glad to see relief flash across her face.

"We have to go!" she shouted, then pointed up.

Garin followed her gaze, and his gut twisted. The entire city appeared ablaze in fire and floating cinders. Caught in his fights, he'd stopped following Heyl's movements.

Now he saw the fire devil had placed a foot not more than a dozen feet away from the house on which they stood.

Panic threatened to claim him, so he turned his gaze down and began climbing back up. His vambraces were rough with the petrified wood, and he drove them, one at a time, against the grooves among the shingles. Slowly, he scaled the roof. Part of him watched Heyl's massive leg out of the corner of his eye, waiting for it to move and crush them, but it remained as it was, as firmly planted as a tree.

Garin reached the top of the roof and stood next to Wren

and Aelyn. He could feel the power boiling off of the mage now. But though his hands were raised toward the demon, no sorcery ripped free of them.

"What's he doing?" he muttered to Wren as he scanned the roofs below them for more Ravagers. Helnor had dispatched the Nightelf and stood guard by the ladder. As their eyes briefly met, the Prime Warder gave him a nod. Uncertain that he deserved the acknowledgement, Garin couldn't deny the warmth that spread through his chest. He returned the nod.

"Silence if I know." Her eyes darted across the Mire. "We can't stay here, though. Do you think we can move him?"

"Can't you feel it? He's brimming with magic."

Her mouth twisted, but she didn't contradict him. "He'd damn well better hurry then."

Garin listened to his muttered words through the continued strains of the Nightsong, trying to recognize any, but they defied his comprehension. Aelyn had once said the more words a sorcerer strung together in a spell, the more dangerous and powerful it became. If he'd been continuing on for this long, he could only imagine what this chant was capable of.

Suddenly, Aelyn's muttering turned into a shout. He stretched his hands up, reaching toward where Heyl's leg connected with its torso a hundred feet above. Garin winced and stepped back, expecting blinding light to flash forward from the mage. But as far as he could tell, nothing happened.

Then the leg severed.

As its leg broke free, Heyl lurched, off-balance and swaying dangerously. Its arms moved as if to catch itself. The leg, already aflame, flared up even greater, then dissipated in a cloud of smoke and ashes. Garin threw up an arm as the cloud blew over them, closing his eyes and coughing.

When the air had cleared enough to see again, he saw that, far above them, Heyl's head turned down toward them, its attention finally awoken. Despite the fiery air surrounding him, a chill shocked through him. One of its immense arms moved around, aiming for them.

Before him, Aelyn swayed, then tipped over. Despite his fear, Garin instinctively reached forward. Someone else was quicker — Helnor had climbed up onto the roof and caught his brother in his arms. Gently, he cradled him against the shingles.

But Heyl hadn't forgotten them. Its arm moved slowly, but inevitably, one mammoth hand descended toward them.

"Go!" Garin screamed, then scrambled down the roof toward the ladder. Only when he reached it did he realize that the others weren't following. Looking back, he saw Helnor's expression was hard with resignation. Wren stood by their side, tears tracking through the ashes on her face, but her mouth set and determined. Above them, the burning hand descended like a falling sun.

They wouldn't make it, he realized, not with Aelyn as he was. They would die.

But you will not. Ilvuan's thought broke into his mind. *Flee, little Listener. There is nothing you can do.*

"I won't abandon them," he whispered, not moving toward or away. "Not again."

You will, or you will die. You cannot stand before Yuldor's Fury. Run!

"NO!"

His limbs twitched, but Garin was ready for it. He fought Ilvuan's attempts to seize control of his body, fought with every ounce of will left in him. The Singer roared in his mind, and the Nightsong cleaved through him in sharp shrieks.

You swore to me! Ilvuan boomed in his head. *You swore to come serve your purpose!*

Garin could only manage a strangled denial, his tongue too much in the devil's grip to form words. But somehow, he'd gained ground. Slowly, only managing a crawl, he forced his arms and legs to inch him back toward where his friends awaited their deaths.

Stop this human foolishness! Ilvuan's protests were edged with fear now. *You cannot save them!*

No, I can't, Garin thought back as he pushed his limbs forward, gaining inch by inch. *But I can die with them.*

A fresh roar thundered through his mind — then Garin found his movement freed. Not stopping to doubt, he rose on shaky legs and scrambled up the rooftop. Wren's eyes were wide with surprise, and he saw her lips mouth something, but he couldn't tell what.

Heyl's hand blazed with the heat of a hundred forges. As it closed over them, flames licking in hungry tongues over it, Garin threw himself in front of his friends and held out his arms. It was a foolish, vain act, he knew.

Yet, as fiery death closed around them, he was glad they'd know he wasn't a coward.

Tal stood. The weakness from moments earlier had dissipated before the firestorm burning within him. His vision doubled, but now he saw another reality beneath the first. Veins of magic ran from the Thorn, through the kintree, to end burning in Heyl below. A chorus of whispers murmured in his mind with half-understood words. *The unspoken truths of the World,* he thought, and a small smile claimed his lips.

The Thorn shouted and raised his hand toward him. But through his second vision, Tal saw it building up long before the vines grew from his hand to fly toward him. He ducked and dodged around them, marveling at how easily and fluidly his body moved now.

Ulen Yulnaed had reacted as well, his rapier darting forward as magic words rolled off his tongue. Tal had barely to think to snuff out the Dancing Master's sorcery. As quick as he'd always proven himself to be, Ulen seemed slow as Tal dodged around the blade and moved in close. He wrapped an arm around his chest as he positioned a leg behind his — then, with all the molten energy inside of him, he threw him.

He barely heard Ulen's surprised cry as he tumbled off the platform.

Turning, Tal faced the Extinguished once more. Sorcery again built within the Thorn, pulsating lines drawing up from the World into him. Tal summoned his own power and formed it into a cutting edge, then drove it forward. He heard the distant scream as the Thorn collapsed, his magic severed midway through its casting and lashing back at its summoner.

Tal turned his head toward the Heartstone dagger, sitting in the pool of his blood, and summoned it. Tendrils of magic used kinetic force and wind to draw it toward his hand, and he caught it. The black stone was an icy pain against his skin, and he scowled at its weakening touch.

Yet he didn't drop it, but strode swiftly to the rising Thorn. For the first time, Tal saw fear in his eyes, but it was the other emotion that stopped him.

"You are his heir," the Thorn whispered. His hand trembled as it reached up toward him, his eyes wide with awe.

Tal dodged around his touch and stabbed the Heartstone dagger through his eye.

The Thorn gasped, sagged, and fell. He twitched, his mouth hanging open in a silent scream.

Then his body fell into ashes.

Garin held up his arms before the devil's hand.

The flames closed around him.

Pain arced across his flesh.

He shut his eyes.

A roar rose in defiance.

Garin jerked. Even amid the hellish blaze surrounding him, some other sensation erupted from within him, enveloping and protecting, then rearing and striking forth.

His eyes jerked open, but he couldn't understand what he saw. A blue light shone around him and along his limbs, the curves that formed it too foreign to differentiate. Then, as the parts became whole, comprehension sunk in. Wonder joined his fear.

Is this you? he thought to Ilvuan. *Your true self?*

But if it was the Singer, he didn't respond. The spirit beast closed its wings around them, and Garin found his arms curving with them, as if the wings grew from his own limbs. As one, they buffeted outward with a force that made the wind snap around them.

Heyl's hand rebounded, and the places where Ilvuan had struck were devoid of flames. A moment later, the clawed hand clenched into a fist, and it was driving back down, faster than before.

Ilvuan roared, throwing his head back on his long neck in challenge, and Garin's head jerked back in a cry of his own. The sound of that roar vibrated in his chest. The Singer surged forth, his sinewy body rippling with glowing power as it pulled free of Garin. He strained after Ilvuan, his arms outstretched, his lips parted in a snarl.

Ilvuan struck the descending fist.

For a moment, it seemed Heyl would prevail, his arm still driving down — then the Singer's head snaked around to snap his jaws over the blazing wrist. The demon's hand broke off in a cloud of ash and smoke, and the taste of sulphur flooded Garin's mouth.

Then he found himself down on the roof, his arms covering his head and face, as the debris fell over him. He hacked and coughed and didn't dare look up for fear of inhaling more. A man could die of too much smoke — Smith back in Hunt's Hollow had told him of it once as a cautionary tale for any blacksmith. Yet his muscles twitched, each of Ilvuan's movements tugging on his body. He longed to see their continued battle, but he knew better than to risk it.

Then a chill settled over him, welcome in the fiery chaos. The Singer had returned to him.

Ilvuan? he thought. He could barely sense him. As he strained after the devil, it felt like peering at a pebble resting on the bottom of a deep pool. *Was that you?*

Rest... the Singer said, his voice distant and thin.

You rescued me. Garin could scarcely believe it, but he knew it was true. *You fought the fire devil.*

Fading...

Though his presence was faint, he flung his question after him. *Was that what you looked like before? Were you once a dragon?*

Flee...

Then Ilvuan slipped free of his mind.

Knowing he could do nothing for the Singer, Garin slowly raised his head. His stomach clenched tight at the burning legs still standing before him. But in addition to the leg Aelyn had severed, an arm was now missing. Ilvuan had managed that much, even though it had come at a price.

"Garin!" someone called weakly behind him, then fell into a coughing fit.

He raised himself up, brushing away ash and swallowing in a vain attempt to moisten his parched throat. Wren crawled across the rooftop toward him, her eyes bloodshot and red-rimmed.

"Wren," he croaked back, and began moving toward her.

As they met, he drew her close to him. They held each other so tightly that it squeezed a cough from his chest. When they came apart, she leaned close against him and whispered in his ear, "We're still alive."

"Somehow."

"You saved us. I don't know how you did it. But when you threw up your hands, Heyl started to come apart."

She couldn't see Ilvuan. "I'll explain it later. We have to go now."

She squeezed his arm. "You're right. Aelyn's starting to wake. Helnor hopes we can get him down."

Before he could respond, a brilliant flash of light turned both of their heads. They couldn't see where it originated, but its target was apparent — for as it struck, another arm detached and fell away into ash. The fire devil turned its head around to face this new assailant.

Wren was already moving and tugging his arm. "Come on! We have to help!"

Garin had his doubts about what aid they could offer. But he followed, and they scrambled as quickly as they could across the rooftop to see who challenged Heyl now.

Tal stared down at what remained of the Thorn.

Amid the ashes and the Heartstone knife, he felt a stirring, a whisper against the roar of sorcery pouring through him. The essence of the warlock was filtering away. Part of him wondered if he could stop it and end the cycle of the Extinguished completely.

But a more urgent task awaited him.

He moved swiftly to the edge of the platform and leaned over the broken railing. Heyl had barely shifted from where Geminia's body had fallen, but its fires spread quickly throughout the city. Elendol burned even more than it had two decades before.

There were signs of resistance. Charred stubs showed where some of the fire devil's limbs had been cut away by great workings of magic. Yet for all the efforts of the Gladelysh mages, Heyl's rampage continued on.

Flames surged over the lip of the platform, and Tal took a quick step back and glanced around. The royal kintree was wreathed by flames. Amid the storm of his surging blood, Tal had barely noticed. Yet he knew he might as easily die of fire and smoke if it were left unattended.

He closed his eyes and tapped into the fires blazing around him. Summoning a sorcery without words, he coaxed the flames to disperse into heat, then rise in a harmless mist. He worked, the pulse of magic pumping through him, until he felt all the fire around him die away. As he opened his eyes, a veil of smoke poured over him from the deadened fires.

Stepping back to the edge, Tal looked down. As he did, a surge of energy washed through him, and a brilliant flash from the street below shot up to collide midway up one of Heyl's arms. A moment later, the limb fell away into ash, leaving the fire devil one arm shorter.

Tal concentrated on the magician below. Though he was too far away to see much beyond a tiny figure, he knew him. Yet it was impossible. How could he, of all people, be here?

Then he remembered Geminia's words of a guest he wouldn't expect, and a smile split his face.

Father, he thought to Kaleras the Impervious below.

He couldn't tell if the surprise he felt in response was imagined or real, but he had no more time to waste wondering. Heyl bent toward the warlock, and Tal had mere moments to help. Even an artifact as powerful as the Ring of Falkuun might not withstand the infernal fires of Heyl.

It came to him a moment later. Running back to where the Thorn's ashes stirred in the hot winds, he bent and gripped the Heartstone dagger. As soon as he touched it, he felt it draining his sorcery, trying to pull the power into itself and suck him dry. Wincing, he sprinted back to the edge of the platform. Heyl stretched its six remaining arms toward where Kaleras stood, shining with pent-up power. But even still, the devil would overwhelm him.

Tal raised his arm and, with sorcerous force, shot it forward.

As the black stone dagger flew out of sight, Tal focused his magic into a sharp, cutting edge and drove it into the devil's core. Heyl, fueled by Geminia's sacrifice, surged its resistances against him, blunting the edge of his sorcery, then retaliating. Withering flames whipped through his mind and body, and pain such as he'd never known burned deep inside him.

But he pressed on, ignoring its attacks and throwing forth all the sorcery coursing through him, pushing and cutting and driving toward the power at its center. He could almost touch it — he pried at the devil's defenses, knowing he needed just a moment, one moment, to expose its vulnerable core and kill it—

He felt the cold vacuum that was the Heartstone knife pierce the last barrier — then all resistance fell away.

A wave passed through him, threatening to shake him free of himself. As it passed, Tal became aware that he gripped the edge of the platform, the dizzying height falling away before him.

Nowhere in sight did the fire devil stand.

A slow smile stretched across Tal's face. "Heyl is dead," he whispered to the broken city.

The smile faded as he wondered how many had died with it.

TRAITOR'S FATE

GARIN WATCHED THE DAWNING SUNLIGHT CATCH ON THE SMOKE swirling through the air. His eyes traveled across the canopy, the Nightsong still whispering through his thoughts.

The battle came back to him in pieces. Kaleras had challenged the fire devil and dealt him a wound. Heyl had turned toward him, stretching all its power toward him, and Garin had known they could do nothing to save him. Yet the Impervious had stood his ground, battling valiantly on, striking blows against the devil that couldn't be ignored. The man's courage outdid his reputation.

But it hadn't been Kaleras who dealt the final strike.

As all seemed lost for the former Magister, another joined the fight. And from them, power radiated like the sun, scorching Garin's every sense. They drove forth from on high, their sorcery piercing into the heart of the devil—

And, in a burst of fire and ash, Heyl was gone.

With the devil's departure, the fires of Elendol had died, as if the creature's fell sorcery had fueled them. But enough destruction had already been done. In a large circle around the Elendola kintree, the Mire had been obliterated, many of the houses burned or crushed to rubble. Only hundreds of feet away did the city appear touched by only ash. Above, there were many gaps in the canopy where kintrees had burned to husks and their leaves crumbled away. As he looked around, a dozen of the mighty trees had suffered damages from the fire, and two were charred beyond salvaging.

Yet through the openings in the canopy, the sunlight crept in, illuminating the forest floor where it hadn't for thousands of years. Garin held out a hand and, despite the battle and death surrounding them, he couldn't help but smile a little as the sun touched his skin.

We survived.

Wren, who'd been standing in a similar stupor next to him, tugged at his arm. "Come on — this isn't over. The devil's gone, but the Ravagers and Sympathists aren't."

Though he felt her urgency, her words reminded him of something else. *Ilvuan?* He quested after the Singer's presence, probing his mind for any sign of where he lingered. But he couldn't sense him. Panic rose in his chest. *Ilvuan!*

He was gone.

His emotions swirling, he followed Wren over to Helnor and Aelyn, who stood at the end of the alley. The memory of the Singer as he'd defied Heyl... It hadn't been how he expected a devil to look. Now, he wondered if he was a devil at all.

He pushed the thoughts down. *If you're going to mourn a demon who possessed you, it can wait until later.*

"You're standing," he noted to Aelyn.

It actually looked as if it were Helnor holding up the mage rather than his own legs, but Aelyn gave him an imperious smile. "Could you expect anything less of your teacher?"

Garin surprised himself when he made the gesture of respect to him. By Aelyn's widened eyes, he'd shocked him as well.

"Thank you," Garin said sincerely. "What you taught Wren and me probably saved our lives."

Aelyn's mouth twisted as he looked away. "I only did my duty," he said stiffly.

Wren stepped forward and lightly punched him on the arm. "You did it well," she said, winking at his outrage, then turned away. "But come on — we have to make sure the others are alive."

"Yes, we do." Helnor's brow creased, wrinkling the tattoos into unfamiliar shapes. "We must see our sister and nephew to safety."

If such a thing exists anymore, Garin thought with a morose look around.

They kept their weapons clutched tightly, Garin having recovered the saber he'd let fall from the rooftop. But no Ravagers appeared. Distant sounds told of the battle's continuation elsewhere in the city, but for the moment, they were spared it.

Then figures emerged from the gray haze that covered the streets. Garin kept up his guard until their faces became visible, and only then did he sheathe his sword. He barely had time to grin before Ox's stout arms swallowed him in a hug.

"You survived!" the Befal trouper exclaimed. He'd gathered Wren in his other arm and squeezed them together with a laugh. "We all survived!"

Though danger still surrounded them, they came together for a moment of reunion. Around the shaking of hands and embraces from the troupers, Garin glimpsed Helnor gathering his sister into his arms, then kneeling before his nephew and ruffling his ashen hair. Aelyn tried to get away with respectful gestures, but Ashelia didn't tolerate it, instead gathering her adopted brother close. After a long moment, the mage reluctantly held her back. Even Brother Nat took part in the embraces, while Brother Causticus hugged nothing but the bag he'd clung to throughout the night.

Then Garin stood before Ashelia himself. For a moment, they only stared at each other. Then he blurted, "Thank you."

Her brow creased. "I did nothing, Garin."

"You gave me courage."

"If you found courage, it was within you all along."

He shrugged uncertainly. "Not much of it."

To his surprise, Ashelia gripped him by the shoulders and looked him full in the face. "I'm proud of you, Garin. There's no shame in fear, and much wisdom to it. And I know you're courageous because you overcame it."

"Or stupid," Wren noted from behind him.

Ashelia released him with a small smile. Garin couldn't turn his face away fast enough. "Thank you," was all he could mumble once more.

He forgot his awkwardness as something prickled in his mind. *Ilvuan?* He sent a questing thought after it. But as he turned his head, he felt that it came not from within, but without. In a way he couldn't understand, he felt a presence peering down at them from afar.

He raised his head. High above, a figure stood on the edge of House Elendola's platform.

For a moment, he imagined their eyes met, and he recognized him.

"Tal Harrenfel…"

Garin startled, thinking for a moment he'd spoken his thoughts aloud. But as he glanced to the side, he saw Brother Causticus staring up at the platform, his eyes wide and hungry, hugging his bag as if someone might try and steal it from him.

He could hardly blame the monk for breaking his oath of silence.

Garin turned his gaze back up to Tal. If the man standing above recognized him in return, he gave no sign. Yet Garin felt more certain with each passing moment it was him. And as the fragments from the battle fell together, he remembered where the blazing forge of magic had surged from.

How did you do it? he asked Tal in his mind. *How did you save us?*

After a long moment, the man turned away. As he disappeared from sight, Garin felt a prickle of unease. But he ignored it and turned back to the others. If Tal had survived, it wouldn't be long before he saw him again. There'd be time enough to ask him all his questions soon.

As Tal stared down at Garin, he felt himself unraveling.

The sorcery flooding through him had receded for the moment, spent in his battle against Heyl. But it still brimmed beneath the surface of his skin, bubbling in his veins, slowly and inevitably amassing. With the dissipation of the fires, the air quickly cooled against his skin.

But inside him, a forge still burned.

To make matters worse, the magic no longer extended its protection against his ills. Exhaustion, pain, and grief crashed over him with every passing moment. The nub on his hand pulsed with each heartbeat, and the sensation of the finger still lingered, tantalizing and maddening. His side throbbed. He'd looked at it, pulling up the rags of the fine shirt and coat that Ashelia had gifted him, only to see the old wound had turned from a seam of unhealed flesh into a scab, the blood crusted over as if the wound were days old rather than minutes.

Other wounds were hidden from view. He'd overcome Heyl, but victory had come with a price. The unseen burns of the demon's attacks lingered, a wrongness oozing from the sorcerous scars left on his being. With his expanded awareness, Tal recognized the corruption for what it was: chaos, magic unwound, spreading throughout his body.

But his wounds were the smallest of his griefs.

My fault.

When it had first ended, he'd gazed upon the burned-out kintrees surrounding House Elendola. Several were destroyed beyond repair, entire Houses gone in less than an hour, and perhaps their families dying within them. The canopy had been ripped open, baring the forest city to dawn's light once again. Butchery had occurred below — he'd seen the bodies of the guards, the Warders, and the Ravagers, all fallen together indiscriminate of their loyalties.

Ravagers. Someone had allowed the battle-trained Easterners into Elendol to lay waste to it. Someone had smuggled them weapons and armor and housed them. But the Imperials hadn't been alone in their blood-thirst. He'd seen the mobs, too, before they'd dispersed before Heyl, Gladelysh hells-bent on slaughtering their refugee fellows, and the Easterners just as determined to fight back.

All my fault.

Part of him knew it was too great of a burden for one man to shoulder, yet he tried. Accusations lined up, one after another, to push their barbed questions into him. Who pushed the Thorn to act so swiftly after he arrived? Whom did Yuldor seek so ardently he'd destroy cities and nations to claim? Who knew he was a hunted man, yet continued to let his friends shelter him and suffer for it?

No more.

With magic extending his vision, he could see the lad's face. Garin stared up at him, his brow creased as if puzzled by what he saw. Perhaps he wondered who stood upon the throne's platform staring down at him. Perhaps he knew and wondered why Tal didn't come down to join their friends.

Take care of them, lad, he thought to his one-time apprentice. *It's the last thing I'll ask of you.*

He released the spell and turned away. His resolution had firmed with each moment he looked upon Garin's face. He knew it was the right way, the only way he could spare them. The safest path amid a jungle of brambles.

Flee.

He would go East. Away from the politics of the Westreach. Away from where he might hurt the ones he loved. Away from

417

everything he knew, and into a hostile and foreign land he'd visited only once before.

He would flee Elendol. But only to go to his final reckoning.

"I'm coming, Yuldor," he murmured. "Though not the way you wanted me."

The pounding of feet on the stairs interrupted his thoughts.

Tal stiffened and listened intently. From the sounds they made, two or three men or women approached. From the lightness of their steps, he could tell they were elves. He looked at the scene around him, and dread gripped his gut tightly. The bodies of the four Onyx Tower mages lay around him. Blood stained his sword and clothes and crusted over his skin. The Thorn had dissipated into a pile of ashes. The Queen was missing, and the corpses of her loyal subjects lay dead beneath her throne.

A sour smile stretched his lips. Even in defeat, the Extinguished had stolen the last laugh.

Knowing time was short, Tal searched the ground, then found what he was looking for. Bending over, his stomach pitched as he picked up his severed finger, the Binding Ring coated red with blood. He tried to pry it loose, but when it wouldn't come off, he put it, finger and all, into one of his pockets.

The elves appeared at the top of the stairs, glaives extended before them as if expecting a fight. By their armor, they were city guards. Their bright, spinning eyes darted around the scene before they fanned out around him.

"Tal Harrenfel," the middle one said, his voice hard. "Lay down your weapons and come with us."

Tal was vaguely surprised to find *Velori* in his hand. But he knew there were only two ways this could end.

"I might. If you tell me who sent you." Tal shifted his weight from one foot to the other as if completely at ease.

The two outer guards glanced at each other, but the middle

guard's gaze never wavered. "Peer Lathniel," he said sharply. "But it is irrelevant. Our authority is the same."

"I wasn't aware that House Lathniel commands the city guard. Nor that the city guards' providence extends to the royal kintree."

"You are a stranger and foreigner here, and a murderer as well, it seems," snapped one of the other guards. "You know nothing of Elendol!"

Tal shook his head, his smile stretching wider. "Murderer, am I? Whom precisely am I accused of killing?"

The hothead guard shifted his glaive forward threateningly. "You damn well know who, you bastard!" he hissed.

"Menalyn!" the first guard spoke in warning before he addressed Tal again. "This is your final warning, Aristhol. You stand accused of killing the late Queen of Gladelyl, Geminia Elendola the Third, and four Onyx Tower mages yet to be identified, and the Ilthasi and guards within the throne room. Lay down your sword and any other weapons and come with us peacefully, or we will use force."

Tal raised his eyes to the beams of light catching on the smoke and ashes floating above. *Inevitable.* Like vines choking a young tree, he saw that this moment had been a long time coming. All of their paths, both those alive and dead around him, came to this.

Now, only two roads stretched forward. He could go with the guards and experience the ferocity and unfairness of House Lathniel's justice. He could rot down in a dungeon, all the time knowing enemies threatened his friends, and he'd done nothing to protect them. Inevitably, he'd be sentenced to execution.

Or he could choose the second path.

As he lowered his gaze again, he found the guards had advanced minutely. He donned a smile that Gerald Barrows might have once worn and settled into a balanced stance.

"Looks like you'll have to force me," he said quietly.

419

The guards wasted no time in rushing forward, glaives lowered before them. They had longer reach and numbers, and all of them looked fresh, as if they hadn't taken part in the fighting below.

Tal was anything but fresh. But as they charged, he broke open the dam inside him, and sorcery rushed through him once more, boiling his veins and searing in a way both painful and pleasurable.

Tal raised his sword and spoke the words of the World-tongue, and reality rippled around him.

"He fled East?"

Garin could scarcely believe the words. He looked from Ashelia, who had given the news, to Wren biting her bottom lip, to Falcon avoiding his gaze, to the others standing in the broken feast hall of the Venaliel kintree: Kaleras, Helnor, Aelyn, and Rolan. The boy had finally released his mother's hand and wandered around the room, observing the destruction with obvious disinterest. The troupers of the Dancing Feathers had retired to their rooms, determined to pack as quickly as they could and head back to Halenhol. Brother Nat and Brother Causticus had declared they were returning, too. Part of Garin wished to go with them, at least as far as Hunt's Hollow. *Home.*

It was a vain hope, he already knew.

Ashelia nodded, her lips pursed tightly together. "According to Balindi, that's what the guards at the Sun Gate reported."

"And he attacked the city guards in the royal kintree? Because they claimed he'd killed Queen Geminia and the others with her?"

"When they tried to arrest him, yes. But none were seriously injured. He seemed more intent on running than fighting."

He crossed his arms tightly against his chest. *Why, Tal? Why do this?* Just when he'd thought he was beginning to understand the man, he did something that turned everything on its head.

"Fine," Wren said with plain exasperation. "Since no one else seems inclined to ask the obvious question — why go East?"

He found himself sharing a look with Aelyn, of all people. The mage smiled snidely, though the bronze in his eyes swirled with buried feeling.

"Why else?" Aelyn held up his hands. "To vie with the Named himself."

"Fool man," Helnor muttered.

Kaleras shifted, and with that slight movement, captured their attention. Garin wondered how the man maintained such gravitas. Even while he perched upon a chair split up the back, all of his energy spent from his battle with Heyl, his posture remained erect.

"I came to Elendol to speak to him," the warlock said, every word as crisp as an Avendoran aristocrat. "From his time in Halenhol, I learned several things I wished to discuss further. As soon as I was recovered enough from my wounds to travel, I did so, intending to attend the Winter Ball at Queen Geminia's invitation. But then I was waylaid upon the road to Elendol. Ravagers beset me in the night, intent on my death. Had I not set wards, they might have succeeded — but as it was, they only delayed my arrival until after the Winter Ball had concluded."

He cast an accusing look around their circle, as if he held each of them responsible for how that had turned out. Garin wasn't the only one to avoid that hawkish gaze.

"Now, I find he has slipped away from me again. I won't stand for it. Tal will answer to the questions he has raised in my mind." The warlock nodded his head sharply, as if that settled the matter.

It took Garin a moment longer to understand what he'd said. "You're going after him?"

As Kaleras' piercing eyes settled on him, Garin winced, but held his gaze.

"Yes," the warlock said. "I am entering into the East. And while I require no companionship, traveling a foreign land is better done with a greater party."

Kaleras didn't look away from Garin, and he swallowed, trying to dredge up a response. *Into the East.* Every story of the barbaric, mountainous lands and the monsters that wandered them rushed through his mind, tying his tongue into knots.

"I'm going, too."

Garin's stomach sank as he glanced at Wren. Her words weren't as surprising as the spots of pink on her cheeks as she stared boldly at the Warlock of Canturith. Yet he wished she hadn't said them.

He finally found his voice. "Wren, are you sure?"

Falcon, who had been uncharacteristically silent, had sat up at his daughter's announcement. "Wren, please. Don't."

She stared defiantly at each of them. "I have just as much of a right to go as any here."

Garin tried not to let his anger show. "Haven't you heard what the East is like?"

"Of course I have. I've heard more stories than you, Garin Dunford."

"But you haven't *seen* them — all those monsters that come down from the mountains. There are griffins and chimeras and quetzals—"

"And draugars?" The gold in her eyes raced. "And dragons? I've met them both."

"It wasn't an actual dragon." His mind spiraled down a different path for a moment before he sharply reined it back in. There'd be time enough to consider that later.

"Wren, daughter, I'm begging you." Falcon had stood and crossed their circle to kneel before his daughter. He tried to take one of her hands in his, but she crossed her arms and watched him silently.

"Please," the bard continued, his voice growing softer, his eyelids fluttering as if to keep tears at bay. "Don't do this."

"We each have to make our own decision, Falcon," Ashelia cut in. She was looking at her son as he gingerly stepped around the shards of broken glass, then continued his circuit around the room.

Falcon looked sharply at her and stood again. "How could you say that? You, who have a son?"

"I'm well aware of how it feels to have my child's life at risk, Falcon. This past night has been a lesson in that. And it is only the beginning."

Ashelia turned her gaze to the old warlock. "I, too, will travel with you, Kaleras. Tal carries a hope that the Westreach desperately needs. And Rolan will travel with us."

The warlock stared hard at her now. Garin wondered if he knew what lay between her and Tal.

"You're taking Rolan?" Despite his earlier complaints of weariness, the Prime Warder was on his feet. "You'll get him killed!"

Rolan had looked over at the sound of his name, startled. After a moment, Ashelia waved him over, and he picked his way across the shattered furniture and glassware.

"There is nowhere safer for him than with me," she said quietly.

Falcon gave one last forlorn look at his daughter, then slowly returned to his seat, shaking his head. Wren, for her part, stared with open admiration at Ashelia.

As the boy reached his mother, Ashelia folded him into her arms, and the storm in her eyes stirred. "Our home is forfeit, *Belosi*," she said to Helnor. "The Sympathists have won."

"Only if we flee now!" the Prime Warder retorted.

She shook her head. "As Geminia was heirless, I was second-in-line for the throne. Maone Lathniel was first. Before the week is gone, she will be named the Queen of Gladelyl. But even if we challenge her claim, even if we scrape back power and the throne, what then? Our nation is broken. The Named and his Nameless have done what they meant to do. There is no will to resist Yuldor and his cult any longer."

Helnor clenched his jaw, but after a moment, he nodded stiffly. "You are the Peer of House Venaliel. And you are my sister. Where you lead, I will follow."

"You can stay and fight, Helnor. Your heart is here."

"And wonder if I let you and my nephew go to your deaths in the East?" He shook his head. "No, *Kolesa*. I go where you go."

Garin had to look away from him, the anger in the scout captain's eyes almost painful to behold. He felt enough of his own fury at Wren's pronouncement.

But a greater weight pressed down on him. He glanced at Aelyn to find the mage watching him. It took all his force of will to hold his gaze.

"And you, Garin?" Aelyn asked, his voice soft, but with all the danger of a prowling jungle cat. "Are you traveling with this merry company as well?"

Garin swallowed. He knew only the barest hint of the threats that would face them in the wild lands of the Empire of the Rising Sun. Yet what he knew was enough to cut him to the bone with terror. He didn't dare look at Wren, fearing he would again see her disgust at his cowardice.

His gaze traveled to Ashelia instead, and he remembered her words that had helped to give him courage — *I know you won't leave our friends to fight alone.*

He thought of Ilvuan and his sacrifice, and some of the only kind words the Singer had said to him: *You have harder scales than I believed.*

Despite a fear that had frozen him in place, he'd run after Wren and the others and fought beside them against the Ravagers. As Heyl turned toward them, he'd thrown himself in front of them, knowing there was nothing he could do.

But he'd still been willing to die for them.

Come.

Garin startled, then quickly reached after the faint echo in his mind. *Ilvuan! You're still alive!* He felt so relieved he didn't even feel guilty. Devil or no, Ilvuan had saved him.

He was his devil now.

Then, nestled deep inside his thoughts, he felt the faintest outline of the Singer's presence, like seeing a silhouette against a dark night sky.

Come, Ilvuan whispered once more, then slipped back into darkness.

"I'll come," Garin heard himself say. His gaze had fallen to the floor, and he raised it as he repeated, "I'll come, too."

Aelyn's mouth twisted in a bitter sneer. "Well, then. I wouldn't want to be left out, would I?"

Ashelia smiled at her House-brother. "Keep up the pretenses if you like, *Belosi*. We know your heart is soft."

As the mage scoffed, Garin glanced at Falcon. The bard was the only one not to declare his intentions. Wren's father stared at the ground, a heavy weight seeming to rest on him.

After a time, Falcon must have sensed the eyes on him, for he raised his head and looked around, then sighed. "Obviously I'm going. Though I have no martial skill and only one hand, I could never let Wren go into peril I wouldn't dare myself."

Wren had let her arms fall at her sides. "Father, as much as I appreciate, you don't have to go. Do you think I want you to risk your life, either?"

The Court Bard smiled sadly at his daughter. "It isn't the same at all, Songbird. But even if it wasn't for you, I might still go. After all, the Legend of Tal is my life's work — and I must be the one to see the song to its end."

"If it means so much to you." But a small smile crimped the corner of Wren's lips.

Garin looked around at all those with him. *My companions.* They would go into the East with no guarantees of survival, and no goal but to track down a man who didn't want to be followed.

He found a smile spreading. *A fool is permitted to do what a wise man never could,* Tal had once told him. They were a company of fools, that much was true — but the bravest fools he could imagine.

No matter the reasons you've fled, and the reasons you stayed away from us, Garin thought, *we're coming for you, Tal.*

And maybe then, they'd finally settle their score.

EPILOGUE: TO THE EAST

IN A LAND HOSTILE AND FOREIGN, WITH SCARS SPLIT OPEN AND pockets flattened, stood a man gazing over a snow-laden valley, all around him still and silent — all except the storm raging inside him.

He had opened the gates, and the sorcery had poured in. Now, his veins burning hot and his skin feverish even in the winter winds, he could not stop it. Slowly, inevitably, he felt its possession of him closing in, and his grip on reality slipping.

But his purpose was fixed in his mind. His eyes, dark in the dusky light, were set in one direction.

East, where the Enemy awaited.

East, where the mysteries would be answered, and the questions would cease.

East, where the pain would end.

He smiled a wolf's smile and turned to travel back down through the snow.

In a city not far to the west, a young man stared up at an archway.

Made of petrified wood, it formed the gate that lead east, and was carved to commemorate it, a sun's passage across the sky carved into the arch. The lad stared at the carving as if it held answers to the questions he'd been asking, as if it might speak of what lay beyond its passage.

The wood whispered no words, and the devil in his head offered nothing more.

Standing with the young man was a company of humans, elves, and those halfway between. A small boy stood among them. Their fellowship, hastily formed, had a unified purpose.

But their intents were not shared in common.

Four went to aid the noble cause of a friend.

Two sought to reconcile with one who had wronged them.

One hunted for justice for the death of a queen.

The gate opened, and the young man led them through, not knowing what was coming, only knowing that, finally, he could face it.

ACKNOWLEDGMENTS

A big round of thanks to:

Kaitlyn, my fiancée, first reader, and mapmaker. I don't know how I'd write these books without you.

René Aigner, for his beautiful cover illustration — he outdoes himself every time.

And thanks to *you*, dear reader, for spending your valuable time sojourning with Tal, Garin, and the rest. Thank you for coming along!

- Josiah (J.D.L. Rosell)

ABOUT THE AUTHOR

J.D.L. Rosell is the internationally bestselling author of the Legend of Tal series, The Runewar Saga, The Famine Cycle series, and the Godslayer Rising trilogy. He has earned an MA in creative writing and has previously written as a ghostwriter.

Always drawn to the outdoors, he ventures out into nature whenever he can to indulge in his hobbies of hiking and photography. Most of the time, he can be found curled up with a good book at home with his wife and two cats, Zelda and Abenthy.

Follow along with his occasional author updates and serializations at www.jdlrosell.com or contact him at authorjdlrosell@gmail.com.

Made in United States
Orlando, FL
12 January 2022

13327028R00264